Spartan Publishing

Published: December 15, 2015

Copyright: Margaret M Williams

The moral right of the author has been asserted

All rights reserved

No part of this publication may be reproduced, stored in a retrieval system, or transmitted in any form or by any means, without the prior permission in writing of the publisher, nor be otherwise circulated in any form of binding or cover other than that in which it is published and without a similar including this condition being imposed on the subsequent purchaser without the permission of the publisher

ISBN: 978-0-9873841-7-1

Spartan Publishing

www.spartanpublishing.uk

THIS OTHER EDEN

For Rachel, Deborah and Jonathan

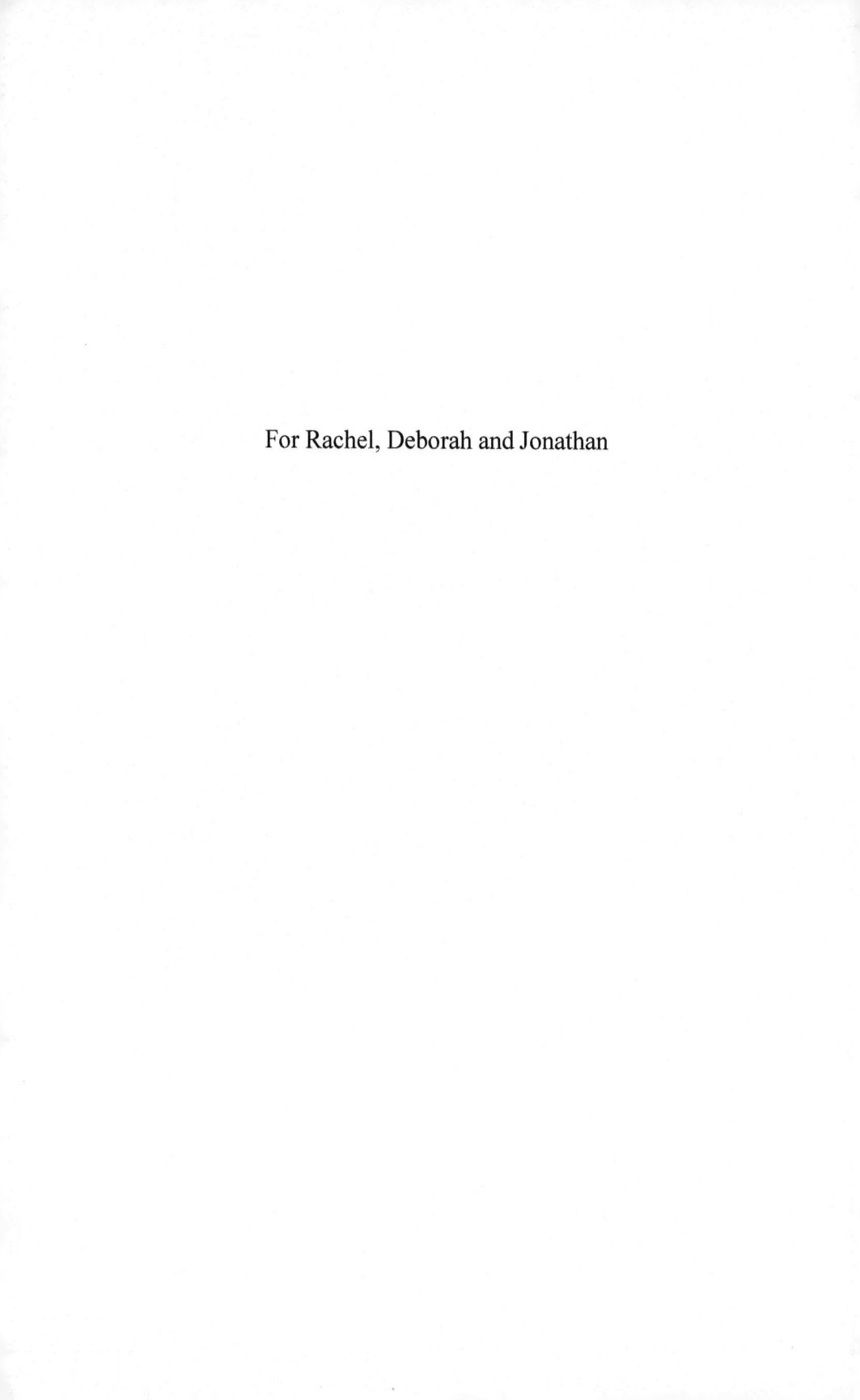

This royal throne of kings, this sceptr'd isle,
This earth of majesty, this seat of Mars,
This Other Eden, demi-paradise....

William Shakespeare. (Richard II)

Acknowledgements

My thanks are firstly due to my son, Jonathan Henley Williams for his invaluable help and digital expertise in the preparation of this novel.

To my father, John Bowerbank, and my primary school head teacher, Mrs. M. C. Appleton, who both by their fascinating stories of past peoples and events, were the first to awaken in me an enduring appreciation of the wonders of history and literature.

Also to Lauren Mackay, in association with Spartan Publishing, and author of her recently published work "Inside the Tudor Court." In her, I immediately recognised a kindred spirit in our mutual attraction to the Tudor period of history.

Lastly, I appreciate the efforts of Lancashire County Library, Ormskirk Branch, for their assistance over several years in locating my many requests.

PREFACE

This novel encompasses a twenty-five year time span. It begins in the final third of King Henry the Eighth's thirty-eight year reign, i.e. from 1535 to his death in 1547. It continues through the shorter reigns of his young son, Edward the Sixth, and his elder daughter, Mary the First, concluding at the beginning of the reign of his younger daughter, Elizabeth the First.

This was a time of turbulent changes, religious and political, for the two were intertwined. Henry's pleas to the Pope for a divorce from his Spanish wife, Katherine of Aragon, on the grounds that his marriage to his brother's widow, despite dispensations given at the time, was contrary to God's law, resulted in stalemate. Spurred on by his overwhelming desire to marry his new love, Anne Boleyn, and his equally pressing need for a legitimate male heir, Henry took the bold step of breaking with Rome and declaring himself to be Head of the Church within his own domains. The houses of religion were being closed, and with the competent diligence of Thomas Cromwell, his Chief Minister, their wealth was being speedily appropriated to the King's use. This was a step deeply resented in the conservatively religious north of England.

The River Eden, flowing through the old county of Cumberland, is central to the unfolding of the tragic events that touched the lives, not only of the great and famous of that time, but also the people who were native to that beautiful area of northern England. The river was witness to the transit of the rising considered to be the greatest threat to King Henry's authority, catching him embarrassingly unprepared to deal with it militarily. Yet it often earns little more than a passing mention in recorded history.

The Pilgrimage of Grace, as the rebellion became known, was doomed to end in bloodshed in Carlisle, and the appalling aftermath of the King's vengeance is reflected in the savagery of the sentencing of those unfortunate prisoners who stood trial there.

Against the political and religious intrigues of the famous and powerful of this and the following Tudor reigns, I have contrasted the lives of the simple labouring folk of Cumberland. For them, in the harshness of their daily lives, the earning of their bread was of paramount importance, irrespective of whatever religious wind was blowing. Amongst these, my own forebears, the Bowerbank family lived, tanners and saddlers, born in the village of Lazonby, near the market town of Penrith. Interlaced with their imagined lives, I have portrayed, at the beginning of the novel, some of the last few nuns whose names are recorded as occupying the nearby small Priory of Armathwaite, to which I have given its earlier name of Heremitithwaite.

In the early 18th century, when the old nunnery buildings were being dismantled, in an aperture in one of the walls, a small painting on copper of a Benedictine nun was discovered, veiled, and holding a book in her hands. A short distance from the convent lay the Nun close, the plot of land where the Sisters of the House were buried, and there the head of a monk wearing his cowl, roughly cut in stone, was found. Also, at the site of the Friary in Penrith, the leg bones of a man of unusual height were discovered during excavations for the building of a house in Friargate. Upon these facts, I have based the character of the Big Friar.

These were years of deeply held and conflicting beliefs, the adherence to which cost many, of whatever status in life, a terrible price. Over the passage of nearly half a millennium, in some of their own words we can hear the anger, the pathos, and the courage of some of those who were destined to live during those years of turmoil. Even at such a distance, it is still possible to recoil at King Henry's fury, evident in his merciless instructions to the Duke of Norfolk, as to how he is to punish those unfortunate rebels to be tried at Carlisle Castle. To read the letters that passed between them, and the depositions taken when the bereaved women of those executed prisoners were taken to task over their pitiful attempts to bury their loved ones, is indeed harrowing.

In the succeeding Tudor reigns, how can we not feel sadness for Edward, a boy not sixteen years of age, so ravaged by an incurable disease that he can say, "I am glad to die?" So too, Queen Mary, who whilst a princess described herself as being "The unhappiest lady in Christendom."

Her ardent words before her marriage to Philip of Spain - "I will love him perfectly," were spoken in hopeful anticipation of fulfillment, after a life spent in denial. That life was to end in sorrowful resignation of hopes unrealised, as expressed in her will "that God has sent me no fruit nor heir of my body."

At the safe distance of almost five hundred years, would it not be presumptuous of us to pass judgment on those men and women who lived through such perilous and confusing times? Therefore, it has been my intention in writing this novel, to be completely impartial, and certainly non-judgmental. For how can we know what our own reactions might have been, faced with similar circumstances, when unlike the freedom of choice and conscience we enjoy today, survival might well have depended upon one's ability to ride the ups and downs of a religious see-saw? How apt is the North American maxim, to never judge a man unless you have walked a mile in his moccasins.

CHARACTERS

At Heremitithwaite Priory
Dame Dinah Wharton, Prioress
Sister Galfride Chambers
Sister Anne Dartwentwater
Sister Marguerite Standley
*Sister Isabelle
*Sister Mary
*Robert Winter, Woodcutter
*Isobel Winter, his wife
*William Winter, his son

At the Friary, Penrith
*Brother John, "The Big Friar"

At Baronwood
*Edward Bowman, forester
*Genett Bowman, his wife
*Benedict, his son

At Lazonby Tannery
Andrew Bowerbank
Mary Bowerbank, his wife
John and Dinah, his son and daughter

At Wetheral

*John Aspedaile, farmer

*Sarah Aspedaile, his wife

*Margaret Aspedaile, his daughter, also known as "the nun's child"

*Janet Burton, Margaret Aspedaile's foster mother and later John Aspedaile's third wife

*Joe Grinton, farmer

*Bernard and Ralph Grinton, his sons

*Ellen Grinton, his daughter and later William Winter's wife

At Court

King Henry VIII

Anne Boleyn

Jane Seymour

Anne of Cleves

Katherine Howard

Katherine Parr

King Edward VI

Queen Mary I

Queen Elizabeth I

Thomas Howard, 3rd Duke of Norfolk

Charles Brandon, Duke of Suffolk, friend and brother-in-law of

Henry VIII

Katherine Willoughby, Duchess of Suffolk, his wife

Edward Seymour, uncle and Lord Protector to King Edward VI

Tom Seymour, his brother and later husband of Queen Katherine Parr

John Dudley, Earl of Warwick and later Duke of Northumberland

Thomas Cromwell, Lord Privy Seal

Sir John Cheke, Tutor to King Edward VI

Prince Philip of Spain, husband of Queen Mary I and nominal King of England

Susan Clarencius, lady in waiting to Queen Mary I

Jane Dormer, lady in waiting to Queen Mary I and later Duchess of Feria

Katherine Ashley, lady in waiting to Queen Elizabeth I

Robert Aske, Great Captain of the Pilgrims

Lord Tom Darcy of Templehurst, Yorkshire

Thomas Cranmer, Archbishop of Canterbury

Margaret Cranmer, his German wife

Dr. Richard Layton, Royal Commissioner Dr. Thomas Legh, Royal Commissioner

*Thomas, Royal Commissioner's agent

Sir Thomas Wyatt, Leader of rising against Queen Mary

Sir William Butts, Physician to King Henry VIII

Barnaby Fitzpatrick, friend of Edward VI

Baron of Upper Ossory, father of Barnaby Fitzpatrick

Will Somers, Henry VIII's fool

Others

*Jack Pedlar

*Rosa the Gypsy

*Walter, labourer on the Earl of Pembroke's estate at Wilton

*Fictional characters

PART I HENRY VIII
1535 - 1547

The silver treasure of Heremitithwaite - The Lazonby Tannery - Murder in Penrith - Baronwood, rape in the forest dwelling - At the Friary in Penrith - Heremitithwaite, visit of the King's Commissioners - Two brothers, and a sister - Barking-time in Baronwood - Closure of the Houses of Religion - The year of three Queens - Rebellion - The tanner's family at Heremitithwaite Priory - The Pilgrimage of Grace - Aftermath, and the King's justice - the last days of the Priory of Heremitithwaite - Rape of the nun - The bullbait in Penrith - In Eden's depths - Prisoners in the Tower of London - Springtime in Wetheral - Hampton Court Palace - Birth of a Prince, and death of a Queen - Birth of a winter babe - The cattle plague - A Princess from the Rhineland - The Cleves marriage - The fall of Privy Seal - Wounds from the "thornless rose" - Death of the last Prioress of Heremitithwaite - Will Somers, the King's fool - Mistress Cranmer, the Archbishop's wife - The Queen from the north - Boulogne, the last campaign - Loss of "The Mary Rose" - The fall of the Howards - End of an era - The road to Windsor - the Lazonby tanner's last journey.

PART II EDWARD VI

1547 - 1553

Coronation, too large a crown - The sword of the spirit - The schooling of a King - Pedlar Jack - The King's two uncles - The new religion - The rise of John Dudley, Earl of Warwick, Duke of Northumberland - Barnaby Fitzpatrick, the King's Irish friend - Gypsy Rosa - The Lady Mary's Mass - The Summer Progress - Decline, Sir John Cheke, the beloved teacher - Two Devices - "I am glad to die."

PART III MARY I

1553 - 1558

All things possible - A crowned Queen Regnant - The pedlar's tale - Marriage negotiations with Spain - The Wyatt rebellion - The Lady Elizabeth - The Tower and Woodstock - A June wedding, and wild roses - The Exodus to Europe - The bridegroom from Spain - Kenninghall, the Duke of Norfolk's last battle - England's return to Rome - Plague - On Eden's flood - Christmas at Wetheral - A birth at Wetheral - The child that never was - The Heresy Laws - Philip's departure for the Netherlands - Burning of the Bishops - The trials of Sir John Cheke - The Battle of St. Quentin - The loss of Calais - On the waters of the Cam - Queen Mary's will - The race to Hatfield - Elizabeth Regina - A time of new beginnings.

PART I

HENRY VIII

1535

September - The Priory at Heremitithwaite

The striking of the bell at the Priory of Our Saviour and the Blessed Virgin Mary at Heremitithwaite in the county of Cumberland, summoned the Ladies of that community to break their fast upon eggs and bread, and the customary small ale of the convent's own brewing. There was a sharpness in the air. It whetted their appetites, and foretold early frost, for despite the soft brilliance of the mid-September day, Cumbrian winters, as likely as not came early, and lasted long.

Sisters Anne Dartwentwater and Galfride Chambers waited with barely concealed impatience, as Sister Marguerite Standley ushered the convent's two longest serving nuns to their places. In her aged condition, Sister Mary's eyes had the milky hue of near blindness. But such was the sweetness of her nature, and her uncomplaining acceptance of her disability, that she never failed to thank God that in laying this burden upon her, He had nevertheless lightened it. For Sister Isabelle, though profoundly deaf herself, was her constant guide, her other eyes, and her unfailing comfort in age. Between them they managed tolerably well, sharing their remaining faculties as best they might, and contributing where they were best fitted, in the many domestic tasks of their small community. This day, they dined without their Prioress. Dame Dinah Wharton had much upon her mind, chatter would not help the pondering of which she feared, and so she elected to take her food alone in her chamber. Her fingers toyed delicately with the manchet of bread before her, systematically reducing it to bite-sized pieces. These she absentmindedly dipped into the soft yolks of the dish of eggs upon her table, smiling that she had reverted to this childish practice of her youth.

That youth now past, when indeed she had been thought comely, Dame Dinah was still a well-favoured woman. She was possessed of much good sense and great capability. Yet despite her calling, she veered, on occasion, to the sin of pride. Always, even without conscious thought, she was aware of her pedigree. By her mother's blood, she was descended from the old local family of Staffield. It was they who had given their name to the scattered hamlet on the opposite bank of Croglin Beck. That name had now been extinct for well over a hundred years, and if ever Dame Dinah vaguely admitted to any flaw in her ancestry, the fault, she felt, lay with those last Staffields who, in the time of the fifth Henry's reign, had neglected to produce male off spring so necessary for the perpetuation of that name.

Of late, the Prioress had found herself recalling many things from her distant but well-remembered childhood. Days spent in her father's manor house with its servants and horses, her proud mother, who ordered the household with unfailing yet kindly competence. And James, her adored twin brother, alas, now dead so many years.
"God rest his soul," Dame Dinah murmured hastily. She crossed herself, and felt the prick of tears behind her eyelids. James, she could see him clearly, her twin, her other half. With him, she had roamed the countryside in the sweetness of each childish summer, as often as not returning home with many a rent in her gown. That last summer, before the sickness took him, they were in their fifteenth year. It was late June, the memory of it still sharp and clear.

They took a basket one sunlit morning filled with pasties and a cold spit- roasted fowl, with bread and small ale. They followed the waters of Croglin, as it tumbled over boulders, now rushing, now flowing evenly to meet the wide River Eden. In the heat of noon, they lay under the shade of overhanging trees, deep in the newly unfurled fronds of bracken, to eat their fill. The broad waters of the river ran deep and sparkling in the mid-day sun. All day they explored along its banks, scrambling over the great slabs of sandstone where the river neared the towering walls of the wondrous gorge.

It was James who discovered it. He climbed high above her, and then he gave a warning yell as his foot dislodged a piece of loose rock. Instinctively, he clutched at the tangled mass of ivy and brambles, the weight of his body tearing it away from the rock face. There, the mouth of a cavern lay exposed before their astonished gaze.

"The nuns' cave," James yelled. "I've found it."

He forgot the pain in his hands, where the bramble thorns bit into his palms. He swung himself onto a nearby ledge of rock and peered into the entrance of a tunnel wide enough to stand upright in.

He peered down at Dinah's upturned face.

"Don't you remember?" he called down to her. "Mother used to scare us when we'd done something bad. She told us the raiders would come down from Scotland and carry us away, like they took the Convents precious things, and the Sisters had to hide in a cave till they were gone."

A sad smile played briefly about the Prioress's lips. She recalled her sense of outrage even then, that such sacred and valuable things should be laid hands on by thieving knaves. Especially so when she was told that some of the booty carried off to Scotland had been willed to the Convent by her own ancestors, as was the custom of the 'dead man's hand.'

"I would have hidden the richest of the treasures, had I been Prioress then," she declared hotly to James that day, as they peered into the dim recesses of the nuns' refuge.

"Pish." James exclaimed, as he had often heard his father declare.

"You, a nun? And a Prioress, forsooth." His merry eyes travelled with amusement over his sister's disheveled state. Her fair hair had escaped from its binding, and curled in loose tendrils about her rosy face, tangled and teased free by the overhanging branches of the trees fringing the ascent to the cave. "Sister," he announced, and wagged a mocking finger in her direction. "There would not have been time to think of hiding treasures, then. Believe me," he teased, "the sight of those wild Scots would have sent you and your nuns fleeing like squawking hens before a fox." He let out another guffaw as his mind's eye pictured his sister in the habit of a Benedictine nun.

Then, he sobered suddenly, remembering that the unruly Scots still posed a threat to lands in the north, and that rape as well as robbery was a well-practiced accomplishment of such unwelcome marauders.

"Promise me little sister," he urged half seriously, half in jest. "If ever you should find yourself in such a situation you will hitch up your skirts and run." He laughed again, and Dinah glared at him, discomfited that he did not take her seriously. She
little guessed that for an instant, the boy in him became the man he was never to be. Nor that it was with a man's eyes that he glimpsed the full beauty of her promised womanhood.
With the edge of her veil the Prioress wiped away a tear that rolled down her cheek. Alas, there had been few such jaunts after that, for before the summer's end James had sickened.

She sighed. The sweat, they called it. And before the ripening berries had blackened on the brambles and swelled with their rich purple juice for making into her mother's jellies, James's young body was consigned to its untimely rest. Sorrow, deep and dark, pervaded the great house then. Though the daily necessity of the ordering of the household, its maids and serving men and the stable lads continued, yet something vital was gone. What purpose then was there to life and effort, and a joylessness overhung each day. As with the Staffields, the last link in the chain that was the name of Wharton was broken. No more of that name would follow.

Then it was that her parents decided that young Dinah should be sent to be made a nun. She was not asked if she thought the religious life would content her. Neither was she consulted when tentative marriage negotiations were discussed.

It had not been so when her elder sisters were betrothed to suitable landed gentlemen. In any case, at that dark time, Dinah cared little how they disposed of her life. She felt the keenness of her brother's loss as only a twin can feel. He had been her constant companion since birth, their lives two halves of one self-sufficient whole. What became of any possible betrothal plans, Dinah never knew, nor cared. No one, she thought, could ever replace James in her affections. And, as she was well aware, affection mattered little where marriage contracts were concerned.

If it existed, or came later, that was an unlooked for sweetener in an otherwise mercenary arrangement between landed families.

"It will be to your best advantage" her mother informed her one day, as they worked together in the stillroom. She arranged the rows of newly made preserves upon the shelves as one in a dream, and sighed. There was a tremor in the usually authoritative voice.

"You are our last child." She choked upon the words. Then she paused to compose herself, and continued with resolution. "Your father and I agree that it is meet we should give a child to God. After all," she continued with some bitterness in her voice, "He has already taken the other." With an intuition beyond her years, Dinah then perceived that, locked in the totality of their own grief, her parents not only salvaged no comfort from the presence of their remaining twin, but in her saw only the magnitude of their loss.

And so, when spring came, Mistress Dinah Wharton became a novice in the Benedictine Order of nuns at the small House that lay close to the Wharton lands.

The portion she brought with her was a goodly one, for her father was ever generous in his gifts. Thus, with a heart grown immune to feeling, the future Prioress of Heremitithwaite entered upon the religious life. Notwithstanding the double loneliness of separation first from her twin, and then from her parents and home, Dinah proved she was not her mother's daughter for nothing.

Coming as she did from a long line of capable women, in time, the newly professed nun far outstripped her contemporaries in natural skill and acquired ability. Whatever office she occupied in the small community, Dame Dinah performed the duties thereof with exemplary diligence, so that even the most exacting of superiors could not but give her credit for her endeavours.

It was therefore but a natural progression that when their old Prioress died and was laid in the earth of the nearby Nunclose, as was their right, the community elected Dame Dinah in her place. The House prospered under her competent rule, and in time, upon the death of her parents, Dame Dinah, and therefore the nunnery, benefitted considerably under the bequests of the Wharton will. For, as well as the handsome financial endowments the will entailed to the Prioress and her married sisters, it was the magnificent gift of a finely wrought crucifix of silver embedded with gems, a chalice and great candlesticks, also of heavy silver, that now occupied Dame Dinah's mind.

"They shall not have them," she vowed to herself when it became known that the King's Commissioners were visiting every religious House in the land, in order to evaluate its assets. What right, she reasoned, had the King, even though he now styled himself Head of the Church, what right had he to steal what had been given to God?

The sound of a commotion below broke in upon the Prioress's musings.

Indignant voices could be heard raised in anger, and from the narrow window of her chamber, Dame Dinah looked down upon the protesting figure of Robert Winter, the nunnery's woodcutter. He was flanked firmly on either side by Sisters Anne Dartwentwater and Galfride Chambers, and was being chivvied along by these two Ladies. It was obvious that he was being propelled in her direction for arbitration in some domestic dispute.

How many times, Dame Dinah wondered with exasperation, had the feckless Robert been warned about snaring rabbits in the woodlands, which formed part of the convent territory? And he, it was suspected, was not averse to helping himself to the odd fowl now and then from the Sisters' henhouse, for which loss foxes had likely been blamed. The Prioress sighed wearily, and descended the stairway to confront the irate complainants.

"Oh, Madame," Sister Galfride panted. Her portly frame was not accustomed to undue exertion and her round face glowed, with effort as well as anger. "We caught him again, Madame, setting his traps," she gasped. "And that's not all.' Here she was forced to pause in order to regain her breath, whereupon Sister Anne thrust the glowering woodcutter squarely in the Prioress's path and snapped. "Indeed, 'tis not, Madame. Old Sister Isabelle was collecting eggs, and she suspected one of her hens to be laying away.

We were searching for its nest within the copse, when she caught her foot in a trap. And we saw him."

She pointed an accusing finger at the sullen figure of the woodcutter "with a snare in his hands, trying to hide in a thicket." Sister Galfride, now sufficiently recovered as to become voluble again, opened her mouth to rejoin the fray, and then subsided before the upraised hand of the Prioress.

"Where is Sister Isabelle now?" she demanded, perceiving that in their quest for the meting out of justice on the hapless Robert, both nuns appeared to have forgotten the plight of Sister Isabelle.

"Still in the copse, Madame. Sister Marguerite is with her," Sister Anne replied.

"Then go back there, and help Sister Marguerite to bring her to the infirmary. I will deal with this matter," Dame Dinah pronounced, and cast a cold glance at the cringing Robert.

"Madame, I meant the Lady no harm," he whined, as his accusers departed.

"I believe you, Robert," the Prioress spoke wearily. "But how often have I instructed you not to set snares so close to the convent? And see now what your disobedience has caused."

Robert remained silent, but shifted his weight uneasily from one leg to the other, and twisted his greasy cap nervously between grimy hands.

"I tell you, Robert," Dame Dinah continued sternly, "this is your last warning. If you offend again, you will be turned out, you and your family, though it would grieve me to do so for their poor sakes. One more time, and you will lose both your living and the woodsman's dwelling you occupy here.

"Do you understand me?" She spoke sharply. He darted her a look of sheer malice, nodded, but was silent.

"Then go, and take heed, for your poor wife's sake. I would not see her suffer for your misdeeds."

Thus dismissed, he slunk as chastened as a whipped dog, and inwardly smarting, from the Lady's authoritative presence

November

When it was believed that a visit from the King's agents was imminent, (the Big Friar from Penrith having brought news of their arrival there) Dame Dinah acted swiftly. First, she gave leave to Sisters Anne and Galfride to visit their respective families, both by good fortune residing within reasonable travelling distance of the nunnery, and by happy coincidence, each family about to celebrate a marriage at so convenient a time.

It would be safer to have those two out of the way, the Prioress reckoned, for that which they did not know, they could not tell, should questions be asked of them later. Neither, it was certain, had the wits to stand up to the probings of experienced interrogators, which the King's agents must surely be. Besides, and the Prioress's mouth tightened in disapproval, Sister Galfride was always readily disposed to blabber unnecessarily about things that did not concern her.

As to old Sisters Isabelle and Mary, the former was now profoundly deaf, and the latter so dim-sighted that she was almost incapable of finding her way about safely without Dame Isabelle's constant watchfulness. The Commissioners would be hard put to get any sense out of them. But Sister Marguerite, though not yet fully professed, was a different matter. The Prioress's eyes softened, for in that young nun she recognised a kindred spirit, a reflection perhaps, of her former self.

The full bloom of that Sister's beauty could not be entirely concealed by the habit she wore, and her eyes, alive and sparkling with a ready wit and keen intellect, gave mobility and animation to a face of arresting beauty beneath the veil. Yes, Dame Dinah reasoned, she would have to know enough of the plan to be on her guard.

It was therefore on a night in late November, that while the convent slept, the Prioress and Sister Marguerite crept silently into the chapel. The red spark of the perpetual light glowed steadily, and a brilliant shaft of moonlight filtered through a high window, and fell full upon the altar. It caught at the jewels embedded in the silver crucifix, and where the white beams played upon the great candlesticks and chalice, the cold metal gleamed softly.

Both women knelt briefly in silent prayer, and before rising, the Prioress gazed upon the altar, knowing in her heart that she was unlikely to see it so again. Then, she rose, and closely followed by the young nun, gathered all from their positions on the altar. By the moon's light, they hastily wrapped each piece in rags ripped from worn-out habits deemed to be past mending, then gathered them into one bundle and secured the whole well with knotted cords. That done, Dame Dinah unlocked the aumbry recessed into the thickness of the chapel wall and lifted out a simple latten crucifix and candlesticks.
These, together with a chalice, were of little value, and had been in use before the gift of the Wharton treasures. These simple items she put in place upon the bared altar. Both women made their obeisance,

and withdrew into the greyness of the night's shadows, carrying their precious bundle between them. The air was chilled with frost, and they pulled close the thick, hooded cloaks they were accustomed to wear whilst occasionally riding abroad.

A tall figure, hooded as they were, watched for them from the shadows of the gatehouse wall. He lifted his hand in silent greeting, and without a word, shouldered the burden the Ladies carried. They kept within the shadows of overhanging trees, leafless now in the austerity of early winter, their dark figures merging swiftly into the darkness.

Somewhere, away on the fellside, the unearthly scream of a vixen announced her approaching fertility. Then, miles away, her call was answered by the staccato barks of a sharp-eared dog fox, eager to respond to her invitation to mate.

In his own mind, the Big Friar from Penrith doubted greatly that the Lady of Heremitithwaite would be able to find the cave she had spoken of that was the ancient nuns' hiding place she and her brother had discovered in their youth. Nigh upon twenty years had passed since that time, and it was past reason to expect that she could find the place again, in the darkness of night. But the Prioress was a determined woman, and he had given his word he would help her.

It was hard going. The sound of Croglin Water in full spate grew louder. There was a place where its boulder-strewn bed narrowed and fell into a steep ravine. Here, the rushing torrent was forced to cascade far below into a natural cauldron of rocks. Dame Dinah shivered, partly from the night's cold, and partly from a long-standing fear she had always had of the place. They descended into the ravine. The night-dark walls of solid rock rose sheer and menacingly, and glistened damply where the foaming waterfall created a constant spray.

The Friar went first, testing the way. It rose and dipped in the rutted sandstone, difficult to traverse and not without danger. The Ladies scrambled after him as best they might, panting with exertion, and barely able to conceal their fright.

They were still within sound of the rushing water when Dame Dinah caught her foot in a tangle of tree roots, for such was the shallow covering of earth atop the underlying bedrock, that they spread like a network of knotted veins probing in every crevice for nutriment. Her cry of alarm rose above the sound of rushing water. Friar John turned swiftly, but too late to break the Prioress's fall. She lay prostrate, half-stunned by the force of her fall, her nostrils pressed close into the earthy odours of decay, of rotting bracken and the musty dankness of mouldering leaves. Above her, she heard the murmur of voices, one tremulous in its concern, the other calm and reassuring.

She felt herself lifted and held in strong arms like a babe. Then, the shock of frost-cold air upon her face revived her senses A pain seared through her ankle, and brought her back to full consciousness, and the realisation that it would be impossible to cross that dangerous way ahead.

An angry tide of frustration boiled up in her, that she must acknowledge the limitations, not only of her sex, but also of increasing age. She reflected bitterly that once, with the confidence of youth, she had trod these rocky paths with ease, and pulled herself up the steep ledges by the slender boles of young saplings. It had been easy then, to walk sure-footedly upon the boulder-strewn edges of Eden's deep waters.

Now, lamed by her fall, giddy and shaken, she lay under the star-pricked blackness of the winter sky, and acknowledged with a sense of loss, that all life was an imperceptible ebbing away, little noticed as day followed day. It was a bitter draught to swallow, and Dame Dinah sighed deeply.

There was pressure upon her hand. Sister Marguerite knelt by her side and gently chafed it to warm it between her own. Her dark form blotted out the sky, but when she raised her head, her hood fell back and moonshine played full upon her face, encircling it in a halo of brilliant light.

Concern, compassion and yes, love, such as a daughter might feel for her mother, all these were written there, and to the aching soul of the Prioress, it was as balm.

"Oh, Madame," the girl exclaimed, and raised the hand she held between her own to her lips.
"Praise be to God, you are alive." She hesitated. "I feared that you were not."

"Peace, child." Dame Dinah smiled ruefully. "It seems that God still has work for me to do."
Then came a strange peace, a sensation of comfort. It enveloped her in a feeling of warmth, though the air was sharp with cold. She listened to the water, rushing, lapping, and gurgling in the riverbed below. The sound created a dimension of timelessness that was of an eternity enfolding all human life. She felt no inclination to stir, and despite the night's chill, was content to lie as one cocooned in that all-enfolding warmth, the origin of which was unknown to her.

She felt suspended between heaven and earth, as one in a dream. Why, she reasoned, should she feel so at peace when God had revealed this very night her frailty and failure? Truly, was the only answer that His was indeed a mysterious way?

She sensed a movement behind her. Only then did she become aware of a strong arm supporting her. The Friar's thick cloak was folded beneath her for protection from the cold earth, and she lay against the broad bulk of his chest. This was peace indeed, such as she had never known or dreamed of. Friar John turned her gently upon his arm. Now was the moment he knew he must dissuade this determined woman from her self-imposed mission.

"My Sister in faith," he spoke quietly, but with authority. "You cannot continue. It would be madness."

He expected her to protest, but strangely, she did not.
"You are right, Brother," came her mild reply. "It is so, I know it, and I am at fault."

She looked up into his face, so close to her own. Something awoke in the Prioress's consciousness. An iron hand loosened its grip upon her heart. Vaguely, she remembered James, and the warmth that had existed between them. But this was different. This nearness to the Friar was unnerving, and obedient to her long training, she drew away as from the warmth of an embrace. Her voice was low, as she sought to speak.
"Tonight, God has shown me that my pride has caused me to endanger your life." She drew Sister Marguerite towards her.

"And, God forbid, the life of this loving child He has placed in my care." Her voice gathered strength, as her conviction grew. Looking up, she held the Friar's eyes in an earnest gaze, and continued steadily. "Most truly I thank Him, yes, with all my heart. For He has revealed to me where true worth lies. The treasures I have burdened you with are as baubles in comparison to your care, and the love of this dear child. "She took his hand. He did not resist, despite the teaching of his Order to avoid familiarity with women. With her other hand, she drew Marguerite close to her. Spellbound, and silently then, and with hearts too full for words, they sat together, unheeding of the cold, and joying in the new aspect of each other's company, each sensing the mystical bond that would inextricably bind together their several destinies.

Each knew that such precious moments of intimacy could never again be theirs, the constraint of their shared monasticism inhibited even now any intimation of the joyous opening of the floodgates of the heart. Mortal love, in its several forms instigated by nature - that of lover, parent, child, mingled with that of their higher calling. It flowed into each receptive soul, and tempered in its purity, selfless and untainted by worldly lust, it engendered such radiance within, that each realised in wonderment the bestowal of an unlooked for grace.

It was the transit of the moon across the sky that stirred Friar John to action. He reached for the bundle that lay beside him, and with his movement, the trance was broken.

"Come." he spoke softly. "What we began must be finished."

The Prioress made as if to rise, but the Friar's hand restrained her. He spoke decisively. "No, I will do it, but alone. Sister Marguerite, see that the Lady stirs not till my return," he ordered.

In the face of such resolve, Dame Dinah's protests subsided, only to re-emerge, but feebly, as he shouldered the bundle.

"But the cave I told you of - you will not find it alone," she protested.

"Sister, I know a place where your treasures can be safely hidden. Besides, I will travel faster alone. See, the night is darkening. No moon now, to light the way."

She caught the urgency in his voice and acquiesced, knowing him to be right.

"Rest easy, now," he said. "The way back will be hard and slow for you, and we must gain the nunnery again while the night still hides us."

He left them within the sound of the waterfall's constant turbulence. Now the way dipped down, then climbed again, then dipped, tree-fringed always, and following Croglin's rushing course as it sped to meet and mingle with the wider waters of Eden. Then, at river level, the moon freed itself of the clouds that had darkened it. Onward Friar John hastened between its broad ribbon of light flecked water and towering walls of jagged rock - the gorge was close

. Now, with infinite care, he must cross the great sandstone slabs, smoothed aeons ago by the river's higher flow.

On summer days, it had often been his pleasure to ease his weary limbs awhile on these smooth outcrops. Then, bathed in sunlight and warmed to ruddy brightness by its glow, this same place emanated a singular peace, away from the intrusive perplexities of worldly things, a peace broken only by birdsong. Perhaps too, as he lay motionless, he might hear the wet slap of an otter fetching his catch from the water.

Now, beneath him, the black water slipped by. So close it surged against the steep side verges upon which he balanced, it was clear that one slip from its narrow shelf would plunge him and the Prioress's precious cargo into the cold embrace of Eden, from which the strong current would be unlikely to release them. Again, he paused to steady himself, his back pressed hard against a massive stone buttress. In places, the towering crags overhung the way ahead and blotted out the little light shed by the moon.

"Into Thy hands I commit myself, O Lord," he murmured. He gripped the bundle firmly. Now the way must be felt, with one free arm outstretched, tracing and never losing contact with the contours of the rock face behind him. He must test each step on the narrow ledge before trusting his body's weight upon it. At times there was barely a foothold between himself and the river.

He tried to remember where the ledge turned, or dipped, or rose again.

And always there was the sound of the river as it raced so close beneath him. His progress was slow, so carefully he edged his way above the fast-flowing water. He paused to rest often, and felt his heart pounding, as much from fear as with exertion.

He seemed to hear his own blood coursing through his ears, the sound merging with that of the water. At length the ledge began to widen. It curved suddenly, veering away from the river into a stony recess where it was safe to move freely.

"Praise be to God," the Friar panted. "The place is near."

It was not a cave, only a wide, hollowed-out tunnel in the fissured rock face. But it was deep, and receded well beyond the reach of a man's arm. It was dry, too, and well above the flow of the river, even in a flood. With haste, Friar John pushed his bundle along the passage between the rock walls until his outstretched fingers could barely make contact with it. He bent down and gathered up loose pebbles that crunched beneath his feet, and cast them down the tunnel's length. The convent's treasures thus sealed in at the furthest end only, the aperture's open mouth belied its use as a place of concealment. What relief he felt then, and the satisfaction of a mission accomplished.

Only the ordeal of the return journey remained, and that, with both hands now free to feel his way in greater safety, he made without mishap. By this time, the moon was well past its zenith. Its brilliance picked out with dancing lights the confluence of the two waters ahead.

Leafless branches of sycamore, beech and oak intertwined above him, to create a dark tracery against the star- studded sky. There was need for haste. The night was well advanced. He threaded his way, as speedily as was safe, between the tree trunks, up a steep bank of dying bracken, and climbed steadily alongside Croglin Water.

The nuns had not stirred. They were waiting, chilled and anxious, and huddled close together for warmth in the place where he had left them.

"All is done," he answered the unspoken question evident upon their upturned faces.

"Your treasures are safely hidden. Though I shall not tell you where, for fear you might be pressed one day for an answer."

A look passed between the women, and it was obvious they had discussed such a possibility during their wait.

"We would not implicate you, Brother," Dame Dinah announced with dignity.

"When the King's men come, and if it becomes necessary, then it is I who will take upon myself the sin of perjury, both as to the existence of our valuables, and their whereabouts. And," she added contritely, "May God forgive me if, by this night's work, I have endangered either of you, in body or soul."

An owl screeched nearby, and swooped upon its prey.

Sister Marguerite shivered.

"Oh, come Madame, let us leave this place. It frightens me, the water and the darkness." She hesitated, and began to tremble, though its cause was not the night's cold. "And," she whispered, "What we have done."

As parents might strive to reassure a fearful child, they sought to comfort her. With a mother's instinct, the Prioress's arm encircled the young nun.
She held her close, and gently rocked her to and fro, as she might a child. The Friar stooped low beside them and spoke earnestly.
"Peace, my daughter. Forget this night. Your part has been only that of obedience to your superior - no blame there."

He stood upright, and for a long moment, he contemplated the brilliance of the stars. Then he spoke with great resolve.
"For my part," he said, "I shall never speak of this matter again.""No," he continued, "not even in confession. For if" he added thoughtfully, "there has been sin this night, I shall lay it only before my Maker."
In the darkness that preceded dawn, they toiled at Dame Dinah's painful pace, at last into the precincts of the convent. There, only the wary eyes of a fox watched them, and he was intent solely upon the havoc he was about to cause within the Sisters' henhouse.

But no, it was not so. Close by, other eyes, craftier even than the fox's, noted with interest that the Prioress of Heremitithwaite walked abroad in the night.

They had watched her leave, the young nun with her, and saw that they carried a bundle between them. Upon her return, he noticed with interest that a tall Friar accompanied her, and that his arm encircled her waist. And the bundle? It was gone.

Robert Winter, for it was he, slung the carcasses of a brace of newly snared rabbits over his shoulder, and slunk from the cover of nearby bushes. He turned homeward to the woodsman's dwelling, a smile of satisfaction upon his face.

He garnered the information firmly in his malicious mind, for he had learned that such was valuable. There were those, in these days, who would pay handsomely for knowledge of what he had just witnessed.

***

How best to prepare the Ladies for the impending visit of the King's agents? And the disappearance of the altar silver? In her anxiety to ensure its safekeeping, Dame Dinah had given scant thought as to how to justify that. Haste was essential. Before the return of Dame Anne and Dame Galfride, there was no time to lose in preparing a plausible explanation for the reappearance of the Priory's humble latten ware that now replaced the silver upon the altar.

For a full day, Dame Dinah kept her chamber and rested. The convent was quiet, Sister Marguerite anxious, and though she tried to conceal her feelings, it was clear she was obviously troubled by the previous night's events.

Dame Mary and Dame Isabelle, as usual, looked after each other, in blissful ignorance of aught amiss. With as much regard for the truth as she could muster, the Prioress sought to fabricate a series of events that would satisfy, not only the returning nuns but also, of vital importance, the dreaded Visitors that the king's Chief Minister, Thomas Cromwell, would send in his name.

The first frosts of oncoming winter briefly rimed the grass that covered the nearby burial ground in the Nunclose. In a few days, Dame Anne and Dame Galfride returned, fingers and toes nipped by the cold. Dame Dinah's ankle still hindered her, so when the little community was complete, they were glad to gather together cosily in her chamber and warm themselves by a glowing fire.

When the happy prattle of the absent Sisters' telling of the recent events in their respective families subsided somewhat, the Prioress raised her hand for silence.
"There is news I regret I must tell you," she began, "for it grieves me. Our beautiful altar silver has been taken. It happened one night while you were away."

A moment of stunned silence prevailed before the impact of the Prioress's words found their mark. Dame Anne was the first to find her voice.

"Robbers, thieves," she shrieked. "I heard my brother say they're about in Inglewood Forest again. And more than deer they take," he said. "Oh, Madame, 'tis a mercy the House was not set alight."

Dame Galfride hastily crossed herself, and silently offered up her fervent thanks that she herself had been absent on that night, then joined Dame Anne in bewailing the loss of the convent's most valuable possessions.

The two old nuns, the blind and the deaf, sat side by side by side in the shadow of the soft light cast by the burning rush tapers. None noticed, for it happened often in these their latter years, that Dame Mary's head was nodding in the easy sleep of old age.

Her companion marked with mild interest the agitation of her two fellow nuns, but not a word could she understand. She therefore contented herself with watching the rapid opening and closing of their mouths.

Sister Marguerite, as instructed by her superior, was glad to remain silent. With bowed head, she sat a little way apart under the soft pool of light cast by the burning taper, and stitched with care upon the rich velvet of a cope, for the thread she embroidered with was purchased at great expense.

The wild imaginings of Dame Anne and Dame Galfride ran on until they had worked themselves up into a state of near hysteria, at which point the Prioress raised her hand.

"Silence," she commanded, and such was her authority that the sisters' frenzied chatter ceased forthwith, and she spoke earnestly to the two.
"I have prayed much over what has befallen us, and it has come to me that we have been in grave danger of committing the sin of pride." They looked at her blankly, without understanding.

"Yes, pride, Sisters," she reiterated, "misplaced pride in the beauty of a crucifix fashioned of precious metal and fine workmanship, and enriched with precious stones." She met the questioning gaze of Dame Anne and Dame Galfride. Dame Isabelle looked on uncomprehendingly, and Dame Mary slept on. Only Sister Marguerite looked down, and pulled back the thread she had stitched in error from the Bishop's cope.
"Our blessed Savior's cross was but of rough-hewn wood - no value there, no beauty nor artistry," Dame Dinah continued. "Yet, to all of Christendom it is of value beyond compare. Sisters, let us not grieve for what we no longer possess. Rather, let us remember with humility where true value lies, each time we look upon the old latten crucifix the poor nuns of this House were wont to use, which I have now placed upon the altar."

Christmas
The tannery at Lazonby, the Friary at Penrith, And Baronwood

It was the morning before Christmas Eve Day, frost-crisp, and in the early sunlight, beautiful to behold. A powdering of snow covered the hard-frozen earth, and the River Eden in Cumberland ran darkly between its icebound verges.

Edward Bowman, employed as a forester in the great Forest of Inglewood, sat his horse splendidly and presented a goodly sight to the maids of the village of Lazonby as he rode by. And it was not only the hearts of the village maids he caused to flutter, for many a matron, married doubtless to a lesser favored fellow, cast even bolder looks in his direction.

Edward was well aware of the pleasurable agitation his presence aroused, and with a cheery greeting, he doffed his cap to each of his admirers. His accompanying smile caused his blue eyes to twinkle engagingly and he rode on. Many a man would have taken advantage of such a situation, but not he. For Edward was ever mindful of his good fortune in wedding the incomparable Genett. She he loved dearly, and it was his earnest hope never to give her cause for grief.

The road took him straight through the village. He passed the Church of St. Nicholas where, long years ago a sapling yew had been planted at its entrance.

A greybeard whose dwelling was close by swore that he had it from his own grandsire that in the time of the fifth Henry, the same tree had been ancient then, and that from certain of its branches were fashioned bows that had wrought such havoc on the French at Agincourt. Now, a covering of frozen snow, which, having begun to melt at the hint of yesterday's thaw had frozen again in the night and now formed long icicles that glistened in the morning sun, softened the darkness of its great outline.

Edward breathed deeply of the sparkling air, savouring its clean coldness in his nostrils. He was bound first for the tanner's dwelling, and this lay some distance from the village, where the road began to rise towards the open fell. Accustomed as folk were to the stenches of daily life, no one it seemed cared to live in close proximity to Andrew Bowerbank's tanyard. His dwelling, known thereabouts as the Skin House, was a long, low structure built of warm hued sandstone, hewn from the fell. It lay close by a knoll of ground upon which a group of ash trees clustered. A small stream ran down from the fell before emptying into a pool bordered by rushes. Here, Andrew's tanpits were to be found, iced over now in the winter weather.

"Andrew, I bid thee good day," Edward drew rein and called out. The sound of his voice had the desired effect.

The burly figure of the tanner strode into view, still clutching a stout ash staff with which he had lately been breaking through the ice in his pits in order to prod at the few remaining skins soaking there.

"Have you got the deer hides for me, friend?" Edward called. "I'll take them with me to Penrith if they're ready."

"Caught the poachers yet, then?" Andrew queried as he carried the skins he had tanned for his friend.

Edward's face darkened. "Nay, but they're still about, I know. But two days gone, I found bloody patches in the snow where the killing was done. I'll wager they're selling the meat hereabouts. They'd not risk taking it into Penrith, or they'd soon be caught."

Edward dismounted swiftly, and together they packed the red deer skins into the two panniers slung across his horse's back.

"Ah, well," observed Andrew, ramming the skins home, "at least the friars will gain some benefit. Good, soft boots these will make for them, I'll swear, when they say the night office."

He was pleased to see Edward. They were firm friends. It had been so since boyhood, since the day they had roamed together on the fell, and captured a young foulmart there. The tiny creature was well nigh lifeless, with no sign of a mother nearby. Most likely it had been snatched up by a bird of prey on one of the rocky outcrops of Crossfell, where foulmarts were known to breed, and then dropped from its talons into the thick furze below. They had managed to rear it to maturity, and so used to the lads it had become that it was not averse to being carried about in a leather bag into which they had pierced air holes.

On one never to be forgotten occasion, it had accompanied the pair to Mass at St, Nicholas's Church, and there, no doubt judging its release to be overdue, it had chewed its way through the bottom of the bag and made its escape among the folk assembled there. In the clamour that ensued, the foulmart understandably panicked.

It bit deep into the fingers of the priest who cornered it and retaliated in the nature of its kind by emitting the foulest of stenches. In no time at all, the scent of burning incense was effectively overpowered, and subsequently both lads paid dearly for the foulmart's misdemeanour. But the sound beatings they each received from their respective fathers, to say nothing of the penances imposed upon them by the foulmart's injured captor, only served to strengthen their bonds of friendship.

"Come into the houseplace Edward and take some ale for the season's sake?" Andrew urged and added encouragingly, "Mary will be glad to see thee."

Being of a social nature, Andrew enjoyed nothing better than a good crack. But it was a pleasure he was often denied, as the aroma pervading his premises, especially in the summer months, was a strong deterrent to any prolonged conversation. Edward hadn't the heart to refuse, though he had much to do in Penrith and make the return journey before nightfall.

"One beaker, old friend, then I must be away. The market bell will be ringing in Penrith, ere long."

It was several beakers later, and full of the warm glow, not only of Mary's good ale, but also of friendship rekindled, that Edward remounted and was ready to leave. Andrew's plans for the betterment of the tanning trade had been mulled over, and as is the age-old custom at Christmas-time, many an old memory relived as the ale flowed from jug to beaker.

"Think you," asked Andrew, with the humour that enabled him to see a comical streak in most situations, "think you that we should have done but half the penance had the foulmart been but a sweetmart, that time at the Mass?"

Between guffaws of laughter, he clapped Edward on the thigh, and the two gripped hands in farewell, each savouring the remembrances of boyhood.

"Take care on the road, friend," he called, as Edward turned his horse's head in the direction of Penrith, and urged his mount to a smart pace. He turned in the saddle and waved farewell. Along the lower fellside, he made good speed where the road allowed, riding in the tracks of those who had taken their merchandise to market early. Nevertheless, by the time he entered the town, Penrith was already thronged with folk. They crowded the alleyways and open spaces, both buyers and sellers, and the hum of their busy commerce was everywhere.

Edward was anxious to join them, for he had much to do and the hours of daylight were short in winter.

But first, he must unload the skins from out of his panniers, and he threaded his way through the jostling crowds till he approached the House of the Austin Friars. There, he dismounted, and rang the bell at the gatehouse. He made his business known, and the tall figure of Friar John hastened to meet him.

"A welcome gift indeed," he beamed, well pleased at the sight of the skins.

'Friars' feet travel far, and the ways are hard. These skins will make soft night boots for the brethren. Our thanks, my son."

Within the Friary precinct, it being near noon, a bell began to toll, thus preventing any further converse. This, each would have welcomed, since the Friar's last itinerary had not taken him near Baronwood, which lay- within great Inglewood Forest and Edward's dwelling. It had been at the ancient preaching cross in Lazonby where they had first met.

Throughout that bitter day, flurries of sleet had soaked repeatedly into the thick habit the Friar wore, till it hung heavy and chill about a body aching with cold. Few lingered to hear his words, and at close of day, these too melted away homeward. It was then that Edward's tall figure stepped out of the gathering dusk and gripped his icy hand.

"Come home with me, Brother," a warm voice urged.

'Tis not fit to attempt the miles to Penrith tonight." Thereafter, whenever Friar John's travels took him that way, he was welcomed in the forester's dwelling with the same generous hospitality that had warmed him, body and soul, that night. But the tolling bell must be obeyed. Upon some instinct, the Friar made the sign of the cross upon Edward's breast.

"God protect you, my son," he murmured, then he gathered together the deerskins and hastened away into the Friary.

The hours of daylight in the winter day were short, and Edward lost no time in going about the rest of his business. Nevertheless, the pale sun was well down in the sky, and the market folk packing up their unsold wares, before he was ready to head out of town.

His panniers were now full of all necessary provisions should there be more falls of snow to drift and isolate his forest home. Over the fells, a biting wind began to whistle, and with the oncoming night it was certain there would be a hard frost. Edward quickened his horse's pace.

It would be good to get home. Genett, she would be awaiting his arrival with some anxiety, for though she suppressed her fears, he knew she was well aware of the risks lone travellers took upon the roads on market days. There were ruffians a-plenty lying in wait to rob, or worse, and Edward, being a forester; he was no friend to the poacher. To them, he was a constant threat, and it would be no grief to such as they should he meet with any mishap.

On the outskirts of Penrith, signs of habitation were sparse. Only the odd tumbledown hovel remained before his way would take him onto the open fellside, and thence by woodland tracks to home. His thoughts turned again to Genett.

By next Christmas, if God was good, they would have another child. He smiled. Perhaps it would be a daughter, to grow into as lovely a woman as her mother, a sister for young Benedict. Ah, Benedict. A proud smile played upon his wind-stiffened lips. Even a king would covet such a son as he.

If it had not been for the starving mouse foraging in the tufts of grass... if it had not been for the screech of the hunting owl as it swooped upon it.... then probably Edward would have reached his home and Genett in safety. As it was, his startled horse reared high upon its haunches. It whinnied in alarm, and caught unawares, Edward was unseated and slid down its hindquarters.

He kicked his feet free of the stirrups and rolled onto the snowy verges of the road.

Unhurt, but shaken, and cursing roundly, he picked himself up and followed the frightened beast as it bolted down an alleyway into the cobbled yard of one of the deserted hovels.

In the commotion that followed, Edward barely had time to take in the full impact of the scene before his eyes. Whole carcasses of deer lay stacked in the snow.

By the dim light of a lantern, others were being dismembered and the joints packed into panniers by two burly poachers, for distribution, no doubt, to conniving customers under cover of darkness. Caught red-handed at their illicit trade, one of the rogues let out a bellow of rage. He yelled a warning to his companion, and together they leapt towards Edward, their knives bloody from the deer meat. But between Edward and his oncoming assailants, the bulk of his still agitated horse loomed out of the deepening dusk.

Its lashing hooves sent one of the fellows sprawling across the cobbles. The other fell back out of their immediate range. With a gentling hand upon the creature's neck, one leap carried Edward into the saddle. But it was too late. Both poachers now blocked the entrance to the alley, and the road home. Vainly, Edward tried to rush them, but one seized his horse's mane, while the other stabbed at his chest.

The blow missed its mark, but the sharp blade slashed open his thigh. Blood spurted from the wound, and he crouched forward upon the horse's neck, taking the full force of the second blow upon his back. The knife entered deep between his ribs, and lodging there, was embedded almost to its grimy hilt. With fingers wound tightly into the horse's mane, and with all his might, Edward urged the frantic animal out of the yard and onto the road again The taste of blood was in his mouth, welling up, choking him.... he must get help, and fast.

He turned for the town again. The Friary, he must reach the Friary before consciousness left him.

It was Friar John who found him, slumped in a pool of blood at the gatehouse door. Nothing could be done. He was already in extremis, and when the blade was withdrawn, blood poured from the gaping wound and frothed in a bright stream from out of his ashen lips. At the point of death, he rallied briefly.

"Genett, I pray you....care for my Genett....and Benedict..."

Friar John barely heard the laboured whisper before the last flickering spark of life was extinguished.

***

It was growing late. He should have been home from market hours ago. How many times had Genett opened the door of the dwelling to stare out into the night? Her ears strained to listen for the sound of hooves, but only the screech of a hunting owl broke the silence.

"Mother, it grows cold in here when the door opens so much," complained the small boy warming himself at the fire. His mother had baked bread that day, enough to last the whole of Christmas week, and now he dipped the crusty chunks she had given him into his piggin of hot milk, and savoured its fragrance.

"'Tis time thy father was here" she sighed, and despite his tender years, Benedict caught the sharp edge of fear in her voice, and sensed the alarm she tried to hide from him.

"He'll be back soon, Mother, never fear." He smiled up at her with childish confidence in his father's invulnerability. No harm, he believed, could come to him. For was he not strong and fearless, and the best wrestler for miles around? He lifted the piggin to his lips, and drained its contents to the last drop.

"Perhaps his horse has cast a shoe," he suggested thoughtfully. Genett gave him a swift glance. She must not allow her own fears to disturb her son. She crossed the room, and took the empty bowl from his hands.

"Of course," she agreed. "Why did I not think of that? He would have to ride slowly, with his panniers full."

With her free hand, she stroked her son's hair, then let it rest lightly upon his shoulder. Her accompanying laugh reassured him, and raising a small hand, he grasped his mother's hand in his.

Ah, his mother. Benedict was certain she must be the most beautiful woman in the whole world. To his mind, even the Blessed Virgin, of whom the Big Friar often spoke, could surely be no lovelier than she. For a long moment mother and son looked at each other, and the small room seemed to glow in the radiance of their love. Genett knelt down, and in the comforting warmth of the turf fire, made him ready for his bed.

"Mother," excitement sparkled in Benedict's dark eyes, and eagerly they searched her face.

"Think you my father will bring me back a gift from the market, since 'tis soon to be Christmas " he asked earnestly.

Genett laughed.

"I shall be surprised indeed if he does not" she replied, and pulled him close against her thickening body.

"Shall I ever be able to love another child as I love this one." she asked herself. "Will there be enough love in me for this second babe?" Genett pondered those questions that inevitably occur to all mothers of their firstborn, then hastily dismissed them as though they signified disloyalty to her little one as yet unborn. She brushed Benedict's face with her lips, and pressed him close to her again.

The wholesome smell of new-baked bread was upon her, its fragrance one with her thick, shining hair, her skin, her clothes. Afterwards, long afterwards, in the smell of bread, Benedict was to remember those golden moments of intimacy they shared, in the fleeting hours before innocence ended.

The thudding of hooves resounded on the frosted pathways through Baronwood. Two riders, inflamed by copious draughts of strong ale they had lately consumed in Penrith, urged on their mounts at breakneck speed. They cursed soundly when the hard-driven beasts' feet splayed on the ice-rutted tracks. With loud obscenities they dismounted awkwardly, and stumbled on uncertain legs to Genett's door. They tried the latch, but the sturdy door was fastened from within.

"Open up, Mistress. We're in need of hospitality for the night," one bawled, his speech came thick and slurred.

"And entertainment, too," his companion shouted. He laughed raucously at his own wit, and rattled upon the shuttered windows with his whip.

Within, all Genett's fears crystallised into one paralysing knot of terror. It centred in her vitals, then radiated throughout her entire body, so that for a brief moment she was immobilised, still kneeling before the fire, Benedict enclosed in her arms.

Then, the renewed clamour outside the door roused her to action.

She rose, as hastily as her condition allowed, one protective hand laid instinctively over her gently rounding belly. The other, she pressed firmly into the small of Benedict's back, and propelled him swiftly through the passage that led to the haystore at the end of the long, low dwelling.

"Mother," Benedict gasped in alarm, "be they robbers, or the Scots raiders come again to steal cattle?" His eyes widened with fright, as he remembered tales he had heard of the ferocity of these wild men from over the border.

"Nay, son," Genett answered him soothingly. "I think they be but revellers from the Christmas market. There'll be many with too much ale inside them this night in Penrith."

There was only the smallest of windows in the haystore, through which a few beams of moonlight penetrated.

Genett hurried her son into the darkest corner where, with frantic speed, she hollowed out a depression for him to hide in the dry hay. She took off her woollen shawl, and laid it down for him on the makeshift bed.

"Here, lie down on this, my sweeting," she whispered, and Benedict obeyed without question, catching the urgency in her low voice.

With shaking hands, she wrapped the thick shawl around his small body, then piled the loosened hay over him, leaving only a small space for breathing around his nostrils.

"Stay here, Benedict, and be as quiet as a mouse. Not a sound, remember. I'll come for thee when I've sent those noisy fellows away. Do not come out, mind, for any reason."

She kissed the tip of his nose, then pulled the heavy door of the haystore behind her, and was gone. In the warmth of his mother's shawl, and deep in a nest of sweet-smelling hay, Benedict felt snug and secure when he remembered that the Big Friar had told him that Our Lord and Saviour had, when a babe, been laid upon such a bed of hay. He had confidence in his mother's ability to send the Christmas revellers on their way, but he wished heartily that his father was here.

The smell of Genett's bread still lingered in the wool of her shawl. It was still warm from her body, and it comforted the small boy, for whom the long day had been full of anticipation.

Christmas was almost here, and that morning, with the early sunlight causing bright sparks to dance on the night's frost, he had watched his father mount up, then turn in the saddle to wave him goodbye. Then he rode off at- a brisk pace along the forest track through Baronwood, to the market in Penrith.

The weight of his body compacted the hay beneath him. He imagined he was a bird deep in its warm nest. Soon, his father would come home, and surely, so his mother said, there would be a gift for him, hidden in the panniers slung across his horse's back.

Sweetmeats perhaps from Penrith market, some marchpane maybe...Soon he was drifting into sleep, dreaming his last enchanting dreams of childhood.

Back in the houseplace, all seemed quiet again. Genett slid to the floor and prayed fervently for her husband's return.

"Oh, Blessed Virgin, send him home to me.

I need him so," she pleaded. Footsteps! Those ruffians were back! Each beat of her heart resounded like a drum beating in her ears. Something crashed into the door, splintering the stout wooden boards with ease.

"Dear Mother of God, protect us from evil," she gasped.

They had found the axe in the woodstore outside. Another mighty blow, and the great blade of the axe pierced the door. She rose to her feet.

They should not see her kneel.

She confronted the leering pair. "Sirs. What dost thou here at this late hour? Surely all good folk are abed by now."

"True, Mistress," one of them grinned meaningfully. "'Tis exactly what we had in mind." He licked his lips at the prospect. He would have taken her anyway, like the many others, whether fair or ill-favoured, he had ravished between Inglewood and the border. But this one was a beauty. It would be a pleasure to take her, indeed. He advanced purposefully, like a beast upon its prey, his intention all too plain. In disgust, Genett recoiled from him.

There was the stink of sour ale upon his breath, and the accumulation of stale sweat on the shirt beneath his bloodstained leather jerkin caused her to retch violently.

She was trapped by the louts before her, and the hot fire at her back.

Suddenly, she was overcome by a surge of all-consuming fury at this violation of her home. It overtook her fear, and as a cornered animal will turn on its tormentors, Genett seized the long chain suspended at the funnel-shaped chimney rising above the turf fed fire. Here, daily, and with love, she would tend her cooking pots over its heat to feed her family. Here, she baked her bread on the covered plate. Now the chain was her weapon. Anger gave her strength, so much strength that when she swung its free end, the terminal hook, hot from its proximity to the fire, slashed across her would-be assailant's face and embedded itself in one of his heavy jowls.

"Vixen," he yelped. "You'll pay me well for this." Blood spurted from the torn flesh, and when he wrenched the chain from her grasp and withdrew the hook, it trickled freely down his cheek and into the neck of his filthy shirt. It was only then that his companion left off gorging himself on the bread he found cooling on the trestle table. He stabbed his long-bladed knife, with which he had lately carved up a quantity of poached venison, into the crusted surface of loaf.

Then he took a long swig of newly brewed ale, belched loudly, and drew a bloodstained sleeve across his mouth.
He spoke not a word, and as the other vainly attempted to staunch the flow of blood gushing from his cheek he dealt Genett a savage blow across her face.
The force of it sent her reeling, and before she could recover her balance, he leapt upon her with cat-like speed.
Vice- like, he pinioned her arms and thrust her into the panelled alcove, which contained the chaff-filled mattress of her undefiled marriage-bed.

No use to ask for pity, either for herself or her unborn child, for Genett knew she could expect none. Nor would she cry out, no matter what her body might endure. For what if Benedict should hear, and despite her warning to him to stay hidden, what scenes of debauchery might his innocent eyes then discover?

And so she bore both the shame and the pain inflicted upon her, first by the silent one, who took her coldly, with methodical cruelty. Then, when he was sated with his sport, the other, with the bloodied face, advanced upon her. His appetite was made doubly keen by rage, and the pain she had caused him. His lust knew no bounds, and when at last he was done with her, she lay bruised, bleeding, and seemingly lifeless upon the bed.

They supped again, on her bread and ale, before galloping off in the direction of Eden. There, they holed up in one of the several caves overhanging the river, where often men of ill- repute concealed themselves from justice. They lighted a fire at its mouth, and drowsed before its crackling flames. No pangs of guilt or remorse disturbed their dreamless sleep, and the sun was well up on the morning of Christmas Eve before they roused themselves.

Before dawn, Genett's senses returned. Her limbs were stiff with cold. Pains racked her entire body. One pain above all others pierced her consciousness with its persistent regularity. It came, then for a brief respite, it receded.

Then it returned in greater intensity, and with each pulsating throb, the red tide of her life ebbed away, and on its flood carried the small being that was to have been her second son. Between dawn and daybreak Benedict woke.

His mother's shawl no longer kept out the cold, and his breath had frozen like cobwebs in the morning dew upon the wisps of hay around his face. His mother had promised to fetch him when she had sent the noisy men away, but she had not done so. All was quiet now, so he rose, pulled out the shawl from under the heap of hay where he had slept, and wrapping it close, he stumbled, half sleeping, along the passageway leading to the houseplace.

He could tell, even in the dimness of early morning that his father was still not returned, and it troubled him. His mother lay still upon the bed. Her sleep was deep, and she did not stir when he touched her icy hand. In the grey light of the wintry morning, he did not see the blood that spread beneath her. Gently, so as not to wake her, he covered her with the shawl, and crept under it into the bed beside her. With one arm, he encircled her neck, and laid his head in the hollow of her shoulder, and nestling close to her still form, he slept again.

***

In Penrith, no-one save his brothers, rising at first light for prayer, was yet astir. While he saddled up his nag and clattered out of the stableyard, Friar John contemplated, with a heavy heart, the tidings he must carry to the newly made widow and her young son.
The waning moon still shone, and in its white brilliance, the frosted road was almost as light as day. It was of small consequence to him, however, for there was scarcely a road or track for many miles around that was not familiar to him.

Soon, he was through the town, and out into the open countryside. He rode on steadily, and with as much speed as he judged it safe to ride, and where the way was sheeted over with ice, he dismounted and led his horse without mishap. Urgent as his mission was, it was then that he was thankful that he had not neglected to make the beast's hooves slipshod by binding them with rags before leaving the Friary.

Dawn broke over the fells as he approached Baronwood. In moments, the sun rose to its full splendour, to lie like a huge bloodspot over the white sheet of the snowy landscape. As he entered the trackway leading to Edward Bowman's dwelling, the Friar could see by the churned up snow that he was not the only rider to have passed that way of late. No wisps of smoke could be seen rising among the trees. He rode up to the door, and saw that its timbers were shattered.

Friar John was no stranger to scenes of violence. Unlike his cloistered brethren of the monasteries, his journeys carried him far abroad, to preach, to beg alms, but all too often to bind up the wounds of the hurt.

He dismounted with haste, fearing what he might discover, and once within the confines of the small room, he instantly recognised the unmistakable odour of blood. Clearly, there was great mischief done here.

Fearfully, dreading what he might find, the Friar picked his way across the floor of the houseplace.

It was littered with broken bread, and in places still damp from the ale spilled over it hours before. Through the thick bed curtains that kept out the cold, and now only partially enclosed the bed, he could see the still forms of Genett and her small son.

In the grey light of the winter morning, he saw that her face was bruised and swollen, her hair dishevelled and matted with dried blood. She was quite dead, her body stiffening. And the child? With dread, the Friar bent down. He looked closer, then saw the rise and fall of the small chest. He breathed, and despite the chill of the morning, his face was rosy with sleep. Mercifully, he appeared unharmed, and seeking warmth, he pressed close to his mother's body. Slowly, so as not to wake him, Brother John drew aside Genett's woollen shawl, and gasped. There was so much blood. It was darkening now in a great pool that spread beneath her. And yet, his feet drawn up beneath him for warmth, Benedict was untouched by it.

The friar felt a great surge of mounting anger engulf him at the sight. This young child, so cruelly bereft of father and now mother in the same night, he must wake to impart such grievous news.
Carefully, he covered Genett's body with her shawl to hide the sight from Benedict, and he, disturbed by the movement, felt himself lifted from the bed. Strong arms held him, folding him tenderly against a broad shoulder.

"Father," he murmured, with pleasure and relief, sleep still heavy on his eyelids. A voice that was not his father's spoke quietly against his ear.

"Benedict. You remember me, Brother John? The Big Friar folk call me." Benedict drew back in the arms that held him, wide-awake now. The face he saw was kindly, and familiar to him, but it was not the one he expected to see. Disappointment and unease clouded the young face, and in an effort to distract him, the Friar set him down quickly, and knelt down beside him.

"My son, while I attend upon thy mother, I beg you look to my horse for me. The good beast has carried me safely from Penrith this day, and is in need of some hay."

He must work with all speed while the lad was out of the room. The body could not be left unprotected. The door no longer served its purpose. Besides, rats were never far away, and in the harshness of winter, foxes grew bold in their quest for food. He searched in the houseplace, and lifted the heavy lid of a wooden chest set at the side of the fire. It served as a meal ark, and the level of meal in it was low.

It would suffice to secure the body from harm until burial could be arranged, for with the ground frozen hard, it might be weeks before that might be. In another chest, he found a coverlet, and spread it inside the ark. Then, with great gentleness, he carried Genett's ravaged body to lay it carefully within.

In the crook of her arm, he cradled her tiny, scarce-formed babe, and drew the edges of the coverlet over all, so that no hint of the outrage committed below was visible.

With a heavy heart, he went in search of Benedict. The lad had taken hay to his tethered horse, and now sat brooding in the haystore, where he had lately been sleeping.
Friar John took Benedict's small hand in his own and led him back into the houseplace. He was so young to hear the pain of what he must be told.
"Benedict," he began. "I have sad things to tell thee. How I wish it was not so." He knelt down beside the child, and held him close. Benedict felt fear, such as he had never known, rising within him.

"My father," he cried out. "Oh, Brother John, what is the matter? My father never came home last night," he sobbed. "And those men I heard outside! They frightened my mother, I know. She hid me in the haystore, and forbade me to come out." His words tumbled out, demanding an answer. Then he saw the bed where his mother's body had been lying was empty.

"Where is my mother?" His voice rose to a scream as panic seized him. The moment was come. With infinite tenderness the Friar drew the child closer and strove to find words that would not lacerate his young heart. But there was none.

He gathered him close to his breast.

"Little one," he spoke gently. "Thy father and thy mother are both now in God's care." He felt a shuddering against his chest.

"Wicked men killing thy father in Penrith. Then I fear it was they who came here and caused thy mother to die." It was done. There was no way to soften the impact of those terrible words.

When at last the storm of weeping lessened, and the power of shock enfolded the child's exhausted mind in its merciful numbness, he allowed the Friar to lead him to where his mother lay.

"Come, Benedict, let us commend thy mother's soul to God's mercy." Benedict knelt before the meal ark, and surveyed its contents with no sense of reality. It was a bad dream. He would awake from it soon, and if he cried out, as he sometimes did in a night terror, his mother would come to his bedside to soothe him.

The intoned words of prayer he could hear the Friar speaking had no meaning for him. Only the sound of the heavy lid of the meal ark closing over her pale face spoke with an eloquence that words could not, for this was his first understanding of death.

***

Benedict sat astride the Friar's horse and lay back against the broad expanse of his chest. He was barely conscious of its movements beneath his legs. But yester morning, there had been no happier boy in the whole of great Inglewood Forest, as he watched his father ride away to Penrith. Now, the Big Friar had told him that both his father and mother were dead. Evil men, he said, had killed his brave father, as he journeyed home. Were they, he wondered, the same wicked men who had so affrighted his mother last night, and had caused her to die? And, he wondered fearfully, what was to become of him? Friar John was taking him away from his home in Baronwood. Who, then, he asked himself, would care for him now?

On market days, when sometimes he had ridden with his father into Penrith, he had seen the beggar boys, some as young as he. They ran ragged and barefoot, in the streets and alleys of the town, pleading for a coin here, stealing a morsel where they might. A cuff and a curse, more often than not, was their only recompense.

"Brother John," he turned anxiously on the horse's back to peer upwards into the Friar's weathered face. "Brother, must I now beg for my bread, as the beggar lads do?" Anxiety, such as a child should not know, was in the tremulous voice.

"Nay, my son, fear not. I will beg for us both, if need be." With a father's instinct, he drew the folds of his habit around the child's shivering frame, and firmly enclosed his cold hands beneath his own. Benedict sensed their strength as they gripped the horse's reins, and the cold hand of fear that clutched his heart relaxed a mite. Thus they plodded on towards Penrith, each deep in his own sorrowful thoughts.

It was with a deep sense of unease that the Friar contemplated the events of the last few hours. In his earlier years he had renounced his family's considerable wealth in order to serve God by serving the least of his needy creatures, and of that work he had found there was no end.

Long ago, in his youth, he had loved a woman. She was young and very beautiful, and they were promised in marriage to each other. Then, how it happened, he could not tell, for although he loved her dearly, another love, great and compelling claimed him. It was God's call to serve the poor and needy. It was insistent, and would not be denied. And so he submitted himself, body and soul, to the rigour of the Augustinian Rule. But now he had felt the stirrings of that earthly love again. It was when he sat near the rushing waters of Croglin Beck with the Prioress of Heremitithwaite. If neither he nor she had been in holy orders, what then might have been?

No matter what the Augustinian Rule had required of him, be it long hours of prayer or manual labour, journeys far afield to preach to souls ignorant of the word of God, or begging alms for the support of his community in Penrith, he had been faithful in all these things, and more.

Though as to the latter, it must be said, it was not in his natural inclination to beg. Therefore, he prayed earnestly for grace to sublimate his pride in order to fulfil this obligation too.

With regard to women, the Rule decreed the avoidance of all familiarity, any look or touch that might cause temptation to a brother being strictly forbidden.

In this also, he had succeeded in suppressing those natural instincts implanted by God in man for the continuance of the human race. For were not those sworn to celibacy men too? But the presence of the child lying against his breast evoked in him a strange emotion. He felt a great surge of pity for him, made fatherless and motherless in the same night. The scenes he had encountered in the woodland home touched a chord, nay, twin chords, in the very fibre of his being, which, being dissimilar twins, pulled his thoughts in opposite directions.

For the one, it seemed, was of divine origin, born in a flash of revelation suggested by the broken bread and spilt ale.
Was it, he wondered, irreverent - heretical even - to liken that woman's ultimate sacrifice of love, to that represented by the holy Eucharist? Was not her sacrifice a pale shadow, an echo maybe, of that mighty, all-encompassing love whereby all souls might gain salvation? Not so, the other chord: Its origin was worldly. It was an ache for the loss of what he had, in the burning zeal of his youth, barely realised he had renounced. The woman, the child - they represented all that might have been.

Dusk was upon them as they neared Penrith, and so intense was the cold as night drew on, that it seemed to bite their very bones.

As it was past sunset, Vespers were over in the little community, and the brothers assembled. All who had been absent were now returned to be together, perhaps for the last time, on this most blessed of nights.

On the morrow, on Christmas Day, they would light their candles in the chapel. Such had been their custom for nigh on two hundred years. The friars had first come to Penrith in the reign of the first Edward, making their way across the wild northern fells from Newcastle-upon-Tyne. With a grant of land, they established their House in Penrith. But poverty was ever their constant companion, so in an effort to encourage some measure of charity towards the brethren, an indulgence of forty days was granted by the Bishop of Carlisle to all those who should be present to see the candles lit on Christmas Day, and to those who made the friars presents, because they were so very poor. How many of the good folk of Penrith, Friar John wondered, would witness the lighting of the candles on the morrow at the celebration of Christ's holy Mass?

Brother John's thoughts ran deep. These were uncertain times for both Church and state. The King's marriage to Spanish Katherine, after long years of waiting, produced no living male heir.

There was outrage in the land when it became known that he wished to put away his wife in order to marry her dark-eyed waiting-woman, Mistress Anne Boleyn.

King Henry's pleas to the Pope had fallen on deaf ears, and his bold step in breaking with Rome, and proclaiming himself Head of the Church in England was creating turmoil throughout the kingdom.

There was turmoil too in the Augustinian Order itself. In the seats of learning in the south, there were those who had already broken with the traditions of the past, and it was said, were eager to espouse the new Lutheran doctrines from Germany. One of these, it was rumoured, George Browne of Canterbury, had been persuaded to officiate at the secret marriage of Henry Tudor and Mistress Anne Boleyn in January 1533, and he it was who proclaimed Anne, Queen of England in the Church of the Austin Friars on Easter Sunday that same year, to the great scandal and indignation of those present. Then a babe, the King's second surviving child, also a daughter, had been born the following September, and the new queen, even now, awaited with hope, the birth of a living son.

At his back, Benedict felt the rise and fall of the Friar's chest, as he sighed deeply, recalling that it was in that same year too, that the visitation of the religious houses began.

Now, on the orders of the King's chief Minister, Thomas Cromwell, all must swear an oath of allegiance to Queen Anne, and the King's issue by her.

That night, Benedict lay in Friar John's cheerless cell. The heaviness of his sorrow exhausted him, and he drifted into a fitful sleep. For a time, a merciful oblivion blotted out all knowledge of the day's horrors. Then, as in a recurring dream, a night terror, consciousness returned throughout the hours of darkness, and in those waking moments, Benedict could see the dimly burning rush light calmed a bowed figure kneeling in earnest prayer, and the fear that gripped his vitals.

News of the murder of Edward and Genett Bowman spread swiftly. By daybreak on Christmas morning, a body of men gathered at the bridge in Lazonby, and led by the tanner, they marched with furious intent along the banks of the river towards the caves where it was known that men of ill repute denned up to hide from justice. Had not the distant flicker of their fire been glimpsed through the hours of darkness?

It was well, both for the hunters and the hunted, that the killers had fled before the angry posse arrived at their hideout. Andrew Bowerbank stood by the cooling ashes of a recent fire, and raged inwardly.

He gripped one of the sharp knives he had snatched up that he used for shaping leather, and kicked with all his might at pieces of sunburnt logs doused by his intended prey before they galloped north to the Scottish border.

"Too late! We're too late, lads." Andrew's voice shook with suppressed fury. His eyes travelled over the bone-littered floor of the cave where Edward's killers had feasted upon stolen venison.

There was a shout from its dim interior, and in a darkened corner, virtually out of sight, a horse's panniers lay. They were Edward's - proof indeed, if any were needed, that the killers had lain up in this inaccessible spot before making good their escape.

The panniers contained little of the provisions Edward had purchased in Penrith. All that was deemed to be of any value was gone, as of course, was Edward's horse. But amidst the residue for which the robbers had no use, Andrew discovered a pretty comb. It was made of horn and he recognised its quality immediately. Indeed, he was familiar with the craft of the hornworkers. As with his own trade, the stink created by their boiling of the cattle horns in order to render the material workable, deterred any lengthy association with them.

The comb - no doubt it was intended as a Christmas gift for Genett. He delved into the depths of the panniers again, and then in his hands he held a box of sweetmeats - it was a gift to delight a child. For a poignant moment a tear glazed the tanner's eye, and pity took the place of cold fury in his heart.

"Oh, Edward, Edward my friend," came his agonised cry. "God keep thee."

***

Once again, Brother John stood at the gatehouse door of the Friary in Penrith. It was the beginning of January, and Benedict's future was resolved.

For a week, the good friars had lavished their care and prayers upon him. It was fortunate that several fat geese were amongst the gifts received by the community at the lighting of their candles on Christmas Day, as these augmented handsomely the brethren's otherwise meagre diet. Benedict, therefore, as their guest, had dined well. Every effort was made by these kindly men to divert the child's troubled mind, and all agreed that in spite of his natural grief, he was an apt pupil. Now the time had come to give him into the care of his father's friend, Andrew Bowerbank, the tanner of Lazonby, a man known well enough to the community for his honest dealings and generosity of heart.

"God keep and protect you always," the Big Friar said, and laid his hand upon Benedict's head in blessing.

Benedict felt himself swung high into the saddle of Andrew's horse, and the tanner's solid frame behind him felt reassuring.
"He shall be as my own son, Brother, I swear." Andrew's voice was gruff with emotion.

"Come, Benedict. There is a brother and sister waiting in Lazonby to meet thee."

With that, Andrew gathered the reins in one hand, and with his free arm held Benedict close as he urged his horse into a quick trot.

"God speed, Benedict," the Big Friar called after them. He watched their departure until they disappeared from sight, then turned to re-enter the Friary. Why, he wondered, did he feel such a sense of loss, of emptiness and strange uncertainty?

***

Far away, at Kimbolton Castle, in the flat lands of Cambridgeshire, in the afternoon of the seventh of January, the many trials of Katherine, Princess of Aragon, divorced wife of King Henry the Eighth of England, and lately styled Princess Dowager of Wales, were ended. She was not mourned by the King, her husband of some twenty-six years, and certainly not by his second wife and queen, Anne Boleyn. But the common people judged her to be much wronged, and held her in high esteem and respect.

Peterborough Abbey was made ready to receive her mortal remains on the twenty-ninth of January, and on that same day, at Greenwich, Queen Anne lay in the throes of premature childbirth. To the King's fury, she miscarried of a son. It was her undoing, for the King's great love of her was ended.

She had bewitched him into marriage, he claimed, and indeed, was it not true that beneath the long sleeves Mistress Boleyn wore, was hidden an extra, tiny finger upon one of her hands. The mark of a witch! In his former insatiable desire for her, and for a healthy, legitimate, living son, the King had broken with Rome and declared himself, and not the Pope, to be Head of the Church in England, thus throwing the realm into confusion.

Now the enchantment was over. Like poor, cast-off Katherine before her, Anne was destined to bear only a living daughter.

"You'll get no more sons of me," the King raged at her, and he convinced himself that like her predecessor, she too was incapable of producing a living male heir. He must be rid of her, too. Besides, those small, wandering eyes had already alighted upon a likely replacement in the shape of pale and modest Jane Seymour, a lady of both gentle birth and nature. Jane was far removed both in looks and temperament from dark-eyed, fiery Anne, whose waiting-woman she was. Events moved swiftly at Court - the King was in his forty-fifth year, and desperate for a son. Anne must go.

1536

January - Heremitithwaite

One bright morning in the newly dawned year of 1536, horsemen drew rein at the Priory gatehouse. Loudly, in the name of the King, they demanded admittance. Doctor Richard Layton and Doctor Thomas Legh were men both north country born. They claimed to be well acquainted with the religious institutions of the northern counties, and of the disposition of the country folk. Thus, they were appointed the King's Commissioners to visit and record the wealth of each House, and to make enquiries as to the morality of its inmates. "To ride down one side of England and come up the other" was Dr. Layton's boast to Thomas Cromwell of his confidence in a speedy accomplishment of the work to be done.

At the Priory that morning, the ordered tenor of the nuns' lives was rudely disrupted. The hubbub occasioned by the mingled shouts of the riders, the whinnying of their steeds and the clatter of their hooves so affrighted blind Dame Mary, and even penetrated to some degree the silent world of Dame Isabelle, that they fled in alarm, at one with the poultry it had been their pleasant task to feed in the morning sunshine.

Accommodation must be found for the Visitors, for besides the Royal Commissioners themselves, for whom the guesthouse must be made ready, they were accompanied by a Clerk whose duty it would be to record the findings his masters would tease out by expert questioning from each member of the House.

He and the Commissioners' servants must content themselves to doss down wherever they might, be it in the stables or in the outhouses, whichever they judged preferable. Food also must be provided - an unlooked-for drain upon the House's expenses. Robert Winter's wife was sent for and set to work, and the Prioress pursed her lips in extreme annoyance at the upset.

"'Tis a mercy they do not stay long, so I have heard," she soothed the flustered nuns, who grumbled as much as they dared at having to prepare what seemed to them gargantuan meals for unwelcome company.

Outside, Robert Winter made himself indispensable to those who served the Visitors. A motley crew they were, raucous, and indifferent to the suppressed hostility their presence invariably aroused. But Robert cared little for that. He felt no loyalty to the convent - only a seething resentment against the Lady, who had bettered him in every confrontation that took place between them.

Besides, he possessed information he sensed was of value, great value even for the right ears to hear, and he savoured the thought of the profit his secret would surely bring him.

Therefore, he grinned amiably at the men's insensitive banter as he carted mounds of dry bracken into the stables and outhouses for their bedding.

"We shall soon be done here," remarked Dr. Layton to Legh, as the little company of nuns, led by their Prioress, assembled nervously in the Chapter House. With bowed heads, and as instructed by their superior, each made a deferential curtsey to the King's Visitors, with the exception that is, of Sisters Mary and Isabelle.

They stood meekly, like lambs anticipating imminent slaughter, each at either side of Sister Marguerite, unable to fully comprehend what was required of them, and no-one, not even Marguerite, had had the time or patience to try to penetrate their sealed worlds.

The King's Commission, authenticating the visit, was read out. The Prioress bowed and kissed the seal, signifying, as she must, her acceptance of the same. A homily followed on the King's concern upon learning of the laxity with which religion was now kept, and the scandalous behaviour of some of those in holy orders. Of course, Dr. Layton explained, a report must also be made of the possessions of every House, its income, rents, lands and valuables.

The Prioress schooled her face to remain impassive, though, at the mention of valuables, she must strive to suppress a sharp intake of breath. And so it began.

It was noted that Dame Anne Dartwentwater and Dame Galfride Chambres were wont to spend considerable time away from their convent, only recently returning from wedding celebrations within their respective families. Both Ladies felt themselves bristling with anger at the implied suggestion that they neglected their calling by gadding about the countryside to partake of forbidden pleasures.

"Blind" and "Deaf," the Clerk recorded against the names of Dame Mary and Dame Isabelle, when Marguerite gently guided them forward to stand before the Visitors.

"Here's a pretty thing," muttered Layton to Legh. "'there'll be little sense to be got out of these two. Together, they scarcely make up one whole." He waved a hand in dismissal to Marguerite.

"Go, Sister," he said. "We will call if we have need of you."

Marguerite made to loose herself from the old nuns, but Dame Mary would not let go the hand she grasped. She clung, childlike, to Marguerite in fright, as the booming voice of Dr. Legh rose in crescendo in his efforts to penetrate the deaf world of Dame Isabelle.

"Oh, stay then, stay," he shouted above the din. "If that will content the old crone."

Moments passed. Dr. Legh abandoned any hopes he might have entertained in questioning Dame Isabelle. Dame Mary ceased her low sobbing, and a semblance of peace returned in the Chapter House.

Then, with quiet resolution, Dame Mary loosed the hand that clasped her own, and drew up her ancient frame to its full height.

She stared fixedly ahead, unseeing, but accurately gauging the place where the Visitors were seated, and unaware that her milky eyes met and held the surprised gaze of both men.

"Sirs," the old voice trembled somewhat, then steadied and rose in more confident volume. "Sirs, I ask your pardon for my lapse of behaviour, whereby I have caused offence. As you see, Sirs, I am old now, and it has been my duty, aye, and my joy to serve God in this House for more years than I can recall." She paused, uncertain as to how to proceed. There was silence in the Chapter House. Dame Dinah was as nonplussed as the curious Visitors at Dame Mary's sudden transformation from her recent state of abject fear, to this dignity that commanded attention.

"I beg a boon of you, Sirs," the old voice pleaded, "that you recommend to the King that this House shall stand, and we be not put forth."

If she had said no more, all might have been well. Such eloquence in one they had deemed of so little account, ensured a brief moment of surprised silence from the Visitors. And in that moment hung the divining of the fates of both those within and without the Priory of Heremitithwaite. But Dame Mary continued.

"Ah, Sirs, my time in this world can be but short, and it would rejoice me greatly to know that my Sisters in Christ are here to lay me before the altar, and pray for my soul, before my body is laid in the Nunclose." She scarcely paused for breath, though speech was wearying her. Her old face became radiant. So might those who claimed to have seen visions have appeared.

"Yea, sightless as I am, I can see it now, my last night in this dear place. The great candles will be lit, and their light will shine on our silver crucifix. Its gems will cast bright colours upon the altar cloth."
She stretched her arms out towards the place she judged the Visitors to be sitting, in a supplicating gesture. She had their rapt attention now. Like hounds, Layton and Legh picked up the scent, the scent of quarry. Here was a trail to follow.
Marguerite snatched at the outstretched hands. "Peace, peace, Sister," she pleaded. "You forget. Our crucifix is but latten."
The spell was broken. Dame Mary woke, as one wakes from a trance, and in the charged silence that followed, she became once more the pathetic old woman to which age and her disability had reduced her.

She wrung her hands piteously.
"What have I said amiss?" she wailed.
The Prioress must produce for the Visitors' inspection, all documents, deeds and evidence of every sort pertaining to the property and wealth

of the House she ruled.

However, nothing earlier than the year 1480 was to be had. The nunnery, situated uncomfortably close to the Scottish border, frequently suffered from the incursions of marauding Scotsmen, who despoiled it of whatever they judged to be of any value. On one such occasion, more vicious than the rest, the convent had been set alight, and its original charter burnt.

It was then that the incumbent Prioress, one Dame Isobel, petitioned the King for the reaffirmation of all privileges formerly granted to the nunnery. Scant evidence existed for proof of such claims, which, it seemed, the nuns based upon the memory of the original foundation charter. And that itself was suspect to forgery at the time of King William Rufus. Their petition, nevertheless, succeeded.

Many weary hours Dame Dinah spent in searching the dusty records of whatever had survived from such depredations, for anything that might strengthen her hand in the examination she knew must come.

One thing of which she was sure, and it lightened her conscience greatly - those old nuns now lying in the nearby Nunclose, had undoubtedly over the years, tweaked the truth for the greater advantage of their House.

Now," its present Prioress vowed, "It is my turn. If I must perjure myself for the sake of the House, then be it so."

"Let us treat easy with this one, to begin with, at least," counselled Layton to Legh. "She is no fool, I'll wager."

Dane Dinah met their authoritative stare with cool politeness. With a slight gesture of her hand, she indicated the scattered array of documents they had been studying, and asked "Is all to your satisfaction, Sirs?"
"It would seem so, Madame," answered Legh. "It appears you manage your affairs well. Answer me though, a few further questions." Of these, both domestic and financial, the Prioress acquitted herself of with ease.

Then, "Your Ladies, Madame. Are their morals...." He covered his mouth behind his hand, to hide a grin, "ahem, of the highest order?" A pause, and then "The young novice especially, too comely, I think, for the cloister." His companion smirked salaciously, and nodded in agreement.
For a long moment, Dame Dinah regarded both men icily, then replied with superb dignity.
"I assure you, Sirs, all the Ladies of this House observe every rule of their calling."
Then, at last, came the question she hoped she would not be asked.
"And the silver crucifix, Madame, of which the blind nun spoke? Where is it now?" Dr. Layton enquired.

"I cannot tell you, Sir." came the Prioress's calm reply. And that, at least was true, she thought, thanks to the Big Friar's foresight.
"Cannot, Madame? How so?" Dr. Layton enquired.

His voice was smooth as silk, but Dame Dinah was aware of an ominous note in its softness, and strove to quell her rising fear.
"Thieves, Sir. Robbers!" She forced herself to tremble. "Murderers, Sir." She crossed herself hastily, and began to wring her hands. "Oh, Sir, great wickedness has been done here in these parts."

"Calm yourself, Madame," Legh remarked drily. "Pray proceed," he urged.
"Even now, Sir," the Prioress continued tremulously, "our forester lies unburied, he and his wife done to death by those villains who take venison and rob hereabouts. Oh, Sir, this is not the only time our House has been robbed by such as these. 'Tis but a short ride to the border, and there I fear our treasure might also be."
How easy it was becoming to lie, Dame Dinah thought.
"Tell me of it Madame, the way of it." Dr. Layton spoke encouragingly. "When was this, er, crime committed?"

"Late last year, Sir. It was at the time when two of our community were absent. Only the two old nuns and the novice remained in the convent - myself too, of course. When I entered the Chapel one morning, the silver was gone!" That, at least, was also true. At this point, Dame Dinah allowed her voice to drop almost to a horrified whisper.

"Oh, indeed," she continued, with suitably contrived agitation, "if it were not for the protection of our Blessed Lady, we might have been burnt in our beds."
She crossed herself, and with a realistic shudder and simulated modesty, added in a whisper "or worse"
"Quite so, Madame," Dr. Layton spoke solicitously. Then his tone hardened. He leaned forward in his chair, and Dame Dinah was forced to meet his probing eyes.
 "Studded with gems, was it? The crucifix the blind nun spoke of?

Had he believed her? Instinct warned her that this was the voice of greed. She composed herself, and replied.

"Dame Mary has not seen the crucifix for many a year. Her memory fades, as her eyesight has. But yes, our crucifix contained some coloured stones. I know not of what value they were." Silence, apart from the scratching of the Clerk's quill.
"Indeed, Madame, your lack of worldliness does you credit," observed Dr. Legh drily. When she was allowed to go, the two men exchanged knowing glances.

"This House must be watched," they agreed.

***

It was the edge of dark - that indeterminate time when day meets night, and seems neither night nor day. A sharpening wind blew across the fells, keened by oncoming frost, and moaning as it gained in strength. Outside the convent's buildings, in a place safe from the danger of conflagration, a fire was lighted, and men stood around the blaze to warm their shins and numbed hands. They savoured the smell of roasting fowls there, purloined from the nuns' henhouse.

Robert Winter, never far away from the company, ingratiated himself by the addition of a few snared rabbits to add to their supper. As darkness deepened, he squatted with them around the fire, tearing at a rabbit's haunch and chewing on bread from the convent's kitchen.

The Clerk, who considered himself to be a cut above the rest of the Visitors' servants, chose to bed down in a corner of the stables. He knew himself not to be popular with the men, and would normally hold himself aloof from them, and in any event, he reasoned, the steamy heat produced by the bodies of a dozen or so horses would be a source of comfort on such a night. Nevertheless, the sight of the blazing fire lured him outside to join the raucous throng encircling the blaze

He had already eaten, but in the sudden silence that ensued at his appearance, he helped himself to a draught of ale. Someone tossed another log onto the fire, and the murmur of voices resumed. He drank deeply, in an effort to dispel the feeling of isolation his position in life inevitably gave rise to, hinging as it did, poised somewhere between that of master and man.

It was natural that the talk should turn upon the events of the day. Any snippet of information gleaned during the day's work, or any hearsay, was duly turned over and speculated upon. The presence of the Clerk was a rare opportunity to gain first- hand knowledge as to how things stood at Heremitithwaite.

Robert Winter chewed at the last shreds of meat from the rabbit's leg, then flung the bone into the fire.

"Drink up, sirs - I know how to get us more," he boasted. In the convent kitchen, his wife would be alone, clearing up the mess left behind from the day's catering, and it would be an easy matter to bully her into releasing further supplies of the convent's ale. On pretext of refilling the men's beakers, he contrived to seat himself within easy earshot of the Clerk, and he, unable to drink as deeply as his companions, and keep his own counsel, was becoming relaxed and garrulous. One young fellow, emboldened by such unusual amiability, ventured to ask: "Well then, Sir Clerk, have our masters made an end here?"

"Aye, tell us, do we ride tomorrow," the rest demanded to know.

"We ride, all save you, Thomas. You remain here. There's work still to be done. Secret work for you." He fixed the young man who had questioned him with an unsteady gaze, and tried, without success, to rise.

"In the morn, they will tell you, tell you...." His voice trailed off, thick and slurred. Robert caught Thomas's eye. Instinctively, they both moved closer, ears pricked. Robert plied the Clerk with yet more ale. He slurped down another beakerful, and muttered, "Secret, secret...she knows...hidden somewhere.... they all try, the fools..."

"Come, Sir, you need your rest if you are to ride the morrow," Thomas shouted in the Clerk's ear. He had dropped his beaker, and was beginning to droop in the first stages of inebriation before the heat of the fire. Thomas beckoned to Robert Winter, and winked.

"Come, let us get him to the stable." He spoke softly, and together they hauled the unprotesting Clerk bedwards, and deposited him, none too gently, upon a heap of dry bracken in the stable. Robert seized his chance - the moment was opportune. He laid a hand urgently upon Thomas's arm.

"I know a thing," he confided. "Will your masters pay me for what I have seen?"

In the steamy warmth of the stable, a long silence ensued, broken only by the occasional shifting of the sleeping horses, and the rhythmic snoring of the Clerk. In the mind of each man, similar questions raced. What advantage is he to me? Can I trust him? Thomas scratched his chin. Instinct told him there might well be profit to be had here.

"They may pay you a mite." He spoke nonchalantly, at length. "It depends." He looked at Robert speculatively, and then he said, "I would advise you to hold off for a while. Wait until I have my orders tomorrow."

The fire in the yard burned low. Men crouched closer to its dying embers. Some sprawled prostrate, in various states of intoxication upon the bare earth. Only when the winter cold bit deep into their limbs would they rouse and seek shelter.

No-one noticed, or if they had, would have cared, that a dark-cloaked figure walked with uncertain steps away from the convent precincts, and ever closer to the banks of Croglin Beck.

When morning came, they found her. She was quite dead. Her body rested on a flat slab of sandstone at the water's edge. The force of the fall crushed Sister Mary's brittle bones as though they had the fragility of eggshells. In the darkness, she had lingered between life and death, until the bitter cold of dawn drained away what was left of life from her.

Doctors Layton and Legh were less than pleased at the delay in setting forth upon the next leg of their journey. The death of Dame Mary threw the whole convent into confusion. Not only that, but most of the Visitors' servants lay slug-a-bed, and even when roused, went laggardly about the business of making all ready for the road. Only Thomas, who had supped sparingly the night before, was in possession of all his wits, an ability the Commissioners had noted in their work at Houses they visited before Heremitithwaite.

It was therefore almost noon before the semblance of order was restored at the convent. The broken body of blind Dame Mary was carried back to the House and given into the care of the shocked and grieving community.

Secretly, Thomas was instructed as to what the Commissioners required of him, and promoted as their agent. Then, at last, and to the relief of both the Visitors and the visited, the troupe rode off at full speed into the pale winter sunshine.

Dame Isabelle was inconsolable. In the long isolation of her silent world, as the sound of speech disappeared, so too did the remembrance of spoken words. So she grieved silently and deeply, unable to fully understand, or to be understood. Except, that is but for the comfort of touch, and it was Marguerite's hand that supplied that semblance of consolation.

When it was time, Dame Mary's prepared body was carried into the Chapel to be laid before the altar. Upon their knees, the Sisters kept vigil, and it was in the night watch that Dame Isabelle's sorrows too were ended. Only the slight intake of breath, and the whisper of her habit as she slid from her knees to the Chapel floor, alerted the Sisters that something was amiss. They gathered up her small frame, light as a child's, into their arms. A smile of joyful recognition illuminated the old nun's face. With her final breath, words such as had not been heard for many a year, rang out in greeting, clear as a bell.

"Mary, Mary...wait for me."

In the weeks that followed, the Cumbrian winter took hold. Night upon night of bitter frost silvered the snow-encrusted branches of the convent's trees, and in the Nunclose, day after day of whirling snow settled, to lay a coverlet of purest white over the beds of the sleepers there.

Spring

The Skin House - Lazonby and Baronwood

In Cumberland, winter held the earth in its iron grip for many weeks, then, with the coming of a thaw, it was at last possible to lay to rest the murdered bodies of Edward and Genett Bowman. With them, lying in the crook of his mother's arm, lay the little one who, like the Queen's stillborn son, had known no separate life outside his mother's body.

At the tanner's house in Lazonby, Benedict's life was vastly different from that of his sylvan idyll in Baronwood. The processes of the tanning trade were many, and for the most part unpleasant. In time, both he and John, the tanner's son, would be expected to learn each stage of the craft from Andrew, and eventually master the craft themselves.

The lads were nearly of an age, and soon became inseparable, as close as blood brothers. From the moment Andrew set the orphaned child down from his horse at the Skin House door, a bond began to grow between the two. Tentatively at first, and cautiously, in the manner of all true Cumbrians, each took measure of the other in silence, words not easily coming between them.

At supper that first night, Benedict discovered he was famished. He had not eaten since leaving Penrith, where rations at the Friary had reverted to their usual meagre state, the Christmas poultry being long since consumed. Mary had baked bread that day, and the scent of its newness was bittersweet to his senses. Tears pricked behind his eyelids, and when he bit into his portion, despite his hunger, the first mouthful seemed like to choke him. Then, the basic need to remedy that hunger superseded all else, and he devoured his share like a half-starved dog. All the while, John's dark eyes were upon him, and as the last morsel was bolted down, he pushed half his own share across the trestle table into Benedict's hand.

"Eat that up. I'm not hungry," he lied.
Mary, meanwhile, poured new milk into three wooden piggins for the young ones to drink with their bread. On a sudden impulse, Dinah slid down from her stool and ran to her mother's side. Carefully, she lifted the first piggin, foaming to the brim, and clasping it in both hands, she carried it without spilling a drop, and set it down before Benedict. Her blue eyes looked steadily into his, and the smile that wreathed her small face seemed to him angelic, and in that moment the ice that held his heart began to melt.

With the onset of spring, John took Benedict on journeys of discovery around the Skin House. First, they completed whatever tasks Andrew set them each day, and then they were free to roam.
"I'll take thee onto Lazonby Fell this day," John announced one sharp sunlit noon. He was rising eight years old, and therefore almost two years Benedict's senior.

This new- found brother he found to be somewhat lacking in the basic rural knowledge already familiar to himself, and he felt it his proud duty to remedy this defect, and to introduce Benedict to whatever diversions that could be found in their rustic surroundings.

Benedict nodded in agreement at John's offer. He was pleased to fall in with whatever suggestion the older lad might make. Already, he trusted John's judgement implicitly, and felt a warming glow in the companionship he shared with the tanner's son.

That morning, they had helped Andrew to clear out a room at the far end of the Skin House. It was here that the cured skins were stored after being put through all the processes of tanning. The room was dark and somewhat musty, and redolent with the distinctive smell of new leather. They disturbed an owl recently returned from its nightly hunt. The creature had crept in under a, gap in the roofing - a snug place to sleep the winter days away, judging by the pile of its droppings on the floor below its perch. A "Jenny Howlett" Mary called it, and shooed it out of her houseplace with a broom, where it blundered about, dazed by the bright sunlight, and half scaring the wits out of young Dinah.

After noontide, Andrew took pity of the lads, knowing they were eager to be off onto the fell. He stood at the edge of the pool where he soaked his skins, and watched them go, locked in their own boyish world of togetherness. The years rolled back, and he saw himself and

Edward Bowman off on one of their own adventures, and then found himself a task to distract himself.

"We'll look for plovers' eggs," John decided. "Did'st thou know they lay upon the ground?" He cocked an enquiring glance at Benedict, to whom this piece of information was news. It was his understanding that all birds, save domestic fowl such as his mother had kept, laid their eggs in nests they made for themselves in trees. It was so in Baronwood. His own father had shown him last springtime the places in thickets and the branches of the woodland trees where the birds flew to and fro all day, carrying nesting materials in their beaks. But of course, he reasoned, John being older than himself, and more experienced in these matters, must be right.

As they reached the open expanse of the fell, he could see the plovers wheeling and hovering, lifting and dipping in the gusty breeze, then landing amidst the furze where John assured him their eggs were hidden. They searched the open ground like hunters, treading stealthily, and exulting in each clutch of eggs they discovered. The plovers rose up in alarm before them, and soared anxiously above their heads.

When the day began to chill, and the sun dropped low, they carried their booty home to Mary, securely tied up in their homespun shirts.

***

In Baronwood, the sap began to rise in the great oaks. As with the somber ash that bordered the Skin House stream, the leafing would come late.

Not until May would a caste of fresh green, tinged overall with a flush of reddish brown, soften the branches of mature and sapling trees alike. Now was the barking time, and before sunrise, Andrew Bowerbank hitched his broad-backed horse between the shafts of a high-sided cart. He waited with some impatience while the lads finished breaking their fast, and disentangled Dinah's clinging arms from around his legs.

"Oh, please, please, father, let me come too," she begged.

Andrew gently stroked the golden curls that framed his small daughter's face.

"Nay, little wench." He looked down into the speedwell blue eyes that looked up pleadingly into his face.

"'Tis not labour for little ones like thee," he said. "The lads will find it work hard enough."

She pouted, and the glimmer of tears washed over the bright blue. "Besides," he knelt down, and looked fondly into the small face, "what should I tell thy mother if thou should come to any harm? What if a tree should fall upon thee while the woodcutters are at their work?

Tell me, what would she do without thee?"

With an easy movement, as if she were light as thistledown, he swung the child high upon his shoulder and carried her in to Mary.

"There. Help thy mother today." He spoke in a tone of mock seriousness, and set her down on the floor of the houseplace.

Mary's eyes, blue like her daughter's, met the laughter in Andrew's twinkling glance with amused exasperation.

"Away with you," she scolded, and snatched up the empty platters from under the lads' noses.

She pushed provisions for the day into their hands. "Here, take these, and don't eat them before noon," she ordered. Then she chivvied all three of them out of the door. John and Benedict clambered into the cart. Andrew followed, thankful to be on his way, for the sun was now well risen. Mary waved them off, with the still sulky Dinah clinging to her mother's skirts in the doorway.

They rode down into Lazonby like lords.

"I shall be one of the King's great nobles," John boasted, and doffed his cap to an imaginary courtier at the roadside.

"Me too," Benedict piped, excitedly. Such euphoria was catching.

"Not so, you can be my servant. All great lords have servants," John proclaimed with certainty.

. His imagined greatness took hold of him, and he rode in a state of high elation until the cart rumbled alongside the village stocks. There, a small crowd of children were gathered, those that is, who were deemed to be more hindrance than help to their parents. That morning, the stocks provided a rare source of entertainment, for they contained an occupant.

With noisy glee, those who had nothing better to do pelted the immobilised figure of the unfortunate local half-wit with partially dried out cowpats. One such missile went wide of its intended mark. It skimmed past the young lord's ear, whereupon it disintegrated upon the floor of the cart into several noxious fragments. The spell was broken, and the workaday world re-established itself. The erstwhile young noble leapt from his seat to deliver a verbal trouncing in the direction of the suddenly silent culprits. One of these, bolder than the rest, yelled after the receding conveyance.

"What's a bit o' muck to thee, tanner's lad? Or a stink?" Andrew grinned, unmoved by such taunts.

"Peace, lad, peace," he soothed his enraged son. "Whoever heard of a stink hurting a body?"

Past the church, they left the road that would have taken them down to the river, and followed the narrow track leading into Baronwood. Their way lay through tracts of heather, budding yet, fern-fringed and interspersed by the rising spires of foxgloves. Here and there, a gorse bush flowered - a splash of bright gold in the morning sun.

Benedict breathed in great lungfuls of the sparkling air. He savoured it, tasting the smells of the forest that were borne faintly upon it. Oh, this was his element, imbibed by him since birth, as naturally as his mother's milk. He relished it, joyed in it, and when Andrew's cart halted in a clearing of felled oaks, he jumped down and rolled in an ecstasy of delight on the carpet of the forest floor. Baronwood. Home. For a brief space, he lay upon his back and studied the round of soft blue overhead.

It was enclosed by a circle of great oaks, newly clothed in spring dress. Birdsong hung in the air, continuous and sweet. Far away, from a distant part of the wood, came the heavy thud of metal as it struck upon the trunk of a tree to be felled. Then came a warning shout of the woodcutter, as yet another doomed oak crashed earthwards. Benedict raised himself up upon one elbow and stared into the canopy. A memory of snow-clad branches flashed before his eyes. His home had been here. But it had been winter then. Andrew's voice dispelled the vision.

"Come on, lads. Work now. We'll take our ease come noon." With purposeful strokes, his axe bit into the trunk of one of the felled oaks, hacking and slicing at the ridged bark until it flaked off as he worked along the length of the trunk. It was the job of John and Benedict to follow, at a safe enough distance from the swinging axe, to collect the piles of bark thus freed, and throw them into the cart.

Andrew worked steadily, chipping and teasing the bark free of the trunk until it lay naked as the carcass of a newly skinned rabbit.

The sun at noontide beat down upon them, hot and strong, unusually so for the time of year. By common consent, they sought out the welcome shade cast by the interlacing branches of two oaks that grew close together. They opened the provisions Mary had given them, and with appetites heightened by their morning's toil, they devoured with relish the fat bacon and bread she had given them. Then, they swilled all down their parched throats with copious draughts of her small ale.

In the languorous warmth of afternoon, and contented in his newly filled belly, Andrew dozed against the bole of one of the oaks, his breathing punctuated by the occasional snore. John and Benedict lay full length upon their backs, side by side, each deep in thought.

"Benedict," John asked at length, "How old think you the biggest of these trees must be?"
Benedict rolled over, and considered before answering.
"Well," he pronounced at length, "I remember the Big Friar told my father once that trees like these have been growing for hundreds of years."

John's face registered a look of disbelief.

"'Tis so, I tell thee," the younger lad assured him. "Kings have come to hunt in Inglewood Forest many times. They killed great numbers of deer in the chase. Wild boar, too. Oh, I know it to be true. Friar John himself said it was so."

He cast a look at John, defying him to question the friar's knowledge of such matters.

"Then, I wonder if Duke Richard himself came here too, when he lived in Penrith? John mused.

"When was that?" Benedict asked. John considered, then hazarded a guess.

"Oh, about a hundred years ago, I think," he replied. "It was before he went to London to be King."

"Then he could have ridden beneath these very trees, I suppose," Benedict said.

The sun was hot, and lulled by its warmth, they drifted into that borderland of consciousness that is half wakefulness and half sleep. There, they galloped with the hunt on gaily caparisoned steeds through the great royal Forest of Inglewood.

They heard the soundings of the huntsmen's horns, the thundering of hooves and the baying of the hounds as the quarry was sighted, pursued without mercy, and brought down for the kill.

The tanner's sleep was dreamless and deep. His snores increased in volume, until at length he woke himself up with one almighty snort.

They laboured then, until the sun dropped low in the sky, and the air began to chill. They piled the bark into the cart. It was laden almost to overflowing, and the lads scrambled up and lay on top of the heap to flatten it down so that nothing of what they had laboured for should be lost. Weariness overcame them on the homeward journey, and they drifted in and out of a fitful slumber, interrupted by the jolting motion of the cart. Not so, Andrew.

He trudged on at a steady pace beside the horse, one hand resting lightly upon its bridle.

Toil he had been accustomed to since boyhood. But today, at the start of the barking season, the constant use of his axe had woken that familiar ache in the muscles of his shoulders and back. It would ease, he knew, in the coming days, as his sturdy body grew used to the labour, but tonight he would be thankful to reach home.
St. Nicholas's Church loomed into view, and he led the horse into the main highway through the village. The stocks were empty now, the poor fool released. Whatever his error, it was Andrew's belief there

was no harm in the lad. The greyness of dusk deepened, and a white moon was rising as he unhitched the horse, fed him and then bedded the beast down for the night. Next, he roused John and Benedict and sent them, bleary-eyed, in to Mary for their supper. Hunger bit at his own vitals, but before he himself could eat, the cart must be unloaded in readiness for another trip on the morrow... And so it would continue until the barking was done. Then would begin the tedious process of crushing it, a task in which all with the exception of young Dinah, would share.

Summer

The Eden Valley and the Tower of London

The Big Friar made good his promise to include the Skin House in Lazonby as often as his journeys would permit. He was always welcome there, and it was his pleasure to teach John and Benedict, and both boys proved to be apt pupils. But with improving weather, his journeys took him further afield, and by this means, he brought gleanings of news, local, and more disturbingly, of greater events in the seats of power in London and the south. There was much unrest in the land, and much to fear.

There could surely not be any place in England where the King's agents had not ridden in recent years, since his marriage to Queen Anne.
Their task was to enforce the swearing of the hated Act of Succession to her children born to the King. To resist was treason. Even to speak in a derogatory manner of the King's matrimonial arrangements was treason, and treason being punishable by death, many paid so for their opinions. No-one, high or low, lay or religious, was safe.

The Friar shuddered. Only a year ago, in the London springtime, three Carthusian monks suffered terribly for their conscience's sake. Quietly, but staunchly, they refused to acknowledge the legality of the King's divorce from Queen Katherine, and consequently the bastardising of their daughter, the Princess Mary.

For this, they were fastened to hurdles and dragged to Tyburn. They were hanged, then cut down whilst still living, to be disemboweled, mutilated and their bodies quartered. The arm of one of them was then nailed up over the door of his monastery as a dire warning to any others who might consider opposing royal authority.

Nor was the King's friendship any guarantee against his wrath. When the break with Rome came, opposition to his supremacy in the Church resulted in the beheading of his former friend, Sir Thomas More. This death was more merciful than that of another Carthusian, Sebastian Newdigate, once a sporting companion of the King. He, with several other monks of the Charterhouse, were chained in a London street and weighted down with lead. There they were left, in their own excrement, deprived of food and water, and unable to stand upright, until after many days their agony was ended by the mercy of death.

The upheaval of the old order of religion was frightening. Not only those in high places, but the simple folk of England must watch their words. Loose talk in the alehouse, a hasty word, and an unwise opinion overheard, all of these might be reported to the King's agents, and there were informants in plenty, eager to claim the reward offered by accusing friend or neighbour alike.

As Friar John walked the trackways of the Eden valley, he pondered long upon the fragments of news that, in time, filtered through to the isolated counties of northern England. All in religious orders were agreed that Thomas Cromwell, the King's chief minister, was indeed a man to be feared, for had he not boasted that he would make his master the richest prince in Christendom? To do this he had already started to seize the lands and revenues of houses of religion in order to augment the King's depleted coffers. In February, the Cistercian Abbey of Calder in Eskdale was closed. Later, news came that the Benedictine nuns of Seton had been evicted, and to the south, the houses of the Augustinians of Cartmel and Conishead closed.

Those who had known only the cloister were dispossessed, driven out to seek shelter and employment in the world they had renounced. True, it was said that some were to receive pensions, but there were those who would most surely be forced to beg. Many of the smaller foundations were already closed, but the richest houses had the most to fear. Nationwide, their wealth and possessions had already been carefully assessed by Cromwell's agents, and those ripest for plunder were being systematically stripped of everything of value, and their lands and buildings sold to those who could afford to pay for their acquisition.

In spite of himself, the Big Friar smiled wryly as he remembered the disappointed faces of those Visitors who had made enquiry at Penrith Friary.

What had the brethren there of value? Nothing that a King might covet, to be sure. Poor they had always been, begging alms, scratching a meagre living from their few acres of land, living from hand to mouth. In this instance, at least, poverty would seem to be their friend. For whilst their wealthier neighbours were being uprooted, the lives of the poor friars continued as before. But for how long, Brother John wondered, how long?

In the Cumbrian springtime, the earth warmed slowly and with many a check, as if winter grudged to release its grip upon the land. But as the days of May sped by, the Big Friar marvelled yet again, as he never failed to do each year, at the beauty of the awakening countryside. As if it was revealed to him for the first time, he wondered at the brilliant green of the shining leaves of wild garlic that emerged in the damp and wooded places, to be followed by the white spheres of their flower heads, each composed of tiny star-like florets.

And the downy rosettes of foxgloves, overwintered in close anchorage to the drier ground of woodland clearings, now began to raise their tall spires towards the warmth of the strengthening sunlight. The streams were running fast, free of ice and full with melt water rushing down from the fells to join at length with the rivers Eden and Eamont. The people too, seemed to unbend somewhat, and take pleasure in the brighter days. To them, their daily round of toil, and the earning of their bread, was their first care. But they also felt the powerful surge of new life returning after the miseries of winter's harshness.

***

Far away, at Greenwich palace, Queen Anne watched the May jousts, unaware that it was her last day of freedom.

The following day she was arrested, and rowed upriver to the Tower of London. Under escort, she left the state barge, and the boom of its cannon announced her entry there as a prisoner.

Charges of adultery, and therefore treason, were brought against her, one of the charges being of incest with her own brother, Lord Rochford. These she vehemently denied, so too did four of the five men of the Court charged with her. Only poor, unheroic Mark Smeaton, a groom of the King's chamber, and favoured by the Queen for his skill in playing the lute, was induced by his terror of the rack, to confess guilt.

On the fifteenth of May, Anne was tried by twenty-six peers, presided over by her own uncle, the Duke of Norfolk. Not one man spoke in her defence. Each knew the verdict expected of him, and pronounced her guilty. She was sentenced to death, the manner of which to be determined at the King's pleasure, either by burning or beheading. Once that great love that Henry professed for her died, he accused her of entrapping him by witchcraft. And witches were burned: But his "pleasure" spared her the horrors of the fire, and also of the axe. Anne would die by the blow of a sharp French sword.

Execution was to be at eight o'clock on the nineteenth of May. The scaffold on which she would die was erected within sight of her chamber window, and her sleep was fitful on that last night of her life. The clothes for her last public appearance lay ready - a gown of grey damask, a bright crimson underskirt.

Dawn broke. Life could hold nothing more for her. She had gambled for great stakes, and she had lost. But what if Elizabeth had been a prince, or the son she had lost in the winter had lived?

Before sunrise coloured the eastern sky, a blackbird flew up to his favourite vantage point on the walls of the Tower. The pure cadences of his song rang out loud and clear in the early morning, and filled the chamber where the Queen lay. She listened to its silvery notes, remembering a time when she had sat in the shelter of the hornbeam, close to the river bower at Hampton Court. A blackbird had sung then, as she worked at her embroidery, and waited for the King's barge to pull in at the landing stage below the mount there. Henry had loved her then, hardly able to be parted from her, even to attend to affairs of state.

Tears rose behind her closed eyelids as in memory she saw him leaping from the royal barge and rushing to greet her on the grassy slope leading from the river. "Sweetheart" he had called her then. But now the wheel had come full circle.

The King's roving eye had fallen upon one of her own waiting women, as it had when she herself had served Queen Katherine.

The sun was rising, and she could hear the subdued whispers of her ladies as they waited to perform their last duties for her. They dressed her with care, then she knelt to receive communion. She swore her innocence of the charges upon which she was condemned, both before and after receiving the sacrament.
The time came for her to die, but the headsman of Calais was delayed on the road, and it was not until later that morning that the guard came to escort her to the scaffold. The blackbird was silent now, from his lofty perch he looked down with an uncomprehending eye at the scene below.

He saw the Queen remove her headdress. Her hair was closely netted so as to leave her slender neck bare. There was a flash as the sunlight caught the blade of the sword. It descended, and a flood of crimson spread over the scaffold. A cannon boomed, to announce to the people of London that the woman many regarded, as the King's whore was dead, and the blackbird rose in alarm, and flew away.

At Hampton Court Palace, workmen were removing the intertwined initials of Henry and Anne carved in the stonework. One, who had been employed all his working life at the Palace, walked down to the river where the Queen's barge was moored. His orders were to burn away the late Queen's white falcon badge from its prow.

"T'was not long ago," he observed thoughtfully to the younger man accompanying him, "that I was sent to get rid of Queen Katherine's coat of arms from this same barge."

"What think you," the younger man asked, "was Queen Anne really as wicked as men say?"

"Quiet now," his companion replied, "say no more. If the King says she was, 'tis dangerous for any to say otherwise. It matters naught what such as we might think."

***

In Lazonby, the pedlar's visit was overdue. Soon it would be June, and daily the tanner's family at the Skin House listened anxiously for the sound of his pony train. Then, at last, the bell horse came in to view.

"What kept thee, Jack?" Andrew greeted him. "Was it a pony gone lame?"

"Nay," Jack replied. "'Twas the telling of the news I had. Folk could not believe it. But 'tis true, I fear. I had it in York from a pedlar newly come from London. And everywhere I go, folk clamour to hear of it."

"Well, what is this news then," Andrew asked. No matter how late Jack might be, Andrew expected the old pedlar was going to take his time in telling it. But no!

"The Queen, Queen Anne Boleyn, has had her head cut off," he stated baldly. "The King ordered it."

There was silence - a shocked, incredulous silence.
"But what was her crime," Andrew asked, "to deserve such a fate?"
Jack glanced at John and Ben, both wide-eyed and avid to details. Mary too was speechless.

"It seems," he answered, carefully moderating his choice of words on their account. "It seems she had had to do with other men. Four, I understand, and one her own brother."
"But to cut off her head," Mary protested. "Could not the King have sent her to a nunnery for the rest of her life?" she asked.
"Nay," Jack answered. "He is closing the nunneries down. And besides, 'tis rumoured he wanted to be rid of her quickly so that he can wed another lady and get himself an heir."

***

To the Big Friar, it seemed that summer that a new madness seized the minds of men. News travelled but slowly to the remote north, especially in hard winters, when even the sturdiest of travellers were deterred by the inhospitable nature of the terrain. So it was only after the spring thaw that news arrived in Penrith of the closure of the Cistercian House of Calder in February. It was the beginning. The Houses of Seton, Cartmel and Conishead were to follow. Tales of immoral crimes supposedly committed by the religious circulated freely. Everywhere, in the marketplace and the alehouse gossip abounded. As he passed amongst them, the friar fancied the credulous countryfolk looked askance at him, as though seeing him with new eyes.

Women turned aside, whispering behind their hands, and many a raucous guffaw followed him as men discussed with relish the lustful behaviour and unnatural practices of which both male and female religious were accused. The Prioress of Seton stood charged of incontinence with priests, and the accusation, whether founded or not, troubled Friar John. So, for the safety of the sisters at Heremitithwaite, he had avoided all possible contact there, lest any spurious charge be brought against the undoubted purity of those Ladies' lives.

With the closure of each House, many who knew no other life but the cloister were to find themselves obliged to seek employment in an unfamiliar world, or else to wander the countryside to beg. Fear, coupled with the primeval instinct of self-preservation was hardening men's hearts and suppressing the virtue of charity. For was it not rumoured that the Abbot of Furness had driven away even those of his own Order who, when dispossessed, came seeking admittance at his door? The Friar sighed. In the confusion that abounded, it was hard now to preach the love of God and the duty of charity towards neighbours.

It was on a stretch of moorland between Penrith and Greystoke that he sat down to take some rest. Of late, sleep had evaded him. Night after weary night, the ills and uncertainties of the times crowded in upon his subconscious mind. Like the tumbling balls of the jugglers they tossed aloft at the fairs, his fears rose and fell with the changing levels of his wakefulness. His present fatigue was of the mind more so than of the body. The sun beat down hotly upon the treeless landscape. No shade was to be had. It was a desolate place - no sign of habitation was near.

Only the low hum of bees, jubilant in the new blossoming heather broke the stillness of noon. Nearby, a trickle of brackish water reamed off in a narrow channel, which eventually would meet and merge with other streams to form a beck.

John knelt, and from cupped hands drank from it to slake his thirst. Then, what relief to plunge his calloused and sweat-soaked feet into its coolness, and sit upon the dry heather to chew upon bread and a chunk of cheese he carried in his scrip. Some miles back, he had passed through a wooded track where wild garlic grew in profusion beneath the moist shade of intertwining trees.

His piece of cheese he had then wrapped carefully in the cool green leaves, redolent of onions, and now he was pleased to find, that by this ploy, it had kept fresh and was now faintly flavoured by its garlic sheath.

His hunger abated, a sweet drowsiness pervaded the weary body of the friar, such as had eluded him for many a night. It seemed that lead weighted his eyelids, and he sank backwards into the springy heath. A lark sang, high and sweet in the vastness of the blue above him. He listened to its pure notes, then sleep came, deep and untroubled, undisturbed by dreams or dark forebodings.

Was it the angry clamour of crows that roused him? Certainly, no other creature was near. He woke with a start, and heard the fluttering of wings. Their black bodies lifted and fell in jumpy half flight as the angry birds quarrelled raucously over something that lay close by, but hidden from view deep in the heather. Carrion, it must be. John rose to his feet - it was only a few paces across the water channel that a heap of rags could be seen. At the Friar's approach, the birds rose up in alarm.

All except one, and it stood its ground to scratch determinedly amongst the rotting fibres of the rags, and peck voraciously at what lay within.

The body of a traveller was not such a rare sight in the unrelenting wildness of the north. But here, side by side, lay two together, huddled close as if for warmth. By their garb, it was still possible to recognise them as Cistercians, but whether they were old or young, or any other distinguishable feature about them, was known now only to the God they had served in life.

There had been a thaw, premature and brief, in the last days of January, when roads and trackways reappeared again across the fells from under a cover of snow. The weather, soft as springtime, beguiled the foolhardy, and those ignorant of its caprices, to embark upon journeys that too often could hazard life. Such these must have been, lost in the encompassing whiteness of a returning blizzard.

Calder Abbey, John reflected, closed in February, forcing its inmates to disperse. In a torn bundle nearby were to be seen the pitiful necessities these two had gathered together, with which to embark upon a new life. A few writing materials and several newly-sharpened quills lay there, scattered doubtless by the foraging of hungry raptors, or the scavenging of winter- famished foxes. Where had they been bound? Penrith most likely, and by their limited skills, not such as were greatly needed in the harsh outside world, they must have hoped to obtain the means of honest employment.

Pity flooded Friar John's heart, and then anger coursed hotly in its place, for well he knew, as these in their cloistered ignorance did not, the grudging reception they might well have encountered in Penrith. There, molded by an unceasing struggle to wrest their own meagre living from the hostile times, men lived hard and harshly, and uncaring of the plight of others.

The day darkened suddenly. John tore his gaze from the pathetic remains before him, and looked up into the sky. Unnoticed, a dark cloud stood overhead, it appeared as if from nowhere in the hitherto blue sky. It grew, with ominous speed, to blot out the brightness of the sun. John felt his former weariness returning. It engulfed him, as though the menacing cloud above him descended and enveloped his entire consciousness in its threatening folds. He contemplated the two deep in the embrace of the springy heath.

"Perhaps 'tis better so," he mused. "For now you are spared the pain of this world's indifference, and rebuff."

The bright promise of the morning was vanished. That one lurid cloud overshadowing the sun was now merged in an all embracing threat of a gathering storm. Friar John knelt and recited the age old prayers for the repose of souls. Against his closed eyelids he saw a flash of lightening, closely followed by the first roll of thunder.

"Requiescat in pace." The words rose automatically to his lips. "Rest, my brothers, rest in peace."

He stood, and raised his cowl above his head against the onset of drenching rain. He would be soaked to the skin before he gained Penrith again.

Autumn

Hampton Court

Since his marriage to Jane Seymour, the King's temper was mellowed. Apart from those early years of his marriage to Spanish Katherine, scarcely had he known a time of such harmonious contentment. It seemed that Jane's gentle influence soothed away, as a healing balm, the stresses of his previous matrimonial entanglements. But, as the months passed, still the longed-for heir was lacking.

In London's alleys, the accumulation of stinking garbage lay festering in the rank heat of summer, whilst amongst the fetid heaps of rubbish the flea-ridden rats scampered and bred. In the city, blowflies swarmed and held festival upon the obscene display of rotting heads of those unfortunates whose consciences, or loyalties, had fallen short of the King's requirements, and contagion flourished.

The coronation of the new Queen was postponed. It had been planned for September or October, but such was the King's morbid fear of infection that he lost no time in forsaking London for the purer air of Hampton Court.
Her women dismissed, Jane, the Queen found it pleasant to sit alone in the late afternoon sunshine of this golden autumn day.

With eyes closed, she turned her pale face upwards towards the gentle warmth of its rays.

A slight breeze drifted in from the river, and in the new gardens the King had ordered to be made at Hampton Court, the sweetness of lavender and clove-scented pinks mingled with that of a great profusion of roses, white and red, the union of which flowers had come to symbolise the Tudor dynasty.

A small frown creased the pale smoothness of Jane's brow. "And for that reason," she murmured quietly, "I am become a Queen." Though why the King's fancy should fall upon herself, quiet, plain Jane Seymour was as much a puzzle to Jane herself as to the watching courtiers. Ever vigilant, they probed and dissected every aspect of royal life. In the corridors and anterooms of the palaces, they gossiped and whispered together behind raised hands. Speculation was rife, and wagers made as to the outcome, or otherwise, of the King's latest venture into matrimony.

"God send me a healthy son," was a prayer that frequently hovered fervently, but unvoiced, upon the new Queen's lips.

Snatches of female chatter, and the high, tinkling laughter of her ladies floated clearly upon the air. In a distant part of the gardens they wandered at ease, glad of the brief respite their mistress had given them. Still fresh in Jane's mind were her own days of service as a maid in waiting, first to Queen Katherine, and then to the fiery and unpredictable Anne Boleyn. She knew well how welcome were these breaks in the tedium of royal duties, and being of a kindly nature she strove, when opportunity allowed, to release her ladies to enjoy their own brief freedoms.

The hint of a rueful smile softened her plain features, for she was well aware of her ladies' intense curiosity as to the state of their mistress's condition. Freed of her presence, Jane knew well the direction their chatter was likely to take. And so it was.

"I'll wager my second-best hood that Her Grace is brought to bed within the year," young Mistress Anne was heard to declare. "Aye, and with a prince, too," she ventured further, and added pertly, "An the King do his work well." She darted a questioning glance at the lady deemed most likely to be in the Queen's confidence, and was discomfited by the tone of her response.

"Fie, Mistress Anne," was that lady's dry observation. "You do well not to wager your best hood. Take care your tongue does not hazard your head as well." Those ladies within earshot smirked at Mistress Anne's discomfiture. This young newcomer had much to learn at Court, not least that royal matters matrimonial were not a subject for idle chatter. And anyway, as to that hood, everyone knew that Her Grace was not well pleased by the Frenchness of Mistress Anne's attire. Indeed, she was insisting that her whole wardrobe be replaced forthwith by clothing more modest and demure in style.

The day was now well advanced, and soon they must make themselves and the Queen ready for supper. She still sat alone in the spot where they had left her, and until they received her signal that she wished to leave, they remained at a discreet distance, exclaiming with pleasure at the transformation Her Grace's gardener, Chapman, had wrought in that part of the new gardens.

If there had been a choice, Jane would have been content to linger so, in solitude, to drink in the deepening scents of evening. In the weeks since their marriage at the end of May, she had accompanied the King upon royal progresses beyond London. The King was ever anxious to show off his new bride, and so to Sittingbourne, Canterbury, Rochester and Dover they had journeyed, accompanied as always by a vast retinue of courtiers. Wherever they stayed, there had been great feastings, often, to Jane, wearisome in their length. The King, ever an ardent huntsman, lost no opportunity to indulge his passion for the chase. Then, in the full heat of summer, how pleasant had seemed the respite of travelling by barge on the sun-flecked river. And always, there was music...

In the joyousness of his new marriage, Henry never tired of showing his gentle wife to the people. He showered her with jewels, furs, and gifts of great cost. Their days were filled with all manner of pleasurable activities, and their nights - they too were filled with other labours, the urgent need for an heir ever present in the King's mind.

There too, deep and fearful, lurked that germ of canker, seeded by the Boleyn whore's taunts. Now, in the forty-sixth year of his life, that once magnificent body was growing ever more gross and corpulent, and the lustiness of the King's rampaging youth was undoubtedly waning.

The Queen's ladies drew closer, in a tacit reminder of the need to make ready for the evening's festivities. With a sigh, Jane rose, reluctantly acknowledging she could no longer stay in the perfumed peace of her arbour. On an impulse, as if to take with her a token of that special joy she had always derived from a garden, she bent to pluck a rose. It was full open, its scent musky and sweet.

It was the rose of York, white, pure and so beautiful, yet so fragile, too. Thoughts of the King's own mother, Elizabeth of York, flitted into Jane's mind. Alas, poor lady, Jane remembered with a shiver, she whose fruitfulness secured the Tudor line, had been destined to die at her last lying-in, of the dreaded childbed fever. She stooped again and gathered a fine red rose. It was the symbol of the House of Lancaster.

"God grant me a son, a healthy, living son," Jane whispered into the perfumed velvet of the roses' petals.

"Madam, we must make haste. See, there is a storm coming," her ladies urged. The sky was darker now, and the red glow of the setting sun blazed angrily behind a widening bruise of purplish-blue. In the near distance, there was a crack of thunder.

It rumbled ominously around the threatening sky, and sent the Queen and her ladies scurrying for the shelter of the palace. The first heavy drops of rain slanted like arrows upon the warm earth. Once inside they quickly shook off the wet from the skirts of their gowns, before speeding along the corridors leading to the royal apartments. In their wake, the shattered petals of the Queen's roses, both the white and the red, fluttered down unnoticed, leaving a trail upon the floor, the white as flakes of fallen snow, and the red as drops of new-spilt blood.

***

Before a blazing fire in the bedchamber of his house in London, Thomas Cromwell stood, wet through, and hastily divested himself of his sodden clothes. He had ridden on horseback on the last lap of his journey from Hampton Court, where for the moment the King had no further need of his services.

The day had been gusty, driving the rain-laden clouds across a leaden sky. Thomas had come by water from Hampton to London, then ridden into the city in the stinging rain. The October night was starting to close in even as he was mounted, the wind strengthening to gale force. It whipped the rain into sharp arrows that penetrated his thick riding coat. Now, he tossed it aside, the brown and the blue of its colouring barely distinguishable in its dark wetness. When he was quite naked, he coaxed life back into his numbed limbs by the vigourous application of hot cloths handed to him by his manservant.

Then, once in his nightshirt, he quickly slipped into the comforting warmth of his fox-faced bedgown.

A serving wench was admitted carrying a warming pan, with which she deftly stroked away the chill of the bed. Hot wine was brought in, mulled with honey and spices. Thomas gulped it down, and a comforting glow began to course through his body. He poured himself more wine, and sat close to the heat of the fire. He began to feel himself revived, without and within, then he clambered gratefully into the great curtained bed.

The chamber was of middling size, and so was quickly warmed. The blazing fire created a cheering glow in the shadowy recesses, for the single candle his servant had placed close to his bed cast but a limited circle of light. A pleasant sense of lethargy, a feeling seldom enjoyed by the King's chief minister, began to overtake him. In his master's service, many were the long night hours he was used to toil for the King's benefit, for which labour he received, more often than not, but scant appreciation.

Indeed, had he not, of late, been deprived of his own palace apartments so that Edward Seymour, the new Queen's brother, might be accommodated there?

This so that the King and Jane might meet there before their marriage, ostensibly chaperoned, and thus untainted by any possible whiff of scandal.

Thomas sighed. Many were the slights he had endured in the rise to the power he now enjoyed. He was well aware that he was most likely now the most hated man in England. Hated he most certainly was by the nobility, for his common blood. They could not stomach the fact that he, the son of a Putney blacksmith, should by means of an astute mind, and a dogged capacity for unremitting toil, aspire to the ear of a monarch. And the people, his own, they feared his far-reaching powers to tax them, and perhaps more disturbingly, they feared his ability to imperil their immortal souls. To these simple folk, the religion of their fathers, held inviolate for over a thousand years, was a thing too sacred to be set aside for secular reasons.

Outside, the wind howled and gusted, and an eddy of draught crept along the boards of the chamber, setting the candle flame flicker. The heat of the room, and the hot, spiced wine soothed and lulled Thomas's senses. Soon, sleep would come. Quickly, he finished the remainder of the wine his servant had placed at his bedside, and slid down into the feathery softness of goose down.

"Close the curtains," he ordered, and when the heavy draperies were loosed, he was in darkness. His man adjusted the folds, then picked up the candlestick and stepped softly towards the door.

"Goodnight, Sir," he called, and left Thomas to sleep.
In the darkness of his enclosed beds pace, Thomas savoured the quiet of his own house. In the palaces when he attended the King, it was

rarely so, for always at Court there was movement at some time, somewhere, even in the night hours. Though Thomas soon slipped into a deep slumber, another sound other than the wind in the chimney drew him up to consciousness. It wanted still some minutes to midnight. He woke, instantly alert.

There was a clatter of hooves below, and a horse whinnied as its rider reined in sharply and dismounted with haste. There was a mighty hammering on the door, and the rider's accompanying shouts for admittance were matched by curses from within by the recently retired household. Thomas parted the bed curtains and swung his legs over the edge of the bed. Already, footsteps could be heard running up the stair, and his chamber door was flung open.
"Sir, pardon the intrusion," his servant gasped. "There is a messenger ridden from Lincolnshire. With urgent news, he says."

A shadow of annoyance crossed the face of the King's chief minister. He had expected a summons from no less a person than the King himself, who might well require his presence, and think nothing of recalling him back to Hampton Court at so late an hour. However, he was awake now. He might as well see what the commotion was about, or further sleep would elude him.
"Fetch him up, then," he barked, and seated himself by the still glowing fire. The messenger, when he stumbled into the chamber, was barely recognisable as one of Cromwell's own agents.

His sodden clothes were covered in the filth his galloping horse had churned up in the relentless rain on his journey from Lincolnshire.

"Well, what news, man'? Cromwell asked testily.
"Rebellion, Sir. In Louth it began." He steadied himself. So long had he spent in the saddle, his legs pained him when fully stretched.

"A misbegotten crowd set upon two of your tax collectors there," he continued. In the heat of the fire, steam began to rise from his rain-soaked clothes, and a noxious puddle was gathering on the polished floorboards beneath his filthy boots.

Cromwell leaned forward in his chair, and stirred the glowing embers of the fire, then thrust the poker into its ruddy heart. He rose and opened the chamber door.
"Wine. Fetch more wine," he shouted. When it arrived, he plunged the tip of the red-hot poker into the neck of the flagon. There was a sharp hissing as the fiery metal met with the cold wine. When the spluttering within the flagon ceased, Cromwell poured a goblet full to the brim, and held it out to the man.
"Here, drink this" he said. "It will revive you." To the waiting servant, he ordered, " Lay out dry clothes beside the kitchen fire, and set down a mattress for this fellow to sleep on. And find him something to eat" he ordered.

The servant bowed, and withdrew. When the door closed behind him, Cromwell eyed the messenger keenly.

"Now, continue. Your full report, man, and then you can rest."

"Sir, it happened in Louth," the messenger began. "A riot broke out there on the first day of October. It was about the taxes you ordered to be collected. Whether the people could not or would not pay, I know not, for 'tis a poor and miserable county is Lincolnshire, and prone to bad harvests. What I do know is that your two tax collectors were shamefully mishandled by that rioting mob."

"How so" Cromwell asked. His voice was dangerously quiet.

"Sir, the mob was mad with fury. They stripped these two, then bound them in animal skins, and set their dogs upon them." He paused, and took another gulp of wine. "And that is not all, Sir. There is unrest spreading like wildfire across the whole county. The ringleaders are demanding..."

"Demanding! What are they demanding?" Cromwell interrupted. His icy calm momentarily deserted him.

"Sir, it is to do with the changes in religious matters, as well as their tax burdens they rail about. They want the new bishops they look upon as heretics to be dismissed. And they demand an end to the closure of the abbeys, and the restoration of the monks ejected from their Houses. Sir..." he paused, uncertain as to how to continue without giving offence.

"Go on, man," Cromwell urged. "I must know all."

"Sir, they rage at you yourself, and....." he hesitated, gulped down the remainder of his wine, then blurted out, "they demand your person, to do with as they will."

There was silence in the chamber, broken only by the small sounds of the dying fire. The embers were whitening as they cooled, and a cinder fell softly in a shower of powdery ash. For a full minute, Cromwell considered, and then he rose and called for his servant.

"I must return to the Palace immediately," he said. "Fetch dry clothes, and see that a horse is saddled up ready."

"But Sir," the servant protested, "'tis the middle of the night, and you are not rested."

"Nevertheless," came the reply, "I am the King's servant, and it is my duty to apprise His Grace with all speed of what I have learned this night. Saddle up, quickly now. I must be at Hampton by morning."

***

It was a glistening morning. Sunlight danced upon the rain-soaked herbage and dripping trees. In the corridors of Hampton Court there was much activity as servants hurried about the business of the day. The great household stirred early, especially when the King was in residence.

Thomas Cromwell waited. He was stiff and chilled from his return journey in the cold dawn, but determined to gain an audience with the King, in whose bedchamber there was much toing and froing as his Grace's toilet proceeded. Yesterday, the bad weather had dashed all hope of the intended hunt, but this day was glorious, and Henry savoured the prospect of a hard ride. As the great door of his chamber opened to admit servants, Thomas could hear him bawling for his riding clothes, and knew that his own delaying presence, to say nothing of the unwelcome news he must impart, would be likely to try the uncertain balance of the royal temper.

Thomas stretched his stiffened legs and watched covertly as copious supplies of food and drink arrived in order that the King might break his fast in his chamber. The signal to approach the great door would not come yet, for the King's appetite was well known. He shifted his position on the bench where he waited, and in his mind's eye he visualised his master's gargantuan attack on his victuals. The prospect of a hard day's chase required ample sustenance for the now more than ample royal frame.

At length, the door of the bedchamber opened wide, and the King's great bulk appeared. Thomas rose immediately and bowed low. A look of aggravation crossed the King's face, for his Chief Minister's presence inevitably spelt delay.

"What, Cromwell," he barked. "Why back so soon?"

"Sire, pardon, but there is grave news from Lincolnshire, Rebellion..." There was a roar.

"Rebellion? What rebellion?" the King bellowed.

As briefly as was possible, Thomas recounted the facts as he had been told them. At first, there was a deceptive silence. Then, as he had often had cause on numerous occasions, he braced himself for the oncoming explosion. Momentarily, the King's face was a steely mask. Then, as he evaluated the impertinence of this challenge to his authority, his anger mounted like the unstoppable eruption of a volcano. His features contorted with rage, eyes wild, small mouth set hard and cruel.

"Ignorant louts" he roared "They make demands, do they? I'll teach them to make demands."

"Sire, if I might suggest...." Thomas began.

"Muster a force! Put the rogues down." The jewelled hand waved in dismissal, and Thomas bowed to the receding figure of his monarch. The King drew on his riding gloves, and closely attended by a bevy of favoured courtiers, made haste to get mounted. This glorious morning, only the chase mattered.

October

Cumberland – Rebellion

As fire runs through dry grass, the rebellion gathered speed. What began in Lincolnshire spread rapidly through Yorkshire, where Robert Aske, a lawyer, a man with one eye, and old Lord Darcy of Templehurst, took up the cause. Both men were sincere in their belief that the King was wrongly advised by those men about him. From Yorkshire, the insurrection then spread to Westmorland. In Kirkby Stephen and Brough under Stainmore, the cry went up to strike a blow for the restitution of those dispossessed religious already turned out from their Houses, and in the clamour of the ringing church bells, the fervour of rebellion heightened.

Eden ran deep, its waters dark and swollen by the October rain. Down both sides of the river the angry host poured, like the parallel tines of a pitchfork. They were fired by the Oath of Honourable Men, the beautiful Pilgrim's Oath that Aske had laboured to bring forth from his deeply held beliefs. They searched in vain for the landowners, the nobility and the gentry, the priests even, to swear to their cause. But with more to lose than the common folk, should the cause fail, these contrived to keep at a most convenient distance from the uprising. Only at Edenhall was Sir Edward Musgrave found, and compelled to take the Oath.

So the collective mood soured somewhat, and despite the high ideals of the enterprise, there were many who smarted more at the grievances they bore in their daily lives.

The crippling taxes and fines, the oppression of the hated bailiff who would squeeze blood from a stone if he were able, and the threat of the enclosure of common land. So none felt any particular guilt if, in the event of an absentee landlord, a barn, a pigstye, or the occasional henhouse was raided for the sustenance of the many.

On they swept, past Eamont Bridge, to rally a few days later at Penrith. There, on the fellside, amidst scenes of riotous tumult, they were met by the town's appointed Captains who took the names of Poverty, Charity, Faith and Pity. The flame of insurrection spread, and the commons of Greystoke, Skelton, Castle Sowerby, and those townships along and beyond Eden were persuaded to rise.

The Oath was beautiful, honourable, and conceived in the integrity of spirit of an honest, yet possibly naive man, who truly believed that his King was ill-advised by the new men, both the spiritual and the temporal, whose deviation from the old order of things was abhorrent to the conservative northern soul. An enigma of a man indeed, was Robert Aske, who had studied law at London's Inns of Court, and therefore was surely not unacquainted with the vagaries at the heart of government. Was he not aware of the dangers to which he exposed himself, as Grand Captain of the rising now called the Pilgrimage of Grace?

Surely, the Big Friar mused, Penrith could never have seen so great a throng. He edged his way forward with difficulty, until by reason of his great height, he was able to see above the heads of the jostling crowd.

"'Tis the Captains' Mass," he heard a man shout, and the crowd stirred expectantly and heaved forward to see the four Captains march with drawn swords into the Church of St. Andrew. Between them, they escorted the Vicar of Brough under Stainmore, a prophet, some said - a man with fire in his belly.

Sadly, Friar John detached himself from the excited crowd, and made his way to the Friary. So much confusion existed in men's minds now, he reflected. The old faith, so deeply rooted in these northern counties, found itself at odds with the tide of unwanted change surging ever closer from the south. The poor commons, in their ignorance, what could they understand of the unthinkable consequences of their actions? There was precious little support to be had from men of position, those with the most to lose, should the rising fail. Even some of those in religion, for whose sakes, in the main, this great rising had erupted, they indeed showed a disappointing reluctance in wholeheartedly espousing the cause.

***

It was needful for Andrew to deliver a saddle to a farm between Heremitithwaite and Wetheral. It was for the wife of John Aspedaile, a kinsman of the Prioress.

Andrew had lavished much care in the making of the saddle, as the lady for whom it was required disdained to ride pillion behind her husband, as was the custom of country wives. Rather, she longed for her own mount, and he, being affluent, and older than she, wished to indulge her. Therefore, on the recommendation of the Prioress, John Aspedaile had secretly commissioned the riding gear, which included matching harness and reins, from Andrew Bowerbank, who had lately become known for his skills in saddlery.

But when the time came for Andrew to deliver the saddle at the agreed time, he was loath to leave his family alone overnight, because of the parties of agents radiating from Penrith in order to augment the Pilgrim ranks. It was rumoured, with some justification, that undue force was frequently employed to achieve this end. Also, he had heard that threats were being made to the wives and children of those men lacking in enthusiasm for the cause - a device, it was found that speedily encouraged more prompt recruitment to the Pilgrims' swelling ranks.

To Mary's alarm, the cockerel, of late, had persisted in crowing at the door. "'Tis a sure sign that strangers are coming," she said to Andrew. "And soon." Her voice betrayed a note of anxiety, and she drove the offending bird away with unusual ferocity. A quick stab of alarm - the fate of Genett Bowman - resolved Andrew's mind as to how to protect his family whilst he travelled to Wetheral and back. For go there he must.

He had given his word to deliver the goods at the time agreed, and his reputation for reliability would suffer if he was found wanting in this.

Therefore, as the sun was rising on a fine rainless morning in October, whilst Mary roused and fed the children, Andrew saw to it that the sow and her three young piglets had extra supplies of food to last them until the following day. He scattered a generous scoop of grain on the ground for the poultry, though they could fend well enough for themselves, and scratch outside at will. Next, he fed the horse and hitched it to the cart, in readiness for the journey. Then, he joined Mary in the houseplace for his customary platter of bacon and eggs. The lads crowded round him, agog with excitement.

"Mother says we're going on a journey. Where to, where to?" they clamoured in unison.

"I am going to Wetheral to deliver the new riding gear to John Aspedaile," Andrew replied, between swallowing mouthfuls of bacon. "We shall all go in the cart. Your mother and Dinah too - we shall go as far as the Priory at Heremitithwaite. Then I shall unhitch the horse, and ride on to Wetheral."

Andrew dipped a hunk of bread into the fat that oozed from the collops on his platter, and met the questioning stare of both the lads.

"You two, your mother and Dinah, will stay with the Sisters overnight," he explained. "Then, when I come back from Wetheral, we shall all ride home again in the cart."

John and Benedict exchanged looks of disappointment. To stay with the nuns was not their expectation of the adventure they had been anticipating.

"But, father," John pleaded, "cannot we two come with you to Wetheral? Riding pillion? The horse is surely big enough to carry three," he added hopefully, though he was not convinced that this was true.

Andrew swallowed the rest of his bread and fat bacon, then wiped his greasy chin with the back of his hand.

"Not so," he said firmly. "I have to carry the riding gear as well, and anyway, I shall ride faster alone."

The weather held, though the brightness of the early morning was diminished somewhat by the time they rode into the Priory courtyard. Andrew was anxious to be away, but for courtesy's sake, he must accompany Mary and the children to thank the Prioress for the safe keeping she afforded his family, also his grateful thanks he offered for her words of recommendation in the matter of the saddle and gear he now intended to deliver.

Then, his handiwork made secure at his horse's back, he rode smartly off in the direction of Wetheral.

***

In her small parlour, the Prioress's eyes ranged somewhat wistfully over the three children standing in some awe before her.

"So this is the little maid who bear's my name?" she smiled at the small figure of Dinah, pressing close to the security of her mother's skirts.

"You were even younger than she, Mary, when the Sisters found you at our door."

The lads stood awkwardly, shifting from one foot to the other, and heartily wishing that they were with their father speeding on his way to Wetheral. Dame Dinah smiled and reached for a small bell, and in answer to its summons, Sister Marguerite entered.

"Sister, take the boys with you to collect eggs," she said. "Go, children and help Sister Marguerite. She will show you the places where our hens lay away." Gladly, they escaped from the imposing presence of the Lady. The Sister who held her hands out to them to show them the way, they could see was young, and despite her concealing habit, even to their youthful eyes, was very beautiful.

In the Prioress's parlour a small fire was burning, for the chill of late autumn pervaded the dim room. Dame Dinah settled herself at its side, and as she was bidden, Mary seated herself at the other, and drew Dinah onto her knee.

"'Tis many a year now, Mary, since you came to Staffield Hall to be our young dairymaid," Dame Dinah said. "Ah, I had not then been sent to be a nun."

Her eyes softened as she recalled that sweet, remembered time of carefree days... But that had been before the death of her beloved James, her twin, her other self. She dismissed such thoughts, and turned her attention again to Mary.

"Tell me, Mary," she asked, "what can you recall of that time?" Mary met the questioning eyes of the Prioress, and smiled.

"I remember, oh - how could I ever forget? After the nuns of this House found me at their door and took me in and cared for me, your own mother and father, of their charity gave me a home and my livelihood. I bless their memory."

"But Mary, what can you remember of a time before the nuns found you," the Prioress persisted.

Young Dinah shifted on her mother's knee, and Mary's arms closed around her. The sensation seemed to trigger a forgotten memory, something deep and dark, too painful to remember, some memory buried still deeper with each passing year. Mary sighed, and as one struggles to bring to mind the clouded images of a long-forgotten dream, words that she could scarce believe to be her own came hesitantly to her lips.

"A man carried me," she began. "I was so weary of walking. It was dark. So cold...." In spite of the warm fire before which she and Dame Dinah sat, she shivered. "The man kept stumbling along the way," she continued.

"Then his arms slackened about me, and I feared he would drop me.... it was raining, and he shielded me from it in his cloak." She paused, and looked into the glowing embers of the fire."

Dame Dinah waited, lest she interrupt Mary's train of thought.

"Ah, yes, I remember that he coughed a great deal. Then, at last he set me down in the shelter of a doorway. He took off his cloak and wrapped me in it."

Mary stared into the depths of the fire, as though she saw remembered images there. Dame Dinah was silent, waiting...

"He bent down to bless me," the dreamy voice continued. "I must have slept, for when I woke, he was not there, and I wept because I was afraid."

Mary looked at the Prioress in astonishment.

"I did not know that I remembered that," she said.

Dame Dinah nodded. "Yes, the Sisters heard your cries, and found you in the shelter of the Priory doorway. You were so young at the time, and I fear that you were never told later that soon afterwards, a man's body was found on the fell. He had no cloak, though it was bitter weather. And Mary, there were bloodstains on his shirt, but not from any wound.

There was blood, too, on the cloak you were wrapped in. My child, I believe that man was your father, too weak to carry you further."

***

Sister Marguerite found a basket of woven twigs, and led the way to the convent's henhouse. There, she held it in readiness as the lads searched the rows of nestboxes, and carefully deposited their finds within its depths.

Then, she led them outside to the edge of the barnyard where a rough patch of brambles and bracken grew, and pointed out the hidden places where those of the convent's flock preferred to lay their eggs in solitude, away from the raucous din made by their neighbours. Sometimes, they found a clutch of several eggs, hidden in the bracken. John and Benedict gleefully scooped up their finds and carried them in their caps to the Sister's basket.

It was in the last place they searched that Benedict found a hen still sitting determinedly upon her eggs. She glared at him, enraged, as he sought to feel beneath her warm feathers, and pecked furiously at the hand seeking to rob her. With a yelp of pain, he snatched back his hand and sucked at the place where blood began to gather. In a burst of anger, he grabbed the offending hen by its neck, and flung it squawking into the fronds of bracken.

"Ah, child," Sister Marguerite smiled up into Benedict's face, as she bent low beside him to examine the small wound, "we should not be angry with the poor hen.

She only wished to protect her children, the chicks she hoped to rear, though it is late in the year for that."

"Sister," John interrupted, "who are those men watching us, over there?" He pointed, and as he did so, Sister Marguerite glimpsed Robert Winter hastily pull another man, a younger man, into the cover of a knot of trees. But he, the younger one, would not be drawn. He came forward boldly, leaving Robert behind, to lurk in the shadow of the trees. Then, he stood close by, the brambles only barring his way.

"I bid you good-day, Sister," he called jauntily. "Pray do not go on my account," he added, as Marguerite turned to go. He studied the trio with some amusement, the lads ranged protectively on either side of the young nun. Instinctively, Marguerite drew her habit closely around her.

"We are done here now, Sir," she replied. "Good-day to you."

Thomas, for it was he, watched the retreating figures until they were out of sight, then he re-traced his steps to the cover of the trees where Robert Winter was skulking.

"Liked you the little nun, then?" Robert sneered knowingly. "Too comely for the cloister, I'll wager." He laughed into Thomas's face, the mirthless laugh of a lecher, and taunted the young man with salacious suggestions.

"Not yet professed, you say," Thomas began. He heard his own voice, a strangulated sound, thick in his throat with passion. He spat out the words, determined, prophetic. "She will never be professed," he choked, "never!"

Marguerite did not look back until they reached the barnyard again. Why she wondered, had she felt such an instinctive, yet seemingly unreasonable fear? The young man had seemed civil enough, though his frank gaze was disconcerting.

There was something familiar about him, something elusive, though what, she could not recall. But something continued to trouble her, and later, much later that day, revelation came. It was the image of a face, now clear amongst the blur of faces on that dreadful day of the nuns' examination by the King's Visitors. He had been there, and for whatever reason, he had not left with them. He was still here, and it troubled her.

When all was quiet, the little hen ventured out from her refuge in the ferns, and reclaimed the nest from which she had been so roughly ejected. With clucks of satisfaction, and driven by hopes of a hatching, she settled herself carefully again upon the eggs that no-one had collected.

Andrew stayed the night at the farmhouse near Wetheral. John Aspedaile and his lady were well pleased with his handiwork, and Andrew was well paid for it, and well fed, too, at his host's table that evening. Then he bedded down on a heap of dry bracken in the warmth of the stable, with his horse, and woke as dawn began to break. He did not wait for food to be prepared in the houseplace, and before the sun was up, he was away, and riding smartly homeward in the direction of Heremitithwaite.

Once at the Priory, he hurried his family into the cart, hitched up the horse, and was eager to be on his way back to Lazonby. The journey home was undertaken in unusual silence. Only young Dinah chattered to a strangely unresponsive mother. Both parents had much to ponder, Andrew especially.

He had heard disquieting tales the night before at John Aspedaile's table - tales of raiding parties roaming the countryside in all directions, in search of provisions to feed the swelling ranks of Pilgrims gathering at Penrith. Mary mused sadly on the revelation brought about by the Prioress's words, and her own long forgotten memories. The lads, too, had sensed the unease of the young Sister, as a result of their encounter with the stranger, and coupled with the heaviness of spirit of their parents, they began to realise that all was not well with the world.

Andrew drove the horse unusually hard, and the cart jolted mightily over the muddy ruts in the road leading to Lazonby.

In the main street of the village, men who should long since have been about their daily work, stood about in solemn groups, cursing soundly. Andrew slowed the horse to a walk and called out to them, "What news, what news?" yet feared to hear their answer. "Get thee back home, tanner," someone shouted. "God alone knows how much livestock was taken here yester night. 'Twill be a miracle if the poxy knaves spared thy place."

No miracle! It must have been easy to catch the young piglets and cut their throats on the spot. Blood was spattered everywhere. The old sow, she was gone too. Only a few frightened fowls, and the cockerel, minus most of his tail feathers, cautiously began to pick their way over the blood soaked patches of ground where the plucked feathers of their erstwhile companions fluttered in the congealing mess.

***

In his travels, the Big Friar absorbed the news, some fact, some rumour, flying as the wind between village, town and city. Penrith in the east, Cockermouth in the west - these were the rallying points in Cumberland. Carlisle, yet to declare itself, no doubt felt in a position to prevaricate, defended as it was by its mighty castle under the command of Sir Thomas Clifford. It was one thing to wear the Pilgrim's badge and march under the banner of the Five Wounds of Christ - but surely, the Big Friar reasoned, was not rebellion treason? And the King was not famous for clemency.

His representative, that veteran of many battles, the Duke of Norfolk, was on his way north. Already, in Louth, the birthplace of the rising, a furious Henry had refused to treat with the insurgents, and the movement had collapsed. To be sure, the Louth rising had been sparked by the vexed tax situation, but the rising that started in Yorkshire had a deeply religious theme, and it flourished.

Mr. Aske was in York, and by the end of October was said to have a following of some thirty thousand men under arms, and the support of old Lord Tom Darcy of Templehurst.

To his mortification, the King was unable to muster sufficient forces in the north to put the rebels down, and the Duke of Norfolk was obliged to play for time, while at the King's command, the Earls of Derby and Shrewsbury endeavoured to raise troops to bring up north, with all speed.

As yet, the Cumberland Pilgrims had met with no opposition, but despite repeated urgings from those at Cockermouth to take the Oath, Carlisle remained loyal to the King. Therefore, when some fifteen thousand armed rebels gathered at Burford Oak on Broadfield, some seven miles from the city, its citizens were gripped by understandable feelings of anxiety.

Their fears of a siege, however, were allayed when news arrived that the King had agreed to a truce negotiated between the Grand Captain Aske, in Yorkshire, and His Majesty's representative, the Duke of Norfolk. Thus, Carlisle was spared, and with great reluctance, the Pilgrims were persuaded to disperse, and return peaceably to their homes. At the moment of their greatest strength, the most fervent of the rebels encamped at Broadfield resented surrendering their hard-won advantage.

In the main, they made their way back, sullen and disappointed, to homes where little if anything was to lift the burdens of their working existence.

In Pontefract, a list of their demands was drawn up, and the Duke, still playing for time, offered on behalf of the King, promises of agreement and a full pardon for those offences committed before the first of November. Aske, in his naivety believed him, convinced that his prince was ill-informed of the north country's reasons for the late uprising. At Christmastime he went to Court to meet with the King to lay before him the truth of the matter, and to assure him of the loyalty of the north. Did not the Oath of Honourable Men specifically state this? And the King?

The truce was short-lived. Aske was barely returned from London before news came of trouble in the west of Cumberland. These were the men who seethed at the injustices and burdens they bore in the drudgery of their daily lives. This was the impetus that had spurred them to rise and march upon Carlisle. How bitterly they resented the order to disband and return home peaceably, not a whit better off for all their trouble.

Not for them the high ideals of the Grand Captain. His prime concern appeared to be the state of religion, and the righting of its wrongs. Theirs was more mundane - the state of their wretched lives. Therefore, in outbreaks of frustration, some pulled down the fences enclosing land in order for the rich owners to rear sheep, others did violence upon the hated bailiffs and even threatened the landlords unless their demands were met. A second insurrection was not far away. It needed but a spark to reignite the smouldering embers of discontent.

1537
February – Carlisle

It came on the twelfth of February, when Sir Thomas Clifford rode out from Carlisle Castle with a small party of horsemen. He rode to Kirkby Stephen, with the intention of apprehending two of the ringleaders of the first insurrection. Once there, they discovered that these two had prudently taken refuge in the church steeple. Thwarted of their purpose there, his troops rode about the town creating mayhem, which roused the inhabitants to angry resistance. In the subsequent skirmish, Sir Thomas's men were routed - it was the signal for a second rising.

Between four and five thousand men gathered in Westmorland to march to Penrith and Greystoke. Their numbers swelled as they went, and by mid-February, they gathered once more outside Carlisle on Broadfield Moor. They had no leaders as such, beyond the two now safely down from the steeple in Kirkby Stephen. A brave, foolhardy gesture it was. Before them again lay Carlisle Castle, defending the greatest city in Cumberland. But its assault was what they had come for, and this time, fired up by an ardour born of a deep-seated sense of injustice, they shot off all their arrows in its direction. Five hundred spearmen issued from the Castle, and fell upon them.

It was carnage.

Those who were not taken prisoner, scattered before the onslaught, and fled. Sir Thomas, watching from his vantage point in the Castle, and no doubt still smarting at the ignominy of his encounter at Kirkby Stephen, sought to redress his position by galloping out to harry the retreating rabble for several miles beyond the city. Thus it ended, in mire and blood, and in three days time, the Duke of Norfolk would arrive.

***

At the age of sixty-four, Thomas Howard, third Duke of Norfolk and King's Lieutenant, the Duke rode the length and breadth of England, through miry roads little better than cart tracks, to impose martial law upon the wild and troublesome north country. In January, rumour had it that he was coming with twenty thousand troops to put down the new risings there. He had ridden to Hull, Scarborough, York, Richmond and Barnard Castle. Now, in the latter days of February, Carlisle was his destination, and there he would try those miscreants captured at the recent assault of that city. There too, obedient to his sovereign's merciless instructions, he must display the King's banner in the Castle there, and order such dreadful execution upon the guilty, to serve as a warning to any as would defy the royal will.

The Duke eased himself in the saddle in an effort to bring back feeling into his frozen legs. It was a bitter winter. In the south, the Thames had frozen over.

So thick was the river ice that the King and Queen Jane had galloped across it on horseback in order to reach Greenwich Palace for the Christmas festivities.

The Duke himself spent Christmas at his house at Kenninghall in Norfolk. Kenninghall too was a fine palace, rebuilt from the old mansion inherited from his father some twelve years ago. Upon its completion, he had parted, with much acrimony, from his willful wife, and banished her to live in a dower house. That accomplished, and much to the duchess's chagrin, he installed Bess Holland, his mistress of several years, in her place at Kenninghall.

Several of the Duke's attendant gentlemen rode ahead to see that all fitting preparations were in hand for his lordship's stay. At last, the great bulk of Carlisle Castle loomed ahead, dark upon the skyline. It dwarfed the huddle of mean dwellings that crowded beneath its towering walls. The Duke's party clattered through the narrow streets, empty of all but a few curious lads, too young to appreciate, or to care why the great lord came and thence into the castle courtyard to dismount. The cold was penetrating. On the long ride, it entered Norfolk's aging body, seemingly to the very marrow of his bones. It locked his muscles so that he must lean heavily upon the proffered shoulder of a groom in order to steady his descent from the saddle.

Now was the time for Tudor vengeance. The truce was broken. No soft words needed now to play for time. Whatever terms the Duke had felt constrained to offer on the King's behalf, whether on his own initiative or with the King's approval, were negated. Armed with the King's instructions, Norfolk set about selecting for trial those deemed to be the chief offenders.

In the great hall of Carlisle Castle, the King's banner was displayed. His instructions were merciless:

"Our pleasure is that before you shall close up our banner again, you shall cause such dreadful execution to be done upon a good number of the inhabitants of every town, village and hamlet that hath offended in this rebellion, as well as by the hanging of them up in trees, as by the quartering of them and the setting up their heads and quarters in every town, great and small, and in all such other places as they may be a fearful spectacle to all others hereafter that would practise any like matter, which we require you to do, without pity or respect...."

No jury, for local men might well have sympathy for their own kind - a trial by the severity of martial law it would be, and seventy-four of the prisoners taken were condemned to suffer so.

***

With the approach of spring, when folk should have looked up with pleasure at the unfurling of new life in the trees, now they witnessed an unseasonable harvest there. And of this obscene crop, they reasoned, could those whose still bodies turned in the wind, past pain now, could they not be said to be the more fortunate ones? For of the condemned to die, twelve of these, still living, hung in chains at

Carlisle. And of the remainder, because of the scarcity of iron in Cumberland, each prisoner was returned to his native village where the blacksmith must labour at his anvil to forge a chain to gibbet a neighbour.

In the villages and hamlets from Carlisle to Penrith, the Big Friar sensed hostility towards him, a hostility born of fear. The people were cowed, and justly so, for wherever his journeyings took him, there was scarcely a hamlet that did not bear evidence of the Duke's diligence in inflicting so-called justice in the name of the King. How was it possible, he agonised, to exhort these bewildered folk to conform to the King's new order of religion, to acknowledge him, and not the Pope, as Head of the Church in England, as all preaching friars were now required to do? Even harder, how to speak of a just and merciful God, of His pity and compassion for mankind, when one of their own swung from a nearby tree? Brother John's words repelled the few who lingered to hear what he would say, and served only to arouse in them a sullen, bitter resentment.

"What justice or mercy did he get, then?" cried the anguished voice of an old man at the edge of the crowd. "He was my son." The reedy voice faltered, as a tide of grief welled up and choked the words he strove to say, and then, "He only went with them, else they would have fired the house."

A murmur of assent rippled round those who stood near to the old man.

"He speaks true. He was forced to go." A man stepped forward, and stood before the Friar. "'Twas to save his father's house from torching that the lad joined those marching on Carlisle," he said, and he jerked an arm to where a solitary tree grew nearby. Brother John looked up. His eyes rested upon the figure of a youth not yet grown to full manhood.

The body had started to shrink, and therefore had grown lighter as the days since his hanging lengthened into weeks.

It swayed and gyrated slowly in the freshening March wind. Birds had feasted upon the soft areas of his face. The eyes were gone, and where his last gasping breath had left his constricted windpipe, the protruding tongue had soon been pecked out from his mouth. And it was expressly forbidden to take down this pitiful remnant of humanity, this so-called rebel, traitor and enemy of the self-styled Head of Holy Church - the King. It must remain so, as a fearful warning to others, by the order of a vengeful ruler.

A crow flew down and perched on the shoulder of he who had once been human. It thrust its powerful bill down a wizened ear, searching for whatever nourishment that might be found there. Someone threw a stone at it, but it missed its mark and struck the Friar full on the side of his face. There was a long moment of silence, then the one who had cast the stone, a burly fellow, bent down and picked up another. He took aim, not at the crow, but at Brother John.

"Get back to thy House, Friar," he yelled. "We be sick to our bellies of folk telling us what to do, what to think. Leave us to mend ourselves, for no other body will" he yelled.

There was a murmur of agreement from the watching crowd. By some instinct, primeval perhaps - the instinct of the crowd - they acted as one. A hail of small stones rained down upon the Friar. All the pent-up rage, the fear and the grief of the past weeks flared up and relieved itself in action.
"Get thee back to Penrith, Friar" someone shouted.
The man who had first spoken to him looked into Brother John's sorrowful face, and urged, "Go now.'Tis not safe here anymore. Crazed men do crazy things."

"God keep you, my son." John's face was calm, his voice quiet, unutterably sad. He turned to face his assailants. He raised his hand in blessing, and made the sign of the cross. Another stone was flung, then another and yet another, smashing into his face.
"Father, forgive them. They know not what they do," he prayed silently, then turned to go.

Noon was past, judging by the sun's position in the sky. On the road, his progress was slow. He felt dazed. Blood was trickling down his face and into his neck, then soaking into his habit. There was a sharp pain in his ankle where a man had hurled a jagged piece of rock, and he could not help but drag his foot. Yes, he must return to his House, but he feared he would be unable to reach Penrith before nightfall, so slowly he was limping.

Overhead, the sky darkened, blue-black, and a cloud driven by a gusty wind soon emptied its load of rain upon the already slushy track. Twice, the Friar lost his footing and fell into the soft mud churned up by the deluge. A solitary tree stood near to the edge of the track, and he struggled towards it to lean for support against its trunk. In the wind, a rhythmic creaking could be heard, its sound insistent above the pelting of the rain. Brother John raised his face and the coldness of the falling raindrops both bathed his face and cleared the dizziness that made his senses swim.

Then it was that he saw the rope. It hung straight, and swung backwards and forwards in the wind. He turned, and at the other side of the tree's trunk upon which he had been leaning, swung the body of one of those unfortunates, not slain, but captured, condemned and gibbetted after the rebels' unsuccessful assault on Carlisle. And this was just one of the many that could now be seen "hanged upon every bush," after trial by martial law in the great hall of the castle there. The Friar retched at the sight, and was ashamed that he did so.

Now it was evident that Penrith could not be reached before darkness fell. But Heremitithwaite was near. For a long time, Brother John had avoided being seen in the vicinity of the Priory in these troubled times, so as not to compromise the nuns there. There were times when he had suspected that his movements were watched. A rustle in the bracken, a shadowy figure disappearing behind a distant tree, something, someone, moving in the moonlight - was it his imagination, or could it be Robert Winter keeping watch upon him?

Hastily, he dismissed the thought. Shelter he must have for the night, and over the gatehouse of the Priory there was a small guest chamber, little used, but sometimes, when travelling late, he had spent the night there, and been up before dawn and on the road to Penrith again. He knew how to get in without troubling the Sisters. Just a few hours rest he desperately needed, then he would leave again under cover of darkness, without being seen.

March – Heremitithwaite

The day the Ladies of the Priory of Heremitithwaite dreaded now arrived. Despite their fervent prayers, the fate of their small House was sealed. They could only watch in silent fear as, one bright, windswept day in March, a messenger clamoured loudly at their door, in the name of the King, demanding admittance and audience with the Prioress. His work with her was done in little enough time. He had long become adept at delivering bad news, and was immune to the tears, and pleas of those who received it. This woman, however, neither wept not pleaded, but merely inclined her head slightly in his direction. Calmly, she listened to the general instructions he related that were necessary for her to observe for the closure of her House.

"All must be ready to leave before the King's workmen arrive," he stated. They, he informed the Lady, would remove anything of value, and carry it away for the King's use. Here, the Prioress's mouth registered the beginning of an icy smile. What might a King covet in this poor House, that sardonic smile questioned. When he had gone, Dame Dinah steeled herself to meet the onslaught of tearful questions she expected would assail her. Slowly, she went to meet them, Sisters Anne and Galfride - women who in their youth had entered the religious life from the security of their prosperous families. Now, after their sheltered years of convent seclusion, they must no longer wear the religious habit of their calling. They must go out into a world vastly changed from the one they left behind.

For years, the immaturity of these two, as grown women, their gullibility, their sheer childishness, had tried Dame Dinah's patience almost beyond endurance. But now, the sight of their abject fear that held these two, her sacred charges, in a paralysing silence, swept away those years of frustration in an all engulfing tide of compassion.

"My Sisters!" Instinctively, she held out her arms to them, and like frightened children, they clung to her and wept; wept tears of fear, dread and bewilderment, and like a mother, Dame Dinah comforted them with the inborn instinct latent in all but the rarest of women. Never let it be said that pity is not one of the several faces of love!

The moment could no longer be delayed. The long-feared tidings must be told.

"We must be ready to leave our beloved House in a week's time." Dame Dinah spoke softly, holding them still in her embrace.
"So soon?" Sister Galfride whispered.
"Yes, it must be so," the Prioress continued. "But remember, you are both fortunate that your families welcome you back. And you will not want, for you will be granted your pensions. At least, the new order permits that, though I fear it will go hard with those religious who must go out into the world. There will be many who have no family to take them in."
"And you, Madame?" Sister Anne enquired. "How will you live?"

"My sister died, God rest her soul, and her husband is now married again. He has prospered, and built a fine, new house. He is a good man, and of his charity, he has offered me the farmstead he and my sister lived in when first they wed. 'Tis not far away - near Wetheral it is," Dame Dinah told them. "Then perhaps we shall meet again, Madame, when we return to the world," Sister Anne spoke hopefully.

"God willing," the Prioress agreed. "But there is one thing most needful to do before we leave. I must journey to Wetheral to ask my brother-in-law to allow Marguerite to live with me there. She is not a fully professed nun, and now she never will be. There will be no pension for her, and I fear she has no family that I know of. So now, I must ride to Wetheral tomorrow, and be back before the King's workmen arrive."

A look of apprehension passed between Sisters Anne and Galfride.
"I shall be away only one night," Dame Dinah assured them. "I shall be back long before the King's workmen come. You need have no fear."

The journey to Wetheral was not a long one. Dame Dinah and the Winter lad set off soon after daybreak and rode at a steady pace, despite the miry state of the road.

There would be much to discuss upon reaching the Aspedaile household, the farmstead to inspect and the arrangements to be made for whatever the Lady might require for the setting up of her own accommodation. And of the utmost importance was the favour she must ask of John Aspedaile with regard to Marguerite.

At the Priory that morning, assured of the Prioress's return the next day, Sisters Anne and Galfride, though they would not admit it to each other, secretly began to enjoy the feeling of their own importance at being left in charge at their House. However, Dame Dinah had not been gone more than an hour, when to their alarm, the rumble of a heavy cart could be heard upon the cobbles of the courtyard. Surely, not the King's workmen already. It could not be, they were not due to arrive for several days, by which time the convent would be empty. But outside there was much shouting of orders as three men jumped down from the cart, dragging ladders and leather bags of tools.

The Sisters' brief moments of euphoria dissolved rapidly. Someone was hammering at the door demanding entry in the name of the King. They exchanged looks of horror.

With trembling hands Sister Anne drew back the bolts of the heavy door and pulled it back until it stood wide. The young man thus revealed viewed the agitated nuns with barely concealed amusement. "Ladies, I would speak with your superior," he announced.

"But Sir," Sister Galfride's voice betrayed the confusion she vainly sought to suppress. "She is not here. She is even now riding to Wetheral on business," she quavered.

"So, you are alone," Thomas queried. "Apart from the novice?" he added.

"Only for today, Sir," Sister Anne spoke up. "The Prioress will return tomorrow. Can you not come back then?" she asked hopefully.

"Madam, I cannot. The work must proceed," Thomas spoke with authority.

"But, Sir, you have come much sooner than we expected. We thought to have a few more days before we must leave." Sister Anne's voice broke. "Oh, what shall we do?" she wailed.

"You need do nothing, Madam. My men will do all that is necessary, and we will trouble you as little as possible" Thomas assured her.

All morning, the Sisters listened to the shouts of the King's workmen in shocked silence, as language such as they might never have heard before reached their scandalized ears. Workmen clambered up their ladders to hack at the lead that protected their roof, until it could be prised off and thrown down to where a fire of some of the roof timbers was burning in readiness. There, the strips of lead were melted, then shaped and stamped with the royal cypher.

The men worked speedily, with the experience gained by so many similar acts of demolition, county by county, throughout England. So much so that as the day wore on, and the lead cooled, the work of loading it onto their cart was completed.

It only needed now for the carter to hitch the two great horses between the shafts, and the journey to Penrith could begin.

It seemed there was some reason for delay. The carter stood ready between his horses and held their heads until the leadstrippers climbed aboard. There was plenty of room on the cart, the amount of lead gained from the Priory roof was not great, it being a small House. The horses stamped their feet - they were powerful beasts, and hard to hold. The carter fumed. They would not reach Penrith before daylight closed if they did not leave soon. A man not used to riding clung to his horse's neck as he galloped into the courtyard and took Thomas aside.

"The Friar" he gasped. The breath was almost shaken out of him by the speed at which he had ridden. "The Big Friar! He comes this way. I passed him on the road."

Thomas's eyes narrowed. "Did he recognise you?" he asked swiftly.

"No. I rode past him as fast as I could go. Besides, his head was down, and his cowl covered most of his face. He was walking slowly. He seemed to limp."

"We have him" Thomas exulted. "Come with me."

Seeing that Thomas was delayed, the leadstrippers had returned to their fire and were warming themselves by its dying embers, but at his approach, they made ready to jump back onto the cart again.

"Wait," he ordered. "There is urgent business we must attend to before we can leave."

"How long will this business take?" the carter asked. "We must leave soon, and see, the horses are hard to hold."

"Not long, I trust" Thomas replied. He turned to the leadstrippers and spoke urgently.

"A man is coming this way, and I have reason to believe that he has hidden valuables, which like this lead, is now the property of the King. I will pay you well if you do exactly as I say when he arrives."

"What would you have us do?" queried one doubtfully. "We should be on the road by now."

"It will not take long," Thomas assured him. "And easy money for you. He will not see that we are here until he passes. Stay hidden behind the cart, and when I give the signal, take him from behind, and bind him."

They waited, ready with their rope. The carter cursed softly, as his horses became increasingly restive. Then, a dark figure of unusual height, though he stooped somewhat, walked unwittingly towards them.

***

It might have been the sound of the wind stirring the branches in the cluster of trees that fringed the approach to the nunnery. But it was not. The Friar saw not a thing. He only heard the sudden rush of men's feet at his rear, then he felt cords binding his wrists as both his arms were pinioned behind his back. Two men held him prisoner and proceeded to drag him to a loaded cart. There, by dint of much pulling and heaving, for he struggled to free himself, they managed to haul him onto its tail. Then it was that Brother John saw the lead, stamped with the King's royal cypher. A man better dressed than the others, whom he took to be the Commissioners' agent, confronted him, and sidling close by was Robert Winter.

"Friar, I will be brief," the agent addressed him. "You are accused of the crime of stealing the King's property. Therefore, I require you to tell me where you have hidden the valuables you were seen to carry away from this House.
I have a witness." Robert smirked.

As a sheep before her shearers is dumb, so was Brother John. At a nod from the agent, Robert Winter leapt onto the cart. A rope trailed behind him, a noose made ready. Another nod, and the Friar felt the noose slip over his head. Onto the piled up lead the workmen clambered to tie the rope's end securely around a stout overhanging branch.

"Now, answer," ordered the agent, "while you are still able." So taut was the rope that Friar John must stand almost a-tiptoe to prevent the noose tightening around his throat.

Nor could he look down at his interrogator. He looked ahead, and upwards at the vastness of the windswept sky.

"Where then is Heaven?" was his only thought. "Answer" the agent urged.

"I will answer, my son." Brother John's voice rang out, clear and calm, and absent of all fear. "I will answer to my God alone, and He shall be my judge. It is to His supreme authority I shall submit, not to yours, not to any man's."

The fire that was made to melt the lead was almost out, but fanned by a sudden gust of wind, a piece of smouldering timber burst into flame. Someone kicked it, and a shower of sparks flew upwards towards the waiting horses. "Fool" the carter yelled. He struggled to hold the startled beasts, but he could not. The cart lurched forward, and the great bulk of the Friar's body swung out and dropped. Often, in life, Brother John had considered that weight a burden he must bear in his many journeys.

At the end, it was his friend, for the transition between life and death was immediate, in the swift snap of his neck.

What so short a time ago seemed to Thomas a near perfect plan had miscarried in the twinkling of an eye. Rage boiled up in him, dangerous in its impotence.

"Damn you," he swore at the hapless carter. The body of the Friar hung on the swinging rope.

It twitched momentarily, and then was still. This was not how it should have happened, Thomas raged helplessly. No. He had intended this man no lasting harm, but had merely meant to press from him the information that was the key to a young man's advancement in this rapidly changing world - wealth. Robert Winter touched him on the arm. "The young nun, the novice. She was with him and the Lady that night. She knows something," he volunteered.

Ah, perhaps all was not lost, then. The novice. Would she not be easier to coerce into revealing what she must surely know of that night's work? And she, not even a fully professed nun, nor yet to be so now, with no vows to keep!

"I would speak with Mistress Standley," he demanded of the two Sisters at the door of the convent. They could not deny him, but hovered close by in the parlour as he addressed Marguerite.

"Mistress, I would speak privately with you. Pray come with me," he ordered. Marguerite rose and laid aside the embroidered cope with which she had sought to distract herself from the disruption the day's events had wrought in the even tenor of the Sisters' lives.

Both Sister Anne and Sister Galfride exchanged looks of shocked apprehension, but were helpless to do otherwise than comply with the agent's order. So Marguerite schooled herself to a show of outward calmness, and walked as Thomas indicated, through the convent door. He slammed it shut, and guided her towards the courtyard. He walked before her. She followed.

"Mistress," he began, as he turned to face her, "You are soon to leave this place and enter the world again. Even now, you are not a professed nun, nor are you bound by any vows of obedience to those in the religious life. You understand that this is so?" She nodded.

Before they reached the end of the courtyard, he stopped and turned again, placing himself before her, so that she should not see, as yet, what hung at the entrance to the Priory. He continued, and looked intently at her.

"Now, Mistress, I ask you in the name of the King, where is the altar silver hidden that you and the Prioress, and the Friar from Penrith were seen carrying away one night? Tell me." His voice was low, and carried a note of suppressed menace.

Marguerite flinched, then answered steadily, and with honesty.

"Sir, I cannot tell you, for I do not know."

"You know something," he insisted. "And you will tell me when you see how it fares with those who refuse to answer."

With that, he swung around, and clutched her arm. Through the folds of her habit, she felt herself held in his vice-like grip.

"Come" he commanded, and forced her towards the cluster of trees where the Friars body hung. "See, see there, Mistress!" He spoke softly, but his voice was laden with menace.

They watched her in silence. Why did she not show fear, when the sight before her would have loosened the tongue of many a man?

"How say you now, Mistress?" Thomas's demanding voice cut into the silent prayer she offered up for the peace of Brother John's soul. Past all hurt, nothing said now, nor done, could harm him further.

"Only the Friar knew where," she whispered. "He would not tell us where."

It seemed that she sat again with the Prioress within the sound of the waterfall, but the sound that rushed in her ears was not that of its tumbling waters, but that which accompanies the blackness of departing consciousness.

"So, he has taken his secret with him. Damn him." Thomas kicked at the wheel of the cart in a burst of frustration. "Cut him down, and load him onto the cart. Make ready to go." He spat the words out through clenched teeth.

He stooped, and gathered up the senseless form of Marguerite, and carried her towards the Priory. Her face was white, bloodless, her eyes closed, as though in sleep. He could feel the warmth of her body beneath the concealing habit. Madness seized him, and it fuelled the rising compulsion within him, a compulsion that would brook no denial. He laid her down upon the grassy verge of the courtyard, drew aside the folds of her habit, and gloried in the splendor of her body.

Lust slaked, and sanity returning, he heard the clatter of hooves as their mounts were brought ready to escort the cartload of lead to Penrith. He stood for a moment over the half- conscious woman he had just violated.
She moaned, and began to sob, as her senses returned, but he turned away and made for the road where already the powerful horses were stepping out with their load.

The body of the Friar now lay wrapped in his habit upon the cart. At one end, it dripped with blood where in his absence, the head had been hacked away. The hammering he could hear was Robert Winter driving a stake into the ground. He sharpened the end, then with savage enjoyment, he impaled the cowled head upon it. His mean soul rejoiced as he anticipated the effect his handiwork would have upon the Prioress next day. He gloated. After years in which he had been bested in every confrontation he had had with the Lady, now he savoured the sweet gratification of delayed revenge.

Next morning, as dawn began to break, those who rose early in Penrith noticed the departure of the King's workmen from their town. One spat as the cart rolled by, unaware that it carried not only lead to augment the King's arsenal, but also the trussed up torso of one of their own community.

Further on, at Eamont Bridge, the carter halted his horses at a spot where there was easy access to the river. Moments later a dark bundle could be seen in the water. It floated briefly, then sank and was gone from sight. In Penrith, the townsfolk went about their various affairs.

At the Friary, those who passed by paused, then looked away and hurried on, but the one who had spat at the lead-laden cart stopped and stared at the scene of butchery there. Over the gateway of the House hung two severed legs.

They were long, unusually so. Those legs, he knew well could only be those of one man, the one folk called "the Big Friar."

***

In the days that followed the departure of the King's workmen, it rained incessantly. The roof of the Priory began to leak, and the dampness oozed through the unprotected timbers. Rain dripped steadily until it collected in pools of water throughout the convent. Dame Dinah was hard pressed as to what to deal with first, whether the needs of the living, or the dead. The dead, of course, she could not help, except by her prayers, but Marguerite's need, though puzzling, was great. The girl herself was incoherent.

Her speech made no sense, and she herself appeared half demented. Sisters Anne and Galfride besieged her with their versions of the events that had occurred in her absence, and it was only with the tale that

Robert Winter's wife had to tell, that the full extent of the outrage committed the previous day became clear. The return of Isobel Winter's errant husband, now more overbearing than before, and his association with the Commissioners' agent terrified her. So she watched the unfolding of events at a safe distance, hidden behind bushes, and concealed in a patch of bracken. She told of the ambush of the Friar, and the circumstances of his death. She witnessed also, what the Sisters could not, they being out of sight inside the convent - the rape of Marguerite.

The Prioress felt numb. It rendered her incapable of immediate reaction. She sat motionless, speechless, and locked in a state of vacancy induced by the compounding of successive shocks. Eventually, the pleading voice of Isobel Winter brought her back to reality.
"Lady, I beg of you. Protect me and my son from the man I am married to. I fear him greatly now, for truly, he is evil," she sobbed. "He laughed, oh how he laughed as he thrust the Friar's head upon the spike."

Isobel shuddered, fear and horror plain in her voice. Dame Dinah surveyed the cringing woman before her. She was a piteous sight.

"Isobel," she began, "you must know that when I leave this House, and that must be soon now, neither I nor the Order I yet serve will have the power to protect you. I shall be a Prioress no longer, and I shall be beholden to my brother-in-law for his charity in giving me a house near Wetheral to live in."

"Then, Madame, take me with you, I beseech you, as your servant. My son, too. He is a good lad. Not like his father. We would serve you well." Isobel Winter was upon her knees. "I beg you, Lady" she pleaded. Dame Dinah considered. She would need help with Marguerite, that was plain. Also, with the daily work of running her household. At length, she spoke to Isobel, who still knelt before her.

"I will send to my brother-in-law to ask his permission," she said. "But first, today, your son must deliver messages to the families of Sisters Anne and Galfride.
They must leave this House immediately. Sister Marguerite and myself will be the last to leave, and if it will content you, and John Aspedaile is willing, William and yourself may come with us, as you wish."
Isobel reached for the Prioress's hand, and kissed it. "Oh, Madame, it will content me, indeed," she sobbed with relief.

"Then, there is much to do," Dame Dinah replied. "Tell William to be ready to ride by noon. But before he goes, I ask that he undo his father's wicked work. The Friar's head must be prepared for burial. Tell William to remove it from the spike, and bring it into the convent."

She took the still quietly weeping Isobel by the hand, and raised her to her feet. "Then, Isobel." she continued, "Go and fetch whatever you need for yourself and William to take with us to Wetheral. Then, come back here, and stay within the convent. I doubt that Robert will return, but whatever protection this House can yet provide, that I can still offer you."

Isobel sank back upon her knees, and knelt at Dame Dinah's feet. She sat back upon her heels, and raised a face prematurely aged by years of ill treatment at her husband's hands.

"Lady," she spoke with the fervour of one unused to being the recipient of human kindness. "Lady, I shall be your debtor for so long as I live. I thank you from the bottom of my heart. My son and I will serve you gladly - ask of us what you will."

Marguerite lay in her austere cell, and alternated between periods of tormented slumber and trance-like wakefulness.
Always, by day or night, she was tended by either Sister Anne or Sister Galfride.

It was they who had found her, crawling across the courtyard after the workmen's cart had rumbled away.

Her habit was grass-stained, and caked in mud, and when they removed it, they saw with alarm the marks beneath. Isobel Winter's account of what she witnessed, was confirmation of their fear that Marguerite's condition was no longer virgin.

The days that followed were the last days of the standing of the Priory of Heremitithwaite. William Winter proved himself a fast rider, and the Prioress's letters were swiftly delivered to the families of Sister Anne and Sister Galfride, and next day the two Ladies rode tearfully away from the convent they had entered as novices so many years before. With their departure, the House was strangely silent. At intervals, that silence was broken by the sound of rainwater dripping through the leaking roof and falling into puddles on the floor below.

Alone now, apart from the winters, Dame Dinah steeled herself for what she must do for Brother John - that last service for a fellow human before burial. Isobel she directed to sit at Marguerite's bedside, and give her what comfort she might. Then, she undertook the task she dreaded. She bathed the Friar's face, and washed away the congealed blood, darkened now, from the severed head. There had been no time for grief till now, the needs of the living taking prominence before all else!

Only now, alone with her awesome task, the intensity of suppressed anguish overwhelmed her, and she wept. Wept as she had never done since, as a young girl she had grieved for the loss of her brother James.

When at length, the storm of tears subsided, she was calm again, and laid a gentle hand on the Friar's white face, caressing it with a love that was more than that for a fellow religious.

Then she bent and kissed the cold forehead, and breathed, "Forgive me, for I have brought you to this." Tenderly, she folded a piece of linen around his head, bound it in place, then lifted it to lie upon the richly embroidered cope that Marguerite had worked so diligently upon. When she had made all secure, she lifted it, and cradled it in her arms. Never, since James had lived, had she felt this affinity to a kindred spirit, and even now, in the agony of such sorrow, she gained a shred of comfort from it.

Outside, the rain had ceased, and the sun began to shine. On the wet grass of the Nunclose, a thousand points of light flashed in its rays. Dame Dinah laid her burden in the place where she had chosen for William to dig. No priest, no cleric intoned the relevant prayers for committal, but Dame Dinah's prayers were fervent, and from her heart. At length, she turned away, and signalled to William to join her. She watched silently as the earth fell from his spade. It rapidly concealed the brightness of the richly coloured cope, and soon filled up the little grave.

William laid down his spade, and together they stood for a while, each deep in troubled thought. Then William spoke hesitantly, yet driven by his need to ask.

"Lady," his voice was rough with emotion, "think you that God will hold my father's sin against me when we come to judgement?" he asked. "The priest says the sins of the fathers...."

"William," the prioress interrupted. She laid a hand upon the young lad's shoulders. "We all err, and stand in need of forgiveness, but I cannot think that God will hold you responsible for your father's actions, wicked though they be."

She felt William's shoulders sag, as though a great weight had been lifted from them. She drew him close, and continued. "William, if you would purge away this terrible sin he has committed, then live a good and honest life in the future, take care of your mother, and be the good man your father is not."

Later, when dusk came, Dame Dinah retraced her steps to the Nunclose. She carried the latten crucifix that was deemed to be too worthless to be carried away for the King's purposes. When she returned to the Priory in the deepening dark, it was resting upon the new mound of earth that marked it for a sacred place.

All night, the night that would be her last in the Priory of Heremitithwaite, Dame Dinah prayed before the bare altar.

She prayed as she had never prayed before in all the life she had spent as a religious. Not by rote, but from her heart, she prayed ardently for the soul of Brother John, for its peace, and loving reception into the arms of a merciful God. For herself, she prayed in anguish, for forgiveness for her sin of pride, for was it not, she reasoned, that pride that most surely brought about the death of Friar John?

She prostrated herself on the damp floor, and as the hours passed, she felt its chill penetrating the folds of her habit. One outstretched hand lay in a pool of water that had collected on the floor. At dawn, she rose, stiff and cold, but resolute in her determination to serve with love the needs of whomsoever Almighty God should give into her care in the new life before her.

One thing more it was needful to do before her life in religion ended. On the wall of her cell hung a small picture.

It had been there when she was elected Prioress, and there, no doubt, in the time of her predecessors. It was certainly old, but nothing was known of its origin. It was painted upon a sheet of copper, and portrayed a veiled Benedictine nun, with a rosary and crucifix, and in her hands, she held a book. Dame Dinah removed it from the wall, and carried it to the aumbry.

Many years ago, the interior of the aumbry had been lined with oak panelling, but over time, the boards at its base had shrunk, causing a crack to develop in the old wood.

This, Dame Dinah prised upwards, until it was possible to slide the picture down a gap between the stones of the Priory wall, into which the aumbry was recessed. She heard it drop, how far she could not tell, but it had disappeared from sight. The loose wood she then replaced and closed the aumbry door, pleased with her small act of defiance at the closure of her House.

Spring

Lazonby and Penrith

The loss of the young pigs the previous autumn was a sore blow to the tanner's household, so too was the old sow. Moreover, the frightened hens were put off lay, and the cockerel, offended at the loss of his tail feathers, seemed scared of his own shadow. Andrew's fondness for the platter of fat bacon Mary cooked for him every morning was well known.

"Sets a man up for the day" was his happy announcement, as warm fat dripped down his chin and glistened upon his whiskers. Now, with the present flitch from a previous kill fast coming to an end, and with the prospect of nothing to follow, his temper was shortened somewhat, and the lads in particular paid due attention to their behaviour. Thus, one morning, Andrew eyed with some dejection the platter his wife placed before him, from which she had judiciously subtracted at least one collop of his usual amount of bacon, in the hope thereby of making the rapidly diminishing flitch last longer.

Mary, of course, was right, he reflected morosely. She always was in matters relating to the household, and other matters too, he had to admit. He sighed deeply, and thrust a whole, succulent collop into his mouth.

Andrew's teeth clamped down upon the bacon, but he had misjudged his aim, and before he could gulp it down, the collop protruded sideways at each corner of his mouth.

"Father, father, come quick. The old sow's back, "John yelled, and he was out of the houseplace as fast as he had rushed in. Outside, commotion reigned, with the lads' shouts and the sow's squeals, as they drove her safely back into her stye.
"Is she really ours?" young Dinah piped up doubtfully. "That pig's a lot fatter than our old one!"

Andrew hastily swallowed the remainder of his collop, and stared. "By St. Anthony" he choked, "she's in pig. The old girl's come home to farrow." So they laid down armfuls of bracken in the stye, and then left her in peace. Later in the day they could see she had pushed the bracken into a rough mound, and lay sleeping contentedly upon it. Andrew looked at her thoughtfully. Nigh on four months had gone by since Lazonby and the surrounding hamlets had been raided to feed the hungry Pilgrims mustering at Penrith.

On that night when he had stayed at John Aspedaile's at Wetheral, the old sow must have managed to get away in the confusion , and gained the comparative safety of Baronwood, there to survive on the autumn drop of acorns from the forest oaks. On her sides, Andrew noticed there were newly healed scars.

These were not the clean straight cuts of a knife, but jagged marks, surely wounds inflicted by the tusks of a rutting boar.

"A rough wooing the old girl's had," he confided to Mary, when the lads were out of earshot.

Darkness still came on early, while the spring was yet young, and the nights were long. When daylight returned, the sow had indeed farrowed, and six hybrid piglets with long snouts nuzzled closely to her. On their hairy bodies, Andrew could see faint, dark stripes running from neck to tail along their backs, confirming his guess that it was indeed a wild boar in Baronwood that had sired them.

Andrew yearned for bacon, a fair platter full such as he was used to eat before the Pilgrims made off with his half grown pigs. Now, in spite of Mary's judicious rationing, the remaining precious flitch had that morning given up its last collop. The young boar pigs the old sow had produced after her encounter with the wild boar in Baronwood were thriving, but it would be months yet before they were ready for slaughter. He leaned over the pigcote wall and viewed them morosely. That morning, he had been forced to make do with a dish of eggs Mary had placed before him.

He sighed, and even cast a speculative eye upon the old sow. She was in fine fettle now, after her return home. She was well fleshed, and no doubt oozing with fat within her barrel like body.

But no, tempted as he was, it would not do to sacrifice her. She could yet ensure his further supplies of bacon in the future. He forced himself to look away, and turned his attention to the cockerel. His tail feathers were now growing again, and he strutted importantly amongst his contented wives, now seemingly forgetful of the indignity inflicted upon him by the raiding party the year before.

The sound of a horse's hooves now claimed Andrew's attention. A farmer riding bareback came on towards him at a steady pace.

He stopped upon seeing Andrew, hailed him and slid down from his horse's back.

"I've come to see thee about a saddle," he said. "I hear John Aspedaile's well pleased with the one you made for him. What will it cost to make me one to ride to market on?" He fixed Andrew with his sharp gaze, and joined him to lean over the pigcote wall to discuss the merits of various grades of leather, and to both parties, a satisfactory agreement upon cost. Both men turned out to be skilled negotiators, but eventually, a mutually acceptable conclusion was arrived at, and a handclasp sealed the deal.

"Queer looking pigs, those. "Andrew's customer jabbed a finger in the direction of the young boar-pigs busily rooting in the churned up earth of their pen, and Andrew related his theory as to their paternity, at the same time lamenting the loss of his pure-bred piglets.

"Aye, we heard what happened hereabouts," the farmer said. "They missed my place. 'Tis hidden away on t' fell towards Wetheral. My pigs are fattening a good deal now. I'll be killing soon, before the weather gets any warmer." He jabbed a finger again at the rooting piglets, and looked speculatively at Andrew. "I wonder what those will taste like?" he asked.

A golden opportunity occurred to Andrew.
"Now, neighbour," he offered. "I'll give thee one of these to grow on, for a side of thy bacon." The farmer considered. Had he been rash in showing an interest ? More bargaining ensued.
"Half a flitch," he countered at length. "How can I ken what t'meat'll taste like? Might not care for it. Andrew conceded, reluctantly. Half a flitch was better than none, he reasoned. And besides, he himself didn't know what the boar-pigs would taste like, either.

***

Andrew was in need of more hides to tan, so he determined next market day to ride to Penrith and take John with him. He was proving a handy lad, and it would be good for him to learn how to conduct every aspect of his father's trade. Animals were slaughtered mainly at Martinmas in November. Very few were killed after Christmas. But there were always calf hides to be had, as young bull calves were sent for slaughter in the first few weeks of their lives, and their flayed skins Andrew expected to be able to get from the market looker at a fair price.

John was jubilant at the prospect of accompanying his father to Penrith, Mary less so.

"I hear there are dreadful things done in Penrith of late," she demurred. "Men hanged, and left to rot. A priest, too. Should the lad see.."

"That was weeks past," Andrew interrupted. "Those poor caitiffs will be cut down and buried by now." Mary's doubts, however, were not entirely dispelled.

"There was a pedlar came but two days past," she said. "He travelled from Torpenhow and Eaglesfield, and he told of terrible happenings there. And it was the womenfolk there who were brave enough to take those hanged bodies down..."

"Aye, aye, I know. I heard his tale too," Andrew cut in, before she could work herself up further. Did she know, though, he wondered, what those poor women had done? That against the orders of the King, they had gathered up what remained of their loved ones - husbands, sons, brothers - and tried to give them Christian burial? Did she know that the priests there, for fear that they would be held blameworthy, refused to bury those rotting remains in their churchyards?

Who, indeed, he thought, could not help admiring those new made widows who refused to accept denial, and buried their husbands in hallowed ground themselves, under cover of darkness?

Others they buried in ditches, or on the fellside, or wherever their strength could carry them, some with the chains they were hanged in still about them. Andrew cast a swift glance at the still doubtful Mary. What, he wondered, if the same had been done here, in Lazonby? Would she have done the same for him?

Andrew shook his head, as if to rid it of such thoughts. Questions as to the state of this new order a man's mind might dwell upon, and still question without ever finding an answer. But this fine morning, market day again, Andrew had neither the time nor the leisure to dwell upon the rights or wrongs of the present times. Whatever those rights or wrongs might be deemed to be by those great ones in power, a man must still feed his family, and for that purpose, a man must work.
And for Andrew's work, his need of skins was pressing. Therefore, he brushed aside his wife's continued misgivings, "Get in the cart, lad," he ordered his son. "Else we shall still be on the road when the market bell sounds in Penrith."

"Father, what was the cause of all the fighting?" John asked as the cart jolted along the road.
"I have heard it said there was a battle at Carlisle and a great number of the Pilgrims were killed."

"Aye son," Andrew replied, "'Tis so."

"And father, they say in the village that the King was very angry, and he sent the great Duke of Norfolk to Carlisle to hang those who were taken prisoner there."

"Aye, that is so too, I fear" Andrew replied heavily.

"Father, there is a woman in the village" John continued, "and her husband went away to fight with the Pilgrims, though she begged him not to go. But he would not listen to her, because he said it was not right to turn the monks and nuns out of their houses. And now he has not come back.

She is very poor, and cannot feed her five children, so now she must send them out to beg for food."

"That I know," Andrew replied. He gave a deep sigh. "There will be many like her, I fear."

He said little else to his son. How could he judge the rights or wrongs of the present troubles? Where should his allegiance lie? Both the King and the Church demanded his obedience - what was a simple man like himself to do? They bumped along the rutted road that led into the bustling streets in Penrith.

These were narrow and crowded with stalls bearing all manner of farm produce carried in from the surrounding districts, and there was scant room between them to drive. Andrew alighted from the cart, and threaded his way at his horse's head through the jostling crowd. The market bell sounded ten of the clock, and business began in earnest.

Andrew's intention was to get to the shambles, so as to have his choice of skins and embark on the lengthy negotiations it would be necessary to have with the market looker as to price.

He made but slow progress though, picking his way through the heaving throng, until his passage with the cart was completely blocked. A bull was being baited, and an excited crowd was gathered to watch the sport. It was an old animal, and tethered by a rope through its nose-ring to an iron ring set in a block of stone upon the ground.

Because of its age, the beast would need to be well baited before slaughter, so as to tenderise the meat. Already, several dogs were leaping at it as it twisted and turned on the rope. Andrew could see his advantage in the matter of the skins slipping away by his inability to negotiate his horse and cart through the unyielding mass of spectators in front of him.

"Get down here and hold the horse's head," he shouted to John above the din. "Stay here while I get through." His last instruction was quite unnecessary, as there was no way the cart could be moved, either backwards now, or forwards. John did as his father bid him with some reluctance.

Standing in the cart, it was possible for him to see over the heads of the crowd, and from that position he had a fine view of the proceedings.

Now, standing and holding the horse while his father elbowed a way forcibly through the increasing crowd of onlookers, meant that he could see little but the legs of the heaving throng before him.

The bull was bellowing, as the barking dogs infuriated it. They snapped at its heels, and sprang at it from behind, careful to avoid the horns on its lowered head.

One dog, a young one, more foolhardy and less experienced at baits, confronted the enraged animal. Though tiring, the bull was quick. It tossed the yelping dog into the air, then trampled it beneath its hooves. At last, it managed to crawl away from further mauling, whimpering piteously, to lie bloodied and panting upon the cobbles. The other dogs came on repeatedly, biting at the old beast with the savagery bred into them for that purpose, until, foam spattered and weakened, it ceased its futile efforts to evade its persecutors and stood still.

Then the high point of the spectacle was reached.

One of the travelling tinkers arrived with his mastiff. It was a powerful, ferocious creature, and the veteran of many such baits. The tinker slipped its leash, and a thrill of anticipation ran round the crowd. The dogs were called off by their owners and lay panting beyond reach of the tethered bull. Only their excited snarls, and the whining of the injured dog, broke a brief prelude of expectant silence. The mastiff and the tired bull eyed each other warily, each calculating the other's expected move.

The bull lowered its head against the threat of attack, ready to toss the oncoming mastiff, but with a speed and agility that belied its bulk, the dog veered to the side of the bull as the massive head jerked upward. In the same moment the dog leapt for its nose. The mastiff's powerful jaws clamped into the soft flesh of the bull's nose, where it clung tenaciously despite the efforts of the maddened bull to dislodge it. Then, the rest of the dogs were set upon it at its rear. There was uproar. The onlookers bawled their approval, the dogs' owners egged their animals on, the dogs themselves barked incessantly, and the bull bellowed in pain and rage. John struggled to control the horse as it fidgeted in alarm at the din. Suddenly, someone gave a warning shout. The crowd began to fall back, and a farmer jumped onto the cart to see what was happening.

"The bull's loose," he yelled. It was! In its frantic efforts to rid itself of the clinging mastiff on its nose, the strain on its tethering rope had caused the nose-ring to split the flesh at the base of its nostrils. Pandemonium broke out, and the crowd hastily scattered. The farmer leapt off the cart, and brought John's rearing horse under control.
"Get behind the cart, lad. I'll hold him for thee," he shouted. The bull saw a passage opening up before him, and with the mastiff still dangling from its nose, it careered at top speed down the narrow street, to the alarm of those stallholders in its way.

It was as well that John did as John Aspedaile instructed, so close did the bull charge by the cart where he took shelter that he could have touched it legs as it raced by.

His father meanwhile, having satisfactorily concluded his business with the market looker, was again endeavouring to push his way back through the throng in order to load up his cart with the skins he had just acquired. As the bull broke loose, and the crowd made for safety out of its way, he was within sight of his cart. His son was nowhere to be seen, but holding on with all his might to the rearing horse was none other than John Aspedaile from Wetheral. Andrew surged forward in alarm.

"Hast thou seen my lad?" he shouted. "I left him here."
Andrew's voice rose sharp with fear.
"Is that your lad?" John Aspedaile jerked a thumb towards the rear of the cart, behind which, to his father's relief, his son was just emerging.
"Father, t'bull would have knocked me down if I'd stayed where you tell't me," he began.
"That I can see, lad," Andrew agreed. He turned to John Aspedaile.

"I owe thee my thanks," he said. "But for thee...." he stopped, as an awful thought flashed through his mind. "What would I have tell't his mother...?

On the banks of the River Eden

Robert Winter sat on a slab of warm sandstone at the river's edge. It was April, and a rare mild day, though it would not have been surprising to witness a sudden blizzard sweeping down from the lowering bulk of Crossfell, this day was warm, and as welcoming as any might be in an often fleeting summer.

In Penrith, he had parted from Thomas and the leadstrippers, where before a warm fire in a tavern there that night, strong ale loosened the tongues of the King's workmen, and he learned that on the long journey across England, a ready market could be found for metals of all descriptions. Not all would reach its intended destination for the King's use.

Robert gleaned as much information as he was able before the heat of the fire and a surfeit of ale reduced the King's workmen to a state of snoring insensibility. Then he slipped away into the darkness to enjoy the sadistic pleasure of hauling up the severed legs of the Big Friar to hang over the gateway of his House. That accomplished to his satisfaction, there was little enough time for sleep before the grey light of dawn made it possible for him to ride safely over the rut-filled roads, churned up by the passage of the lead-laden cart, back to Heremitithwaite.

It was no surprise to find his cottage deserted and the few meagre belongings of his wife and son, and they themselves gone. Where? He did not care - let them beg in the streets of Penrith, if need be. The Priory too, he found abandoned, and in his cankered mind he savoured with intense pleasure the turning off from her House of the woman he had grown to loathe. He helped himself to the remaining provisions in the convent's kitchen, then he went to look for eggs in the hen-house. With no- one to shut the fowls in for the night, a fox had got there before him, as evidenced by the several sucked-out shells littering the floor.

Also, judging by the abundance of feathers drifting in the breeze, Tod had dined well since the departure of the nuns. He captured one of the terrified fowls that had later returned to the hen-house and wrung its neck. Then he made his way down to the river and lit a fire within a circle of stones. The convent fowl was a plump one, and Robert crouched down upon his haunches, and watched the juices run. When they dripped upon the hot stones, they hissed and sizzled, sending forth an aroma that tantalized his nostrils.

Impatiently, he ripped off a wing, blew upon it to cool it, then thrust it whole into his mouth. His attempts at plucking fell far below the finesse achieved by his wife in that skill, and the quills of the fowl's flight feathers, though burnt down by the fire, still remained within the flesh.

These he spat out, together with the bones of the wing, after gulping down the morsel of meat contained upon it. He dipped a flat stone in the river to serve as a platter.

It dried quickly in the warmth of the fire, and he laid the rest of the fowl upon it, with bread filched from the convent's larder. With succulent hunks of meat gouged from the hot carcass, Robert felt the same repleteness the fox must have felt after his nightly predations in the nunnery's henhouse.

He leaned back against a buttress of rock and closed his eyes. In the warmth of the sun, half-sleep overcame him, and gave rise to a drift of dreams, conjured from distant memories. Often he would come to this place in childhood, to escape the black rages of a brutal father, hiding in a low cave recessed into the rocky banks of the river. In summer, he would light a fire, snare a rabbit or catch a fish to sustain himself until he dare return home again. One winter he had fled here, leaving his mother to bear the brunt of his father's anger.

Under a rain of blows, he had forced from her the secret of his young son's refuge, and came in pursuit. In his terror, Robert had trusted himself to the frozen river, rather than face his maddened father. He reached the opposite bank safely, but the ice would not bear the weight of a man. The day that started so golden was no more.

Clouds hid the sun, the air cooled, and a shower of rain, though short-lived, was heavy. It extinguished the dying embers of the fire, and Robert woke with a start. Hastily, he sought the shelter of the cave, and crouched down at its mouth, for it was not possible for a grown man to stand upright, and waited for the shower to pass.

In those long gone days, when the river bank was a safer place to be than his home, Robert became familiar with every bend and twist of Eden.

He learned how to cross safely in places, leaping upon the great slabs of sandstone that jutted from the river like giant stepping stones when the water was low. He knew, too where the treacherous channels lay, where the shelving of rock fell away, and one wrong step could be fatal. He discovered, too, every small cave and crevice in the fissured rock of the steep river bank. No-one could know that stretch of the river as he did, and here somewhere, he was certain, was hidden the Priory's precious silver.

It was imperative that he find it before the Commissioners' agent returned, and with a horse now at his disposal, he would be away, away from Heremitithwaite forever. A new and better life beckoned, and he began his search in earnest. When daylight merged into dusk, his efforts had met with no success, so he returned to the cave and made a fire at its mouth. Then, as he had often done in childhood days, he lay down and slept.

He woke early and resumed his search. By noontide, he had not missed one crevice in the rock. Before him now stretched that solid wall of sandstone where, in places, it seemed to rise out of the water and overhang the fast flowing river. He pressed his body hard upon the sheer rise of the rock to steady himself and felt his way, bit by bit, along the narrow ledge that barely stood above the swirling water. At length, the bank widened into a bend, and he could walk easy again.

Sometimes, a child, he had come this way, but a man must have strong reason to attempt so hazardous a passage.

So, had the Big Friar come this way, carrying a burden, and at night? Even Robert, callous as he was, could not but feel some shred of admiration for such a man. If that were so, he reasoned, the Friar must have had fore-knowledge of this place. Here were several holes in the rockface where things might be concealed. In one, he found two long bones he had hidden in his youth. When the river froze hard, he had tied these to his feet and skated upon the solid verges of thick ice. Now, he flung them into the water, not wishing to be reminded of past pain.

Yet another opening; this one was packed with loose pebbles, surely not the work of nature. One by one, he cast them out until, at arm's length, the feel of cloth just touched the very tip of his probing fingers.

The aperture was just wide enough to thrust one shoulder inside, one side of his face he must press hard against the rock until it pierced his skin and blood began to flow down his cheek. He strained every muscle to gain a hold upon something that lay within. His fingernails clawed into the cloth, easing it forward until he could grasp it firmly, his hand dragging it towards him. His heart beat faster. Was this what he sought?

He drew it out, and opened up the bundle, and yes, in the sunlight the silver gleamed softly, and the stones set in the crucifix winked at him with shafts of coloured light. There were
candlesticks there, and a chalice, too. Robert allowed himself to speculate upon the future lifestyle this treasure might buy him.

But not for long! The day was well advanced, and he must make the return journey safely with this precious burden. And a burden it would surely be on those perilous ledges above the fast flowing river. With haste, he wrapped all securely again, and tied up the bundle. What was difficult before, now seemed well-nigh impossible. In places he feared to move even the smallest of steps. The weight of the silver he carried rendered him immobile for fear of losing his balance where the foothold was at its most precarious.

Many times he must lean against the rock behind him to rest, and it was only by a sideways shuffle of one foot behind the other that he made some progress. He felt the wetness of his own sweat, the sweat not only of exertion, but of fear. At length, the way opened up, the ledges upon which he trod grew wider, and he could move with greater safety.

The sun was dipping down in the sky when he reached the cave again, and he flung himself down at its mouth to rest. Then, before the daylight faded, he gathered up twigs and kindled a fire. He bit voraciously at the rest of the meat on the carcass of the fowl he had roasted the previous day, and then he lay down before the fire to sleep. So deep was his sleep, he was unaware a watcher lingered nearby.

From a tumble of boulders that lay on the river bank, some distance from the cave where Robert slept, the watcher had marked his return, and strained to glimpse the contents of the bundle he gloated over.
He watched until weariness overtook him, then Thomas, for it was he, moved closer, stealthy as a stalking cat, until he stood over the sleeping Robert. The bundle lay at his side, one arm stretched protectively over it. To pick it up would surely wake him, so with infinite care Thomas began to edge it, oh so slowly, from under Robert's out flung arm. There was a chink of metal as the silver within moved, and Thomas froze. But Robert's snores only grew louder, and at last he had it free.

He considered what he should do next. The darkness was dense, there being no moon this night. It would be too risky to try to negotiate the rest of the river bank now.

There was no help for it, though he needed to put distance between himself and Robert, he must wait for more light. With great care, he picked up the bundle so that the objects within should make no noise, and crept away as silently as he had come.

He gained the place where he had concealed himself to await Robert's return, and lay down upon a flat boulder to sleep. In the morning, even before dawn was fully broken, he must leave this place before Robert awoke to discover his loss. The night's cold, and more so , his fear, ensured that Thomas dozed but fitfully, so sickened he had become by the cold savagery of which he knew Robert Winter to be capable.

It was only the brightness of the risen sun that roused Robert to wakefulness. His sleep had been deep and long, so great was his fatigue. He yawned, and heaved himself up into a sitting position. Drowsily, he felt for the bundle.

It was not at his side where he had placed it before he slept. Alarm rendered him immediately alert. It was gone! He leapt to his feet, cursing volubly, to search the immediate vicinity, but to no avail. Realisation dawned swiftly. So, Robert fumed, he was back, that rogue of an agent who would cheat him of his hard-won prize.

He must have watched him setting out on that perilous journey at river level, seen his return, and what he carried. With mounting fury Robert paused only to buckle on the belt where hung his long bladed knife. Then with all the speed he could muster, he followed in the wake of his erstwhile accomplice.

***

Thomas meanwhile made much slower progress, burdened as he was with the precious load he carried. At length, the pathway widened, and in the fissured rock of the high bank, scrawny oaks and sycamore, over time had managed to find purchase. Their hungry roots snaked ever downwards, over and under the rockface, in their perpetual search for moisture, until at the water's edge they spread in the river itself. Last year's growth of bracken clothed the bank and formed a tangled mass of rotting vegetation, through which the young green fronds of the new growth were emerging. The way ahead appeared to be blocked, and for what distance, it was not possible to tell, for at this spot the river twisted again.

Thomas sat down on the trunk of a fallen tree, and studied the swirling water at his feet. There was a way, if he could cross over the river to the other side on the sandstone slabs that in places outcropped from the riverbed.
And such a place lay before him. The sun was now rising higher into the sky. Certainly Robert Winter would have discovered his loss by this time, and no doubt would be in hot pursuit.

It was not safe to linger.

With the bundle secured as best he could at his back, Thomas stepped out onto a shelf of stone that underlay the river. He picked his way slowly, with infinite care. In places, the slabs rose well above water level, like giant stepping stones, then they dipped below the surface, and he was wading knee-deep in the river. The swirling water was cold, and the current was tugging at his legs, but now he was approaching mid-river, and beyond lay a further line of slabs stretching out towards the opposite bank. He looked back, to see how far he had come.

A man stood at the water's edge. He paused to unsheathe a knife at his side, then stepped confidently into the water. Robert, knowing from his youth the shelving of the river, came on apace, swiftly and safely, determined as a hunter bent upon his prey. Thomas stood transfixed for the merest fraction of time, though to him it seemed an eternity. Robert laughed. It was a triumphant, mirthless sound that carried over the water to where Thomas stood midstream. He saw Robert raise his arm. He held a knife, and the long blade flashed in the sunlight. Move he must. Robert was surging through the water, surefooted as he, Thomas, was not. He turned - a stretch of water lay before him, wider than it had seemed from the bank.
Across it, another pathway of jutting slabs led to the far bank. But between ran a deep channel through which the river poured.

He was trapped, there was only one way for him to go. Fear lent him speed. He untied the bundle, and slipped it from his shoulders, and with all his might, he cast it across the turbulent water. He heard the chink of metal as it landed safely on the further slab, then he leapt after it. So close was Robert behind him that the knife he threw penetrated deep into Thomas's back as he leapt above the water, and he dropped like a stone into its depths. Once, he rose to the surface, reddening the water, and in despair he held out a hand to the grinning Robert. Then the current caught him, had him in its power, and swept his weakening body away.

Not one whit of remorse did Robert feel. Neither man had trusted the other, and had their roles been reversed, Robert would have expected no better treatment for himself. Without a qualm, he turned his full attention to the repossession of his prize. He too must clear the same deep channel in the river, as he had sometimes done in his youth. It was for a wager then, for a paltry recompense in comparison to what lay on the wide shelf of rock across this deep running water. He knew its danger, but to retrieve the treasure, it must be done. He braced himself, and sprang over the torrent. He barely cleared it, so close to the edge he was, but the precious bundle lay within his reach. He made a grab for it, and clawed it towards him. Then his feet slipped on the wet surface of the rock, and he began to slide backwards over the edge. It took all his strength to heave himself up, so that he clung by his forearms over the side of the great boulder.

But not for long. Try as he might to scramble up the slippery rockface, exhaustion finally caused him to lose his grip, and he plunged into the swirling depth beneath.

The bundle that he would not release weighted him down and took him down to the rock-strewn bed of the river. There, by the force of his descent, his foot lodged in a cleft worn by the constant passage of water over a ridge of sandstone. He was trapped. In panic, he dropped the bundle and felt for the knife at his belt. If only he could cut the leather of his boot and free his foot! The knife was not there! Eden held him, and would not let him go.

Spring - London
The Tower & the road to York

Old Lord Tom Darcy of Templehurst, in the County of Yorkshire, lay in the Tower of London awaiting trial. His Lordship was some seventy years of age, and frail now. Despite the milder weather of this southern spring, little of the warmth of its sunshine penetrated the stone walls of his prison cell. So, when a few bright rays of its light illuminated a small patch of the floor, he moved his seat to it and sat within the little warmth it afforded. And being old, he began to doze, and thus, to dream.

The present receded and past events returned in his mind as clearly as if they had happened but yesterday. Ah, those burning days under the Spanish sun - he had been as hot then as he was cold now. It was then that he had felt impelled, like the Crusaders of old, to strike a blow for Christendom, and fight against the invading Infidel there. But that was not to be. The old Lord sighed in his half sleep.

No sooner had he and his little band of northern men arrived in Spain, and awaited King Ferdinand's orders, than news came that the King had made peace with the Infidel, and there was nothing for it but to return home again without a blow having been struck.

And it was then, at that time in Spain that His Lordship's men had worn his badge upon their breasts, that of the Five Wounds of Christ - the same that the present Pilgrims took at their rising.

It was upon this very matter that he was so closely questioned at his examination. Thick and fast those questions came as to how the origin of those same badges touched upon the late insurrection in the north.

"Were those badges new made, or were they the same as you gave in Spain, or what remained of them?"

"Could you not have disposed of the said badges before the insurrection?"

"Did you keep them for that purpose?"

"If they were new, who made them, and where, and how long before the insurrection?"

"For what intent made you those new badges? Was it not for setting forth the insurrection of Yorkshire, encouraging the soldiers to believe their rebellion was for the defence of the Faith?"

Lord Darcy allowed himself a grim smile, then. Yes, it could not be denied that whatever he had done, had indeed been because of his unshakable adherence to the true Faith and Holy Church. But, he countered, had not the Pilgrims ripped off those self-same badges and returned to their homes when the Duke of Norfolk assured them of a pardon after Mr. Aske returned from London? There, the Great Captain had met and spoken with His Grace himself, and assured the

King of the loyalty of his northern subjects.

So many questions! The old Lord's head had begun to whirl at the consummate skill by which his interrogators sought to entrap him. The sun-light moved over the cell floor, and the warm patch where he sat was gone. Then he stirred to wakefulness as his old body became aware of the withdrawal of that little warmth. He gave an involuntary shiver, though from the cell's gloom, not from fear.

"Ah, they mean to have my head, if they can," he sighed. Then, he gave another smile, and proclaimed to his solitary cell. "Well, I would not have grudged to die for the Faith then, in Spain. Nor will I grudge now." Of course, at his trial he was found guilty of treason and condemned to die in the manner accorded the nobility, by the axe.

It was mid-May when Robert Aske was pronounced guilty of treason in Westminster Hall, and then returned to the Tower to await his own execution. Now it was late June.

"Perhaps today, or tomorrow, or very soon," he reflected, "they will come for me, and take me home to Yorkshire to hang." That very morning, his gaoler told him that a scaffold was being erected for Lord Darcy's beheading. Well, if the headsman did his work well, the old Lord would feel no pain. That proud old man would make a good end, and would soon be at peace, Robert reflected.

"But what of me, a commoner?" He shivered slightly. He would not fear to hang. So many had already done so, and he himself had unwittingly been instrumental in bringing them to that end.

But the manner of it? What if they cut him down before he was dead, and opened up his living body to rip out his heart and bowels? It was a prospect he contemplated with dread, for how would he conduct himself then? He groaned and laid his head on the stones of the window embrasure.

Outside the Tower, London basked in the pleasant sunshine. A butterfly landed and spread its wings where the sun's rays warmed the outer stones of the window. Robert studied it intently, for it occurred to him that he might never see a butterfly again. Close to the stone it clung, displaying the beauty of its colours, the like of which he had taken but scant notice when life had seemed to stretch out before him.

He watched it with a heightened sense of wonder, as if seeing its beauty for the first time.

Its velvety body was of the richest brown, the deep colour radiating across each wing in perfect symmetry. Then came a jagged arc of vermilion, reminding him of the bright marigolds that grew at home at Aughton. The tip of each wing was dark, so dark it might have been black, and this was splashed with irregular spots of white. He tried to count the tiny spots of brown upon the line of vermilion at the base of each wing. Were there four, or was it five?

The butterfly folded its wings together, so he was unsure of the number. For all the world it seemed now but a shrivelled autumn leaf. Then it fluttered away into the perfect blue of the cloudless sky, free, as he was not. Yet, we will both die soon, he thought.

***

His Grace, Duke of Norfolk must ride again to witness the King's justice done to yet another traitor. This time, he rode to York, to oversee the hanging of Robert Aske, the one-time Great Captain of the Pilgrims. It was early July when the party set out, and the weather was fair, much to the Duke's relief. His Lordship was no longer young, being well past his sixtieth year, and after the many journeys he had been constrained to make in winter weather to see the King's justice done, his body ached for the softer south. He rejoiced to quit this wild northern country where the bitter cold ate at the very bones of a man. His "little, poor carcass," as he referred to himself in a recent letter to the King, was afflicted in no small measure by frequent stomach gripes often resulting in an inconvenient flux of the bowels.

There was much to contemplate as he rode onward to York. In May, it had come belatedly to his knowledge that the bodies of some of those rebels commanded to be left to hang within sight of their neighbours, had been taken down. If reports were to be believed, the deed had been done by their own womenfolk. Depositions of the examinations of those same women, and pitiful they were, were taken at Cockermouth, Carlisle and Penrith. Nevertheless, the King was not satisfied. Such deeds, he asserted "could not have come only of women's heads," and he laid it upon the Duke to find out and punish the principal doers.

His Lordship, kept in ignorance of such doings, felt himself justifiably vexed . Neither he, nor the King had been well served!

His feelings of aggravation mounted as the miles towards York lessened. The Earl of Cumberland, the Duke ruminated morosely - it was under his rule that the offences had been committed - let him stir himself, therefore, to root out the culprits. A cloud passed over the sun, threatening the earlier promise of a fair day.

"Damn this northern weather," the Duke swore to himself. "Like the people, not to be trusted." Yet he felt compelled to concede, though with exasperation, that there were those amongst them, and not least those women, deserving of respect for their rugged fortitude and loyalty, if not to the King, but to each other. And he, the King's representative in these matters, must prosecute them for that.

Those women! His mind dwelt intermittently upon them; especially the one who, upon examination, told of the gathering up of her husband's remains from where they had lain for nine days after his cutting down. She lay what was left of him upon a sheet. Another three days passed. Was her strength not equal to
moving that ghastly yet precious burden? So it seemed, for it took four other women to help her to drag it away, and then to bury it in a ditch.

Little wonder, thought the Duke, that the King, used as he was to the flattery and self-seeking intrigues of those perfumed ladies at his Court, could not believe what, by their own determination and banding together in adversity, that sisterhood of sorrow had done.

On to York his party rode, where, travelling on the road from London, his and the party guarding the prisoner Aske, would converge.

May - Wetheral

There was an ancient pear tree in the orchard belonging to the farmhouse at Wetheral, so old that the hands that had planted its sapling form had long since become dust. When Norman kings ruled the land, it was said that the lordship of Wetheral was given to a Norman baron for his good service to the crown, He then gave the manor to the Benedictine Abbey of St. Mary at York, and a prior and twelve monks came from there to build a monastery overlooking the River Eden.

How old his pear tree was, John Aspedaile did not know, but when he was a stripling, his grandsire recalled that in his own youth, he remembered it was said that a monk from the Abbey, who was skilled in the culture of the fruit trees that flourished there at that time, had planted the sapling pear in recompense for some service rendered by a long-forgotten Aspedaile. Now it was early May, and the old tree was a glory to see, so covered in blossom of virginal white it was, that the fresh green of its new leaves were all but hidden by the profusion of bloom.

John stood within the doorway of the handsome new house he had built to replace his old farmstead. It was a joy to breathe in the sweet freshness of this May morning. Ah, the old pear tree was a fine sight indeed. A good harvest there should be, if the late frosts kept off. How true, he thought, was the old saying, that he who plants pears, plants for his heirs. A twinge of regret clouded John's enjoyment of the morning, for he had no heirs.

The tiny daughter borne to him by his first wife died whilst yet a babe, and since the miscarrying of their son, no further children seemed likely to bless his second marriage.

There was a movement at the foot of the tree. It was the little nun, though nun she had not been, and never would be now. He walked towards the place where she sat upon the trunk of a fallen tree. She had a basket upon her lap, half filled with the eggs she had been collecting in the barnyard. John had seen little of her since her arrival with Dame Dinah earlier in the year, a distraught half-crazed child she had seemed to him then. Today, she appeared to have a bloom about her, the sun dappling the fuller contours of her face. She rose at his approach, laid down her basket, and dropped a curtsey in his direction.

"Good day to you, Mistress. I hope I find you well, now." John spoke formally, not certain as to how to address her, and was surprised to see, as she raised her head, that a deepening flush coloured her face and neck.

"I thank you, Sir," she murmured, "for your great kindness to me." Not knowing the cause of her embarrassment, and not wishing to prolong it, he nodded his head in acknowledgement, then smiled, and walked on.

In the farmhouse, Dame Dinah and Isobel Winter conferred anxiously. "Her courses have not appeared since we came to Wetheral," Dame Dinah announced. "And this morning, I heard her retching in her chamber, as soon as she rose. Tell me, Isobel, is not that a sure sign that she is with child?"

"Lady, as to the first sign, it sometimes happens that a great shock can delay the natural progress of a woman's courses, but coupled with the second sign, yes - I fear 'tis likely so."

In the weeks since their arrival at Wetheral, the gulf that existed between the two women on account of their differing status in life, began to diminish. For her part, Dame Dinah never ceased to be thankful for the devotion and practical help of Robert Winter's wife. Together, they took turns in watching by Marguerite's bedside at night. They listened to the tortured ramblings of her mind, and soothed her to sleep. By day, they persuaded her out of her lethargy, and encouraged her to take an interest in her new surroundings, and by degrees, they were successful. Marguerite complied dutifully with all she was asked to do, as her training had taught her, but something about her, so difficult to define, was changed. Some joyous spark was gone, only an empty shell of her former self remained.

Dame Dinah sighed deeply. "She is but a child herself," she said.

"She came to us so young, and I doubt she is aware of her likely condition." Isobel Winter repressed a smile. Indeed who, she thought, in that closed community of virgins, would have considered it necessary to enlighten a future nun of those matters that women in the outside world learned early?

"Lady" she said, "we cannot yet be sure. If it be so, then soon she will start to show."

***

The pear blossom was fallen, and the young fruits were swelling in their wake. As the days lengthened, spring progressed into summer, and there was no doubt. Marguerite's slender body thickened, and it too swelled with its own promise of fruitfulness.

"The child will be here come Martinmas," Isobel reckoned.
"A winter babe," Dame Dinah spoke softly. "A child for Christmas. Tonight I must speak with my brother-in-law and Mistress Aspedaile, for they will surely have guessed by now, how matters stand."

When she judged the day's work would be done, and John and his wife taking their ease, Dame Dinah made her way through the orchard, and along the path leading to the new house. Here grew Mistress Aspedaile's pot-herbs she used to flavour her cooking, and their faint scent hung on the evening air. She found John and his wife seated upon their three-legged coppy stools at their doorway, enjoying the last rays of the setting sun.

"Come in sister, we have been expecting you." In his forthright manner, John came to the point without delay. "It is the plight of Mistress Standley, is it not?" he asked.

"It is brother. It is as we feared. Her child should be born come November."

Far into the evening and early nightfall they talked, Mistress Aspedaile rising only to light a rush taper as the shadows deepened. She adjusted its height in its iron stand, then seated herself again at her husband's side. John took her hand within his own, for he knew she still grieved for the little one she had lost, though that was now some years gone by.

"Sister" he addressed Dame Dinah, as they agreed their relationship of brother and sister should be. "Sarah agrees with me that this babe must be welcomed and cared for by us. I can see that Mistress Standley, Marguerite, is as dear to you as a daughter, and she has been greatly wronged."
"You are right, brother. I care for her, and I grieve for her, for she suffers so in her mind."
"But the child," John continued, "is an innocent, to be born into this naughty world. So be assured, sister, I will help you, and so will Sarah, in whatever ways we can."
"John Aspedaile, you are a good man, and I thank you.
And you too, Sarah."

Sarah Aspedaile nodded in agreement, and smiled at Dame Dinah. She was somewhat in awe of her predecessor's sister, and in the main, seldom entered into conversation between her husband and his first wife's sister. However, so taken up was John with this most pressing matter, she perceived that he appeared to have forgotten to relate what news he had learned of happenings in the south.

"John was in Penrith yesterday" she said. He tells me there was a pedlar there who told that Queen Jane is with child," she volunteered the information.

"And not only that," John broke in. "He brought grim news too. He had it from another pedlar who passed through York." He hesitated. But there was no way to minimise the horror of what he must tell.

"Robert Aske, that Great Captain of the Pilgrims - he hangs there in chains from the walls of the city's keep. He lives still, and will do for days yet, until death comes."
The two women crossed themselves. "May God have mercy upon him, and deliver him soon from his pains" Dame Dinah prayed.

Autumn
Hampton Court & Windsor

After old Lord Darcy's head was struck off on the last day of June, and the heat of high summer intensified, the horrors of returning plague stalked in the city of London. The Queen was fearful for her unborn child, and a strict vetting procedure was instituted for the restricted numbers allowed to attend Court.

It was in mid September, a month before the expected birth, that the Queen ceremonially took to her chamber at Hampton Court Palace. She took her leave of all her male officers and courtiers, in the manner laid down by the King's redoubtable grandmother, the Lady Margaret Beaufort. Thereafter, once inside that chamber, where she would, God grant, be safely delivered, only women would attend her. No man, not even the King, might enter there.

"God send you a good hour, Madam," they wished her. She entered the darkened room. It felt stifling. The walls were hung with tapestries, and on the floor lay thick carpets. only one uncurtained window admitted the daylight. Oh, she thought, to be able to sit in her well-loved gardens now at the Palace, in the mellow sunlight. A cooling breeze would be blowing in from the river.

"It will be springtime again before I can take my pleasure there" she murmured.

The days shortened as the autumn progressed, and with them, the gloom within the chamber became more pronounced. October came, and the sense of anticipation amongst those her served her became palpable. The midwives prodded and examined her swollen belly, and conferred amongst themselves. All, it seemed, was well.

There was an alter within the chamber, and daily Jane prayed fervently for strength for her coming ordeal, for safe deliverance, and above all that the child within her would prove to be the longed-for prince. For what if it was not? In the night hours this was a question that troubled her sleep. If this child too should be another princess, what would the King do then? Already two of his wives had failed in this queenly duty.

One, the good Queen Katherine, whom he herself served, he had put away, and Anne? In tortured dreams Jane imagined that horrific scene at the Tower of London, the swift blow of the French executioner's sword, and the Queen of England's head rolling upon the ground. She groaned, and so vivid were the dreams that she would wake with a cry.

"Madam, was it a pain?" asked the attendants who slept close by.

When her pains did begin, they were slow, and her labour was long and painful. For three days and nights she strove to bring the child to birth.

Then it became clear that her body was weakening under the strain and fears grew for the lives of both mother and child. But with the last of her strength, before dawn broke on the twelfth of October, a living babe was born.

"A prince, a prince" the midwife cried. "Madam, you have a fine son." Swiftly, a message was carried to the King. His joy knew no bounds and he wept when his longed-for son was placed in his arms.

In the city, there was great rejoicing. Bonfires were lit, and wine flowed freely from the conduits. When the baby prince was three days old, he was baptised with great ceremony at midnight in the Chapel Royal at Hampton Court. He was given the name of Edward, having been born on that saint's day.

Jane waited in her own apartments to greet her son after his baptismal ceremony. She lay upon a richly dressed bed, the King sitting at her side. Her ladies had swathed her in a robe of crimson velvet, and raised her up in the bed on cushions. This was the hour of her greatest triumph. The son she had borne to the King was her pride, and her salvation too. She gave him her blessing, so too did the King, with tears of joy in his eyes. In the early morning hours, after the prince was returned to his nursery, though weary and week, she received the congratulations of those favoured guests who had witnessed his christening.

Then, in a few short days Jane sickened and became fevered. She died, her infant son not two weeks old. The King was distraught, and immediately left Hampton Court to return to Whitehall. There he shut himself away to grieve for the cruel loss of the woman who at the cost of her own life, had given him his heart's desire. In those dark days, it was not the platitudes of his own nobility and advisors he could bear to hear. But one man, Will Somers, his so called fool, witnessed the King's distress and found the right words with which to solace his master.

Outside the door of the Presence Chamber, the Duke of Norfolk waited, hoping for admittance. Another marriage would be necessary, though not yet - it would not be politic to raise the subject too soon. The King's temper was volatile, even when he was in good humour. But the succession could not be left to hang on the left to hang on the life of a two-week old babe. He was vexed to see Thomas Cromwell appear, obviously with the same intentions as himself.

"Well, Cromwell," he snapped, "what brings a fellow like yourself here?"

Cromwell smiled, that irritating, sardonic smile that masked thoughts he had no intention of divulging. Before he could reply, the door opened to let out Lord Hertford and his brother Tom Seymour. The Duke rose to his feet in anticipation of admittance to the King's presence.

"His Majesty will see no-one," Hertford informed him.

Then added derisively, "only his fool."

***

In the Queen's presence chamber at Hampton Court, those ladies who had served her if life performed their last duties in sorrow. They laid her out, then with great care, they dressed her body in a robe of gold tissue, and placed a crown upon her head. Around the bier, lighted tapers burned, there was a sad sound of dirges being sung, and masses were said for her soul. Upon their knees, the Lady Mary and her ladies kept vigil by day, and priests by night. All the ordering of the pomp and ceremonies relative to the death of a queen was laid upon the Duke of Norfolk. Then, at the end of the first week of November, the time came for the Lady Mary, as chief mourner, to ride out accompanying the Queen's funeral cortege on the road to Windsor.

There, on the twelfth of November, exactly a month after the birth of her son, Queen Jane was buried with great ceremony in St. George's Chapel. Grief at her untimely death was general and genuine. But to the Lady Mary, she was that rare thing for royalty, a friend. It was she who had brought about her reconciliation with the King, and the ending of her years of banishment from Court.

December - Wetheral

For all that they called it St. Martin's little summer, when the mildness of late autumn often seemed reluctant to depart, the days of early November began to grow colder, and signalled the onset of an early winter. The wind whistled across the fells, scattering the last of the yellowing leaves that still clung to the branches of the orchard trees at Wetheral. As they fell, they whirled in little eddies in each sharp blast of rising wind; soon the dark branches stood gaunt against leaden skies, only in the old pear tree a few ragged leaves still clung tenaciously, flapping in a shrivelled travesty of their summer exuberance.

Martinmas came, and went. Below her bodice, the folds of Marguerite's homespun gown were thrust outwards, so that it hung uplifted at her feet. Her breath was short, and she tired easily. The former grace of her movements was replaced by the clumsiness of advanced pregnancy. It was not until December came, and a sharp night frost rimed the ground to a sparkling whiteness, that Marguerite woke in the early hours to a dull ache in her back. Then, it receded, only to return at intervals, each time growing in intensity. She placed her hands at her back, and the pressure eased the ache. Dame Dinah poked her head around the door of her chamber and saw her thus, and immediately went in search of Isobel Winter.

"Yes, she has started," Isobel confirmed. "we must make all ready." William she dispatched with all speed to the Aspedailes, and soon both John and Sarah were at their door. John carried a wooden cradle, hooded, and fixed upon rockers.

He laid it down before the fire, and gently set it in motion. "Your little niece lay in this," he smiled up at Dame Dinah, as he continued to rock the cradle, its movement evoking memories both sweet and sad.

"And so would Sarah's babe have slept here, too" he said. Sarah turned aside. The sight of the rocking cradle pained her. Quickly, she opened the bundle she had brought with her, and laid it upon Dame Dinah's lap. Everything for a new-born was there, each tiny garment stitched in hopeful expectation of a new life to come.

"I made them for my own child." She spoke in so low a tone that Dame Dinah barely caught her words. "But they were never needed." Sarah's hands lingered momentarily, caressing the small clothes as if in a farewell blessing. Dame Dinah caught the hands in her own.

"I thank you," she spoke softly and earnestly to Sarah, "for this most precious gift. And you, John, for yours."

Isobel entered. She had left Marguerite's bedside only to change the flat stones that had cooled down in her bed. These she wished to exchange for the ones already heated in a cauldron set in the turf fire. Three pairs of anxious eyes searched her face.

"Is all well", Dame Dinah asked.

"It is, but slow. Her pains come on but slowly. She is sleeping now." Isobel laid down the cold stones she had taken from Marguerite's bed, and drew the great pot to the side of the fire.

From it, with the aid of tongs, she deftly extracted the two hot stones it contained, and wrapped each one in a thick cloth, one to lay at Marguerite's back, the other at her feet.

Dawn came, and daybreak, and as the day wore on, Dame Dinah and Isobel, and Sarah too, took turns to watch over Marguerite. Despite the cold, as night closed in, beads of sweat stood out upon her brow, and as the pains of labour sharpened, Dame Dinah prayed silently and fervently to the Virgin Mary to assist her child, and with great tenderness, she wiped the sweat from Marguerite's face. Never, she vowed, would she ever cease to be thankful for Isobel Winter's presence this night. It was approaching midnight when Isobel said, "I can see the head. It cannot be long, now." Marguerite had not cried out until that moment, but then, as she strained with all her might, she screamed, because she must, as the sharpest pain of all assailed her. Moments later, she brought to birth her tiny daughter.

The owl, perched in the old pear tree, was listening. He listened for even the slightest sound that might alert him to the presence of a foraging mouse below. He fluffed his feathers against the cold, and his great eyes widened in puzzlement as his keen hearing picked up sounds he did not recognise. Not the scream of the vixen advertising her willingness to mate did he hear, nor the piteous cry of a rabbit as the snare bit deep into its flesh. These cries, unknown to his species, were the anguish of birth pangs, and the thin, first wail of human kind.

***

Dame Dinah loved Marguerite's child from the moment, shortly after her birth, that Isobel laid her in her arms. The same rush of maternal feeling was not, it seemed, evident in Marguerite. Whilst Isobel performed all the necessary care for the new mother, and Dame Dinah laid the infant in the crook of her mother's arm, Marguerite stared uncomprehendingly at her daughter. It seemed to be no part of her, but a puppet, a doll child. A look of consternation passed between the two women tending her.

"Let her sleep now. Let us all sleep, the babe too, we are all weary," Isobel said. So they wrapped the babe close in its receiving cloth that lay warming by the fire, and laid her gently in the wooden cradle.

"Her wits have flown," Sarah Aspedaile pronounced, at length. And this was the opinion the three women caring for Marguerite were forced to admit. Even the insistent howling of the babe for nourishment did not move her, and only by dint of persuasion and encouragement did she suckle the hungry infant. As the days wore on, however, ever obedient, she did as she was bidden, though it was evident that the former Marguerite was gone, and only an empty shell remained.

It was mid December, and a whirling blizzard blew across the fells as the grey light of the short day deepened to darkness.

"We shall have drifts by morning," John Aspedaile spoke from the overhang of the doorway. He shook himself to dislodge the film of snow already settled upon his clothing, and stamped his feet to rid them of the melting clods that clung to his boots. From the byre, the milking done, he and William brought the fallen log that had lain drying out at the foot of the pear tree for more than a twelvemonth. This, their Yule log, would burn well and give out a good heat at Christmastime. He handed the pail of new milk he held to Isobel, who carried it down the corridor to the dairy at the end of the house. Tomorrow, she intended to set Marguerite the task of buttermaking in the up and down churn.

Tonight, Marguerite seemed content to sit on the wooden settle by the fireside. At her feet, the babe lay sleeping in her cradle, and Marguerite, her foot upon the rocker, gently swayed it from side to side. John surveyed the domestic scene with some satisfaction. All seemed snug and secure, and maybe now a degree of normality was returning to the household. He smiled at the now calm Marguerite, and bid all goodnight. Then, out into the fast falling snow, he hurried home to Sarah. In the farmhouse, Dame Dinah, Isobel and William slept deeply that night.

All were wearied by the extra work of preparing for the Christmas feast. When the little one woke and began to cry, Marguerite gathered her child in her arms and nursed her, then she laid her back in her cradle, warmly wrapped against the cold.

In the first show of tenderness, she stroked the downy head, and watched until the babe slept again Then she went to the door of the houseplace and unlatched the heavy door. Outside, the snow no longer fell, and a full moon shone down upon a white world. It was as bright as day. Clad only in her shift, Marguerite looked out. The snow was piled high against the door and she broke the drift as she stepped outside through the wall of whiteness. She could see the pear tree glistening in the moonlight, and in her disordered mind, it seemed that spring was come and the white blossom frothing in profusion along its branches again.

She tried to run towards it, but the deep snow reached up to her knees. At first the bite of cold upon her bare feet was an excruciating pain, then a numbness crept up her limbs, so that she could not tell whether she moved or not. She reached the pear tree at last and fell into the drifted snow beneath it. The cold enveloped her, and soon, all feeling was gone. There was no pain as her body slowly froze, only an overwhelming desire to sleep. Deeper and ever deeper, sleep transported her to another place, to a haven of unparalleled light, of warmth, and peace.

All sorrow spent, all the care of the sad world flown, it seemed a voice called somewhere from a world away, "Come."

In Marguerite's mind, at the last, lucidity returned. "Ah, though I was robbed of the gift I would have offered, perhaps in His mercy, He will accept that loss as the only sacrifice I can give now."

Near dawn, it snowed again, a fine powdering snow. It laid a crystalline coverlet over the body of Marguerite. Thus, they found her in the early morning, a vision of purity personified.

John Aspedaile reached down into the white drift, and gathered up the icy body of Marguerite in his arms. Her face was pale as the purest marble, of which the images of the blessed saints were carved, and the bright rays of the morning sun created the illusion of a nimbus about her head. John carried her inside and laid her down upon the board of the long table that stood in the houseplace. Her child, in Dame Dinah's arms, wailed for nourishment. At the fire, Isobel warmed milk, into which she dipped the end of a cloth, to hold in the babe's mouth to induce her to suck.

There were no more preparations for Christmas. Instead, Dame Dinah took charge of all that must be done. John saddled up his horse and rode through the virgin snow to the priest's house at Wetheral to arrange burial. Sarah came, and seeing the plight of Isobel in her efforts to feed the babe, now motherless, spoke urgently to Dame Dinah.

"I know of a poor woman in Wetheral, delivered of her child last month. It lived but a two, three weeks. If you are willing, would it not be best to see if she will come and be wet nurse to this little one?"

"Think you that she would come?" Dame Dinah paused in her work of washing Marguerite's snow-encrusted body, and looked hopefully at Sarah.

"It would be a charity, I think," Sarah replied. "She is a broken woman, I fear, and with good reason. Her husband was pressed to join the Pilgrims when they marched on Carlisle. He never returned. She lives alone now, in a poor sort of dwelling. If it were not for the succour of her neighbours, she would be destitute."

Sarah looked hesitantly to where Marguerite's body lay. "Let me take the child and Isobel to stay with me" she offered. "There is room for all of us, and the Wetheral woman too, if she will come. It would be better until...." Her meaning was clear, though she shrank from uttering the words.

"Yes, you are right, Sarah. Until we must take my Marguerite to be laid in the cold ground." Dame Dinah's voice was low, suppressed in her effort to contain the grief that threatened to overwhelm her.

"I shall be glad to be alone with her until that time. Look at her, Sarah. Is she not beautiful, even now?"

It was so. Even in death, Marguerite's beauty was not diminished.

Before the light faded on that dreadful day, Sarah brought two precious candles of fine wax, bought at great expense, to set upon the board where Marguerite lay. That night, Dame Dinah lit them and placed them, one at Marguerite's head, and one at her feet. Then, upon her knees, she kept vigil, in deep sorrow and heartfelt prayer.

1538

New Year Hampton Court Palace

Such was the King's anxiety for the health of his precious heir that every day the paths and corridors leading to the Prince's nursery apartments were diligently swept and washed. No pages were allowed in the vicinity, as the habits of young boys were thought to be questionable, and dogs and beggars were strictly kept out of all the courtyards and approaches to his household.

It was unfortunate therefore, that one late afternoon in the New Year, the King rode into Hampton Court and hastened in the diminishing daylight to see his son. It was even more unfortunate that just as the courtyard had been cleansed, for the third time that day, a young pup belonging to one of the courtier's pages slipped its leash where it was tethered, and wandered into the forbidden area.

Unnoticed, in the gathering greyness of early evening, it fouled the pathway upon which the King and his gentlemen trod. It was not until they reached the watching chamber that guarded the approach to the Prince's nursery, that the soiling of the toe of His Majesty's riding boot was noticed.

The royal temper flared, and the noise of the uproar that ensued came to the ears of the Lady Mistress of the Prince's household, and to the alarm of the rockers at his cradle.

The precautions the King took to protect the life of this longed-for child were phenomenal. The Prince's whole household, and any person remotely connected to it, was subject to the strictest rules of hygiene, both culinary and personal. The Tudor line was tenuous, as Henry well knew. His own consumptive father coughing up blood from his disease-ridden lungs, Arthur, his elder brother who should have been king, his own bastard son, Henry Fitzroy, these last two were both dead before reaching the age of twenty. Those male infants, too, born to him by Katherine and Anne, the phantoms of all these drove his near mania to guard this most precious heir.

He needed to marry again, it was true. Jane, his gentle queen who had given him this precious gift of a son, was barely in her grave at Windsor before the pragmatic Cromwell was searching the European courts for her successor, and as soon as he dare, was encouraging the grieving Henry to "frame his mind" to marrying again, for the sake of the succession. More sons were indeed desirable, or at least, a Duke of York, should Edward, God forbid, fall prey to those childish illnesses that carried away so many little ones in infancy. There was the recurring threat of plague, too, the infection of it so easily brought to Court, and his own injured leg - it never healed. It was in 1528 that a sore first appeared on his leg. At that time, his surgeon had cured it, but it appeared again later. The pain of it became excruciating when fragments of bone worked their way out of his flesh and the poisonous puss that built up in the angry swelling had to be drained.

And to cap it all, the King fumed, Francis and Charles, those two turncoat brother sovereigns of France and Spain, egged on by the Pope, even now, so his spies reported, were negotiating an alliance together against him. Henry's ire rose especially at the perfidy of Francis, as he recalled the French king's fervent protestations of brotherly love and peace between their respective nations, when they had met in splendour at the Field of the Cloth of Gold in the year 1520. Was it any wonder, Henry asked himself, that his temper was somewhat short?

Just a brief year ago, it seemed that God prospered him. Those traitors who dared to call their rising against him, their Prince, the Pilgrimage of Grace, were put down. The north was subdued, and there was the promise of an heir to bless the harmony of his third marriage. Now Jane was dead, and the Tudor succession left hanging on the life of an only son.

Why, he wondered bitterly, for perhaps the hundredth time, was God so stinting in blessing him with sons, when to even the lowest of his subjects He was wont to bestow the Biblical quiverful of progeny? Did it amuse the Almighty, he wondered morosely, to thus humiliate a king, whilst even the most feckless beggar in the kingdom could, without thought for the morrow, achieve with ease what he, thrice-wed King that he was could not?

Winter – Wetheral

Before deep winter sealed the earth in its iron-hard grip, they dug a grave in the burial ground of Wetheral Church for the one people called "the little nun." In the village, though few had seen her, all were aware of the outrageous happenings at Heremitithwaite. This very week, too, had not their neighbour, poor Janet Burton, her own babe dead, gone to be foster mother to the nun's child? Though they had shared the little they had with the young widow, want was never far from any man's door, and it was his obligation to see to his own first.

Janet was already half-starved in spite of what little charity they could afford to give her, and it seemed she cared little, in her sorrow, whether she lived or died. All knew that had it not been for the good offices of Sarah Aspedaile, it might not have been possible to sustain her through the privations of winter.

A cheerless Christmas had passed by, in heaviness of spirit. Marguerite's child was baptised, and John Aspedaile gave her his own name. With Janet now housed in the farmstead with Dame Dinah and Isobel winter, well fed and warm in the cold winter weather, both she and little Margaret Aspedaile began to thrive.

The young widow was indeed young, only a few years older than Marguerite herself.

If it pained Dame Dinah to watch her, nursing and humming a lullaby to her tiny charge, she fought down the ache that rose up inside her, glad at least that the little orphan flourished. Often, in those early weeks, Janet's voice, as she lulled the babe to sleep, would falter, and she must wipe away the tears that over-spilled her eyes and rolled down her cheeks. Isobel noticed with satisfaction that the girl's cheeks were less hollow now, as a result of her own insistence that if only for the sake of the babe's nourishment, she herself ate well.

In the gloom of early evening one February day, Dame Dinah set the rush light in its iron stand, and adjusted its height. She came upon Janet peering out into the darkening day. More snow began to fall softly, as feathers shaken from a feather-stuffed bed.

"It was at this time, a year gone, that he left me to go to Carlisle," she sobbed. "I begged him not to go, but the Pilgrims forced him." She wept quietly. The glow of the lighted rush taper caught the gleam of her tear-wet face. Dame Dinah drew her gently to the settle, then gathered her close, and waited until her sobs subsided.

"Tell me of it, child," she urged. "Let us share your pain.
You have never spoken of it since you came."
Slowly, the words tumbled out, halting at first, then they came as a torrent fed by the release of pent up grief.
"They came like a pack of animals," she sobbed. "So wild, so forceful they were. His friend George was with them.

They had taken him too. So they went together, George and my Luke." Her voice dropped to a whisper. "I never saw him again," the words barely audible, now her head lay in the hollow of Dame Dinah's shoulder, and in the age-old instinct of motherhood, she rocked the weeping girl to and fro. A deep sigh, then Janet continued.

"His friend came back, but not my Luke." Another sob escaped her, and then with a low moan, she went on.

They were together when the pikemen rushed out from the castle and set upon them. They both fell. My Luke took a spear full to his heart. George, only to his shoulder. He lay for dead until nightfall, among the dead and dying, then he managed to crawl away. It took days for him to come back, hiding in ditches by day, for fear of the soldiers. One night, he came to my door to tell me that Luke was dead." There was a long silence, and Dame Dinah held her close. At last, she raised herself from Dame Dinah's shoulder, and looked up into her face.

"Then, I found that I was with child," she cried, "and Luke would never know."

There are no words, Dame Dinah reflected, to comfort sorrow like this. She is too young to bear such burdens. Like my Marguerite, she is but a child herself. So she gathered the child-widow in her arms again, and watching the glow of the turf fire, she rocked her gently, and comforted by touch alone.

***

Spring, and the River Eden was running high and wide, fed by the melt water of thawing snow and ice. It carried with it a tangled mass of interlacing branches, some ripped off from trees by the ferocity of winter's gales. John Aspedaile and William Winter walked home from Wetheral village where John had some business to attend to. They walked on the river path that took them past the Abbey where long ago the departed monks had made their fish traps, and watched the turbulent flow of the river. A small crowd was gathered at the bank, pointing to something half submerged that rose and fell as the motion of the water stirred it.

Someone brought a long hook and dragged the mass of branches, and the thing that was entangled in it to the side of the bank. What appeared at first sight to be a bundle of clothes, revealed the remains of what had once been a man. No surprise there; the river swept many a body into the barrier created by the monks to catch fish for the Abbey, but there was something unusual about this one.

"Been in the water a long time, he has" observed the man with the hook, and indeed, he spoke with authority. His was a service he had performed many times for those unfortunates the river took. It was so. Time, and the perpetual action of the water, the winter ice, and the rocks within the river, had all conspired to rob this man of his identity.

"Look at his boots," another said. "Fine boots they be for riding."

They turned him over, so that his ravaged face lay upon the bank, and recoiled in shock. A knife protruded from the man's back, embedded deep, almost to the hilt.

"'Tis a marvel," John Aspedaile spoke first, "that the knife is still held fast in his body. The blade must have gone deep, even through bone."

At his side, he saw William flinch. "What is it, lad?" he asked quietly. "Do'st know this man?"

"Not the man," William faltered. "Though I can guess who he was. 'Tis the knife. I know it well." He turned aside, so that only John caught the note of fear in his lowered voice. "'Tis my father's knife."

John drew him aside from the group of men still speculating on the possible identity of the stranger, for his dress, though spoiled by the water, indicated that he was a man of some standing.

"And the man?" John queried.

"One of the Royal Commissioners' agents," William replied. They left him at Heremitithwaite for some reason after they left. My father met with him many times. I think they were plotting something, though I know not what it was."

"Come away lad," John Aspedaile whispered. "You know nothing."

Summer
Rush gathering and the murrain

Northern summers, as likely as not so shy to arrive, and equally as eager to depart, nevertheless so sweet could be their brief stay. Mary woke as the light of the sun's rays dispersed the last lingering vapours of the dawn mist, and knew that the day would be hot. Today, she would be free, she and Dinah, once Andrew and the lads were from under her feet. It was their intention to make one of their periodic visits to the outlying farmsteads along Eden to collect the hides of any aborted calves.

These were much prized for the making of vellum.
There was always a ready market for such in the past, when the monks transformed the cured skins into the pages of their gloriously illustrated manuscripts of holy writings. But now, with the closure of so many religious houses, Andrew wondered where he could find another outlet for such skins, as the higher price they realised was a welcome source of income to his earnings.

Mary rose quietly without waking Andrew. He and the lads would have a long day before them, tramping over the fells in the hot sun. She packed them provisions of bread and cheese and a copious supply of small ale for the journey; it would be thirsty work.

Then, when they had broken their fast, she watched the three set off, each with a sack thrown over his shoulder to carry the skins in, and Andrew in charge of the food and drink.

Mother, mother, what shall we do today?" young Dinah's face appeared around the door. She handed Mary the basket of eggs she had just collected in the henhouse, and fixed her blue eyes upon her mother's face. This day was hers, hers and her mother's alone - no over-riding clamour of the demands of the departed menfolk to claim Mary's prior attention. Truly, this was a situation that was rare, and to be enjoyed.

Mary smiled, and led her daughter to a chest. From it, she took out two bonnets, of unequal size.

"Do you remember when I tore my gown upon a nail your father had not hammered far enough into the new fence he was making to keep the pigs from roaming?" Dinah nodded. She well remembered the berating her father had received from his angry wife at the spoiling of her best gown.

"Well" her mother continued, "I had to cut away the rent portion, and from it I have made these two bonnets. We will wear them today when we go down to the river to cut rushes. It is going to be a hot day, and these bonnets will prevent our necks and faces from burning in the sun."

"Oh, no one else has such a bonnet," Dinah squealed with pride, and tied the strings beneath her chin. Then, she danced outside, and paraded happily in the sunshine to test the effectiveness of her mother's claims as to her new finery.

Meanwhile, Mary collected all that she needed for the expedition to the river, and donned her own bonnet.

Poor Andrew. She laughed softly as she recalled his stricken face that day she caught her gown upon a nail. Never so quick with words as she, he was practically speechless before her angry tirade.

"Shouldn't have been near the pig pen in thy best gown," he grunted, when she paused for breath.

"It was a drink I was bringing," she had retorted hotly.

"For thee!" It was true, and not for the first time when Andrew and his wife had occasion to differ, he conceded defeat.

Mary gathered up all that she had collected together, and took Dinah by the hand. They walked through the village, covertly aware of the looks, some envious, though mostly admiring, that were cast in their direction. She nodded in acknowledgment to those who greeted her, and Dinah beamed with undisguised pride before the goggle-eyed stares of less fortunate little maids with mothers less skilled with the needle than her own.

One, unable to conceal her envy, made a face and poked out her tongue as they passed.

They reached the church, near the end of the village. Mercifully, in this heat, the stocks were unoccupied this day. The path dipped to the river, and in the shallow water meadows, here and there, cattle came to drink. Mary made for the nearby reed beds, and took off her shoes. These she placed with Dinah's above the water line, and in her bare feet she stepped into the cool water and proceeded to cut the long green stems of the rushes.

She trod carefully along the fringe of the bed, so as not to get beyond the level of her gown, hitched high to her knees. The rushes made a whispering sound as she moved through them, and as she bent low to cut, they towered in a curtain of green above her. Dinah splashed gleefully at the water's edge, forbidden by her mother to follow further.

Mary cut steadily, and when her arm was full, she tossed each sheaf to Dinah to gather together into neat bundles.

She worked so until the sun was overhead. Noontide it must be, and a goodly heap of rushes lay submerged at the water's edge to keep them moist. Then, she stowed her sharp knife into one of her shoes, and called to Dinah. They found a place shaded by bushes, and sat down to eat the provisions Mary had brought, and to slake their thirst.

When they had eaten their fill, Dinah's bright head began to droop. Soon, she lay down upon her side and slept the easy slumber of a happy child. Mary eased the bonnet around her face, so as to shade one rosy cheek. Then she cut for a further hour or so, while her daughter slept. When she reckoned she had cut as many as she and Dinah could carry home, she raised them from the water's edge and shook off most of the moisture.

When Dinah woke, they put on their shoes, and laden with the damp rushes, they hastened back through the village. Once back at the Skin House, they laid their rushes into a pool, to leave until such time as they should have leisure to peel away the outer sheath, and dip the core into fat.

"Shall we go again, mother, to gather more?" Dinah asked hopefully that night. Mary arranged the bedcovers over her already drowsing daughter.

"Yes, we must," she replied. "And soon, before the summer ends. Then we shall have a great store of rush-lights ready to light us through the dark winter nights." There was no sound from Dinah. Already sleep had claimed her, and her childish chest rose and fell rhythmically in time with her soft breathing. Before she left her sleeping child, Mary made the sign of the cross over her bed, and breathed a prayer for her protection through the night.

This was a ritual she never failed to perform, for once, in years gone by, she had heard the old dames in the village muttering when they saw the lovely child her baby daughter had become.

"That child is too beautiful to live" one whispered to another, "the angels take such as she, to join them in Heaven!"

***

Meanwhile, Andrew and the lads trudged from farm to farm to collect calf skins. Often, these dwellings were isolated, built in lonely places on the fell, and it was necessary to cover considerable distances between each one. Andrew was well- known in the district, and had been for several years, since, like John and Ben, he had accompanied his own father on such expeditions.

Also, apart from the small recompense the farmers could recoup in trading the small skins of those calves dropped before their time, Andrew was, as a general rule, a welcome carrier of news.

This day, however, the tanner's visit was received with less enthusiasm. Wherever they went, the farmers eyed morosely the rapidly filling sacks they lugged from farm to farm, their worst fears confirmed.

"'Tis the murrain again, I tell thee, tanner," said one Andrew had known since his father's days, when he himself had been learning his trade. The old man produced several small skins he had ripped from the bodies of recently aborted calves. Andrew counted them. There were more than he expected. He pressed the agreed number of coins into the old farmer's hand.

"Thy gain, my loss" he spoke despondently. "'Tis a bad season, I tell thee, tanner."

At noon, when the sun was high and hot, the three rested in the cool shade of a friendly farmer's barn. There, they remedied the pangs of their clamouring bellies, and long swigs of small ale restored their parched throats.

"I was like to spit feathers," Andrew gasped, after draining the last drops from the neck of a leathern bottle. John winked his eye at Ben, and from behind his father's back, he laid his head upon his folded hands, and gave a surreptitious snore. Ben grinned, and nodded. Both knew that soon Andrew would doss himself down on a heap of dry bracken, and snore contentedly while his food digested.

"Got blisters on my heels," Ben complained.
"Well, go barefoot, then, for the rest of the way," John advised. "We've only two more places to go."

Ben kicked off his boots, and peeled off his stockings. They were new ones, and Mary had smeared the heels with tar, and rubbed them in ashes from the turf fire. Good to preserve the life of the stockings, but when newly treated so, less kind to the wearer's heels. Ben stuffed the offending stockings into his boots, and flung them into his sack.

"They'll stink in there, with those new skins" John told him.

"Don't care," Ben laughed, and wriggled his toes in relief, in the dusty floor of the barn. "This is so much better."

Andrew slept on. Now and again, his snores reached crescendo pitch, at which point the noise of them threatened to wake him. But each time, he changed his position slightly on his couch of bracken, and subsided into further contented slumber.

"Watch this," John sniggered. Feathers from moulting fowl lay scattered over the barn-yard floor. He selected a soft, downy breast feather, and leaned behind the sleeping form of his father. Time and again, he waggled the feather beneath his father's nostrils.

Each time, the tanner's hand made as if to brush away an annoying fly, until with a great snort, full consciousness returned, by which time, his son and the feather were prudently removed to a safe distance.

"No peace in here for flies," Andrew complained. He yawned mightily, then eyed the smirking lads, but could see no reason for their merriment. "Well, let's be on our way again, then."

They gathered up their sacks and set off across the fell. The way by which they had travelled swung round in an arc, so that by the time they reached the last farmstead that day, they joined a pathway south of Wetheral which would take them in the direction of Lazonby again. It was a dismal sort of dwelling they approached. The farmer was known to be a brutish man, born of a brutish father, and himself the father of brutish sons. When the cattle plague had struck before, believing that the smoke from a smouldering fire was an effective remedy for the condition, he had driven his cattle, coughing and sneezing through the acrid smoke of old thatch and damp bracken.

Then, he drove his ailing wife through the same smoke, she being a poor body ground down by years of unremitting toil, and racked by a persistent cough. As far as the cattle were concerned, it was difficult to tell of what benefit such treatment had been, for in the fullness of time, the plague disappeared.

But the wife sickened further, until death released her from her unhappy state. Only a daughter now remained to serve in the capacity of a thankless drudge to her father and two brothers.

Joe Grinton met them by the midden, close by the long, low farmstead that crouched into the back of the fellside. He was in a surly mood, but that was nothing fresh. He kicked at the barking dog, giving warning of approaching strangers, and growled what passed for a greeting.

"Well, what dost thou want, then?" He eyed Andrew with suspicion, until he recognised him as the Lazonby tanner. Then, he brightened a jot. "Skins, I suppose?" he said. "How many?" asked Andrew, not wanting to prolong his association with his unsociable customer. The man had a reputation for cruelty, which, from what Andrew knew of him, he little doubted.

"Two, dropped this morning," Grinton replied. "was going to feed them to't dog. Not skinned yet. Do it thyself." With that, he lifted off the retaining wall of the midden two tiny half- formed bodies of aborted calves, still in their bags of amniotic fluid, and flung them at Andrew's feet.

"But they're no use to me - too small," Andrew objected. Grinton all but snarled. But before he could utter the curse that rose readily to his lips, a commotion in his cowshed claimed his more immediate attention. First, it was the piteous sound of a distressed cow, followed by the agitated bawling of the rest of the herd. It was milking time, and the Grinton brothers had driven in the stragglers ready for their sister to milk.

At the cowshed door, the eldest emerged with a spade and quickly opened up the soft earth at its threshold. It had, it seemed, been recently dug, and it took him little time to hollow out a small trench. He straightened up and seized a pitchfork that stood at the doorway.

"Come on, then. Fetch it out. I'm ready for thee now," he called to his, brother. Out came a younger lad, thick-set like his brother. He held a pitchfork too, an aborted calf skewered on its prongs.

"Cast it there," the elder one instructed, and jabbed a grimy thumb in the direction of the hole. The lad shook the calf's body free of the fork, and it landed with a small thud in the trench his brother had dug.

The dusty earth powdered its still wet form, and then it moved, its stick-like legs twitching.

"It might ha lived, if tha hadna stuck it," Joe Grinton bellowed at his younger son. "Well, 'tis too late now." The elder lad shrugged, and drove his own fork into the still quivering body. Whatever tiny spark of life might still have lingered in the small creature was quickly and mercifully choked out, as spadefuls of earth rapidly filled up the small hole.

By the midden, the Grintons' dog was tearing at the bodies of the two aborted calves Andrew had rejected. Ravenous it was, and half-starving, it survived on what it could catch. Joe Grinton grudged to feed it, maintaining that there were plenty of rats to be had in his barnyard.

"Come away" Andrew urged, and for a while, each was silent with his thoughts, as they tramped homewards across the fell.
"Father, could the calf have lived, if they had not injured it?" John asked at length.

"It might," Andrew replied, "if they had tended it, for it seemed it wanted but a little time to full term. But folk are loath to spend time cosseting a weakling beast. Besides, when a cow has dropped its calf early, some hold that 'tis a powerful charm against the cattle plague to bury it at the entrance to the byre, whether the creature be alive or dead."

"And how think you, father," Ben asked. For though he still remembered, his own father, the memory of Edward Bowman was becoming blurred, and it troubled him sometimes that he could not always call to mind his face.

Andrew looked keenly at the lad he regarded as his second son,

"I say 'tis an old belief, held since time long past. The murrain comes, and it will pass, whether there be such buryings or no."

***

I hear those Grinton lads have been making trouble for Marjorie Whitelock again." Janet was sitting in a shaft of autumn sunlight in the houseplace of the new house at Wetheral. Deftly, she folded a pile of newly washed and dried smallclothes, while a tiny, dark-haired child clung for support against her knee. The little one staggered unsteadily upon legs that frequently collapsed beneath her, and then she would crawl rapidly upon all fours to wherever she sought to go. The face of young Margaret Aspedaile already had ample promise of her mother's beauty. It was, Sarah thought, akin to the face of an angel. She gathered up the pile of folded smallclothes from Janet, and looked sharply at her.

"How came you to know that?" she asked.

"It was William," Janet replied. "He heard the tale in Wetheral, a two, three days past.

It seems Marjorie went to the Grinton place to beg milk, just a little for herself and her cat. Ellen Grinton would give her some at milking time, if her father and brothers were not around, for they grudged even the smallest drop."

"Aye, that I know," Sarah nodded in agreement. "A grudging, grasping family they have always been. Except for the girl. Put upon, like her poor mother, God rest her."

"You are right, both her father and her brothers treat her shamefully," Janet said.

"So, what was the way of it?" asked Sarah.

"Well, 'tis said that Marjorie had been gathering blackites to give to Ellen in exchange for the milk. But the brothers came into the byre just as Ellen was pouring her some milk from the pail. They shouted and raged at her, and flung the basket of blackites on the floor. Then, the cow that Ellen had just been milking took fright at the din, and kicked over the pail. She trampled the blackites and the spilt milk into a purple mess, just as Joe Grinton came in to see what all the shouting was about.

When he saw the spilt milk, he seized a stick and roundly cudgelled his daughter's back with it, and drove poor Marjorie away in fear of her life."

Sarah's eyes flashed in anger.

"Does John know of this," she wanted to know.

"I think not," Janet replied. "He would surely have told you of it, would he not?"

"Indeed," agreed Sarah. "And when John comes in," she continued, "I shall ask him to send William to Marjorie's dwelling with milk, and to tell her to come to us for it in future. Though," she added thoughtfully, "'tis a way further for her to walk, I fear."

"I am sure she will do that gladly," Janet smiled. "He is a good man, your John."

A loud wail put an end to further talk. Young Margaret sat upon the floor beneath a west facing window. The late afternoon sunlight streamed in, and above her, upon the warm stone of the sill, his back arched, and hissing in annoyance, stood the rudely awakened old tabby cat.

He resented the prying fingers of the young child exploring through his fur, and retaliated with a swift dab upon her outstretched, dimpled arms. He stood staring at his young tormentor with wary eyes. He reinforced his initial warning to her with another lightning strike from his sharp claws, and another even louder yell of fright broke forth.

Seeing Janet's hasty approach, he deemed it wise to remove himself to the peace of the barnyard until dusk should fall, and he judged it time for him to hunt.

Janet took the sobbing child upon her lap, and rocked her gently to and fro until she forgot her fright.

"Yes," she continued, "Marjorie has had sorrow a plenty in her life. Her son, he was her only child. He was one of those hanged at Carlisle when the Pilgrims were caught, though he only went with them because he feared they would fire his mother's dwelling if he did not." A shadow crossed Janet's face. "My Luke knew him well."

Her words were scarcely more than a whisper, and to hide the tears that rose to sting against her eyelids, she bent her head until her cheek rested upon the dark curls of the now quieted child.

November – London

The King contemplated the new ring upon his finger - the Becket ring. He moved his hand back and forth, and watched as the pale beams of November sunlight caught the gem, and ignited the fire within the heart of the great ruby. Once the jewel was named the Regale de France, and for more than three hundred and fifty years it adorned the tomb of St. Thomas a Becket at Canterbury. King Louis the Seventh had offered it at the saint's shrine when he had prayed there for a sick child. Now, that shrine was bare, relieved of three centuries worth of rich offerings of gold and precious stones, and the relics of the saint unceremoniously dispersed. All this in the past year, since he himself and Jane had made their own offerings there.

He sighed deeply. Melancholy was never far from him, his spirits low. Before him lay the orders for the execution of traitors. They awaited his signature. In a flash of memory he remembered a time, a golden time when these same men had been his youthful companions of the joust, and hunting and hawking. They had all been young then, in those heady days of youth and young manhood. His hands rested upon the table, fingers drumming. His hand hovered over the orders for their execution. Then he seized the quill and signed. Again, a beam of sunlight caught the ruby and cast a pool of crimson upon the orders. He flung down the quill.

A king can have no friends, he reflected grimly.

There was trouble looming on the continent, as well. The French and the Spanish had put aside their differences, and agreed to make no further alliances with England. Henry found himself isolated and immediately began to prepare for the looming threat of invasion. The southern shores of England, the first expected points of attack, he defended by a line of fortified castles, and paid for the same by utilizing his recently acquired wealth from the dissolved religion houses.

And the other pressing matter - remarriage? Cromwell favoured a princess from the Duchy of Cleves, a small German state in the northern Rhineland. Cleves, like England, had become a non-papal Catholic country, and therefore a like- minded ally with whom to join in matrimonial relationship.

Hans Holbein was duly despatched to Germany to paint the likenesses of the Princesses Amelia and Anne, the two sisters of the Duke of Cleves, and it was upon Anne that the King's choice fell. A marriage treaty was signed, and before Christmas Anne began her journey, travelling though France with a great retinue, where the dress of her German ladies gave rise to much unkind mirth. In Calais, she waited for a storm to abate, and the English party escorting her endeavoured, with some difficulty, on account of her limited grasp of English, to teach her card games, knowing that this was a pastime the King enjoyed.

Then, when the Lady landed upon English soil, Henry was impatient to inspect his bride.

On the first of January he rode off to Rochester with a few of his gentlemen. There, the Lady Anne was resting after her long journey from her homeland, and not knowing the King's penchant for disguisings, was disconcerted when six men, all dressed alike, and wearing hoods, abruptly entered the chamber. One of these embraced her, saying he carried gifts from the King. Understanding little of his speech, Anne was confused by such behaviour, and Henry, seeing her lack of reaction to his playful game, revealed his identity.

The meeting was a disaster. The face of the Lady who stood before him was pock-marked, and her nose - how long it was! No wonder Holbein had not painted her in profile! And the King, a fastidious man, was appalled by what he termed the "very evil smells about her." He took his leave, as quickly as good manners would permit, and the furs he had brought to give to his bride, he took back with him. His fury knew no bounds. He felt himself cheated, trapped into a marriage he could not stomach, and misled by everyone who had had a hand in negotiating this now repugnant union. He sought desperately to find a way by which he might extricate himself, and it was upon Thomas Cromwell, Lord Privy Seal, that the burden of blame descended.

"I like her not," he barked at Cromwell, who was, in truth, the architect of the proposed union with Cleves.

"If I had known as much before as I know now, she would never have come into this realm."

Nevertheless, next day, with a great company, bejewelled and arrayed in purple and gold, he rode to meet his bride with every courtesy.

The English ladies who received Anne en route to meet the King were apprehensive at what they saw. It was not only her personal appearance, but the absence of those accomplishments desirable in a queen that were lacking. She spoke no other language but her native German. She had never hunted or been taught to dance or to play an instrument. These were accomplishments not thought to be desirable in a woman at the Court of Cleves. Her mother, the Duchess, had brought her daughters up to be dutiful wives, but had neglected to inform them as to what such duties would be.

So with the princess already on English soil, the date of the wedding fixed, and no valid obstacle being discovered in time to prevent it, the king found himself in the rare and invidious position of being forced to stifle his own personal objections, and honour the alliance contracted with the Lady's brother, the new Duke of Cleves. Therefore, on the 6th January, the last day of the Christmas festivities, Henry felt constrained, reluctantly, to marry her. The occasion was a brilliant spectacle, the costumes, the jewels, the furs, and the studied courtesy with which Henry received his bride, all belied his underlying aversion to a union so distasteful to him, that the marriage was never consummated.

And in her innocence, Anne did not realise there was anything wrong. "He kisses me goodnight and good morning," she told her ladies, in response to their diplomatic questioning, and was aghast when one informed her "But, madam, there must be more if ever we are to have a Duke of York."

Indeed, it was his claim when subsequently seeking an annulment that, "he left the Lady as good a maid as he found her." All the while, he cast about for the means to be rid of his German wife, though wife he said he doubted she was, and seized upon the existence of a pre-contract that had been made for her in childhood with the son of the Duke of Lorraine.

Thomas Cromwell, Lord Privy Seal, worked late into the night. It was more often than not his practice. It was spring, soon to be Easter, and the King was impatient to be free of the woman he had reluctantly married, but said he could not love. Patience was not a virtue bestowed upon His Grace, and to make matters worse, he was now bent upon pursuing a flighty chit of a girl younger than his eldest daughter. This time, the object of the King's suddenly recovered lust was, much to Lord Privy Seal's annoyance, another sprig of the prolific family of the Duke of Norfolk. Mistress Katherine Howard, in Privy Seal's opinion, constituted an entanglement hardly to be desired, considering the career of that other Howard niece, Nan Bullen.

As for the Duke, Cromwell was well aware of his enmity. Like the rest of the nobility, he despised new men, like himself. He was jealous of the power that Privy Seal now wielded, and would bring him down, if he could.

The night breeze was cold. It blew in from the open casement, and he rose to close it. How stiff his legs were! He had lost count of the passing hours seated there, trying to devise the means by which the King might sever the knot that bound him to Cleves. How, he racked his brain, could this be done without causing offence to the Lady's brother, Duke William, its new ruler. The night was far gone.
Soon, it would be dawn, and still he had much to do. He poured some wine, and paced the room as he drank, in an effort to bring back feeling to his numbed limbs. A shiver came over him. Was it cold alone, or did he recall in the depths of his mind, the plight of his former master, Cardinal Wolsey, in whose service he had learned his trade?

He too had faced a similar task - how to extricate this same King from the bonds of a marriage from which he was intent upon breaking free. The King's conscience, Privy seal reflected, was a fickle thing. It had come into play when, after so many years of marriage to Spanish Katherine, and the loss of those doomed offspring, it was tardily suggested that Katherine could not be his true wife on account of her prior, though brief marriage to Prince Arthur, his own elder brother.

It was proof, the King claimed then, that despite a Papal dispensation at the time, his own marriage with his brother's widow, was sinful. Had not God shown his displeasure, he asserted, in granting him no living son?

Now, Cromwell though wryly, that same conscience was stirring again, this time conveniently awakened by his natural aversion to the Lady of Cleves. The marriage was no marriage; the King claimed, unconsummated as it was.

Some means must be found by which he might free himself, some loophole must be found... Could it be the Lady's pre-contract made for her in childhood with the son of the Duke of Lorraine? Cromwell sighed. It was weak, but it must serve, and speedily. Not this time would there be the long drawn out and abortive negotiations with Rome that was poor Wolsey's lot, no Legatine Courts to pry into the innermost privacies of the married state, that dragged on for years; this matter must be concluded swiftly. The King's temper was shortening with age.

Dawn began to break, but warmed by the wine, Cromwell resumed his seat and worked till early light. There were many other matters he must attend to, including the grant to the Royal College of Surgeons of four dead bodies for dissection from criminals hanged on the Tyburn gallows.

A servant, up and about his day's toil, noticed that a light was still burning in Lord Privy Seal's chamber. He placed one eye at a crack in the shrunken wood of the door, then hastily withdrew. Was it true, then, what people said, that the man never slept? Or, what was worse, that he was in league with the powers of darkness? Some certainly thought so!

***

What had he feared, Lord Privy Seal wondered, in those dark night hours, when the past cast long shadows? And the future, who could tell what that held? Always, he knew, he must guard his back.

Those old reactionaries, Bishop Gardiner, Norfolk, Suffolk and Southampton, he knew they dripped poison into the King's ears, seeking to discredit him. But today, the seventeenth day of April in the year of our Lord, 1540, he, Thomas Cromwell stood in his splendid ceremonial robes, about to be created Earl of Essex. He allowed himself a rare smile.

Those long nights of work in the dark hours bred fantasies unfounded. Today, with the bright sun shining, his gut feelings of unease were dispelled. Surely, he reasoned, this was the culmination of all he had striven for, the King's recognition of his worth. He, the low-born son of a Putney blacksmith, raised to the peerage, an equal with those who despised him.

For three sweet weeks the newly ennobled blacksmith's son savoured his elevated status. Oh, he was well aware of the thinly veiled disdain and the barely suppressed sneers of those born to nobility, so how could it be that he, the most well- informed man in England, whose spies were everywhere, and knowing so many dark secrets, seemingly had no knowledge of impending events that day in June? But there was one, as wily as he, one adept and long-practiced in the art of hiding the hand he meant to play, one who summed up one facet of his own many sided character thus: "There was never a man I have made but what I can break" - the King.

It was upon his orders that Thomas Cromwell was arrested as he entered the council chamber at Westminster. Gleefully, Norfolk and Southampton pulled off his seal of office and Garter insignia. He protested, of course.

"I am no traitor," he yelled at them, and struggled mightily with those who would constrain him. All to no avail - the Tower awaited him.

What thoughts are those of prisoners that languish in that place - fear, certainly, rage, rebellion, escape? And at the last, perhaps - resignation. But for Thomas Cromwell, the last was not yet come. He saw Norfolk's hand in this. Always, the Duke had looked down that long, aristocratic nose of his, resenting the power of base-born fellows such as himself.

He wrote to the King, but his letters were ignored, and finally, as he awaited execution, condemned on charges of treason and heresy, his last despairing cry to his prince was for "mercy, mercy, mercy."

Execution was to be on the twenty-eighth day of July. By the Act of Attainder passed against him, he would go to the block as plain Thomas Cromwell, deprived of his short-lived nobility.

Those last days of life when a man knows he is to die, who can tell what images from the past leap up in his mind? For Cromwell, those childhood days in Putney, when he watched his father labouring in the heat of his smithy, he had not thought of him for many a year.

He had a sister, too, and after he returned from his wanderings in Italy, there was Elizabeth, his wife, dead now for how many years? She was never to know how high he would rise, nor now how low he would fall. And Gregory, his son, who, in their wildest dreams could have imagined that he, the blacksmith's grandson, would aspire to marry so high, she the Queen of England's sister, Elizabeth Seymour, the widowed Lady Uchtred?

That last night? Was it wakeful, as so many past nights of toil had been? What passed in the inscrutable mind of the once powerful Lord Privy Seal?

A great crowd, in holiday mood, thronged the route to Tower Hill to see him die. Below the scaffold, a sea of faces watched him, Privy Seal, come to spill his blood in the place where he had sent countless others to the same fate. Some yelled abuse, brave in the anonymity of the crowd. Most stared up at him, stony-faced, implacable in their hostility. If there were any present, who in his earlier years of power, he had given his help, they were voiceless that day. Only one man, Archbishop Cranmer, had had the courage to speak up for him to the King, asking "Who will your Grace trust hereafter, if you may not trust him?" And strangely, because they served different masters, the Imperial Ambassador, Eustace Chapuys had found Cromwell congenial company, perhaps appreciating that to serve royalty, as he himself had done for many years, was no sinecure.

The moment was come. He declared himself a true Catholic. Who believed him? Guilty of Lutheran sympathies, of protecting those suspected of heresy, and most heinous of all, denying transubstantiation, the Presence in the Mass - there would be no last minute reprieve for crimes such as these. He laid his head upon the block, and a murmur of anticipation ran around the crowd. Then they fell silent. The headsman raised his axe. But what ailed the man? Blow after blow he struck before his clumsy butchery succeeded in severing perhaps the most brilliant head in England from its body.

The performance was over, and the crowd began to disperse. It was generally agreed that the entertainment had been splendid. Some lingered to watch the clearing-up on the scaffold. Others who had brought food with them, seated themselves on the ground nearby, and ate with relish in the summer sunshine. Two men appeared with pitchforks, whose job it was to gather up the blood soaked straw around the block and throw it onto a waiting cart.

Then they swilled the scaffold with bucketfuls of water, and brushed away the reddened flood until it overshot the edges of the scaffold and dripped through the spaces where the timbers met.

"So, the churl is dead," observed the younger man, and cocked an enquiring eye at the other, inviting comment.

"Aye," the second replied. He leaned upon his broom, and with precision spat upon the mess of bloodied straw piled up on the cart.

"He has trod the same path he forced others to tread" He considered for a while, then he regarded his companion solemnly and said. "I call that justice." He looked thoughtfully at the little groups of people eating and drinking, and seemingly untroubled by the grisly scene they had just witnessed.

"Aye," he repeated. "There is many will rejoice in England at this death"

Cromwell's blood was not yet dried in the heap of straw they flung from the cart that day, when Henry Tudor was joined in wedlock to Mistress Katherine Howard, his rose without a thorn. He doted upon his pretty wife.

At forty-nine he felt himself young again. His health improved, and consequently his temper, too. The troublesome leg was quiescent now, and in spite of his vastly increased bulk, he rode and hunted again. Jewels, rich gowns and furs he showered upon her, and Queen

Katherine danced and made merry. In the political and religious tug-of-war, her Uncle Norfolk and the Howards rose high once more, to the chagrin of the new men.

It was a Christmas of great splendour - there was a queen again. Anne of Cleves came to Court, and showed no rancour towards the younger girl who had supplanted her, well satisfied, it appeared, with the King's generous provision for her continued life in England, and her new title - "the King's sister."

1541

Summer - Progress to York

In February, the King's leg ulcerated again. It forced him to endure weeks of inactivity, while the pus was allowed to drain. In moments of depression, he was to reflect that Cromwell was "the most faithful servant he ever had." But with the approach of spring, his black mood shifted, the rebellious leg calmed, and mobility of sorts was restored. The idea of a royal progress was conceived. To the north then, to York, he would show himself in those rebellious parts of England he had never seen. A coronation for Katherine at York, perhaps? That was one of the suggestions that traitor Aske had made when he came to court that Christmastime of 1536. Well, the King thought wryly, in a way neither he nor those so-called Pilgrims had foreseen, circumstances had conspired to bring about one of their most pressing demands, the "expulsion of villein blood" from the Council. i.e. Cromwell's death.

And why not invite James, his sister Margaret's son, the King of Scotland, to come south and meet with him at York? There was need of talk between them. The lad seemed incapable of governing those Lowland Border Scots of his, who continued to enjoy their wild sport of conducting raiding parties over the Border into northern England, even as far as the town of Penrith.

So, it was arranged, and the great northern progress was ready to set out at the end of June. It was a magnificent display, almost on a par with that of the Field of the Cloth of Gold in France, some twenty years before. By degrees, the awe-inspiring procession made its way through towns and villages whose inhabitants had never seen their sovereign, and as intended, were suitably impressed. On roads that were sometimes little more than tracks, the glittering troupe traversed the wilder territories of the realm, until at last, in mid-September, the city of York was finally reached. It was a relief after the long journey, to enjoy the luxuriously appointed buildings of a former religious house made ready to receive the Court there, and that of King James, too, when he should arrive.

Pedlar Jack was anxious to begin his journey home. In the Summer he had travelled to York to buy provisions. Now, at the summer's end, it was time to return to Carlisle, serving those villages in the remote country districts en route before the winter began. But now, with the arrival of the King, not to mention the expected arrival of the King of Scotland, how could he not linger in York awhile longer? It was news, and he would be the proud narrator of an event the north had never witnessed before.

York was packed with folk who had flocked there to see the arrival of the great cavalcade, and the stable where Jack slept with his pony train was invaded by other travellers seeking a lodging.

He struck up a companionship with a travelling tinker, a fellow who, like himself, was always journeying to make a living.

"Tomorrow," his companion informed him as they ate their shared meal, "the King is to receive the public submission of those rebels he pardoned after the great rising hereabouts. You remember - the Pilgrimage of Grace they called it."

"Aye, I remember it" Jack replied, "and so do many in York." He lowered his voice, fearing to be overheard by any in the stable where they supped. "There was scant merriment in York then, when Robert Aske was hung here in chains."

"So I have heard," the younger man replied. "My own father saw it."
Next day they joined the jostling crowd early. It was a rare sight, the brilliant apparel of the royal entourage, the clergy and York's own city fathers, anxious that no mishap should occur to mar the proceedings.

There was a stir as the King arrived, and a roar of welcome. Jack and the tinker watched. Some two hundred men knelt down in the street before the King. These were those former rebels fortunate to have escaped the noose when the King's justice was meted out when that fateful rebellion failed.
They had already been pardoned, but now they were required to make their further submission.

"What are they giving to the King?" someone in the tightly packed crowd asked.

"Purses," another replied, "and there's gold in those purses, I'll warrant."

"Ah," an old man spoke sadly, and drew his sleeve across his eyes.

"The price of so many lives," he sighed.

King James of Scotland however, never came to meet his uncle - no message was ever received from him. At length, by the end of September, it was obvious that the King of Scots was not coming, much to his uncle of England's annoyance. However, despite the young pup's rudeness, and the fact that there had been no coronation arranged for Katherine, Henry was pleased with the majority of the enterprise, and it was especially so at York, where he was pleased to receive the abject submissions of those who had been beguiled into rising against him by the Pilgrims.

He had shown himself in his splendour, to those subjects who inhabited the wilder regions of his realm. To them, he must have seemed a distant figure, a name only. Now they had seen him in reality, and witnessed his colourful ceremonies.

He had heard their legal complaints, and dispensed justice. The King, for his part, had seen and wondered at the stern beauty of these northern regions of England, the gaunt treeless moors and dense stretches of forest where wolves were said to still roam. Here was a harshness of life that bred hardness and endurance in its people.

It bred too, he reflected, the Pilgrimage of Grace in mind, a tenacity and stubbornness that enabled them to resist any change they considered contrary to their ideals.

By the end of September, there was the threat of worsening weather, and the return journey could be delayed no longer. They packed up the tents that were pitched in the Abbey grounds intended for the accommodation of the overflow of both the English and the Scots Courts, and then they began the long journey back to the softer south.

The shock of what awaited Henry immediately upon his return to London struck him with the velocity of a thunderclap. Disbelief was his first reaction. It could not be! They were malicious lies, those allegations concerning his sweet Katherine's wanton behaviour whilst living in the household of her step Grandmother, the dowager Duchess of Norfolk. She was accused of improper relations with a certain Henry Mannox, employed by the Duchess to teach her music - surely she could not have been much more than twelve or thirteen years of age at that time. But, more seriously, there was Francis Dereham, some sort of distant cousin, come recently to Court, and seeking employment in the Queen's household. He had a loose tongue, and he claimed that they were pre-contracted, and that therefore she was his wife.

That, together with the testimonies of some of the young women who shared the same bed-chamber with Katherine at the Duchess's establishment at Lambeth, made the accusations of her promiscuous past incontrovertible, The King wept. Then came rage, explosive in its intensity, following hard upon his grief. That rage spilled over too against those who had supported his intention to marry again, especially the Howards. Had not Katherine's own uncle, the Duke himself, assured the King of his niece's "pure and honest condition?"

Serious as the matter was, if it had rested there, perhaps the marriage could have been declared invalid, and Katherine herself banished in disgrace. But more, and worse, was to come, Whilst the King had lain sick in February, Katherine and his much-favoured Gentleman of the Privy Chamber, the young and handsome Thomas Culpeper, had, it seemed, entered into a secret liaison. Perhaps it was inevitable that she, shackled to an old and ailing husband, and he, rash and beguiled by her beauty, should throw discretion to the winds, and with the wild abandon of youth take so terrible a risk. Night after night, wherever the recent progress halted on the way to York and back, they contrived to meet, Lady Rochford standing guard outside the locked door of the Queen's chamber.

The situation was dire. Both Culpeper and Dereham were arrested, and Katherine, thoroughly frightened, was divested of her title of Queen, and placed under house arrest at Hampton Court. Then, she was sent under guard to Syon House.

On the first day of December, the fate of Culpeper and Dereham was sealed. They were tried and convicted of high treason, and condemned to death, though not as originally sentenced, to that most cruel death of hanging, drawing, and quartering. Perhaps it was the King's former fondness for the wild, young Culpeper that prompted him to commute the sentence to the mercy of simple beheading. On the tenth of December sentence was carried out, the two heads thereafter being impaled on spikes on London Bridge.

November – Wetheral

Isobel set down the pail of milk she carried from the dairy. She moved quietly about the houseplace, for she saw that Dame Dinah was sleeping. The Lady, for that was how she still called the former Prioress, drooped forward in her chair at the side of the fire, a hand cradling her breast. Isobel felt a stab of fear. She sensed that something was amiss. She stood and surveyed the sleeping woman, the Lady to whom she owed so great a debt.

Since they had left the Priory, there had been a change, not immediately obvious, but a gradual loss of energy, and of interest too, even in the little one, Marguerite's child, though Dame Dinah loved her dearly. Did she still grieve for her, her lost Marguerite, Isobel wondered? Yes, of course she did, and would do so, doubtless, always.
But was it grief alone that caused this increasing lassitude, this loss of her former vitality? And surely, the Lady's robust form should not have seemed to shrink in the last two years or so? The once comely face was pinched now and sunken, the skin tightening across the high cheek bones. Isobel's fears came together now, and took hold of her vitals in a sickening grasp.

"My own mother looked so," the awful thought sang in her head, repeating itself time and again. Then, wed but a short time to Robert Winter, a neighbour came to their door to tell of her mother's sickness. Though Robert looked suspiciously at the man, she rode with him, pillion, to the nearby village where she had been born. Thereafter, she walked to tend the ailing woman as best she could, but to no avail. Robert meanwhile grew peevish and sulky, grudging the time she spent away. Finally, his black mood erupted into rage when one night she was caught in a thunderstorm and sheltered in a barn, and so was late home. In his pent-up fury, he rained down blows upon her, punching mercilessly until his wrath was spent. That night, the child she had but lately conceived, that would have been her first-born, flooded out of her bruised body in a pool of blood.

The sleeping figure stirred, as if aware of another's presence. Immediately, she straightened up in her chair, and withdrew the hand that clutched her breast.

"Lady, how is it with you? I fear you are not well." Isobel's anxiety was plain to see, and despite the pain that was now her almost constant companion, Dame Dinah forced herself to smile.

"Isobel, have no fear. "Tis naught. I begin to grow old, I think, and with age you must know, some pains must come." She eased herself slowly in the chair. "But then," she spoke as though to herself, "Tis not given to all to grow old."

But despite her brave words, and the iron will that fought the pain, and the increasing weakness of her body, as the year turned and the fading leaves swirled in small eddies around the farmstead, Dame Dinah was forced to take to her bed. Sarah came, and give her a soothing syrup to make her sleep. Janet too came every day with her small charge, and Dame Dinah watched with loving eyes as the child played happily on the floor of her chamber.

Only in Isobel's presence did the indomitable spirit waver. When the effects of the syrup wore off and the pain returned in all its intensity, though the Lady bit upon her inner lip until the blood came, it was Isobel at her bedside who took the thin hand in her own, and marvelled at the strength of her grip as the crescendo of pain mounted.

In the last days of October, there was a merciful respite from the rigours of the pain's intensity. Dame Dinah lay still and peaceful upon her bed, and watched the rays of weak autumn sunlight play upon the walls of her chamber. Only Isobel sat with her, with her sewing, ever watchful.

"Isobel." There was a renewed strength in the voice that of late was little more than a whisper. "Isobel, bring William to me soon, There is something I would say to him, and ask of him."

"Lady, I heard him in the houseplace but now, bringing in the milk from the dairy. Do you wish to see him now?"

Dame Dinah nodded, and settled herself on the pillow that Isobel placed at her back to raise her. When William entered, having hastily made himself more decent to enter into the Lady's presence, Dame Dinah began to speak.

"Sit here by me, Isobel." She pointed to the chair at her bedside.
"You must know," she continued, in a voice low, yet steady and calm, "that I am not long now for this world. No, Isobel, you must not grieve." She lightly touched the shaking shoulders, and laid a thin hand upon Isobel's bowed head.
"I hope, by God's grace, to join those I have loved in life." A look of sheer joy, for a brief moment, lit up and transformed the wan face. "So do not grieve for me." She lay back on the pillow, and rested for a while, then she gathered her strength and continued.

"William, I have spoken to my brother-in-law. He is well pleased with your service to him. After I am gone, if it pleases you, this is to continue to be your home, and that of your mother, of course." She paused to rest again, then smiled gently as though she looked into the future. "And that of your wife and children, when that time shall be." Again, she rested, for to speak at length was wearying for her.

"Pray give me a little time," she said, and looked with contentment at mother and son.

"I would have been blessed to have a son such as yours, Isobel," she said, if I had not been sent to be a nun.

William's voice was rough with emotion as he strove to speak.

"Lady," he said, "I thank you most heartily for your care of my mother. In our great need, you gave us your protection, and we owe you much.

I thank you too for your part in raising me in the world."

Dame Dinah lifted a hand to silence him.

"No, William, there is no debt, and if ever you should think there was, your mother's devotion to me has cancelled all."

With an effort, she leaned towards him and looked intently into his face.

"William," her voice was low now with fatigue, "you remember that time we stood together in the Nunclose, and the purpose for which we were there?"

"I do, Lady, I will always remember it," he said "You know the place there I speak of?"

"Yes, Lady, I know it."

Earnestly, Dame Dinah's eyes held William's own, as she asked, "Of your charity, William, will you do a last service for me there?"

"Lady, whatever is in my power to do for you, that I will gladly do" William assured her.

With a sigh, Dame Dinah fell back upon the pillow, and turned to Isobel. "The little coffer that stands upon the windowsill - please bring it to me, Isobel." Then, while Isobel held it, Dame Dinah lifted the lid, and brought out a small carved box. She held it between her hands, as if she shielded it from harm.

"My mother gave this to me when I entered the religious life," she said softly. "It contained a holy relic then. It was one of her most treasured possessions." Her voice dropped to a murmur, "'Tis empty now. Alas, I found it cast down on the floor of my chamber, after the King's workmen were gone. It was a thing of no value to them - the relic gone."

The sun slipped low in the western sky, and the soft greying shadows of evening gathered.

"Isobel," the tired voice was all but a whisper now, "When I am dead, I ask you to cut off a lock of my hair, and place it within." She unfolded her hands, and lifted the lid of the box. "Then, William, this is what I ask of you, that you will carry it to that place in the Nunclose and bury it there, in the place of which you know I speak. Will you do this last service for me?

William bowed his head. "Lady, it will be my honour, though grievous to me 'twill be."

When night came, there was no need of Sarah's soothing syrup to help Dame Dinah to sleep. Already, she lay in a deep slumber, for once undisturbed by pain. Morning found her refreshed and serene, and possessed of an inner peace. It shone from the sunken face and when she spoke, a note something akin to triumph rang out.

"Isobel, I dreamed of Marguerite in the night. She came to me in a shining cloud of white light. She stood as close as you are to me now, at the foot of my bed."

"Lady, did she speak to you?" Isobel asked.

"No," Dame Dinah replied. "She smiled, and held out her hands to me. Alas, I could not reach to touch them. She was radiant.

She stood in a cloud of light, and when she moved away, she was beckoning all the time for me to follow."

Isobel crossed herself.

"Last night was All Hallows, Lady, when 'tis said the spirits of the dead do visit us."

"Ah," Dame Dinah nodded. "I did not know it was All Hallows."

She drowsed intermittently throughout the day, blessedly undisturbed by pain. Noon was well past, and the day shortening when she stirred and rallied.

"Isobel, ask Sarah and Janet to bring the little one to me," she asked.

"And John, I would give him my thanks for his great charity to me."

They came, heavy of heart, knowing the end must come soon. Something of the solemnity of the chamber hushed for a while the young Margaret's childish chatter. Then, on a sudden impulse, she shook off the restraining hands that held her, and made her way purposefully to where Dame Dinah lay. There, she flung wide her dimpled arms, and smiled up into the loving eyes that saw the child's and her mother's face intermingling.

Dame Dinah reached out her hand, and rested it lightly upon the little one's dark head. "Bless you, my child. God keep you in His love, and guard you from all ill." The thin hand fell away, and with all that was left of human strength, she raised it to make the sign of the cross.

Soon, because she was so weary, they took their leave of her. She blessed each one, as they knelt at her bedside, though John and Sarah returned to sit and watch the night away. She never saw the morning break, but in those hours when All Hallows merged with All Souls, and though the watchers heard no sound, Dame Dinah uttered a cry of joy to greet two radiant beings come to guide her on her journey between worlds. One was young, a youth still, who had loved her from their shared infancy; the other older, taller, and he had loved in a different way.

"My brothers" she called out to them gladly. They held out their arms to her and beckoned, "Come." Her spirit reached out to them in an ecstasy of rapture. Their fingers touched, entwined, and joined irrevocably in the handfast of eternity.

1542
February - London

Between the beheading of Katherine's lovers and the passing of her own sentence, Christmas intervened, as sorry and mirthless a time as the previous Christmas of 1540 had been gay. In the new year of 1542, Parliament re-convened, and on the eleventh of February, the former Queen's death warrant was issued. Next day, she came under guard from Syon by river, so terrified she had to be forced aboard. In the dim light of evening, the barge sailed under London Bridge, where the sightless heads of her two lovers stared blindly out across the dark water.

Once within the Tower, a strange courage took hold of Katherine. She acted with a dignity born perhaps of a sense of past generations of noble breeding, or perhaps, maybe, just the acceptance of those resigned to die. It was a brave request she made, that the block upon which, the following day, she must lay her head, be brought to her prison cell, so that she might practice what she must do.

When the morning of her short life came, that brief courage deserted her. Terror immobilised her limbs, and she needed help to mount the scaffold. She sank to her knees, the headsman raised his axe and the head of the King's fifth wife was struck off.

Pain, rage, torment of mind, and pain again; the cycle turned endlessly, like the revolving of a wheel, and always returning to pain. But a king's pain must not be public, lest it be seen as weakness. It must be endured. But rage was another matter. Rage could be justifiably expressed. Rage at betrayal, and most bitter of all, betrayal of love and loyalty by those deep in a king's affection. Katherine, most loved of wives, no pure virgin and young, Culpeper, a fond favourite, so trusted that he slept upon a pallet at the foot of the King's bed.

A wounded animal will seek solitude. It will lie up in isolation, to recover, or to die. Instinctively, Henry sealed himself away, wounded in heart and in pride, to grieve, to rage, and fight that great, black beast later generations would name depression. In his worst moments, it held him without mercy, cornered him when he tried to escape, dragged him back, as a cat with a mouse, allowing it a few moments of freedom, then capturing it again and again to torment it further.

So few had access to the King at that time, no courtiers with their insincere pity, to flatter and fawn, then later to sneer at his plight. He knew their ways. But one man gave him solace in those days, the dark days of his soul. He was a man who, over the years had cheered him with his merry wit, whose mind was sharp, and fine enough to discourse with a king on weighty matters, a man who never flattered, but spoke true, knew when to speak, or when to keep a companionable silence.

That man gain, was Will Somers - jester by profession! Was it the wisdom of a fool that restored the balance of a king's mind?

Of the multitudinous Howard clan, a goodly number now languished in prison, nervously awaiting the capricious royal pleasure. But not the Duke, the old survivor. Only too conscious of the damage done to his family and faction by the fall from grace of two of his nieces, he wisely removed himself to Kenninghall to attend to domestic matters, lest his presence at Court further inflame a vengeful monarch. Then, old soldier that he was, towards the end of the year, his King had need of his undoubted military skills, and with Lord Hertford, he was again on his way north, this time to the Scottish Borders.

Reluctant as King James had been to come south the previous year to meet his uncle at York, now with his Lowland army he was threatening to cross the Border by way of Solway Moss. It was his undoing, On the twenty-fourth of November, his troops suffered a terrible defeat in the mudflats of the treacherous Solway, and James himself, retreating to Stirling Castle, appeared to simply lie down and die. He left as his heir a week old baby girl, Mary, Queen of Scotland in the first week of her life. His uncle gloated - a marriage between his own precious heir, Edward, and this infant Queen? Perhaps herein showed the hand of God for the peaceful unification, under Tudor sovereignty, of two long warring nations?

1543

Summer - Germany

Mistress Margarete Cranmer lived the life of a non-person, unacknowledged, hidden away in country places, moving between England and her native Germany. In Lutheran Germany, it was permissible for a cleric to have a wife, and it was there, in Germany, that she had met and married Thomas, the now Archbishop of Canterbury. But England was not a safe place to live for one of her persuasion, whose uncle was a Lutheran theologian in Nuremburg. So, back in Germany in the spring of 1543, she learned little, though enough to worry her, of the purge of heretics in progress at the instigation of Bishop Gardiner.

Her husband Thomas was himself accused of heresy by Gardiner, and had good reason to fear the intrigues of those reactionaries who sought to bring him down. The King, too had got wind of the fact that his Primate was married, and not being the bravest of men, this was a time when Thomas Cranmer feared for his life.

Margarete sighed. Religion! How she had come to hate the word, the cruelty, the divisions and hate it engendered in those who professed to believe in the Gospel of Christ, and His teaching of compassion and love. How then, she reasoned, could His true believers sanction the burnings, the torture, and the hideous practices committed in His name? She shuddered.

How vividly she remembered hearing in her uncle's establishment what appalling methods were employed to punish those so-called heretics, of which she knew herself to be regarded as one.

Great was her relief when at last she heard that the King himself had come to the aid of his Archbishop, and roundly berated those plotters who sought to destroy him. Might it even be possible, she wondered, with the King's protection, for her to return to England again soon, to Thomas? But no, Thomas had sent her back to Germany for her own safety, his too, and it would not be wise to compromise his position by her presence in England.

***

Hampton Court

It was July, 1543, and another Katherine stood at the King's side at Hampton Court to become his sixth wife. This was a lady, born Katherine Parr in Kendal castle, in the northern county of Westmorland. At some thirty years of age, Katherine was the widow of two elderly husbands. Here was no flighty chit of a girl, as her predecessor was. Katherine Parr, Lady Latimer, was a steady, kindly and intelligent young woman, no beauty, but comely, and endowed with a gentle grace. Like Queen Jane, of blessed memory, she was balm to the King's soul. Their marriage was to last for three and a half years, his sixth, her third. She exuded a gentling influence upon an often testy, ailing monarch, restoring him to good humour by her skilful and intelligent conversation, yet wisely contriving, in the main, to defer to his presumed greater knowledge.

1544

Summer - London & Boulogne

The next year, there was talk of war again. Across the Channel, France was a continuing threat to England's security, and needed to be taught a sharp lesson. This, the King decided with relish, he would administer himself. He would lead his army into battle in person, despite his unreliable health. Dr. Butts, his physician of many years standing, sought in vain to dissuade him from the venture.

"Sire, I would be lacking in my duty if I were not to appeal to you to reconsider. For you to hazard your person, in your state of health..." he began.
"My person and my state of health are always rejuvenated on campaign," the King snapped, and Butts knew better than to continue to proffer unwanted advice.

Nevertheless, a new Act of Succession was ratified by Parliament, should Henry, Heaven forfend, not return alive to the kingdom. Firstly, Edward and his heirs should succeed, then Mary then Elizabeth, and their respective heirs, lastly, the heirs of the King's younger sister Mary, late Queen of France and her husband Charles Brandon, Duke of Suffolk, but not those of his sister Margaret, late

Queen of Scotland. England under Stewart rule, King Henry could not countenance, but he was ever hopeful of negotiating a marriage between his own son and heir, and the infant Queen of Scotland, thus uniting the two lands under Tudor rule.

Surely, he reasoned, then England's back-door would be safeguarded from the continuing threat of Scots incursions in the north.

With that done, and Queen Katherine Parr appointed Regent, he embarked for Calais in mid-July to join those experienced commanders, Norfolk and Brandon. Both were veterans of many a past campaign, Norfolk was still soldiering at the age of seventy-one, and Brandon, his friend since youth, was now sixty. A brave show it was, the King riding out into the French countryside, resplendently armoured and weaponed, at the head of his army. He rode astride a mighty courser, the mounting of which, no easy feat, was achieved by the necessary use of a winch.

It was Brandon who was given charge of the siege of the walled city of Boulogne. It resisted until mid-September, then when its walls were breached by the heavy English ordnance, it was forced to surrender. The King returned home in triumph. For him, the activity of the campaign had restored, albeit briefly, some of the energy and vigour of his former years. But it was not to last. His leg troubled him again, his spirits were low, and the French, in league again with the Emperor Charles, were keen to regain their lost possessions. And the cost of the war, and the expense of maintaining French territories, was draining the treasury.

In the end, reluctantly, but because it was prudent, France was allowed to buy back her city of Boulogne for a ransom of two million crowns.

1545

July - Southsea Castle

Another year was gone by, and there was impending war again with France. That perfidious Francis, allied with the Emperor Charles, was busy assembling a fleet, a veritable armada of fighting ships at le Havre and other French ports. England was isolated, friendless in Europe, and faced the very real danger of invasion by sea. The King thanked providence, and God, for his own foresight in fortifying his southerly coastline with a line of modernised castles bristling with up-to- date artillery. Southsea Castle, hardby Portsmouth, was only just made ready, and it was to there that he rode to review his assembled troops. It was a fine show, the mounted King, clad in cloth of gold and tawny velvet, riding up to his castle, a white plume nodding atop his black bonnet. From a vantage point high up on the castle walls, he was able to view the uninterrupted vista encompassing Spithead and the Solent, and away to the Isle of Wight.

If Henry felt any apprehension, as well he might, he hid it well that day. Through his spies' reports, he had learned the count of enemy ships was prodigious, some two hundred and thirty five. His own, less than one hundred. Of English defenders, on land and at sea, ten thousand only stood ready to repulse thirty thousand Frenchmen.

"St. George, defend this your land," was his silent prayer that winged its way heavenward. The nineteenth day of July dawned hot, and unusually, not a breeze ruffled the calm of the sea, nor stirred the motionless sails of the English fleet. Not a ship could move. God, it seemed, was bestowing His favour upon the enemy.

Ahead of the great fighting ships of the main fleet, the French loosed their galleys, those agile, armoured row-boats that needed no wind, They darted like a pack of terriers hither and thither across the still water, harrying the becalmed English fleet. Their ploy was to lure the English out into the open water, and by giving chase, to render them prey to the heavy guns of the French ships waiting off the Isle of Wight. The boom of heavy guns and the crack of lighter artillery resounded across the water. The nimble little galleys pestered the becalmed English like a swarm of gnats, teasing and enticing them to follow, hopefully to their destruction.

Then, all changed. A sudden wind blew from landward. God and St. George, it seemed to the King, watching from the battlements of the castle, had heard his pleas. The wind filled the sails of his two great carracks, the Mary Rose, and the Great Harry, old vessels both, but newly refurbished at great expense, and fitted with extra guns. They began to move, gun ports open, ready for firing. Great Harry, the King's flagship, led the way, followed by the Mary Rose, named for the King's sister, and the Tudor emblem. She carried the newly appointed Vice-Admiral, Sir George Carew, whose wife proudly watched on the battlements beside the King.

Their sails billowed in a sudden gust. But what ailed the Mary Rose? She began to turn, but upon that turn she was heeling over, dangerously so. Her open gun- ports were level with the water, she was lying down upon her side, the sea rushing in and flooding her decks. There were hundreds on board, trapped both on the lower gun-deck and on the one above, where anti-boarding netting fastened in those on board like captured fish. The pitiful cries of the drowning carried to land, to the ears of the horrified onlookers. Mary Rose sank like a stone, only two of her topmost masts could be seen above the waves. So very few were saved, six hundred perished.

The French were jubilant. It was their belief that their own gunfire had caused the Mary Rose to sink. Their joy, however, was short-lived. The English fleet bore down upon them, wreaking havoc, and sending them packing. God's hand had prevailed. But the cost? It had caused a king to weep.

***

Late in the year, the King sat in his chair in a pool of hazy sunshine, and worked on the speech he would deliver when he addressed Parliament in December. His head began to ache, so he pulled away the gazings that were clipped onto his nose, and rubbed his tired eyes. Of late, he had been glad to wear these lens made from Venetian rock crystal, to remedy somewhat his deteriorating eyesight.

This last year, despite the trouncing the French had been given in July, had been a year of loss, of sorrows, and the falling away of former time-held certainties.

The Mary Rose, her loss the King felt deeply. Only weeks later, the sudden death of Charles Brandon, Duke of Suffolk, was a blow he felt keenly. Companions they had been since their youth, and one-time brothers-in-law when, to his initial annoyance, Brandon had secretly married his sister Mary, the lately widowed Queen of France. But Mary had loved Brandon, and before she could be persuaded into her reluctant and short- lived marriage with the aged and ailing old Louis of France, she managed to extract from her brother the promise that when she should be free to marry again, it would be to a man of her own choosing.

Henry had sent Brandon to escort his widowed sister home from the French court, after the specified time she must wait to ensure she was not with child. In spite of himself, Henry gave a rueful smile. The minx! She had obviously felt it prudent to make sure that he did not renege on that promise, and yes, he had to admit, it was a promise unwillingly given. His sister was a valuable pawn in the diplomatic marriage market. Those two, they had presented him with a fait accompli - they had out- manoeuvred him, and thereby had incurred his severe displeasure.

But what could he do? She was his favourite sister, and Brandon was the closest a king might have as a friend. So he relented eventually, and created them Duke and Duchess of Suffolk. Now Mary was twelve years dead, her namesake, the Mary Rose gone too, her widowed husband Charles had married again, speedily, it must be said, and now Charles himself, like the Mary Rose, was gone, buried with great pomp and solemnity at Windsor.

Windsor. That was where his dear Jane now lay, and in God's time, he would join her there. How long, he wondered? Those fits of melancholy visited him frequently now. Did all men feel so, with advancing age? This relentless letting go of youthful vigour, of activity, and the exhilaration of health and strength? He eased his now massive body in the chair, a body grown so gross and corpulent, puffed-up and unwieldy that it must be lifted and moved by mechanical means, for his greater comfort. And if he wished to hunt, now he must often remain stationary, where they had built the Great Standing, and wait to shoot at the deer as they were driven by - he who was used to wear out three horses in the duration of a day's hunt!

He closed his eyes, and rested his head between cupped hands. His head still throbbed, but there was so much he needed to read. No, this year had not been a good one, his own fitful health, change, loss, the two rival factions jockeying for supremacy, and Edward, not yet a man to deal with them, should he, the King...No, he would not think of it. He must strive to continue till his son...Someone was hovering at the door, despite his express desire not to be disturbed.

"Enter," he called testily, and glared at the hesitant messenger. "Well?" he snapped.

"Sire," his Gentleman bowed. "I regret to tell you that Sir William Butts is dead." There was silence in the room. The King laid a hand upon his forehead, and leaned forward, his elbow upon the desk. The Gentleman waited, until the King wordlessly signalled his dismissal with his free hand. The patch of sunlight was gone, leaving the room in the grey gloom of November. Someone came with lights, and outside the window the gloom eventually turned to thick darkness.

How long the King remained so, he could not tell. He was remembering the many years of kindly service, the loyalty and discretion of Sir William, his trusted physician. At length, he straightened, and leaned back in his chair.

"Oh, William, I will miss you," he said at last, and his regret was sincere. "So close to me you were, a comforter through all my years of pain.

"Physician, heal thyself', it says in holy writ. But you could not, for all your undoubted skill. Nor could you heal me."

1546
London

Sometimes in the following year, the King would walk in his gardens, when the pain in his legs permitted. Occasionally, by the aid of mounting blocks and hoists, he was well enough to sit a horse again, and then enjoy, to a limited, degree, his old pursuits of hunting and hawking. Then, inevitably, he would endure those bouts of illness that laid him low and steadily eroded that once magnificent constitution. Then, as if by some miracle, and contrary to expectation, he would rally, and make light of the pain and consequent weakness that inexorably bore him closer to the inevitable end. And all the while, at Court, the plotting and intrigues of those around him escalated.

He knew that the schemers looked beyond him for their furtherance in the next reign. Skilfully, he continued to play them off, one faction against the other, and by force of his own willpower, he managed throughout that last year to maintain control. He had made his will, and laid down the order of succession, and the terms of a sixteen strong Council of Regency to serve until Edward's majority, in particular, no one person taking precedence in this event.

In December, it came to his ears that the Duke of Norfolk's son, Henry Howard, Earl of Surrey, had substituted a crown for the coronet on his coat of arms, and added the letters H.R. - Henricus Rex.

It was damning evidence of his family's future treasonous aspirations, and a threat to his still vulnerable heir. Both Surrey and his father, the Duke were promptly arrested and lodged in the Tower.

1547

London Whitehall

Surrey was tried at the Guildhall in mid-January, and despite his vigorous protestations, was found guilty and condemned to death. Upon his return to the Tower to await execution, Surrey made a desperate, but unsuccessful bid to escape by way of his privy, the vertical shaft of which emptied into the river via a moat. At low tide, he began to lower himself down towards the water, but was caught and shackled. Then, on the twenty-first of January Henry Howard paid the ultimate price for his folly on Tower Hill.

Parliament passed an Act of Attainder against both father and son. It would deprive them of both their lives and their lands. The old Duke languished in the Tower for a further week after his son's beheading, awaiting his own fate.

In the meantime, the King was failing.
"Sweetheart, it is God's will that we should part," he told his last Queen, and sent her away weeping. Perhaps he never realised the end was so near, for when at last it was brought home to him, that "in man's judgement, he was not like to live," and though it was Archbishop Cranmer he wished to see, first he would take a little sleep, then as he felt, he would advise on the matter.

The little sleep deepened, and began to merge with that great sleep from which there is no awakening.

By the time the Archbishop arrived in the early morning of the twenty-eighth of January, the King's powers of speech were gone. Cranmer leaned over the great bed and took the King's hand in his own.

"Give a sign that you die in the faith of Christ," the Archbishop urged, and felt the tightening of the King's hand clasped in his own. What remained of consciousness sank into oblivion, and by the second hour of the morning, King Henry's life had ebbed away.

Not far away, in the Tower of London, the old Duke of Norfolk awaited execution. It was fixed for that same day. The winter sun rose, and he listened for the arrival of an escort to convey him to the scaffold. It did not come, not that day, nor in the days that followed. Perhaps his King, remembering the Duke's long life of military service on his behalf, and that he himself, king though he was, would soon stand before an authority higher than his own, and in need of mercy, had ordered a reprieve. Or in those latter days, did he ever sign the order for execution? Or perhaps, in the face of the King's impending death, the plight of the old Duke was simply forgotten.

The King died at Whitehall, and he would be interred at Windsor, close to the body of Queen Jane. The journey there would take two days. By the middle of February, he had been embalmed and cered, and lain in state. Then, his magnificent funeral procession set off from

Whitehall. It bumped along the murky roads, some of which had been hastily widened to facilitate its passing.

The vast procession rested at Syon overnight, that place of unhappy memory, to the very date five years previously of the confinement of the terrified Queen Katherine Howard prior to her forcible ejection from there to face execution. Next morning the cortege resumed its journey to Windsor, and the end of an era.

Few could remember a time before King Harry's reign. It had lasted for thirty eight years. But if there were a few greybeards who watched the king's last earthly journey make its way to Windsor Castle, and wondered at the magnificence of the richly robed and jewelled effigy that topped the towering hearse, they would have remembered, though perhaps dimly, a time when Englishmen had taken the handsome eighteen year old prince to their hearts as their King. Truly now, an era was ended.

February - Lazonby

On the same day that King Henry's vast coffin was lowered into the earth beneath the paving stones of St. George's Chapel in Windsor Castle, and his officers and household broke their staves of office and cast them into the void, an event of little consequence occurred in faraway Cumberland. Of little consequence, that is, to the great and the good, and of the several not so good, assembled there. It was only that one of the late king's subjects died, a labouring man, one of the many such nameless and unremarked that would die that day too.

In Lazonby, it was coming daylight, and Andrew Bowerbank woke with a start. Mary was calling, and the smell of frying bacon reached his nostrils. But the smell made him feel queasy, and when he rose from his bed, his head felt strange. There was much to do that day, and he must be about his work. More saddles were promised, and he was thankful that John was proving to be a quick learner, and Ben almost equally so. He could hear their voices outside already. They must have swallowed their platters of bacon and eggs Mary cooked for them over the houseplace fire, and were eager to make an early start on the work ahead.

Andrew felt his head swimming round, or was it the room? He steadied himself, then pulled on his breeches and the rest of the clothes he had flung off the night before.

"Father, your food is ready," Dinah was calling from the houseplace. He staggered down, his legs felt strangely unreliable, and he was thankful to slide onto his seat at the board.

At the fireside Mary's back was turned towards him, so she was unaware that anything was amiss. She handed the platter she had been keeping warm for Dinah to carry and set down before her father. Nausea overcame him at the smell of the bacon, and bile rose up from his gut. He left the food untouched, and made for the door. Outside, he began to retch violently.

"What ails your father?" Mary' asked, "He's never not eaten his bacon before."

Andrew was sweating, though the morning was cold, but it was a relief to get outside into the fresh air. The pig needed feeding, so he made his way to the pigstye with the intention of giving its lone occupant the bucketful of household scraps Mary gathered up each day. The pig saw the bucket, and greeted him with loud grunts of anticipation. He fumbled for the gate fastening, and once inside, emptied the slop into the pig's trough. Then blackness overcame him. He fell insensible, his face twisting to one side, and the pig, finding a hand lying within its trough, began to chew on the lifeless fingers.

John found him, and with Ben's help, together they carried the inert body into the houseplace. Time to grieve was not a luxury those who laboured for their living could afford, but in shock they carried out all the tasks that death made necessary. In a state of frozen disbelief,

Mary set a cauldron of water over the fire to heat. Then they stripped Andrew of his fouled clothing and washed his body. Dinah sobbed quietly, whilst Mary went to a low chest, and with shaking hands took out two fair linen sheets, the ones kept solely by those who could afford them, to cover their dead. When all was done, John and Ben lifted Andrew's body up onto the board and covered him decently, there to lie until he was simply coffined.

A newly dug grave awaited them in Lazonby churchyard, and when it was time, John hitched up the horse, between the shafts of Andrew's cart. With Ben, together they lifted up the plain wooden box that contained their father's body, and carried it out of the houseplace. It began to snow, a soft, filmy mist of white, as they loaded it up onto the floor of the cart. Mary watched, dry-eyed now, as the lads, one either side of the cart, led the horse and turned it onto the road that would take them through the village and down to Lazonby Church.

Dinah joined her, and their heads bent against the now whirling flakes, they walked behind the cart that carried Andrew to the place where all roads must end.

PART II

EDWARD VI

Winter - London, The Tower

On the morning of the 30th January, three riders galloped south in the direction of London. They had left Enfield, where the Princess Elizabeth was lodged, well before noon, and aimed to reach the capital before the short winter day closed in. Before them lay a four-hour ride, though no risks must be taken for the sake of speed. The life and health of the young rider they flanked was paramount.

Edward Seymour, Lord Hertford, glanced frequently at the slight figure of his nephew, and now his sovereign, riding at his side. The lad rode well, he thought, but then, he did most things well, if his tutors were to be believed. However, he felt sure that the young prince had never before undertaken so long a journey on horseback. Nevertheless, it was vital that he himself, as Lord Protector, secure the person of the nine-year old King, and lodge him safely in the Tower until his coronation. Mercifully, the weather was not inclement for travelling this winter day.

They were making good speed, and by late afternoon, a sprawling blur of greyness in the distance confirmed that they were within reach of London.

The little King urged his horse forward and drew ahead of his uncle. Riding at his other side was Sir Anthony Browne, his father's loyal Master of the Horse. In the royal wake, clods of earth flew up in an arc from his horse's hooves, to the discomfiture of His Lordship, who received one such missile full on the mouth. Edward Seymour spat vigourously, and contemplated the rise and fall of his royal nephew's trim backside. It was, he observed wryly, a most congenial sight in comparison to that of his lately deceased sire. King Henry's vast rump, in his latter years, was prone to overhang both the saddle and the broad back of any steed he was capable in his latter years, of mounting.

"Ah, Henry," Seymour mused, "six wives, and all those years of striving to beget an heir! And it cost my pale Jane her life to give you this slip of a lad. Surely 'tis fitting that I, his maternal uncle, should bear the weight of government, until these slender shoulders are strong enough to carry so weighty a burden?" Thus he sought to salve his conscience, for even before breath had left his dying brother-in-law's body, he had paced the outer spaces of the death chamber, seeking to overturn the now speechless King's will. The sixteen strong Council of Regency that King Henry had laboured on to ensure that no one person should have greater power than another, this he schemed to overturn, and take sole power as Lord Protector for himself, to govern during young King Edward's minority.

Ahead loomed the Tower, from whose guns a thunderous salvo of welcome boomed out, and ships on the river let off their own ordnance in greeting.

Crowds were waiting in the streets to catch a glimpse of the slender boy who was now their new monarch. They cheered ecstatically, and took the slip of a lad to their hearts. The Constable of the Tower was waiting to receive his new King, and Uncle Hertford motioned that he should ride forward alone into the precincts of the Tower.

There, Edward dismounted. His legs felt unsteady, stiff and cramped by the long ride. He feared they might buckle beneath him, but then, the sound of his cheering subjects sent a thrill of excitement through his body. His spirits lifted, and there before him knelt his godfather, Archbishop Cranmer, and a gathering of noble lords, kneeling also, though of these, he could not name them all. With due gravity, despite his tender years, Edward received their homage.

"I am Edward Tudor, King of England," was the thought that ran repeatedly through his head. ,"With God's help, I will be a good King," he resolved.

That night, dog-tired and somewhat saddle-sore, he was thankful to sink into the warm softness of the great bed prepared for him in the private apartments he must now occupy in this forbidding place, until it was time for him to leave, and be crowned at Westminster.

Thoughts, images, questions, all interchanged repeatedly in jumbled confusion in his brain, born of the apprehension of the last awful days since he learned of the death of his father.

The King, that great, towering, all-powerful figure, whom he revered next to God, was no more. They told him that Archbishop Cranmer had raced through the night to reach his father's side as he lay dying.

He had assured him that the King had been able to signal to him that he died in the faith of Jesus Christ. Therefore, his father's soul was now safe with God, and the knowledge was a comfort to him.

Nevertheless, alone in the dark night, his childish fear of the unknown rose to hinder sleep. He felt tears welling up into his closed eyes and over-spilling onto the soft pillow beneath his head. That dreadful moment when he and his sister the Lady Elizabeth learned of the death of the King! How she had held him to her, and in their shared grief, they had wept together for the loss of the father they saw but rarely, yet who was to them the bright star of their universe.

In the curtained bed, the slight figure began to toss and turn. All was blackness within the bedspace, the heavy hangings drawn close against the cold of the winter night. But near the bedhead, a small sliver of light where the curtains met penetrated the darkness, and by drawing back the folds, Edward watched the moving shadows through the gap. They danced on the walls of the chamber, created by the flames that flickered in the great stone fireplace. He heard the wind begin to rise. It moaned and sighed, a sad sound, he thought. Yes, and this was a sad place too, of that he was well aware.

People came here, to the Tower, to die, to have their heads chopped off, like Elizabeth's own mother. And traitors, like the old Duke of Norfolk. He was here too, somewhere within these same walls, waiting, wondering how long he would live.

Then, he remembered there was that dreadful story about the two young princes. They were brothers, and one was a rightful king, young like himself, who came here, never to be seen again. Only it was not a story, it was true. They were his own grandmother's two brothers. But they had a wicked uncle, and he stole the throne from them, so people said. Edward shivered, though it was not from the cold. Perhaps they were still here, quite close, their bodies hidden somewhere in the walls of this great fortress. The fire was dying low now. Its red embers glowed faintly, and the shadows ceased to dance.

"I have uncles, two of them. Uncle Hertford and Uncle Tom Seymour...what if...?" No, he must not think so. They were his mother's brothers. He let the parted curtains close again, and slid deeper down the great bed. He drew its coverings close against his body, and with one hand, he drew the fur that lay over all around his head, so that only the tip of his nose protruded above the covers. Thus, tightly cocooned, and crouching instinctively in the defensive foetal position, sleep began to soften the edges of consciousness, and warmth and weariness at last lulled him into the deep slumber of childhood.

February
London - Westminster Abbey

Between the burial of King Henry the Eighth at Windsor on the seventeenth of February, and the coronation of his son, Edward, at Westminster, only two days elapsed. Since his father's death, whilst Edward was lodged in the Tower, as was the custom for monarchs until their crowning, there was much to be achieved. Uncle Hertford, with his nephew's consent, was formally proclaimed in Council, Lord Protector of the realm and governor of the King's person until his majority, and shortly afterwards, Hertford was elevated to the Dukedom of Somerset. The Lords, as always, intrigued, jockeyed for position, and selected friends or foes amongst their own ranks, to be used, or abused, as occasion might demand, for their own furtherance in the future.

All were astir early at the Tower, from the least minion to the noblest lord. It was the day before the young King's coronation, and today his procession into the city would leave the Tower and thread its way through the streets of London to Westminster. Excited crowds were gathering, despite the rawness of the winter dawn, jostling each other in order to secure the best positions to see their new King ride by.

All morning, the formation of the vast procession took shape. The nobility and statesmen, the clergy, the courtiers, foreign ambassadors and diplomats, each was assigned his place to ride in the cavalcade.

The clink and clash of weaponry, and the shouts of the ordering of the thousands of men at arms, who would bring up the rear of the procession on foot, resounded in the courtyards and surrounding precincts of the Tower, and continued well until noon. By one of the clock all was ready, and the King's horse, richly caparisoned in crimson satin, awaited him in the main courtyard. The King himself shone in cloth of silver, overworked in gold.

At his waist, he wore a belt of silver filigree, set with rubies, diamonds and pearls. His doublet and boots were of white velvet, so too his cap, studded with similar gems. Once mounted, the small, shining figure rode out of the Tower to the wild acclaim of his waiting subjects, and the cannon in the Tower's arsenal boomed out. The city conduits ran with wine, much to the satisfaction of the crowds, who were chilled by their long hours of waiting in the winter cold.

All along the route, Edward was greeted by singing and recitations by small children who, awed by the grandeur of the occasion, strove with mixed degrees of success to deliver the lines they had been taught. On raised platforms, tableaux of allegorical scenes were enacted before him, whilst flattering discourses alluding to his person and future reign reached him, in part, above the din of the moving procession.

By mid-afternoon, they had reached Cheapside, where the mayor and city fathers waited to offer their homage in the shape of a large purse stuffed with a thousand crowns. Edward leaned down from his horse to accept their weighty tribute from the kneeling mayor, but it was too heavy for his small hands to hold. How was he to manage?

He needed both hands, one to doff his cap to the cheering throng, and the other to hold the reins of his horse. He looked to Uncle Hertford, no - it was uncle Somerset now, and it was he who resolved the situation.

"Give it to the Captain of the Guard to carry," he advised, ignoring the suspicious looks of the city fathers, who misliked seeing the transfer of their assiduously garnered riches to the questionable keeping of the military. On they went, until they approached St. George's Church.

Here there was a spectacle that so enthralled him, young boy that he was, for all that he was a king, that Edward signalled the procession to halt so that he might watch the daring performance of an acrobat. The man lay on a rope fastened from the church steeple to the ground, and by balancing his body by his outstretched arms and legs, he propelled himself downwards on the rope, as though he were an arrow in flight.

When he had descended safely, he approached the King and kissed his foot. He was a Spaniard, he said, Aragonese by birth, and a native of the homeland of the King's late father's first wife, Spanish Queen Katherine. He was as agile as a monkey, a creature of which that lady was especially fond, and he scrambled upwards again on the rope, then walked upon it, balancing first upon one leg and then the other, to the delight of both the King and the watching crowd below. It was some time before Edward could tear himself away from the scene, and the procession moved on again. Then, they went by way of Fleet Street and Temple Bar, and arrived at Westminster as daylight waned.

***

"God save the King" the people's cries rang in Edward's ears as he slipped that night into happy sleep. In the streets, despite the cold, the crowds lingered as long as the wine flowed from the conduits, and many a loyal toast slurred upon the lips of the new King's sated subjects. No feelings of dread, or strange fears disturbed his slumber that night in the Palace of Westminster, such as those that troubled his mind that first night he slept in the Tower. Tonight, he felt exhilarated, and secure in the outpouring of adulation and loyalty, and the warmth, and even love, of those crowds who had waited in the winter cold to greet him.

Tomorrow, he would sit in the Confessor's chair, and the Archbishop would place the crown of England on his head. Sleep would not come, tired though he was. For a child of his yet tender years, the day had been exhausting. He stretched his legs in the softness of the ample proportions of the bed. All afternoon, he had ridden on horseback, and his legs were still cramped and stiff.

But, oh, the thrill of the spectacles he had seen, the noise, the colour, the cheering as he passed through London. The acrobat! That agile little man from Aragon, he had been fascinated by him. All the images of the day began to interchange and merge as, at length he drifted into sleep.

Early in the morning of Sunday, the 20th of February, he was awakened. It would be a long and arduous day. The ceremony at the Abbey would last for some seven hours. The banquet at Westminster Hall would take another four hours, and after that would be the reception of ministers and foreign diplomats. Then would begin the entertainments.

Again, he was robed in velvet, rich crimson, overworked in gold, and overlaid with ermine fur. Upon his head was perched a black velvet cap. When all was ready, Uncle Somerset, resplendent in his own newly-acquired ducal finery, led him with a body of nobles to the state barge waiting on the river. They travelled via Whitehall to Westminster Hall, and from there it was but a short walk to the Abbey. On this most solemn day, they went in formal procession. There would be no yelling crowds to witness the priestly rite that would consecrate the coronation of a king.

As he approached the great door of Westminster Abbey, the significance of the occasion, and what lay before him, was daunting for one so young.

Then, what pleasure, what warm reassurance he felt when he saw waiting for him those boys of high rank with whom he had studied in the days of what seemed to him now his princely freedom. How good it was to see their familiar faces on this day that already he felt was setting him apart. They took up their places, walking behind those high nobles who bore the crown, the orb and the sceptre, and each was given the honour of carrying some item of the coronation regalia.

They reached the Abbey door, and the joyous cadences of the choir burst forth to greet them. The Dean bowed, and led them up the aisle until each assumed his appointed place, leaving the crimson-robed figure of the little King to go forward alone, and be seated in St. Edward's chair. Then Archbishop Cranmer presented his godson as the rightful and undoubted inheritor of the crown and dignity of the realm. "Yea, yea, yea. God save King Edward," came the united response. Cranmer knelt at the altar, and at the foot of the steps lay the acknowledged King. The Archbishop prayed, the choir sang, and despite the sense of awe pervading him, an errant thought flitted through Edward's mind.

"This is how the knights of old kept vigil throughout the night before they received their accolades." Those stories of knightly chivalry - he had read of them with pleasure in his school books.... When the anthem ended, it was time for him to rise, to be anointed with the sacred oil. The most hallowed moment was come.

They removed his upper clothing, and upon his breast, his back, his forehead, and upon the palms of his hands, he felt the oil touch his skin like cold silk. Then, he was re-robed, and led to St. Edward's chair, to be seated there and crowned. Three crowns were used. First, St. Edward's golden circle, then the crown Imperial, which being too big for the head of a child, the Archbishop simply held above him, and lastly a small copy specially made to fit, was placed upon his head.

He was invested with the rest of the regalia, and made his kingly vows. It was done; the nobles of the realm were coming to kneel before him in homage, their anointed and crowned King of England.

To Thomas Cranmer, Archbishop of Canterbury, the sight of this child King seated in the ancient chair upon which Christian monarchs had been crowned for centuries, signified both the end of one era and the fresh dawn of another.

This child was trained from his tenderest years by scholars of the new learning. All his already considerable intellect accepted its teaching, and this day King Edward's crowning represented a landmark in the history of the realm. For since his father's break with the Papacy, this coronation was unique in that it was sanctioned outside the reach of Rome.

This ardent young soul himself was, under God, the Supreme Head of the Church within its own dominions. And it warmed the Archbishop's heart, when leaving the Abbey and walking under his canopy of estate to the banquet in Westminster Hall, the young King asked as to the reason why three swords were being carried before him.

"They are the symbols of your three kingdoms, Sire," he was told. "One is wanting'," the young King observed. "The Bible. 'Tis the sword of the spirit." And as he had halted his progress into London to watch the performance of the Spanish acrobat, the procession waited.

"Let the Bible be brought from the lectern in the Abbey," he commanded.

"It must be borne before these emblems of earthly power."

***

It was spring again, and Edward the Sixth, the new King resumed his studies with his old school fellows. Of these, Henry Sidney and Barnaby Fitzpatrick were chiefest in his affections. This bright morning, let out from lessons, they were practising shooting at the mark. The King took careful aim, not wishing to be outdone by his older companions.

The arrow flew, but a sudden gust of wind deflected its flight, and it went wide of its intended target.

"S'blood," swore the newly consecrated monarch, so recently invested God's Vice-regent and supreme Head of the Church.

The outburst reached the ears of his tutor, John Cheke, who promptly took his young charge to task. "But kings do swear. My royal father did so. 'Tis expected of them," was Edward's reply. Cheke regarded his much-loved pupil with a mixture of amusement and concern. It was true, such irreverent references to the blood of the Saviour were frequently on the lips of both the nobles and councillors with whom the young King was now mixing. However, this reprehensible practice must be nipped in the bud. It was not fitting that such profanity should be disregarded. Besides, fully aware of the mischievous nature of boys, Cheke suspected that Edward had been led on by his older fellows, for sheer sport.

"Who told you so?" he probed, but to no avail. Edward refused to betray his informant. When later the culprit owned up, punishment was meted out. Barnaby, for it was he, that irrepressible sprig of the Irish nobility who withstood the whipping his friend the King was made to watch. As prince, Edward had on occasion, been beaten by his tutor, Dr. Cox, for neglecting his lessons. But as King, he was spared this indignity, and felt keenly for his friend.

"Tis nought," Barnaby assured him when it was over, as he rubbed his stinging backside.

"My father did lay on much harder, at home in Ireland."

That his nephew should continue his usual routine of lessons suited the Protector well, while he took power to himself, and imposed his own increasingly autocratic rule upon his nephew's realm. But it was Tom Seymour, the Protector's jealous and discountented brother, who intrigued in pursuit of his own reckless ambition.

Within months of King Henry's death, he secretly married the widowed Queen Katherine Parr.

Now he was styled Baron Sudeley, Lord High Admiral of England, though in truth, matters of a maritime nature took up but a scant portion of his time. He curried favour with his young nephew by supplying him with funds his other uncle, the Protector, had not thought to make available for the boy's use, and by insinuating himself into Edward's good graces, he hoped to undermine his brother's authority, and even assume the protectorship himself.

***

But then, his Queen died in childbirth in the autumn of 1548, and with one royal wife dead, the Admiral began to look for a match with either of the King's sisters. However, neither of these two ladies were willing to compromise themselves, particularly the Lady Elizabeth, whose reputation had been brought into question whilst she lived at Chelsea under his and Queen Katherine's care.

Any well-intentioned advice from his elder brother Somerset fell upon Tom Seymour's closed ears, and a rift between the brothers widened. Both were possessed of violent tempers, though Somerset was more in control of his than Seymour. Now the King became alarmed by his Uncle Seymour's intrigues, and took care never to be alone in his presence.

The upshot was that reckless, beyond belief, on the night of the sixteenth of January 1549, the Admiral somehow managed to approach the King's bedchamber unobserved. But Edward had a little dog that lay outside his door. It began to bark, and the Admiral panicked, drew his pistol and shot it dead. Uproar followed, and his Lordship, pistol in hand was promptly arrested and speedily conveyed to the Tower. Those of whom he had made enemies, and there were many, were quick to lay charges against him. He was condemned, and the following month went to the block.

There were those who said the Lord Protector never lifted a finger to save his brother, perhaps unjustly so. Undoubtedly, on Somerset's part, there had been brotherly regard for his hot-headed sibling, and more than once he had given him the benefit of the doubt when his brother Tom's nefarious schemes came to light. But Somerset was perceived by the people to be a cold, unfeeling fratricide, and the Admiral a likeable, open-handed charmer of both men and women.

Besides, there was another, waiting, and not recognised by the Protector, who sought, in time, to supplant him..

Relations with France were improving. There was talk of a French princess as the King's future bride and Barnaby Fitzpatrick left for France, to make himself agreeable at the court of King Henri II.

"I shall miss you sorely", Edward told his dearest friend, but he was well aware that Barnaby must needs further his career, and make his way in life. So, he devoted himself to his studies, and the Protector pressed on with his reforms, growing ever more short-tempered and intolerant of opinions that did not coincide with his own.

***

The celebration of the Mass was forbidden, and in its place, the Liturgy of the first English Prayer Book was ordered to be used in all churches, and the English language used in services instead of the familiar Latin. But the common people were apprehensive of change, and clung to the comfort of the rituals they had always known. And to compound their discontent, those who depended on the land for their existence, suffered from its increasing enclosure by those landowners who turned it into deer parks for their pleasure, or sheep runs for their profit, the trade in wool being a lucrative business. Come summer of 1549, things came to a violent head on both religious and economic fronts. There were risings in the south east and the south west of the country, and the military was dispatched to put them down. Thousands died in the slaughter that ensued, and the country verged upon civil war.

Immersed as he was in the punishing programme he had set himself, overworked and seemingly myopic in his vision, incredibly the Protector failed to detect (or did he ignore?) the undercurrents of dissent, the machinations and false friendships of his Council colleagues. Especially of one in particular, so subtly did that one conceal his hand, waiting, scheming.

Winter and Spring – Wetheral

No longer ever mindful to be on his guard against the vengeful outbursts of his father's uncertain temper, and the unkindly guidance of John Aspedaile, William Winter flourished. Ever would he be beholden to John for the refuge afforded to himself and his mother in their time of need, he determined to repay that good man's generosity in the only way he was able, by his own unstinting labour. Therefore, he learned avidly all John Aspedaile could teach him in the management of the farm of Wetheral, and never grudged in his labour on John's behalf. Consequently, the farm prospered abundantly by this efforts, and John was therefore relieved of much of the burden of his maintenance.

Isobel watched as the pair rode into the barnyard on their way home from market. There was an easy familiarity between the two, though her son never failed to show the older man respect.

"William," she said, when he had eaten and they sat at their ease at evening's gate, "I would that thy father had been a small part as John Aspedaile is to you. I fear I have failed you in that, my son."

"Mother," William replied gently, "'tis no fault of yours that he did those evil things. How could you have known his true nature before you were wed?"

Isobel sighed deeply.

"I knew of his own father's mistreatment of him and his mother. Robert once told me how he feared his father, so when his rages were upon him he would escape to the riverbank to hide away for days until he dare return home again."

"I never knew of that" said William quietly.

"William" his mother seized his hand in hers and looked intently into his eyes.

"When the time shall come, I pray God, for you to have a son, I beg you think of John Aspedaile as a father. Look to his goodness, and take him as your example. Let this chain of brutality that has passed from father to son be broken."

Winter and Spring

Lazonby

In those winter days after Andrew Bowerbank's burial, Ben's grief for the man he called father, was deep. His own father was now a childhood memory, though still a painful one, and his love of Andrew, his father's friend, was beyond measure. Vividly he recalled again those terrible days of his own bereavement, his childish terror and bewilderment, and that experience gave him an innate wisdom in his understanding of John and Dinah's loss.

Dinah, her sorrow for her beloved father she held within her, only shedding bitter tears when she thought herself to be unobserved. Ben watched, and offered comfort where he could. As children, a bond had been forged between them on this day at the Skin House. She had carried a bowl of milk her mother had poured, and set it down for him to drink. from that day forward he had loved her in childish innocence. They took to roaming the woods and riverbank together.

"Look after thy sister," Andrew would tell him. "See she comes to no harm." And Mary too, apprehensive always for her daughter's safety "Look after Dinah, Ben," was always her plea when they went exploring the countryside together.

Dinah had no fear of the water. She would skip merrily along the river path, throwing wide arms as if to embrace the water.

"Don't go so close to the bank, Dinah," Ben would often call to her, but she would simply laugh, and dance a few steps closer to the edge. Then she would run back to him and brush his cheek with a kiss.

"Silly," she would say, "I won't fall in." But now those childhood days were gone. He was eighteen. She was sixteen, and a new love, deep and tender, was awakening.

***

In the south east and south west of England there had been protests against the rapid changes in religion, and also at the enclosures of land. In the first week of October, the young King was at Hampton Court. So too was his uncle, the Duke of Somerset. As night fell, a great crowd gathered outside the Palace. The Duke was alarmed for the safety of his nephew, as Hampton Court was easily defensible. He roused the sleeping King, and together they mounted their horses and galloped away, riding through the darkness to the fortress of Windsor Castle. Much was made of the move - the King's person seized, this time by his other Seymour uncle. The Protector's absolute power was resented by the already disgruntled Council. This was not what King Henry, in his last days, had intended when he appointed a Council of Regency to serve until his son's majority. To his surprise, Somerset found himself lodged in the Tower.

Now John Dudley, Earl of Warwick, fresh from his part in the crushing of the eastern rebels, showed his hand. One of the sixteen strong Council of Regency, no doubt he resented what he regarded as the Protector's usurping of power, even as King Henry lay dying.

Now, he judged the time was ripe to make his subtle move. But he was in no hurry to make an end of his rival.

It was too risky. In the city, where it mattered most, the Duke still retained some popularity, and beyond, because of his genuine concern for the people's welfare. To many, he was still their "Good Duke." So in the early weeks of the new year of 1550, Somerset emerged, unscathed, from prison, but deprived of his Protectorship, and diminished in power.

***

In John Dudley's London house at Ely Place, the old cat was dozing, as he did most of the day, lying in the patches of sunlight that filtered through the window. But as darkness drew on, he became a different creature. A servant entered and brought candles, and by their light, Warwick dealt with the pile of correspondence before him. It was growing late, but at this time of relative quiet, he could work swiftly, with less chance of interruption, and before long the formidable heap began to lessen. He poured himself a goblet of wine, then sat back in his chair to watch Mouser.

Hopeful for prey, the old cat had not moved for the last hour, intent as he was, watching at a tiny aperture in the wainscot where the wooden panelling of the wall met the floor.

He crouched, alert, eyes fixed, and waited. The Earl sipped his wine and regarded the old tabby with amusement. He drained his goblet, and leaned forward to set it down in order to fill it again. In that moment Mouser sprang, his speed making a mockery of his years. His eyes gleamed in the candlelight. They flashed green, then golden, as he moved his head from side to side.

He surveyed the Earl dispassionately, then dropped the still living mouse he had clamped between his jaws. He allowed it a brief taste of freedom, then as it tried desperately to reach the safety of its hole in the wall, he leapt upon it again. The end was quick, and before Warwick had filled his goblet again, Mouser had chewed off his victim's head, and was making short work of the rest of its small body.

"You teach a good lesson, Mouser" the Earl laughed. "Watch, wait, be patient, then 'tch.'" His hand struck his neck in a slicing movement. He replaced his goblet on the table, but it overturned on the littered surface, and the dregs of wine at the bottom splashed out in a red pool on the pale parchments lying there. And so it was, in time, that Warwick's own quarry was caught. He had played for time, and bided his time, until he judged time to be right. Time to play the seeming friend, though false, time even to marry his son to Somerset's daughter, time to set snares, amass information, to prove, or if that was not possible, to fabricate his victim's guilt, time to turn the King's mind against his uncle, to convince him of a treasonous plot in the making.

In October 1551, the trap was sprung, and events moved swiftly. Warwick was raised to the vacant Dukedom of Northumberland, and an unsuspecting Somerset arrested again. He was accused of high treason, and again committed to the Tower, there to be joined by his wife and children. Trial, conviction and execution, it all ended for the "Good Duke" on the early morning of the twenty-second of January, 1552. The crowds that gathered on Tower Hill were for him; he still retained their regard. Even on the scaffold, they hoped for a reprieve. But none came. He died well, with undoubted dignity, true and faithful, he said, to the King's majesty.

Lazonby & Wetheral
1547, 1548 & 1549

In Lazonby, the brothers toil was unremitting. Each day and every day, they laboured from dawn to dusk, and often into the night hours by the glow of rushlights. They missed Andrew sorely, not only for his knowledgeable presence, but also most acutely, for his merry good humour that lightened their daily tasks. He had taught them well, and if sometimes, they had regarded him as an exacting taskmaster, now they came to appreciate the high standard of workmanship he had demanded of them. For if a mistake should be made, it could be a costly matter to put it right, both in time spent, and also in spoiled materials.

Andrew had been justly proud of whatever he was called upon to make, be it a saddle, harness and reins, or perhaps a horse collar for a draught horse. He always worked with infinite care, and his reputation for reliability and excellent workmanship was known in the farmsteads in and beyond Lazonby. So the lads worked with care. Andrew's memory was dear to them, and they resolved that it must not be sullied by any neglect on their part. Steadily and slowly they worked and their hours of toil were therefore long.

There were those who doubted their ability to manage their trade without Andrew to guide them, but as time went by, not one of those who put work their way had occasion to complain, and even the doubters were reluctantly forced to admit to a grudging admiration of their abilities.

In the houseplace, too, Mary's and Dinah's work seemed never-ending, though work was their salvation. If they had had leisure to grieve, it would have been their undoing. So with heavy hearts, they cooked and cleaned, fed the pig and the fowl, and washed the malodorous clothing of John and Ben. In the evening hours, if they had some freedom from their household tasks, they occupied themselves with twisting together linen threads, coated in beeswax, to make the strong cord needed by John to stitch together the leather he fashioned into saddles and horse collars.

At the fireside, mother and daughter worked together in silence, each busy with her own thoughts. Dinah's fingers were deft and swift. She worked steadily, her pile of twisted threads coiling in a heap at her feet..

"Mother" she glanced at Mary, "Surely the pedlar should be here by now?" she asked. "We need more thread. There is very little left now for us to twist."

"He is late this time I know," Mary agreed. "But it has been a hard winter. There is likely to be snow still blocking the tracks across the fells. And the helm was on Crossfell but a few days ago, so the force of the wind would make it dangerous for him to travel till it dropped."

And so it was, then, a week later, the smart clip clop of the pedlar's black-coated fell ponies could be heard approaching the Skin House. Each sturdy beast carried a bulging pack upon its broad back, and followed the bell-horse, the leading pony, in a single train. Jack, the pedlar, walked alongside the bell-horse, one hand holding lightly upon its bridle. He was whistling merrily. Folk were always glad to see him, as much for the news he brought from far afield, as for the much needed goods he carried.

He came in the spring, when winter had passed, and again in the autumn before bad weather in winter made it too dangerous, if not nigh impossible to cross the high fells in safety. Between times he travelled the less hazardous routes, skirting the towns and cities.

"I passed through York again a while ago," he told them as he opened his packs for them to select from his wares.

"The great Duke of Norfolk is clapped in the Tower of London, and like to die a traitor's death', he told them.

"Well, he sent many to their deaths hereabouts," John observed grimly. "'Twill be hard to find any in Cumberland to pity him."

"Aye, 'tis so in York, too," agreed Jack. "Folk there cannot forget t'was the Duke caused Robert Aske to hang there alive in chains one market day. He was one of their own, their great Captain of the Pilgrims, and they remember well that they watched him die slowly, and suffer for days until he moved no more." Jack was silent for a moment, then he loosed the rest of his packs from off his ponies' backs, and displayed his wares. All the while, he related snippets of news he had gathered from wherever his journeyings had taken him.

"The new King is but a lad, but nine years old he is. They say his uncle rules for him, the Lord Protector he's called."

The pack horses champed contentedly at the grass at the wayside. Mary and Dinah gathered up quantities of linen thread and household necessities they would need until Jack came again. John selected some new needles for stitching leather, strong ones, some straight, some curved. "Red ribbons to your fancy, young mistress?" The pedlar's eyes twinkled in his weathered face, as he waved a knot of gay ribbons in Dinah's direction.

"The milk-maids favour them greatly to hang in the dairies. They hold them to be a powerful charm against witches." He laughed. "Nonsense, I call it. But folk believe in strange things, and if they want them, I sell it them. 'Tis my living."

Their purchases made, Jack began to gather up his packs, and swing them over the backs of his waiting ponies, taking care to distribute the weight equally on either side of their broad backs.

"The helm wind blew cruelly down Crossfell a while ago," he said as he began to move the pack train ready to go.

"Aye, we saw the cloud atop the summit," Mary said, "We knew the wind would be fierce."

"I heard tell a shepherd was killed bringing, his flock down from one of the high slopes," Jack said. "The wind rushed down the side of the fell, so furious it was it blew him over the edge, his dog too. So I waited until the wind died down to cross over."

Then, he was ready to go, and with a cheery wave he led the bell-horse out onto the road. The other three ponies followed, nose to tail, in a single line.

"Go safely, Jack," Mary called after him. "We'll see thee again in the autumn, God willing."

***

The summer was fleeting., slow to come and swift to go. The onset of autumn drew on apace, and a fine rain, light but unceasing, gave rise to a grey mist that enveloped the fells, so that the great spread of Crossfell could not be seen for days on end.

Within the Skin House, it was dim. Little light penetrated into the houseplace on sunless days. It was a dreary time, and for Mary and Dinah, the sadness they felt at their loss of Andrew was intensified in the grey gloom. It was time, however, for the annual task of dipping their peeled rushes into melted fat, to create a goodly supply of rushlights to burn in the dark hours of the winter nights to come.

Both worked together steadily, speaking little, but joined in mind, until John and Ben came in, hungry and wet. Then they resumed their task after all were fed, and gathered before the glow of the fire.
John stretched his legs across the hearthstone, carefully avoiding the pot of liquid fat his mother and sister placed between them. Most of the day he had spent sitting, knees bent, stitching together the two tubes of leather to form the main part of a horse collar ordered by John Aspedaile for a draught horse to drag felled timber in that part of his farm that contained woodland.

The leather he had held clamped tightly between his knees, and with one of the new curved needles purchased from the pedlar, he had guided it in and out of the equally spaced holes he had already pricked into the leather with an awl. Now it was bliss to ease his cramped muscles at the warm fireside, and soon he began to doze.

Ben too sat by the smouldering turves, and before long a noxious smell began to rise in the steam from his damp clothing. All day he had laboured at the beam, scraping away hair and flesh from new hides destined for the tanpits.

At length, the one burning rushlight beneath which Mary and Dinah were seated, began to flicker and give warning that its light would soon burn out. It was the signal for all to end the day's labours and seek their rest.

The dying light of the rush taper flared suddenly, and shone upon a glistening tear as it rolled down Dinah's cheek. Only Ben noticed, as she hastily brushed it away. Beneath his lowered eyelids, he had watched her face all night. Though more than a year had passed since Andrew's death he knew that she still grieved deeply for her father. He leapt up, and in an instant, he was cradling her in his arms, her own arms were flung, tightly around him.

She laid her head wearily against his shoulder, and he felt a great sigh stifled against his chest.

Never before had he held her like this, in all their years as sister and brother. Often then they had wandered together hand in hand, their arms around each other in the innocence of childish companionship. But this was different, compelling and urgent. He bent his head and kissed away the wetness from her eyelashes, and stroked her hair.

"Hush, hush," he whispered tenderly against her ear.

"I loved him, too." By some power unknown to him before, but driven by primeval instinct, then he kissed her mouth, and it was not the kiss of a brother for a sister. For them both, time stood still.

They did not see Mary's eyes upon them, knowing and alarmed. Nor could they have told how long they clung to each other so. It might have been but a second, or it could have been an eternity, but when they drew apart, it seemed to Ben that he was bereft of the most precious thing the world contained for him.

For Dinah, in Ben's embrace, she found the blessed comfort she so needed in her sorrow, balm for her sad soul. And something else! It was something she could not name, but it stirred her from the lethargy into which she had sunk since her father's death, and she felt alive again. In that kiss, a strange excitement was born. It fluttered into life, hesitantly at first, then it rose, gathered strength, then possessed her, and she knew she would never be the same again.

The rushlight smouldered briefly. The last spark died away, and John slept on at the fireside.

***

It was a harsh winter, and the cough Sarah Aspedaile developed racked her body in its intensity. She became feverish, her eyes unnaturally bright, and her cheeks flushed by two patches of bright colour in her otherwise pale face. By spring, every bout of coughing tore at her chest. It exhausted her now frail body, and she could get little rest.

This day, however, though the weather was milder and the sun shone brightly, she was too weary to make the effort to rise and dress, so all day she kept her chamber. Janet entered with a bowl of nourishing broth, and moved the pillows at Sarah's back to raise her up in the bed, then encouraged her to swallow the broth she proffered by the spoonful.

"Where is John?" Sarah asked. Janet laid aside the bowl, well pleased that Sarah had taken all of the broth.

"He is in the houseplace, I think," she replied. "I left him nodding at the fireside after he'd eaten."

Another fit of coughing seized Sarah, and when at length it was over, she lay back on the pillows in exhaustion.
"He can get no rest at night, Janet. I disturb him so," she said when she was able to speak, "Well, it will not be for long, I think." She laid her thin hands on top of the bedcovers, and Janet reached forward and grasped them.

"What mean you, Sarah?" she asked, unable to control the note of alarm in her voice. "The weather is getting warmer now, and by summer you will surely be better again." Sarah smiled, knowing that Janet spoke in hope rather than in conviction. She gathered Janet's hand in her own, and her smile was one of resignation.

"No Janet. I fear the summer will not cure me. I spat blood last night." She felt Janet's hand tighten beneath her own, then she loosed it gently, and felt beneath the pillow she rested against. In her hand she held a cloth. It was stained with streaks of darkened blood. She met Janet's shocked eyes, and went on.

"I know the way of it, Janet. It was so with my mother. 'Tis a disease of the lungs, and it gets worse, not better."

She began to cough again, and pressed the cloth to her mouth. When the bout ended, Janet could see that new blood stained the cloth, and that it was bright red. Tenderly, she wiped away a dribble of bloodstained spittle from the corner of Sarah's mouth, and sat in troubled silence at her bedside.

It was sometime before Sarah could speak again, but when she did, it was with resolute determination. Again, she took Janet's hand, and their eyes met.

"Janet," she spoke calmly, for she had thought much of the matter, so urgent it was to her now. "We must make plans, Janet. For John, and young Margaret.... for when I am gone. Will you care for them for me... when that time comes?"

Tears coursed down Janet's face. "You know that I will, Sarah" she choked in reply. "I owe my very life to you and John, and I love Margaret as my own child." There was a pause.

"And John?" Sarah persisted. "He will grieve for me, I know. But when the pain eases, as it must in time, it would content me to know that you and he might find another happiness.....together. Might it be so?" Her eyes met Janet's startled gaze unflinchingly, seeking an answer.

There is not a better man than John Aspedaile in the whole of Cumberland," Janet replied at last. "And I swear to you, Sarah, for all the goodness you both have shown me, that I will care for your John as it may be best for him. I cannot say more, for I do not know his mind. Will that content you?"

Sarah nodded, and lay back upon the pillows. Her eyes wandered past Janet's bent head, and it seemed that a curtain was lifted briefly upon those years she knew she would not see.

"It will, Janet. Oh, it will, and I thank you."

She lingered until the summer, and when the days were bright with sunlight, they set a seat in the doorway of the houseplace, and John lifted her, warmly wrapped, to sit and enjoy the sweet scent of her potherbs that fringed the pathway. Margaret stayed close, helping Janet with the work, and sitting with Sarah to keep her company. Isobel came too, and as often as he could, John would join them, bringing news he had gathered in Penrith on market days.

On such a day, they gathered in the houseplace at evening's gate, lest at sundown Sarah should take a chill in the cooler air, and the fever return. John and William Winter had ridden to market that day, and found the town agog with news.

"The young King has forbidden the celebration of the Mass," John told them. "'Tis against the new laws he has made.
He is making great changes in the way folk are to worship now. Even more than his father did before him."
Four pairs of startled eyes met his own. "Aye," he spoke heavily, "it seems there is a new religion in the land now."
"Religion!" Janet's voice was bitter. "It seems to me religion is twisted by men in power to suit their own ends."

"Janet, it was always so, I fear," Sarah agreed.

William came in, the milking done. He handed a pail of new milk to Janet, and she took it into the dairy.

"Sit down, William," Sarah said. "John has just told us of the news in Penrith."

"And there is another law passed," John continued. It allows the marriage of those who once lived in religion, and were cast out of their Houses. So now, a monk or a friar or a nun, might now wed."

William nodded, and looked at Isobel. "Mother, you call to mind the time we lived at Heremitithwaite, at the Nunnery there?"

"Dear God, how could I forget it? The end was terrible," Isobel replied.

"Sister Galfride - you remember her?" William went on.
"I do. She went to live with her brother when the nuns were turned out. To care for his children, I think. He had an ailing wife. Yes. I remember her well."

"And so do I, mother. Well, when the Friary in Penrith closed too. Sister Galfride's brother offered a place in his household to one of the friars, to educate his young sons, and now Sister Galfride and the friar are wed. The new law allows it."

There was silence in the houseplace for a while.
"My mother was a nun, was she not?" young Margaret's voice broke into their thoughts. "I have heard the village folk call me "the nun's child.""

Janet rose from her stool and took the girl in her arms, holding her close.
"She would have been a nun, child, if the old King had not closed her House. And she was greatly wronged," Janet added. There was a note of sadness in her voice.

Sarah lasted until the summer's end. Then, when the gales of autumn sent the withering leaves of the old pear tree scattering across stormy skies, and the bite of early frost nipped the tips of her potherbs, the spark of her life burned ever lower, until one night it faded as she slept. No-one could with certainty tell the moment of her passing, so gently she slipped into the sleep of eternity. But all were agreed that the transition had caused her no pain, for in the morning sunlight, a smile of contentment played about her face.

It softened the sharpness of its sunken contours, and it seemed she did but sleep peacefully.

1550

Autumn – Wetheral

There was trouble at the Grintons' place. Old man Grinton's tyrannical rule over his family was over. His sons did certainly not regret his death. Rather, they were jubilant. For the first time in their lives they were free of his ill-tempered rule over them, and in their unaccustomed freedom, they ran wild. For Ellen, the absence of her father's controlling influence in her life, simply meant that she exchanged one servitude for another. It was from their father that Bernard and Ralph, her brothers, had learned to become mean-spirited bullies, and she was their drudge.

One market day, William Winter was late when he rode home to Wetheral.
"I like not what is going on at the Grintons' farm, mother," he said to Isobel when he came into the houseplace. "I overtook young Ellen walking alone on the road from Penrith."

"Walking, and alone?" Isobel queried. "Had she not ridden there pillion with one of her brothers?"

"She had," William answered. "And she had sold all of the butter they had taken to market, while he was drinking most of the afternoon."

"They are a bad lot, those Grinton men," Isobel said in disgust. "But the girl, I hear she takes after her mother, a gentle, hardworking soul. Those two brothers work her like an animal. So, tell me, why did her brother not ride her back home?"

William's face tightened. "It was her elder brother, Bernard," he said. "He took up with a woman where he had been drinking, and she it was riding pillion behind him. They left Ellen to follow on foot, but she could not keep up with them, and they rode off and left her."

"The shame of it," Isobel declared. "It would have taken her hours to walk all that way back, and in the dark. Besides, there can be robbers about on market days, and worse. Was she frightened?" she asked.

"She was weeping a little, when I found her," William replied. "So I took her up and rode her back home. 'Tis a cheerless place, though, the Grintons' is. I doubt there is any comfort for her there." He sighed deeply. "And she is a fine young woman, too good for the likes of those two."

He spoke forcefully, and his mother looked sharply at him. Never had he spoken so of a woman before. She said at length choosing her words with care, "I am glad you saw her safe home."

At first, it worked tolerably well. The woman Bernard Grinton brought from Penrith with him had enough wits to appreciate the considerable improvement in her circumstances.

She could not tell her age, but she remembered she had been born to a Romany mother, who quickly taught her to beg and steal. When the encampment moved on, Rosa had dawdled behind with a gipsy lad, and they had lived then as best they could.

Rosa, her mother had so named her, for she said she had been born when the wild roses bloomed by the wayside. The young child matured early into a comely enough wench, dark-haired, and with eyes that could have been entirely black. She learned early how to please, and if a man had the means to keep her for a while, she could be generous with her favours.

So when, in his half-drunken state, Bernard Grinton leered at her over the top of his beaker, she had no difficulty in convincing him of the benefits to be had by their further acquaintance.

To say Rosa did nothing to help in the house would not be quite true, but her housekeeping skills were negligible, and she was slovenly in her habits. Her attempts at cooking were disastrous. The resultant mess she produced drove Ellen to near distraction by her waste of good food, but at least the old, half-starved dog was the better fed.

The greatest contribution Rosa made to the benefit of the household was by her mesmeric hold over Bernard. He was besotted with her, and in his state of euphoria, he quite forgot to mistreat his sister. The only loser in this new ménage was Ralph Grinton. Night by night his envy grew as he watched his brother carousing with Rosa, and though he would join them in their drinking, the surfeit of home-brewed ale consumed only left him the more morose. He felt a rising tide of frustration when Rosa's dark eyes flashed mockingly at him, as Bernard hustled her out of the houseplace and into the big bed where their father had been used to sleep, and their shrieks of laughter sounded down the passageway. Then Ralph would jump up from his stool and seek his own bed, unable to sleep while the sounds of merriment continued far into the night.

As usual, the last to sleep was Ellen. Nightly, she cleared away the mess left by the drinkers. Wearily, she mopped up the slopped ale from the board and the floor, and wondered anxiously what would happen should her supply of home- brewed ale run out, since they were drinking it faster than she could brew it.

One morning, Rosa let it be known that on account of her lack of culinary skills, she might do better in the dairy, and it was with some relief that Ellen felt inclined to agree with her, especially as Rosa claimed to have been a milk-maid at some unspecified point in her career.

"Have you not a red ribbon to hang in the dairy?" she demanded of Ellen, when the first milking of the day came in, and Ellen set her to work.

"'Tis a powerful charm against witches, I tell thee," she announced. "And where is the rowan stick to stir with? It must be rowan, for that too has strong powers."

Ellen laughed. "I do not think there are such things as witches," she replied. "Only lonely old women."

"Then you are a fool, Ellen." Rosa swung round, and surveyed her in amazement. "I am sure that there are. They turn milk sour if they look at it, and they can do worse mischief as well. "I remember my mother once told me she had seen one being drowned because she had caused a man to die after she had cursed him."

Rosa shuddered. "I am afraid of witches" she stated emphatically. When the summer days slipped by, and autumn came, and berries ripened, Rosa picked up a basket and set out across the fell. When she returned, Ellen saw that her basket was filled to the brim with bright orange rowan berries.

"Give me a needle and some thread," she asked Ellen. "I will make necklaces of these berries to wear in the dairy." Then she sat at the fireside, threading diligently, until she held up two strings of bright berries.

"There" she exclaimed with satisfaction. "I shall feel safer now. And I've made one for you, too, Ellen, even though you say you don't believe in witches."

She twined the rope of berries into a double coil around her neck, and twirled around the houseplace, well satisfied with herself. Then, she gave Ellen a disconcerting look.

"I saw an old woman picking blackites away down the fell. Who is she?" she demanded.

"Oh, that was most likely old Marjorie," Ellen replied. "She likes to gather the blackites as soon as they ripen. She says the Devil spits on them after Michaelmas day." Ellen laughed. "What nonsense," she said. But she felt uneasy. This talk of witches would do old Marjorie no good if her brothers came to hear of it.

Rosa's accomplishments in the dairy were, it must be said, superior to her efforts in the houseplace. Unfortunately, they were not maintained. Before long, she began to lie slug-a-bed far into the morning, despite the inviting smell of Ellen's bacon frying at the fireside. Even Bernard could not shift her. When the milking was done, and there was still no sign of her, Bernard's temper was not to be trifled with. He whistled to the dog, and grasped the stick he carried when driving cattle.

"We'll take the herd down to the far pasture today. The one nearest the river," he told his brother tersely. "Then I'm off into Wetheral.
You stay here, and muck out," he ordered Ralph. With that, he drove the cows out onto the track that led down to the Eden, and Ralph had no option but to follow.

It was a fair distance from the farmhouse to the river pasture, and little speech was exchanged between the brothers. They passed the hovel that was shelter to old Marjorie, a tumbledown old place now, since there was none to mend its increasing defects. Bernard jabbed a finger in its direction.

"Rosa thinks that old dame's a witch." He glowered at Ralph. "I think she's very likely right."

It was unfortunate that at that precise moment, Marjorie appeared in the doorway, a basket on her arm, intent upon more blackite picking in the brambles that grew in a patch close by the river. It was even more unfortunate that her young black tomcat chose to follow, anticipating the prospect of searching out mice that might be lurking in the bramble thicket. He was in a frisky mood, and ready to make a dart at anything that moved. He sat for a moment and eyed the ambling herd as it made its leisurely way down to the water meadow.

Maybe the scent of milk reached his sensitive nostrils. Then, for whatever reason, he joined them, dashing between their legs and rushing in and out of the way of their trampling hooves. One cow panicked, and spooked the rest of the herd into a stampede for the water. Not the furious shouts of the Grinton brothers, nor the frantic barking of their dog could stop them until they were wallowing in the river.

Unwilling to get his feet wet, the little cat stopped short of the water, and stood on the bank surveying his handiwork.

Bernard Grinton set the dog on him, and when he was half worried, he picked up the small, savaged body and tossed it into the river.

Old Marjorie was distraught. She came hobbling up as fast as her old legs could carry her.

"Swim her, swim the witch," Bernard yelled to his brother, and together they seized her defenseless body, and flung her headlong into the water. She sank, where the riverbed shelved deeply, then surfaced and floated near to the edge of the bank, only to see her tormentors standing above her. Bernard Grinton pushed her down with his stick, again and again, and did so repeatedly until she ceased to struggle. Then the current caught her, and carried her away from the bank into midstream, and onwards towards Wetheral.

They said nothing of what had taken place that night. Both brothers drank heavily, and there was an unusual air of suppressed elation about them. Ellen watched them warily. She had never seen them so before, and a strange thread of fear ran through her.

Only Ellen rose early next morning. It was Tuesday, market-day in Penrith, and already she had her butter packed into panniers ready to be hoisted over the back of the pack horse. She and Bernard should have been mounted by now and on their way before the market bell began to ring in Penrith to signal the start of business.

But the late night drinkers were laggardly in rising, and when Bernard appeared, he was sullen, his head throbbed, and Ellen had only just finished the morning's milking. He wolfed down some of the bacon she had cooked earlier, the fat from the collops already congealing around them on the platter.

Then he went in search of Ralph, and threw him out of bed. He aimed a non-too-gentle kick at his brother's backside as he sprawled half-awake on the floor.

"Drive the cows to the near pasture, thou lazy slug-a-bed," he barked. "And get mucked-out." He paused. "and get that good-for-nothing Rosa to help thee with the late milking. I'm off to Penrith with the butter." He aimed another encouraging kick at Ralph's hastily retreating rear, and bawled for Ellen to help him adjust the panniers so as to distribute their weight equally over the horse's back. That done, and Ellen mounted, he swung himself up before her and headed with all the speed he could muster for Penrith market.

Ralph could hardly believe his luck. His overbearing brother was out of the way, and would not be back till late. Till then, he would have Rosa to himself, and he intended to take full advantage of the situation. He rubbed his smarting rump where Bernard's boot had made contact, and hastened to pull on his breeches. Then, he tiptoed down the passageway to where, each night his brother and Rosa cavorted in their father's bed, Quietly, he pushed open the door. Rosa still lay there, her black hair spread out about her head in a profusion of tangled curls.

Ralph stood and watched her for a while, unable to wrest his fascinated gaze from the rise and fall of the coverlet that only partially concealed Rosa's considerable charms. Then, he swooped. He tried to pin her arms at her sides, but Rosa was instantly awake, and slipped like a snake out of his grasp. Not for the first time had she found it necessary to repel an unwanted invader from her bed.

Her kick was well aimed, and she was standing at the bedhead looking down at him, laughing mockingly as he lay face downwards upon the bed, spread-eagled in the place where she had been lying.

"I'll tell Bernard," she teased.

Ralph raised himself up, and watched sullenly as she searched about for her scattered clothes. She was not in the least afraid; rather, she was enjoying his embarrassment.

"Thou'lt not do that, vixen," he said thickly. "He's away to Penrith with the butter. Ellen's gone, too, and thou'rt to help me with the dairying, he says."

A flicker of amusement crossed Rosa's face. Ralph's intentions were all too plain, and for her part, she purposed to lead him on to the point of distraction, before allowing him whatever favours she might decide to bestow upon him. She found the garments she had been searching for, and cast a coy look in Ralph's direction.

"Then thou'd better shift thyself from here sir, for I do not dress myself before strange gentlemen" she taunted.

The cattle were bellowing to be let out and driven down to the near pasture before Rosa appeared in the houseplace. Together, she and Ralph finished off the rest of the cold bacon that Ellen had cooked hours before, and it was approaching noon when Ralph whistled to the dog, and drove them down to the pasture nearest to the farmstead.

For the rest of the day, Rosa flitted in and out of the dairy, though her efforts there accomplished little. She kicked over a pail of the morning's milk, and it drenched the bottom of her gown. On hearing her cries of annoyance, Ralph left off carting muck from the cowshed to the midden, to find her in the yard, hitching up her skirts above her ankles, and in the process displaying much of her shapely legs.

"Do not come near me, for you stink," she cried in mock alarm, though her eyes said otherwise, and Ralph withdrew in confusion, seething with frustration.

When the sun was low in the sky, the herd must be driven in from pasture, and the evening milking done. This was the moment Rosa had been anticipating with relish for most of the day. She set her gown to rights, and tucked a new red ribbon into her bodice. Then she flounced into the cowshed to join Ralph at the milking. Many were the bold looks she cast in his direction, her eyes inviting now.

"Bernard will be back from market soon," she taunted him. It was true. The day that earlier had seemed to hold so much promise, was now doomed to end without the realisation of his hopes. It was too much for flesh and hot blood to bear. He could not, would not spend another night watching this tease flaunting her charms for Bernard's sole benefit. She was watching him, and there was an expression in those unfathomable dark eyes he had never seen before. Suddenly, she kicked aside her milking stool, and brushed past him, yet lingering so close, with pouting lips and fluttering lashes.

He seized her and held her fast, pinioning her arms behind her back. She was smiling up at him provocatively, and he felt the warmth of her yielding body as it merged with his own. She knew her ploy would end thus. By long denial, she had brought his desire to fever pitch, and now it would brook no delay.

She did not struggle or protest, as he half expected she might, and he made to lay her down upon a heap of dry bracken in a corner of the byre. She whispered against his ear, "Not here. Inside."

The daylight was fading fast, and the houseplace, with its small window, was grey and dim. They paused only to set the rushlight burning, then with the speed born of urgency, Ralph swung her off her feet and carried her down the passage to his bed.

They did not hear the steady tread of the pack horse returning in the yard, nor did they hear Bernard and Ellen enter the houseplace. It was Ellen who heard the sound of their voices first, and she froze with fear. Bernard had drunk more than usual in Penrith that day, and he was in a sour mood again. Suddenly, he heard them, his brother's voice jubilant, as he had never heard him before, and Rosa's, the unmistakable sound of her laughter telling plainly how she was employed. He gave a roar of pure fury, and kicked open his brother's door. Rosa gave a terrified scream, and rushed into the houseplace. Ralph he dragged from his bed, and shook him like a dog worrying a rat, until his teeth rattled.

Then they fought, along the dim passageway, blow after blow. Ralph's blood was up, and he gave as good as he got. Into the houseplace they struggled, where Rosa cowered in the shadows behind Ellen.

"I'll kill thee, thou worthless slut, when I'm done with him," Bernard growled at her through clenched teeth, his voice low, suffused with rage, and menacing.

They wrestled each other, brother against brother, well matched. They fought in deadly earnest, each striving to throw the other, their breath coming in guttural grunts. At last they loosed, neither able to bring about a fall. But Ralph was winded. Bernard seized him by the shoulder and took careful aim. Ellen screamed a warning, but it was too late.

Bernard's clenched fist smashed into his brother's face. The sight of his spurting blood only served to increase Bernard's mad lust for revenge. He struck relentlessly, again and again, until Ralph's face was a bloody pulp, and a last powerful swing beneath his chin floored him. Ralph fell backwards. There was a dull thud as his head hit the flagstones of the hearth. His body twitched in a convulsive spasm, then he lay still.

In their struggles they overturned the iron sconce that held the rushlight, and the houseplace was plunged into darkness. There was silence, except for Bernard's heavy breathing. When his eyes became accustomed to the gloom of the unlit houseplace, he cast about seeking Rosa.

"Where art thou, thou sly bitch?" he roared. "I'll teach thee to play me false." But Rosa was gone. In the darkness, she ran out to the stable, and Ellen followed.

"Take the horse, and get to Penrith," Ellen urged. "If he catches thee, there's no knowing what he'll do to thee." They loosed the horse and Ellen helped Rosa up onto its back.

"Come with me, Ellen. We could do well enough in Penrith," Rosa said. She held out her hand to help Ellen mount up behind her, but Ellen shook her head.

"No Rosa. My brothers will need me when their tempers have cooled. Now go, before Bernard finds thee." Rosa nodded, then she kicked at the horse's sides and leaning low over its neck, she rode bareback out of the yard and onto the track that would lead her to the road to Penrith. Ellen watched until she disappeared into the darkness, then as she had so often done when her brothers rowed within the house, she laid down on a heap of bracken they used to bed down the cattle, and slept the sleep of exhaustion.

In the houseplace, Bernard heard the clatter of hooves as Rosa made her escape. He rushed towards the door, but slipped on a patch of grease that Rosa had not thought to wipe up after she and Ralph had broken their fast earlier that day. He did not fall, but the crack to his forehead when it hit the board made him reel. He groped for a stool they had upturned in their fight. He righted it, and sank down upon it at the board.

A wave of faintness overcame him, and he slumped forward. Then, with his head cushioned upon his folded arms, weariness, and the drink he had consumed in Penrith, overcame him, and he slipped into sleep.

In the overturned sconce, a feeble spark still smouldered in the rush taper. It cast no light, and would have died away had it not lain so close to the patch of congealed fat that spread over the floor. Its tiny glow was sufficient to melt a droplet of fat where it had fallen. Then, it flared into life and soon became a growing sheet of flame as it followed the greasy trail upon the flagstones. It licked at the legs of the coppy stools that stood about the board, and where the falling sconce had knocked over a box containing Ellen's newly-dipped rushlights, it fed upon the scattered contents with voracity.

Soon, the houseplace was alight, and of the two brothers sleeping there, one would never wake again; the other, roused at last by the inferno that raged around him, he could find no means of escape.

***

William Winter was riding home from Wetheral. He had been delayed there unexpectedly, and so he only left the village on the edge of dark. He quickened his pace in anticipation of the meal his mother would have waiting for him, and his empty belly rumbled mightily, for he had eaten little since breaking his fast that morning. As he neared the farmstead, he noticed a strange light glowing across the fell.

He dismounted in the yard, and watched as plumes of flame leapt skyward, then collapsed upon themselves in showers of blazing sparks. It was the Grintons' farm, it must be. No other dwelling lay in that direction. He felt a sharp stab of fear. Ellen! He threw down the reins and left his horse standing in the stable yard. He rushed to the door of the new house, and hammered upon it urgently. When John Aspedaile appeared in answer to the din, he pleaded, "John, I beg thee come with me to the Grintons' place. The house is on fire." He hardly waited for John to saddle up and mount, before they rode at speed over the fell, their horses stumbling over the rough ground in the darkness, until they reached the track that led to the Grintons' farmhouse.

The heat from the blazing building met them in a scorching wave as they drew near. Their horses whinnied in fear and shied away, as they slid from their backs. There was no sign of life, only the bellowing of agitated beasts in the outbuildings could be heard above the roar of the flames.

"They must all be inside," William screamed, and rushed towards the door that was already a blazing mass of crackling wood.

"No." John pulled him back. "Do not go in. 'Tis too late. See, the roof is gone. No-one can be alive in there."

William fell to his knees on the cobblestones, and covered his face with his hands. "Ellen, Ellen," he moaned.

"Nay, see, she's there, surely." John pointed, and a woman's figure, dark against the bright light from the blazing fire, came running towards them.

"My brothers," she screamed. "I thought you were my brothers standing there. Where are they?"

"There was no-one here when we got here," John told her gently. "We came too late to get inside."

William caught her by the hands as she rushed towards what had once been the door, but was now a gaping hole through which a billowing wall of flame rose and fell inside.

"No," he said quietly. "'Tis not possible to get inside. See, the roof is gone."

They held her between them, and tried to comfort her. She sobbed uncontrollably, weeping as though her heart would break. She shuddered, and William encircled her with his arms. It seemed such a natural thing to do, though he had never held a girl so before. And Ellen, just as naturally, rested her head upon his shoulder, and her sobs began to quieten.

"They had been fighting," she said at last. "It was over Rosa. I thought they would kill each other, and I was so afraid. Rosa got away, so I ran to the byre, and slept there. Then the cows woke me with their bawling."

There was a crash, as a wall of the house collapsed. The wind was rising, and the flames roared with greater intensity.

"Come away, Ellen," and John drew her back from the scorching heat. "You cannot stay here, and there is nothing we can do tonight. But we will come back in the morning." He looked at William, and asked, "Isobel, will she care for her, think you?"
"We will both care for her," William replied, as he stroked Ellen's hair.

"Come Ellen," he said. "Come with us."

They rounded up the horses, and John helped Ellen up pillion behind William.

They rode away, and eventually the fire passed its peak, and subsided into a smouldering heap. When morning broke, the blackened timbers of the burnt-out house were beginning to whiten under a powdering of soft ash.

1551

Spring – Wetheral

Margaret Aspedaile sat upon the swing her father had fashioned for her beneath the stout branches of the old pear tree. It was her favourite place, and she came to it often, especially when she wanted to think. This morning, she had walked in the bright spring sunshine with her father and Janet to the church in Wetheral village, where the two people she loved most had been wed. In the house, there were wellwishers aplenty, for both were held in high regard. John held open house for his neighbours, it being a bidden wedding, and many there were who came to do him honour.

Margaret pushed at the ground with one foot to set the swing in motion. She looked up into the tree's branches. It was spring again, and the pear blossom clung in snow white clusters along its branches so thickly she could hardly see the sky. She was thirteen now, going on fourteen at the end of the present year, and already she was emerging from childhood into early womanhood, the promise of her mother's beauty evident to see.

For some reason unknown to her, this place beneath the pear tree held some special affinity for her.

Always, it had drawn her towards it, and now she felt the need to slip away from the noise of the happy wedding celebrations in the house, and reflect on the events of recent months.

With Sarah's death came her first acquaintance with real sorrow. Mother she had called her since babyhood, as she had called John father. And yet, there was another she loved dearly, one she did not call mother, yet with whom she felt a deeper bond. Janet, it was Janet who soothed away her childish hurts, and chased away her fears, and comforted her imagined sorrows.

In the dark days after Sarah died, each mourned her in their own particular way. John would sit silently each evening when he took his ease, wordless in his grief. Then Margaret would nestle close to him, not knowing, as yet, being still a child, what words of comfort to say. And Janet, living out her promise of care, was an unfailing source of quiet strength to both when they were gripped by inevitable sorrow.

Then, as Sarah had predicted, a time came when the sharpness of that sorrow eased, More than a year was passed since her death, and those who were left grew ever closer to each other, bound in interdependence and appreciation, each with the other. When Christmastime came round for the second time, and they celebrated Margaret's thirteenth birthday, John kissed his daughter upon the brow and asked, "My child, I know that you loved your mother Sarah, and I know that you love Janet, too.

Would it please you to have her now, for your mother? If we were to wed, I mean?"

"Oh, father, it would. It would make me so very happy, if it would make you happy, too," she cried.

And so, this joyful morning, the deed was done, and the newly wedded pair walked home from Wetheral under a sunlit sky of cloudless blue. Each radiated an aura of quiet contentment, each aware of, and appreciating the worth of the other. On this happy day of new beginnings, each knew and accepted that the other would, indeed must, remember with some inescapable sadness, the ones they had loved and lost in former years.

From her seat on the swing, Margaret could see some of her father's guests leaving to make their way home before nightfall. Already, the sun was beginning to sink lower in the sky, and there was a hint of sharpness in the air, for despite the unusual warmth of the day, it was still early spring. She slid down from her seat on the swing, and was about to run back to the house when she noticed William Winter and Ellen Grinton walking slowly back to the old farmhouse. William's arm was around Ellen's waist, and her head rested on his shoulder. Margaret waited until they had passed. They were so close, yet they did not see her, each having eyes only for each other.

"Ah" Margaret said to herself, "Perhaps we shall have another wedding soon," and she began to walk back to the house.

Then, she stopped, and stood quite still. Another couple wandered into view. It was Dinah Bowerbank and her brother Ben, about to ride home to Lazonby. There was a slight curve in the path that led to the house, and when it seemed to them that they could not be seen from there, Ben halted the fell pony they had ridden on to Wetheral that morning, and drew Dinah into his arms.

Margaret stepped quietly back, and upon a sudden instinct withdrew into the shadow of the pear tree's trunk. Ben and Dinah came closer, his head resting above hers. He stopped, and pulled her round to face him, and bent to kiss her mouth.

"Ben, we must not. T'would not be right. We are brother and sister", Dinah whispered. They were so close. Margaret could see the look of sadness on Dinah's face, and that very gently, she placed her hands on Ben's chest, and made to push him away.

"Nay, Dinah. We are not brother and sister, not by blood." he said. Surely 'tis not a sin to love as we do." He pulled her close again, and kissed her lips, a long, lingering kiss from which neither could, nor wished to break free. Their senses began to swim, and time was suspended, the spell only broken by the merry sounds of the departing guests shouting their jovial goodnights to John and the new Mistress Aspedaile. Dinah was the first to pull away.

"We must get back, Ben. 'Twill be dark before we reach Lazonby," she said.

Reluctantly, Ben loosed her, and Margaret waited until they were mounted and out of sight before she emerged from behind the pear tree. Then, she smoothed out the creases from her gown, and ran swiftly back to the house.

In the houseplace, Janet was clearing away the remainder of the food and drink from the trestle tables set up to accommodate the bridal feast. Isobel Winter was helping her, and Mistress Mary Bowerbank was seated before the fire waiting for her son John to ride her the miles home to Lazonby. He too had come on horseback that morning, his mother riding pillion behind him. Now, he was laughing, in animated conversation with John Aspedaile, whose eyes were twinkling with amusement.

"I mind the time, John Bowerbank," he quipped, "When you were but a lad. Thy father left thee in charge of his cart in Penrith one market day, and the bull got loose" he laughed merrily at the recollection. It would have trampled thee, for sure, if I had not shifted thee behind the cart."

"I mind it, too", John replied with a rueful smile. "I think I owed I my life to thee that day, sir."

"Ah, Margaret." John Aspedaile turned as he spied his daughter enter the houseplace. "Where have you been?" He did not wait for her reply, but resumed his conversation with John Bowerbank.

"John," he said, "This is my daughter, Margaret."

At that moment, Margaret felt that something turned over inside her. Was it her heart, she wondered? A pair of dark brown eyes swept over her, causing a fluttering to occur in that region.

"I bid thee good-day, Mistress", John smiled down at her.
So tall he seemed.
"We have met before, I think. But you were but a very young maid then" he said. "I doubt you would remember." He gave a little bow, and in return, she dropped a curtsey. Was there a note of amusement in his voice, she wondered? Did he tease? He was so handsome, she thought, and older than she was. But he had just addressed her as Mistress, as though he regarded her as a woman grown. No-one had ever addressed her so. It seemed to her that the young saddler from Lazonby had just invested her with a new dignity, and she felt a strange thrill such as she had not known before. As she rose from her curtsey, she looked up earnestly into his face, and smiled.

"But indeed, I do remember, though it was a long time ago. I recall that you came with your father to bring a saddle he had made for one of our horses. Yes, I remember it well."

"You are right, Mistress. It was so. Your memory does you credit" John replied. And being so addressed again, Margaret's face flushed with pleasure.

It was near sunset when John Aspedaile assisted Mistress Bowerbank to mount up behind her son. Janet and Margaret waved their goodbyes, and holding the horse's bridle, John walked down the herb-fringed pathway, past the old pear tree, and set them on their road to Lazonby.

"I like that young fellow", he confided to Janet that evening. "He has learned well from his father, and now he is a skilled craftsman himself. It was a heavy burden he took on when Andrew died, and many a one doubted he would manage."

When nightfall came, Margaret slept alone in her chamber for the first time. Always, even before a time she could remember, Janet had slept close by. But tonight, and henceforward, Janet would join her father in his chamber, as was the custom of married folk. Tonight, they had gathered her close between them, and kissed and blessed her before she retired to the chamber she had occupied all her life. In Janet's loving embrace, she had clung close and whispered "Mother, dear Mother" against her ear.

She was tired, the day had been long, but sleep did not come easily, try as she might to shut out all the many happenings of the day. The image of one face, that of the dark-eyed, handsome young saddler from Lazonby repeatedly insinuated itself into her visions of half-sleep, and when at last the deep slumber of the young overtook her, even then, that same face predominated in her dreams. This night, it seemed, the world was changed. She was changed, of that she was certain, and this night she knew she would remember it always.

Winter – Ireland

In Ireland, the Baron of Upper Ossory lay still in his great bed, sick, it was feared unto death. His oldest son, Barnaby, born of the Baron's first marriage, eased his cramped limbs in the heat of the glowing peat fire. He was careful not to disturb the old wolfhound that lay dozing on the warm stones there. Jess sensed that all was not well, her master lying so still in the bed. She disliked the traffic of those of the household she knew, and most particularly of those she did not, who invaded the territory of her master's chamber. She raised up defensibly as Barnaby shifted his legs, and glared at him menacingly, then emitted a low, warning growl. Barnaby smiled. He held out his hand to the old bitch, and she sniffed at it in puzzlement, before giving it a cautious lick.

"Ah, so you do remember me, then? Remember how we used to sport together, when we were both young pups?" The old hound lay down again, and watched, then allowed herself to be scratched beneath one ear. Something stirred faintly, but persistently, in her brain; a dim memory of a small boy who had smelled like this stranger.
This her keen nose could detect, even through the rain-soaked leather of his breeches, heavily impregnated as they were with the conflicting odours of the several horses he had ridden

by the brown heather-covered boglands since landing at the coast. She slipped into a shallow sleep, still wary of the stranger with the confusing smell. The years receded, and she dreamed that she rolled in the dust of the stable-yard with a boy whose smell was the same as that of the man who shared her place in the chimney nook.

Barnaby too slipped into a state of half-sleep, though his was fitful and troubled. It was December, and his friend, King Edward, was expecting him at Court in time for the Christmas festivities. He himself had been in France for a whole year in the service of King Henri II, when a messenger hastened from Ireland with the news that his father was dying, and summoned him home. He was the Baron's eldest son, and he required him to attend to his affairs. It was imperative that he obeyed.

Edward would understand his situation, because of the generous nature that he possessed. King though he was, he would recognise where his friend's duty lay. So Barnaby left France with all speed, and embarked on a vessel that rolled and dipped alarmingly in the tumultuous waves of a winter storm. For most of the voyage he had lain prostrate below deck, so sick that he could almost have wished for shipwreck, just to stay that awful motion.

A hand touched his shoulder.

It was Fergal, his father's serving man; the same man who had many times defended Barnaby from his father's wrath, in consequence of some boyish misdemeanour.

"Your father's awake now, sir. He's asking after yourself." Fergal's voice roused him to full consciousness. He rose wearily, his legs unsteady and stiffened by long hours in the saddle, riding through the driving rain.

Oh, how it could rain in his native Ireland, he had almost forgotten how persistent it could be, used as he was to the pleasant climes of southern England, and France.

Jess padded after him, and lay down at his side as he knelt to receive his father's blessing. Fergal brought in another light; the grey dusk of evening was deepening fast. It did little to dispel the gloom of the sick man's chamber. Rather, it served to accentuate the drastic change wrought in his father's face since Barnaby had last been home. But the eyes flashed in joyful recognition of his son, and the Baron strove to reach out across the expanse of bedcovers to lay his hand upon the bent head.

"Help me, Fergal," he whispered, and tenderly Fergal lifted the outstretched hand and laid it upon Barnaby's head.

"Receive thy father's blessing." Fergal's voice shook, and he dashed away a tear. He took the cold hand in his own and laid it back in the warmth of the bed.

"I should have come home sooner, Fergal," Barnaby choked. "Before this...." He pointed to the still figure in the bed, and wept.

"Nay, sir." Fergal laid a comforting arm upon his shoulder. "Nay, your father was content that you were making your way at Court. Proud, he was, that you served two Kings."

"Stay by me, Fergal, while I watch by him," Barnaby urged, and together, with the old dog between them at their feet, they sat long into the night hours while the Baron, content that his son was close by, slept deep and long. A cold moon rose high in the sky, then near midnight, he woke, refreshed, miraculously so.

"Lift me up," he ordered, and between them, Barnaby and Fergal raised the wasted form high in the bed, and supported him at his back and sides with pillows that were stuffed with the feathers of unknown generations of geese.

A smile of contentment played upon the thin lips, and the voice, when he spoke, was low but steady.

"You are here, my son, thanks be to God."

Barnaby's hand sought that of his father, and he clasped it in his own.

"I should have come sooner, father. And I would, had news of your illness reached me in France. I was on campaign with King Henri's army. Forgive me that have been so tardy."

"Nay, Barnaby, 'tis no matter. You are here now, and I can die happy. Be easy now, it must be so. Death comes to all men in time, and this I think, is my time." He paused to gather strength, all the while his eyes devouring the contours of his firstborn's face, grown now to manhood in those years of which he had seldom returned to his family. He held Barnaby's hand in the firm grip his son remembered well.

"I charge you, my son, that after I am gone, you look well to my wishes. You know the ways of the world better than myself. See that all is done in fairness. See no soul is cheated of his portion." He was silent for a while, for length of words wearied him. His eyes shifted to where Fergal huddled at his bedside.
Servant? Yes, but so much more. He had been his confidante and loyal stalwart since the years of their youth.

"And especially Fergal," he resumed at last. Look to it, son, that he wants for nothing in time to come."

"Father, it shall be so. I give you my solemn word." They clasped hands, as good men do when they think to part. The Baron lay back upon his pillows, and a sense of relief flooded his mind. Barnaby would see to all, he was sure, now.

Yes, he had been right to send the lad away, to be one of "the King's children", though it had torn at his heartstrings then. To study, to be tutored in all the courtly accomplishments, to play, it was his son Barnaby, the poorest of all those noble boys, who had become one of the young prince's most favoured companions, and now he was the friend of the King.

He began to fidget with the bedcovers, until his fingers touched the rough hair of the wolfskin that was laid over his knees for warmth.
"Ah, Barnaby," he smiled "Jess remembered you then, or she would not have let you so close." At the sound of her name, Jess thumped her tail upon the wooden boards where she lay at the bedside, and rested her chin over Barnaby's boots.

"I mind the time", the Baron's voice was low now, with exhaustion, but clear, and filled with a happy contentment as his mind strayed back across many years. "Aye, I remember it well, when we hunted the wolf together that day. 'Twas Jess pulled him down, great creature that he was, and held him by the throat until the huntsmen caught up and despatched him." The Baron's hand patted the wolfskin, on the bed, and smiled again.

"Oh, Barnaby, I mind the time, too when you sneaked down to the kennels to frisk with the half-grown pups. You had on your fine, new clothes to receive our guests, and Fergal found you rolling in the dirt. The pups were yelping, and tearing your finery to shreds." The smile never left his face as he slipped into sleep.

In the small hours, one hand dropped at the bedside, and old Jess rose to sniff it. Instinctively, the hand stroked gently beneath her muzzle, then it fell still. In the darkness, Jess licked at the hand until she felt it grow cold beneath her tongue. Then, slowly she padded to the narrow window of the chamber, and bayed sorrowfully to the breaking dawn.

When Fergal stirred from his pallet bed in the Baron's chamber, he stumbled over the stiffening body of the old wolfhound. She lay, as if in sleep, beneath the outstretched hand of her beloved master. The Baron's hand was stone-cold, but though faint, Fergal could still feel the throb of life that pulsed beneath his own fingers.

Barnaby slept, slumped in the chair in which he kept watch at his father's bedside. Fergal roused him, and he started into wakefulness.

"Oh, Fergal, I have slept", he exclaimed ruefully. "I am ashamed. It was my duty to watch while you took your rest. My father? How does he?"

In the bed, the Baron lay motionless. His eyes stared uncomprehendingly at the two, both dear to his heart, who tended him. He did not die, as was expected, but lived on, trapped in that indeterminate state that is a life without life, a life that even death disdains to claim.

Greenwich - Christmas

Preparations for the Twelve days of Christmas at Greenwich went on apace. The Lady Mary remembered with sadness the Christmas of 1550, when she and the Lady Elizabeth had joined their brother there. This year, she would not go to Court. She distrusted John Dudley greatly, and she feared that her presence at Court would give the Council the opportunity to coerce her in the matter of the celebration of her Mass. How long, she wondered wearily, could she hold out against them in not conforming to the new laws? Dear though Edward was to her, and she to him, their conflicting religions were driving them apart.

This morning, her head ached cruelly, so did her teeth. There had been a hard frost overnight, and her hands were icy cold. She laid them against her throbbing brow in a vain endeavour to ease the pain.

"If she were my daughter, I would strike her head against the wall until it was as soft as a boiled apple." Never would she forget those words, nor the insults the Duke of Norfolk and the hectoring bullies her father had sent to force her into submission to his demands those years ago. So her head felt now, as if it had indeed been banged against a wall.

At this time of the declining year, in the grey drabness of its fading weeks, this was when a same greyness seemed to enter her very being.

Now, in these days of her soul's darkness, she must wrestle again with her tortured conscience, as she had done in that dreadful year of 1536. Then, in that final act of submission to her father's will, when her frail body and agonised mind were at their lowest ebb, she had yielded at last to her father's demands, and signed her name to that damning document. It was to her an act of betrayal, of her faith, and to her recently dead mother.

In signing, she acknowledged King Henry, and not the Pope, as Head of the Church in England, and denied the validity of her parents' marriage. Thus, she bastardised her own self. Guilt and sorrow pervaded her life thereafter in no small measure, and her fragile health suffered as a result.

Now her brother Edward's England was a Protestant country, and the celebration of the holy Mass forbidden, yet because of the affection in which the young King held her, she had continued its celebration privately in her own household with impunity. But under Dudley's increasing influence, Edward was now demanding that his sister obey the laws of the land, and when they had met, harsh words were spoken, and both brother and sister shed bitter tears together.

How many times the Lady Mary asked herself the same question?

Had she been foolish in not seizing the chance to escape from England and this continued persecution when those ships sent by her cousin, the Emperor Charles, had lain off the Essex coast, waiting for her to come? She might have fled, first to the Netherlands, and then perhaps to her mother's homeland of Catholic Spain, where she would have had the freedom to practice the religion she held so dear. But no, she was an English woman born, and so she stayed. She would hold on, both to her faith and to her country. But she would not go to court this Christmastide.

How Edward cherished those rare times of privacy. Such times were rare indeed when he could be truly alone. But then, it was a pleasure to retire to his place of private study, and as now, at the end of January 1552, to seal himself off from the importunities that Kingship entailed, and write to his friend Barnaby. Yes, Barnaby was a friend, a dear one, and he missed his company sorely. At fourteen, Edward had not needed yet to learn that a king can have no friends. Even so, like his father, he rarely showed his mind to others, and was finding it politic to keep his own counsel.

Christmas and the Twelfth Night festivities were, he told Barnaby, passed merrily. He brushed the end of his quill against his cheek as he reflected upon some of the irreverent aspersions the Lord of Misrule had cast upon Catholic doctrine then. How Mary would have been offended. It was as well that she had kept Christmas quietly in her own way, away from Court.

In her own way! Ah, that was the nub of the matter, for no doubt she would have been celebrating the Mass, along with her household, knowing that it was against the law now to do so. Edward's eyes hardened. Love her as he did, she must be brought to conform to the law. Could Elizabeth help, he wondered, speaking sister to sister? Unlikely. Like himself, Elizabeth was as entrenched in her Protestantism as Mary was in Catholicism. Besides, Mary hated Elizabeth's mother, blaming Anne Boleyn, as she did, for the start of all her troubles.

What would his father have done, he wondered? He laid down his quill and pushed his letter to Barnaby away. Many heads had rolled in his father's long reign, including those belonging to two of his wives. So close a relationship, yet not one of blood. Of blood! He leaned forward and cupped his head between his hands.

"This is why I need to be alone." He closed his eyes, as though to blot out the memory of events too painful to face.

"Uncle Somerset, and Uncle Tom Seymour, too. My own mother's brothers! What has been done in my name?" He groaned, and pressed his clenched fingers against his eyes.

The sky was darkening before he resumed writing his letter to Barnaby. A servant came in to bring lights, and his reverie was broken. A deep sigh escaped him.

This is a burden a king must bear, he reflected. A burden not to be shared even with so close a friend as Barnaby. He took up his quill again and finished the letter.

"God have you in His keeping," he ended, and signed "Edward R."

1552

Spring, Summer and Autumn, London, and the Summer Progress

It was springtime of the following year, and the young Lady Elizabeth came to visit. She rode in state with her ladies through the city of London, and a fine show she made of it. In their private time together, Edward showed her his plans for the refurbishment of the old palace of Bridewell, St. Thomas's too, and Greyfriars, now in much need of repair. So moved had he been, Edward told his sister, by a sermon preached before him by Bishop Ridley in February, on the ills endured by the poor, that he had decided to gift these three buildings to serve, in time, as hospitals and orphanages for the relief of the many sick and needy of the city.

"There should be schools too, for the education of poor, deserving scholars, and they shall bear my name", he told Elizabeth, with quiet determination. "I shall call it my 'Device for the poor.'

They walked together companionably, in the fitful sunshine of newly sprung April. The sun's rays had little strength, and the Lady Elizabeth shivered as a passing cloud blotted out their little warmth.
"You are cold, sister?" Edward's voice denoted surprise. "I feel a great heat spreading through my body - I am on fire!"

"Is it the sweat?" he asked, when his doctors were summoned.

They conferred hastily, and examined the rash of spots they observed on the King's body.

"No, Sire. Not that, thanks be to God", they assured him. "You have a high fever, and an attack of the measles. Smallpox, perhaps."

"Ah, measles, a childish complaint!" Edward smiled in relief. "Then I shall soon be well again.'

It was so. By the month's end, he was writing to Barnaby that he had been "a little troubled with the smallpox, but now we have shaken that quite away."

***

In the gardens at Greenwich, the King strolled in the sweetness of the warm May days. He regained his strength, and Mary came to visit him, and neither raised the thorny subject of her Mass. He was still at Greenwich in June when he received news that terrified him. John Cheke, his dearly loved tutor, lay sick with the dreaded sweat. So severe was the attack that all hope for his life was abandoned, yet daily, the young King prayed fervently for his tutor's recovery.

"No, he will not die this time," Edward assured the doleful physicians. "I have begged for his life in my prayers." God heard, and Cheke recovered, against all the odds, and returned to his beloved Cambridge to regain his health.

Edward's own recovery was such that by July, he set out with a vast entourage upon a progress throughout the south of England. His spirits rose.

Freed from his studies, the tedium of Council meetings and the importunities of foreign ambassadors, he relished the acclaim of the simple country folk who left their toil and gathered to cheer him as his colourful train clattered by. He felt liberated too, by the absence of the Duke of Northumberland's restraining presence. My lord Duke wisely decided not to accompany his young sovereign, and thus perhaps expose himself to the resentment he knew was felt for him by the common people. They had not forgotten the death of their "Good Duke" and suspected Northumberland's hand in the affair.

The glittering cavalcade wended its way from one great house to another throughout the southern counties of Sussex, Hampshire and Wiltshire. Edward hunted, and dined sumptuously upon the richest fare his hosts vied with each other to lay before him. He breathed deeply of the sweet airs of high summer, and doffed his cap to acknowledge the greetings of those who laboured at their haymaking. Ah, this indeed was what it was to be royal. A surge of strangely paternal affection engulfed him, strange, that is, in one so young. These people, his people, the common people of England - they lacked any surfeit of this world's goods, but had without reserve taken him to their generous hearts.

That night, after the feasting and the merrymaking ended, he prayed an impassioned prayer to the God of his reformed faith, for His guidance and wisdom in the government of these people, as he reached his majority.

"Teach me, Lord, I pray thee, to be a good King, and to rule for the betterment of all my people."

All August, the pace continued, and if Edward, not long recovered from his illness in the spring, was feeling any strain, he did not admit it. On they went, to Portsmouth, Southampton and Beaulieu where, because of concern that he was exhausting himself, he was persuaded to take some rest. The Earl of Pembroke received him at Wilton. There, more hunting parties were arranged for his stay, and his host entertained him with truly magnificent splendour.

***

One bright evening at sundown, two men sat taking their ease at the village hostelry, and slaked their parched throats with copious draughts of ale.

"You saw him, then, Walter, the young King?" one asked of the other. Walter, a labourer on the Earl's estate, had more opportunity than most to catch a glimpse of the King.

"Aye, that I did", Walter responded. He took a long slurp of his ale, but remained silent.

"Well?" The prompt had little effect upon Walter, whose attention was fixed upon the crowd of ragged, but seemingly happy, healthy children playing nearby. In the sunburned face of his companion, a questioning pair of blue eyes shone intently, requiring an answer. Walter leaned close, so that only the blue- eyed one should hear. He remembered well when he himself was a lad, that loose talk concerning royalty could be dangerous.

"I was carting logs from the woodstore to the big house," he began at length, "when I saw him. He was walking with one of his gentlemen in the sunshine."

"Did you see him close?" the owner of the blue eyes queried.

"I did," Walter replied. "He saw me unloading the logs, and I was amazed - he came over to where I was working, and spoke to me."

"Blue Eyes" was agog. He took a gulp of his ale, and spluttered.

"Tis heavy work you do here. Have you not a younger man to help you?" the King asked.

"I bowed to him," Walter said, and told him that the Earl had agreed to take on my eldest son before the winter."

"Ah, you have children. How many?" the King wanted to know.

"I have twelve, Sire, seven sons and five daughters."

"Then," Walter continued, "the King nodded to his gentleman, who reached in his pouch and gave me a coin. More than I can earn in many a while!"

"For your children", the King said to me. "God keep you."
Then, he walked away.
"Blue Eyes" digested the information to which he had just been made privy. It was the stuff of dreams to him that a king should talk with a labouring man. Why then, he wondered, did Walter seem so low? If he had been in Walter's shoes, half the county would have known about it by now. Something was amiss.
"Why so glum, friend," he asked gently. It was clear that something troubled Walter. The sun was fast slipping down westward in a sphere of red gold. It suffused the sky in its lingering magnificence of bright colour.

Those mothers whose children had not obeyed their instructions to return home by sunset, appeared with forceful determination to round up their tardy offspring. Walter watched with amusement as two of his own, his youngest, were being marched rapidly home, one on each side of his irate wife. He felt more than a small twinge of guilt that he had just drunk down what he had earned that day, and worse, the ale he had supped that evening had in no way alleviated the strange feeling of heaviness that descended upon him after his meeting with the young King.

He set down his empty beaker on the rough board that served as a table, and made to go. "Blue Eyes" still stared up at him, locking his gaze questioningly upon his own. Walter stooped, and leaned close towards him.

"I tell thee", Walter spoke quietly, and looked about him to see if anyone was near enough to overhear. "I could wish that the old King had been lusty enough to breed a goodly brood of strong sons to follow him."

"Lusty, Lusty!" "Blue Eyes" almost choked on the last of his ale. "King Harry had six wives, man! Is not that lusty?"

"Hush now", Walter quieted him. "Say no more. But it seems to me that this worthy lad is as a slender twig to the mighty oak that was his father."

***

Summer was passing, and in the shortening days of September, the progress reached Windsor by the middle of the month. It had been on the move for some two months, and when Northumberland joined the Court on the last leg of its journey, he observed in the following days something that troubled him greatly. The King was changed. From the health and vigour of his earlier years, it alarmed the Duke to see him declining into a frail shadow of his former self. He tired easily, and was finding it hard to resume his former duties.

The courteous youth who used to sit patiently observing and making his own notes on the involved wrangling at Council meetings, would at times fly into a temper.

It was at this time that Edward wrote again to Barnaby, suggesting that he might ask leave of the French King to return to Court. Barnaby, however, was reluctant to leave his newly commissioned post in the French army, so with his King's agreement, his return to England was postponed until December, for then the winter weather would necessitate a respite in military activities.

In November, the second Prayer Book was published; no-one was happy with the first. Even then, it was not before an unholy row was resolved between the bickering clergy as to whether or not a communicant should kneel to receive the sacrament.

Opinions differed, and the underlying controversy caused Edward much pain; his care, and that of Archbishop Cranmer for the compilation of the reformed liturgy, was a thing so dear to his heart.

1553

Winter - London

Greenwich & Westminster, and the last summer at Greenwich

It was a keen disappointment to Edward that his friend Barnaby would not be at court for the Christmas celebrations, as he had so eagerly anticipated.

Once more, George Ferrers was Lord of Misrule for the festivities that would last until Twelfth Night, and Ferrers' ambitious schemes knew no bounds. His inventive mind produced plan after yet more costly plan, in which a veritable small army of actors would be required to perform.

The expense of just clothing this army in the sumptuously rich materials that Ferrers demanded, escalated alarmingly. But Edward noted with pleasure that Will Somers, his father's old fool, retired now for many a year with rooms provided for him at both Greenwich and Hampton Court, would be present. No fool, though, was Will. His father had recognised and appreciated that sharp intellect of his, and the deep wisdom concealed beneath his foolery. It was that same wisdom that, on no few occasions, served to solace the sorrow of the King.

And so passed many a merry day until Twelfth Night ended the celebrations, with revelry, masques and feasting, and the laughter occasioned by the crude bawdiness of the jesters that had always cheered the midwinter merrymaking.

Then Edward left Greenwich and returned to the palace of Westminster.

In the winter weather, he took a chill, and it settled upon his lungs. All February he kept his chamber, fevered, and striving to summon the strength to cough up the objectionable matter produced there. And thus began the inexorable progress of decay that long before the winter frosts returned, would rob England of its royal boy of such undoubted worth. He rallied though, but was weakened, yet by sheer willpower, he forced himself to attend Council meetings, and even to open Parliament.

He walked a little in the palace gardens, when the air of early spring was sufficiently mild, and when April came, he left London by barge for Greenwich. As ever, his dear Cheke stayed close, their two fine minds engaged, as in happier times, in study and discussion. In those days, as the weather grew warmer, there was a brief, blessed respite in the King's condition. He strolled in the gardens at Greenwich, enjoying the gentle warmth of the sun. An early dragonfly darted by, and landed on a nearby bush. It spread its wings at rest.

They were translucent, barely visible, if it had not been for the brilliant flashes of gold as the sun struck the fine filigree that outlined them. Edward bent to examine the creature more fully. It lifted its wings then, and they seemed to disappear, its body barely distinguishable from a living twig, touched with green. He looked at it intently, fascinated by the huge eyes that bulged on each side of its tapering body.

"Did you know Sire," asked Cheke, "that the country folk call it the Devil's darning needle?"

Edward cocked an enquiring eye up at his old tutor. "I did not," he laughed. "Why so?"

"Because of its shape," Cheke told him. "They think that it might sew up the eyes, ears and mouth of a sleeping child."

Edward straightened up, and the abrupt movement disturbed the dragonfly. It flew away, the sunlight striking glints of gold from its diaphanous wings.

"Oh, these superstitions, Cheke! How they cloud the minds of our people," Edward exclaimed. "Education! How great is the need." They walked on, followed at a respectful distance by Sir Henry Sidney and Sir Thomas Wroth, both his Gentlemen of the Bedchamber, and Christopher Salmon, whose services in the sickroom were proving unenviable.

Without warning, Edward was seized with a violent fit of coughing, and he spat into the cloth proffered by the watchful Salmon. The foul matter expelled from his diseased lungs was streaked with stagnant blood. The bout exhausted him, and he leaned heavily on the shoulders of his Gentlemen, who half carried him back to the palace. Thereafter, he walked in the gardens no more.

***

Rumours of the gravity of the King's sickness, even of his death, circulated amongst the Londoners, only to be vehemently denied by the authorities. As the pendulum of Edward's life swung relentlessly from relapse to rally, it was evident to those close to him that he was losing his hard-fought battle to stay alive, and continue his God-given work. Even as he wasted away, he forced himself to finalise those charitable projects dear to his heart - the grammar schools that were to bear his name, and the newly named Christ's Hospital for the relief of orphans, created from the refurbished old palace of Bridewell.

In the sweet May days of birdsong and blossom-hung fruit trees, then it was that an overpowering sadness gripped the dying boy. He knew that he could not live, and there was fear. How could it not be so? To die, before there had been so little time to live, why he agonised, had he been born at all, if he must come to death so soon?

"I am like to die, I think", he told the ever watchful Cheke one day, and there was bitterness in his voice.

"Sire, from the moment we are born, we start to die. It is the condition of man" Cheke tried to soothe him, and cursed the inadequacy of his words. The doctors came to administer their foul potions that did little to relieve the ongoing progress of this beloved boy's decline. Cheke withdrew, and gathered up the books that lay upon the King's bed. He carried them to his own chamber close by, and laid them upon a table. One fell from the pile, and lay open upon the floor. Cheke picked it up, and saw that Edward had written something on the title page.

"Live to die and die to live again," he read. Tears rose to his eyes. Did that signify despair, or hope? He could not tell.

Methodically, despite his weakness, Edward continued to deal with matters of state. He gave audience to foreign ambassadors, and councillors and ministers. He followed the progress of his charities, his "Device for the poor," as he called it. But, as he said at his coronation, when he ordered the Bible to be carried before him," one more is wanting." This time, it was a device over which he agonised - the device for the succession! Soon, he knew he must face death, and without issue to ensure the continuance of the Protestant faith in England. By the terms of King Henry's will, the Lady Mary would succeed, and she would undo all he had striven to establish. She would undoubtedly return the country to the faith of Rome. Even the Lady Elizabeth, should she marry a foreigner, would risk the domination of the realm by foreign rule.

But there was a way. A new will - his own. In it, for the maintenance of the Protestant faith in which he believed so fervently, he must set aside the near ties of blood and kin. The claim of both his sisters must be negated in favour of their cousin, the staunchly Protestant Lady Jane Grey. She was of royal descent herself, the great niece of King Henry, and lately married, though unwillingly he had heard, to an Englishman, Lord Guilford Dudley, Northumberland's son. Surely, in time, this young and fiercely Protestant girl would produce male heirs, and thus ensure the continuance of the reformed faith.

And so it was done, his Device for the Succession, though not without the unease of those members of the Council whose consciences doubted its legality, as did the justiciary. Fear that the King might die before the succession could be altered and made legal, drove Northumberland to furious outbursts of rage at the frustration of his plans. So violent were they that such laggards were cowed into compliance, and the device was signed. Yet one vital signature was missing; that of Archbishop Cranmer. His conscience too, was troubled, caught as he was, between his loyalty to the two kings he served. To disinherit King Henry's daughters, named by the late King in the succession after his son, was surely, his conscience told him, an illegal act. Yet, for the love he bore his dying godson, and for the maintenance of the reformed faith, he too, at last was persuaded to add his signature to the document.

By now it was June, and Edward's sufferings were such that he prayed for death to release him. "I am glad to die," he murmured. But that he could not do, nor could he live. He lingered, pain-racked and sometimes delirious, in limbo as it were, between the two states. His body was a cruel travesty of the handsome, athletic youth he once had been. His feet and legs swelled, his hair fell out, so did the nails from his fingers and toes. He was often too weak to cough up the evil-smelling matter his diseased lungs produced, and when he did, it was of a black colour. The agony continued for Edward, and for those who must watch him suffer.

Henry Sidney and Thomas Wroth, and Christopher Salmon stayed close, as they had for weeks. And Barnaby came. The dreadful figure on the bed lay still.

Had the longed-for release come at last, they wondered? Not quite! A low murmuring sound issued from the still breathing body, but none could tell the words it had not the strength to utter. Henry Sidney took his old school-fellow in his arms and cradled him against his breast. Before the whispering died away, perhaps it was the name "Barnaby" they thought they heard, so low no-one could be sure.

Sidney held him, silent now for hours. Thomas Wroth then took hold of the little King on the other side, and together they held him as his young life drained away.

It was evening, the sixth day of July, and outside, thunder clouds were gathering. The faint whispering began again.

"Lord God, deliver me out of this miserable and wretched life..."

In his last moments, he was aware of his companions' nearness.

"I was praying to God," he said to them. Then, the world began to recede.

"Lord God, have mercy on me, and take my spirit," they heard him say.

PART III MARY I

July - South-east England & The Tower of London

Under cover of darkness, a small party of Mary Tudor's trusted household left Hunsdon Manor in Hertfordshire, and rode with her through the warm summer night of the fourth of July. She had been summoned to Greenwich to her dying brother's bedside, but well aware of the new legislation that deprived her of her right to the throne, she feared a trap to lure her into the Duke of Northumberland's clutches. In order to put as much distance as possible between herself and the Duke, Mary made for Kenninghall in north Norfolk, and stayed at safe houses of trusted Catholic sympathisers en route. The King's death on the sixth of July was kept secret, so it was not until the ninth of July, when Mary's headquarters were established at Kenninghall, that she was certain that her brother had died.

Mary had always loved to gamble, whether at cards or for a wager. And often she lost! But that was the thrill of the game. But this was different, dangerously so.

The stakes could not be higher, and the prize - the crown. If she lost, her freedom, and most probably her life itself would be forfeit. But with her brother's death, a change came over her. No longer was she the bastardised princess, only the Lady Mary, but by her father's will, the rightful heir to the throne of England.

Throughout her many painful years of ignominy, deprived of her titles, harassed and bullied by men in power, she had held fast to her faith, and now, she saw the hand of God sweeping away all obstacles to her true destiny.

In the south east of England, Mary lost no time in appealing for the support of the local people, and the Catholic gentry flocked to her side. Her courage and confidence rose, as more landowners raised armed men to her cause. At last, God was with her! But she knew she must fight, and by the grace of God, surely, she believed she would prevail. Soon, she was raising support not only from East Anglia, but also westward, towards London.

She wrote to the Privy Council, as Queen, instructing that she be proclaimed as such. In London, there was amazement and consternation at the speed and boldness of her move. The Lady Mary had been regarded as an ineffectual, indecisive woman. But this was the daughter of King Henry the Eighth, and she had stolen a march on them all. To their chagrin, the bird they had thought to ensnare, had very speedily flown.

In the Tower, another Queen, the sixteen year old Lady Jane Grey had also been proclaimed. There was, however, small enthusiasm for this little-known girl, the soles of whose shoes had needed to be raised so that she might be better seen by the Londoners, on her way to take up residence in the Tower, prior to her coronation.

Mary, on the other hand, had long been known as King Henry's daughter and King Edward's sister, and it was she they regarded as their rightful Queen.

By mid-July, Mary's forces were swelling, and she left Kenninghall for Framlingham in Suffolk. The castle there was moated, and more easily defensible than Kenninghall, and like Kenninghall, fallen to the crown on the attainder of the imprisoned Duke of Norfolk, in Henry's reign.

The Duke of Northumberland rode from London to meet her. His sense of unease was justified. In the city, there was growing enthusiasm for the Princess Mary, and the Privy Council, devoid of his strong hold over them, might see fit to play the turncoat in order to save their own political skins. He was right to be fearful. All his long and careful planning for the succession was unravelling. No back-up of troops followed him from London, and there were desertions amongst his own men. He therefore felt it politic to retreat to Cambridge.

Mary's forces, on the other hand, were still growing, and mustering at Framlingham. Two riders galloped from the capital with the news that the Privy Council had proclaimed her Queen. The Duke of Northumberland had surrendered at Cambridge; not a sword was drawn, and no English bloodshed. The curse of civil war was averted in establishing her as the rightful claimant to the crown, and that night, with a full heart, she thanked God for His miracle.

It was the evening of the third day of August, and judging by the mingled sounds of cheering and marching feet, Queen Mary's journey to London from Framlingham, across eastern England, was now over. Soon, she would be within the Tower. It was the custom for a new monarch to pardon certain prisoners held there, and Thomas Howard, third Duke of Norfolk waited and wondered.

He was eighty years old now, for the last six years of which he had been mewed up within these walls, deprived of his possessions and wealth by the Act of Attainder passed against him in the last days of King Henry's reign, and he had not been one of those released by the young King Edward. He was under sentence of death, but by some quirk of fate, it seemed that King Henry never signed his death warrant before he died. As the days and months dragged into years, he had been hagridden by the unwelcome visits of his troublesome wife.

She and Bess, the mistress he had installed at Kenninghall in the Duchess's place, were both equally determined to snatch whatever they could from whatever was left to him of the scattered Howard fortune. Women! How many nights had he sat in his lodgings in the Beauchamp Tower, and cursed the lot of them? Elizabeth, his high-minded wife, daughter of the great Duke of Buckingham, his mistress, Bess Holland, who had done very well by him, and yet had testified against him, and those two Howard nieces he had steered to queenship, how they all irked him.

And yet, there was one against whom he had not raged, and she was a dim memory now. So long ago, there had been Anne, Anne Plantagenet, the daughter of a king and the sister of a queen; to him, the lost wife of his youth.

The Tower discharged its ordnance, the roar of the cannon momentarily drowning out the wild cheering of the crowd. The Queen was here. The Constable of the Tower was greeting his new sovereign at the gates.

Now she was approaching the green where Thomas and his fellow prisoners stood on the grass, a small yet regal figure clad in a gown of that violet colour of which, he remembered, she was so fond.

He knelt down as she came closer, remembering too that this was the woman he had bullied unmercifully to force her to her father's will. Did she, for her part, remember the episode of the boiled apple, and his own rough language to her when she was a distressed princess? Of course she did. Tudors had long memories for a hurt. Could he now expect mercy from her, from this women, abased, insulted, and by her own admission, the unhappiest lady in Christendom, but now against all the odds stacked against her, Queen regnant? His knees pained him. The ground was not kind to ancient bones such as his. He bowed his head in homage, seeing only the richness of the gold embroidery upon her velvet gown.

"These be my prisoners," Mary's deep-toned voice announced. Then he felt the kiss of pardon upon his cheek.
"Rise up," she ordered. He was free. So too were the other suppliants, lined up beside him, Gardiner and Bonner, staunchly Catholic Bishops both.
In the power struggle that followed, after the death of the boy King, in which the see-saw of political fortunes swung high and low, scant attention was given to the burial of his poor, diseased body. Only those faithful and dearest to him stayed close, and in death did what was necessary, until the sister he had disinherited for the sake of religion, came to claim his throne.

Within a week of her arrival in London, Mary saw to it that the funeral of the brother she had loved as a child, and with whom she had wept in sorrow as religion divided them, was hastily arranged. Dearly she would have loved to return his soul to God by his committal in the Catholic faith, but reluctantly she was persuaded by her newly convened Council, to allow Archbishop Cranmer to officiate at his interment in Westminster Abbey, in the reformed faith in which the late King so ardently believed. So, Edward, the last of that so tenuous line of male Tudors, was laid to rest near the magnificent tomb of his grandfather, King Henry the Seventh, the first Tudor King. Mary, his equally ardent Catholic sister held a solemn requiem Mass for him in St. Peter's Chapel in the Tower.

For John Dudley, Duke of Northumberland, events moved as on a fast-running tide. He was not destined to watch the changing of the seasons from his lodging in the Tower, as the newly released Duke of Norfolk had. Dudley's trial was set for the eighteenth of August, to be presided over by Norfolk, himself newly appointed by the Queen to the rank and duty of High Steward of England. Beneath a canopy of cloth of gold, he dismissed Northumberland's plea that it was no treason to carry out the commands of his sovereign, the late King, in the matter of the succession.

"If I be guilty, so be you" he levelled at the court of his peers. It was of no avail. As was expected of them, sentence of death was pronounced. What was not expected, was Northumberland's request.

"I ask" he announced, "that I might have appointed to me some learned men for the instruction and quieting of my conscience."

In the four days of life left to him, he rejected the beliefs of the reformed faith, of which he had schemed and laboured so long to promote, and returned again to Catholicism, so that when he went to the scaffold, he announced to the many onlookers come to see him die, that he had no shame in returning to God. There were those who said his return to the Catholic faith was a desperate bid to obtain the Queen's clemency. Perhaps it was, but in the face of death, did he fear for his immortal soul too, and turn again to save it from damnation? Perhaps only in the inscrutable mind of John Dudley might the answer be found.

Westminster Abbey

Autumn drew on, and the Queen's coronation was to be on Sunday, the first day of October. All through the mellow days of September, the services of every tailor in London were sought, in order to produce the rich apparel required by the many who would participate in the coronation procession. These men sat cross-legged, each in his tiny workroom, amid the bales of sumptuous materials, and stitched from dawn to dusk, and afterwards often into the night hours, by candlelight, so that all might be ready in time.

On the last day of September, seated beneath a canopy in an open-sided chariot, Mary left the Tower to ride through the city to Westminster. Her gown of purple velvet was furred with ermine, and precious gems sparkled in the golden circle upon her head. A boisterous wind blew, a forerunner of the gales that might be expected in the later weeks of autumn. It whipped the surface of the deep swell of the river into a thousand little peaks, and many a handsome new cap of velvet was ripped from the head of its owner, and sent whirling aloft, to be snatched up and fought over by the city urchins.

Before the Queen rode her newly appointed High Steward of England, the Duke of Norfolk, to whom the swift unfolding of the events of the summer must have seemed as miraculous to him as they did to the Queen herself. To serve princes was a dangerous game, much to gain, and often more to lose, and the line of Howards knew it well.

So it was with a sense of deep satisfaction that, in extreme old age, the third Duke had lived through the tumult of Tudor politics, and survived to see the resurgence of Howard pride and fortune.

Behind him followed four noble ladies clad in crimson velvet, who rode alongside the Queen's chariot. One of these was his own troublesome wife, Elizabeth, the high-born daughter of the executed Duke of Buckingham. Her pride equalled, if not exceeded (if that were possible) that of the Howards. She had been married to him against her will, and had given him ample cause to regret his matching with her ever since. His arrogant duchess had been a loyal lady-in-waiting to Queen Katherine, and all the while, when he himself had striven to force the Lady Mary into denying the validity of her parents' marriage, she had had no reservations as to where her sympathies lay, even going so far as to refuse to attend the coronation of his niece, Anne Boleyn. The Duke sighed. He often did; it was one of his mannerisms. Women! What trouble they were capable of causing!

All along the route to Westminster, the people cheered the Queen as she passed. Children sang, acrobats performed their daring feats, and loyal addresses were spoken, the words of which tended to be blown away by the sharp gusts of wind. And, to the satisfaction of the crowds, there was wine flowing again from the conduits, as there had been at the time of the coronation of the Queen's young brother.

***

"Sirs, here present is Mary, rightful and undoubted inheratrix by the laws of God and man to the crown and royal dignity of the realm of England." Beneath a canopy carried by the five Barons of the Cinque ports, and robed in crimson velvet, Mary Tudor walked in procession towards the high altar of Westminster Abbey. Before her, the regalia was carried, and bearing the crown, her "prisoner," the Duke of Norfolk. Behind her, holding her train, followed Elizabeth, the Duke's longsuffering wife, When, as custom demanded, those assembled were asked for their assent to the Queen's crowning, the cry of "Yea, yea, yea, God save Queen Mary" rose strong and clear. Now she must prostrate herself before the altar, lying upon cushions of cloth of gold.

She listened to the intoning of prayers, then she must swear her solemn oaths, rising to be anointed with holy oil. Not the same oil used at the coronation of her brother; this to Mary seemed contaminated by schism, but pure, and sent in haste, at her request, from Arras in Flanders. A fanfare of trumpets sounded, and Bishop Stephen Gardiner, that other "prisoner," freed by her after years of incarceration in the Tower, performed the crowning ceremony. Now came the moment that signified her union with the realm. She felt the coronation ring, the wedding ring of England, sliding smoothly along her finger, and the singing of Te Deum Laudamus, that joyful song of praise to God, rose from the Abbey choir.

The ring's presence upon her finger reminded Mary that soon she must look for a husband. Marry she must. It was a monarch's duty, unwelcome as the thought of marriage might be to her personally. Since childhood, she had been traded by her father as a pawn in the European marriage market, only to be withdrawn as his political objectives changed, so that she had learned to stifle any hopes she might have felt for a husband and children. Children especially, for children she loved. Even the little bright-haired Elizabeth, the baby who had supplanted her, the name of whose mother she could not even bear to speak, even she, as a little child, Mary's generous heart had warmed to.

She was crowned queen regnant, uniquely so, the first female monarch in England to rule in sole power. She was invested with the sword and the spurs, as if she had been a king, and received the homage of both the nobility of church and state. When the solemn rites ended, she walked in state down the Abbey towards the great door, the crowds bowing as she passed.

In Westminster Hall, beneath the high beams of the vaulted roof, there was feasting and dancing, music and drinking, and when at last the long day ended, and the weary but triumphant Queen retired, she prayed for the strength to perform what she had promised in the solemn oaths she had sworn that day. And there was another prayer that rose to her lips, hesitant yet ardent. It was the plea of a woman near the end of her childbearing years, and not yet even wed. It was for the blessing of motherhood.

Surely God, she believed, who had safely brought her through all her bitter years of sorrow and danger, surely it was His intention, by the fruit of her body, to restore and maintain England in the Catholic faith.

"Holy Virgin, Mother of God, intercede for me," she prayed.

The October night grew cold, but in the streets a ragged crowd still waited at the place where the broken meats were known to be thrown out for the poorest of the poor to scrabble and fight for. To most of these, the superfluous leavings from the tables of the rich would be all that would allay their pangs of hunger that day, and fierce was the competition for the best pieces. There was merriment in the streets that night, its citizens determined to enjoy to the full whatever perquisites that came their way.

Again, as at the last coronation, wine flowed freely from the conduits, and when the following morning dawned, many a maidenhead had been lost, and in due time, many a goodwife of hitherto impeccable virtue, would give birth to a summer babe of whose paternity she could not be entirely sure.

Late Autumn – Wetheral

Mistress Margaret Aspedaile waited with barely concealed impatience for the pedlar's visit. Her heart was set upon new ribbons with which to adorn her best gown, and she had had no difficulty in cajoling her father into promising to defray the cost of these greatly desired fripperies. But Jack, the old pedlar was late this autumn, and the October gales were already blowing over the fells, and sending the yellowing leaves of the old pear tree into scurrying eddies, where they gathered in shrivelling heaps around the walls of the house. Janet too, was anxious for the pedlar's visit. Her needs for the household were growing more each week that passed.

"I hope no harm has come to him," she confided to John. "He is getting old now, and there is always danger on the roads."

Then, in the last days of October, Jack arrived, the sound of his fell ponies' hooves clattering at a steady pace, making for Carlisle. Young Margaret rushed out to meet him, her dark curls flying beneath her linen cap.

"Ribbons, ribbons" she cried.

Old Jack's eyes twinkled with merriment. He put on a sad face, and surveyed her sorrowfully.

"Ribbons, young mistress? I do believe I sold the last of them to the maids in Lazonby this very day." He winked at John and Janet, as they followed hard on Margaret's heels.

Then he loosed the fastenings of a pannier slung across the back of one of his ponies. It fell open, to display a profusion of brightly coloured ribbons, laces and all manner of trifles and trinkets, the sight of which immediately transformed the downcast face of young Mistress Aspedaile from disappointment to gleeful anticipation.

"Is it well with you, Jack?" Janet eyed the old man with concern. "We feared there was something amiss, you are so late this time."

"Nay, mistress. I do well enough for an old body," Jack laughed. "'Twas the news that I carry that delayed me. Everywhere go, folk clamour for the news." He looked at John enquiringly. "You know the young King is dead?" he asked.

"I do" John replied, "I had it in Penrith this summer."
"When I was in York, I heard strange tales." Jack cast an enquiring glance at his audience, and as he expected, he had their attention, their eyes willing him to continue.

From long experience, the pedlar told a good tale, and it was easy to see that the telling of it delayed him wherever he went. But it was the habit of a lifetime to be the carrier of news, and what news he had, so he cleared his throat, and spat vigourously in the same direction as the wind was blowing, and leaned upon his folded arms over the back of his bell-horse.

"In London town, there are some who whisper that the young King was poisoned." Young Margaret left off fingering the ribbons she was choosing, and exclaimed, "Oh, but he was so young to die! He was born in the same year as I was. Is that not so, father?"

"He was, indeed," John replied. "He would have been sixteen this very month. On St. Edwards Day, I recall he was born, and so he was named."

"There were great stirrings in London when he died," Jack went on, "for it seems he left his crown to his cousin, the Lady Jane Grey, when by rights it was the Lady Mary, his sister, who was the rightful heir."

"So, what was the way of it?" John wanted to know. He could see that old Jack was in no hurry, rather he was content to stretch out his tale at length.

The bell-horse took a few steps forward to crop a nearby tuft of grass, and Jack was forced to relinquish the position he had adopted over its back to relate his tale. So when the bell- horse moved, so must the rest of the train. Jack therefore merely transferred his stance to the next following pony, and continued to hold forth with relish.

"Two queens there were proclaimed this summertime," he announced. "Queen Jane was but a little maid, young like King Edward, and the great Duke of Northumberland married her to his son, and had her crowned in the Tower.

But she reigned for only nine days, and now she is a prisoner there. Queen Mary, our Queen that now is, she came to London with a great force, and the people welcomed her as their rightful Queen, because she is the daughter of old King Harry, and named by him to succeed, if young King Edward should not live."

Jack paused for breath, and cocked a querulous eye upon his listeners to ascertain the effect his tale was having upon them.

"So why," John asked thoughtfully, "did not the Lady Mary succeed as soon as her brother died? Queen Jane, what claim had she to the throne?"

"Ah," Jack resumed, "it seems it was all because of religion. King Edward feared his sister Mary would bring back the old religion if she became Queen, and that he dreaded.

So he made his own will, his Device, he called it, and named the Lady Jane his heir, so that the new religion that he so loved, should continue after his death."

"But who is the Lady Jane?" asked Margaret. "I have never heard of her."

"No, nor have many people", Jack replied. "But her grandmother was the Princess Mary, King Henry's favourite sister."

"So how will it go for Queen Jane, now?" Margaret wanted to know. "What will become of her?"

"I cannot tell, little Mistress." Jack shook his head slowly, then said, "But I fear for her."

"Religion!" Janet spoke bitterly. "What are folks like us to make of it?"

"Well, Queen Mary is crowned now", Jack said with an air of finality. "I had it before I left York. A great spectacle it was, too."

Their selections made, Jack began to re-pack his train and make ready for the road again. He took the money they owed him, and laid his hand on the bell-horse's bridle. It nuzzled his pocket in the hope of finding an apple there.

"Nay, old lad. There'll be apples a-plenty for thee when we get home to Carlisle," Jack laughed.

"Wait," Margaret cried, and she ran back to where windfalls lay in the grass of the orchard, and before Jack had the bell-horse turned to lead the train out again onto the road, she was back, with an apple for each of the ponies.

"I thank thee, little Mistress", Jack called. Then he turned. "Oh, I forgot to tell thee. The old Duke of Norfolk is let out of the Tower, and restored to great favour again."

***

Half Spanish herself, it was natural that Mary should look to the land of her mother's birth in her quest for a suitable husband. Catholic he must be, and royal for preference, so foreign he must be also, distasteful though that might be to those of her Council who would have her marry an Englishman. So who then could be more Catholic, or more royal, than Prince Philip of Spain, son of Charles the Fifth, the Holy Roman Emperor? Ah, Charles! Mary's eyes softened. Once, many years ago, he had come to London. He was a young man then, and she a six year old princess who was to become his bride.

But he could not wait for her to grow, and so he married another princess, Isabella of Portugal, and it was their son, Philip, she was now considering as a husband. She suppressed a sigh, and banished the thought that sprang unbidden into her mind. How different her life might have been, married to Charles, empress of the vast Hapsburg territories, as well as now, England's queen. But, to the present; Philip? What did she know of him? He was aged twenty-six - eleven years her junior.

Her heart quailed. How would he find her, her youth now past? He was a widower, too. He had been married young, and his wife, the childish Princess Maria Manoela of Portugal had died, but seventeen years of age, in giving birth to Don Carlos, their son. Rumour had it that the boy was misshapen, his growth stunted, and his mind unstable.

Ah, yes! There was the taint of insanity in the royal blood of Spain. Her own mother's elder sister, Queen Juana had it. "Juana the mad," they called her, and she was Philip's own grandmother.

Also, if rumour had substance, Philip kept a mistress in Spain, and had fathered her two young sons. Alas, Mary sighed again. Royal marriages were made for power, for land, to seal a treaty. For love, princes looked elsewhere. But, she reasoned, Philip was a kinsman, family, and it was for him that her lonely heart yearned.

In the shifting world of politics, the Emperor Charles constantly strove to maintain a state of equilibrium throughout his overseas territories. His astute mind readily recognised the advantage of marrying his son into England. From that small island, Philip would be ideally placed to keep a watchful eye on that most troublesome of his dominions, the Netherlands.

Always, there was some unrest there, and the threat to Holy Church of heresy. Close by was France, untrustworthy France, always vacillating between fickle friend and potential enemy.

And in Germany, there was the menace of the Lutheran princes. If, he reasoned, Spain and England were united by this possible marriage, the balance of power would tip in Spain's favour. And, most desirable too, Charles concluded, with the assistance of the Inquisition, if that should be necessary, his son's zeal to serve

Holy Church would most assuredly restore again that schismatic land to the embrace of Rome.

As to Philip's ardour to meet the embraces of the aging Mary Tudor, that, the Emperor reflected, was another matter. But, unpalatable as the prospect might be, Charles knew that his son would comply.

His duty to the true Faith, and to Spain, would over-rule whatever his own desires might be. In any case, the Emperor mused, if Philip could get the new Queen of England with child, with the Catholic heir he knew she so craved, he need not stay at Mary's side indefinitely. She must be made aware that Philip had duties a-plenty in the great Hapsburg empire, and it would be needful for him to return to Spain, or to wherever in the Empire need might arise.

1554

In the first week of the new year of 1554, five Imperial Commissioners arrived in England from the Low Countries, their mission to conclude the terms of the marriage treaty between England and Spain. They hoped to wrest from a reluctant Council as much advantage as they might for the benefit of their prince, and they knew that their task would be a hard one. These English, they were well aware, were a truculent race, their manners rough, and less than civil. Moreover, they were known to be suspicious of foreigners, and although the Commissioners themselves had been greeted with due courtesy on arriving in this benighted country, their servants had not. These were met, when they walked abroad in the streets of London, with glowering looks and shouted insults, and once, they had been set upon by a jeering band of ragged urchins, who pelted them with a hail of snowballs.

By the third week of January, the treaty was concluded, the final terms of which greatly favoured England rather than Spain. Philip, though sharing Mary's title as King, would in fact wield scant authority in the actual governing of the country. The power of monarchy would remain with his wife. It was a hard bargain these islanders drove. Perhaps, the Commissioners wondered, was there something in this people's residual memory of a time five hundred years ago, when the French ruled their land, and all but obliterated their own identity?

Howsoever that might be, they were obdurate in their resolve to share not a jot of their jealously guarded rights as to the government of their country.

The Council too were divided in their opinion. Some were in favour of the Queen's marriage to Prince Philip. Others would have preferred her to marry within the realm. But the Queen herself was adamant, she was determined to have him, let the Council fret as much as they chose. She would marry, yes. It was her duty to England to do so, but it must be to a consort of her own choosing.

In London and further afield, there was distrust and discontent at the prospect of the Spanish marriage. In the towns and alehouses, people muttered darkly, fearing the influx of foreigners amongst them.

On the Earl of Pembroke's estate at Wilton, when the day's toil was done, Walter and his blue-eyed crony sat together at the inn. An air of restraint hung between them. Their talk was guarded until three riders, strangers passing through, mounted their horses and rode away at speed.

Walter took a long swig of his ale and learn forward towards his companion.

"Who be they?" he wondered. "Not Englishmen, I'll warrant." He indicated the half-drained beakers left behind by the strangers. One had taken a gulp of his ale and spat it out, grimacing in disgust.

"Spaniards, I reckon," the other murmured. "And 'tis not only our ale they mislike." He looked around, and lowered his voice yet further.

"The new religion - young King Edward's religion, Queen Mary hates it. She looks to wed her kinsman, the prince from Spain. There are Spaniards here already, and they seek to arrange the match.

Walter met his anxious gaze.

"'Tis true," he agreed. "I was carting logs for the fire in the big house, and I heard the servants talking. They fear that if the Queen marries the Spanish prince, the Inquisition will come here, and they say there are dreadful things done to those who are not of the old religion. Heretics will be hunted down without mercy here as well." The Inquisition struck terror to men's hearts.

Would that horror be loosed upon Englishman if the Spaniard came? So too wondered a gentleman in Kent. Sir Thomas Wyatt was lately returned from soldiering on the continent. During his service there, in the conflicts between France and the Spanish-held Low Countries, whatever he had witnessed of the conduct of Spaniards there repelled him.

There were others too. In Devon and the Midlands, a plot was conceived to converge and march upon London in the spring. No-one would wish to move in the winter weather. But news of the plan leaked out, and it was left to Wyatt alone to raise his standard at Maidstone, and march with his three thousand Kentish men on the twenty-fifth of January.

Thus, the rebellion against the Spanish marriage began. The weather was bad, and despite his advanced years, the Duke of Norfolk was dispatched to intercept the oncoming rebels. His men, however, began to desert to Wyatt's force, thus compelling the old campaigner to break off the engagement.

In London, the Imperial representatives, their task completed, and fearful for their own safety, made haste to put distance between themselves and the oncoming hostile force and removed at speed back to the Low Countries. Sir Thomas and his men advanced unimpeded. However, the Queen's impassioned speech to her government at the Guildhall ensured that London was ready and armed by the time he reached the capital on the third of February. London Bridge, where he hoped to cross the Thames was so well guarded that he was forced to wait until nightfall, and cross the river at Kingston.

There were running battles in the streets of London that night, and in the early hours, the rebels reached Westminster. There they shot arrows at the palace windows. Inside, armed men filled the Queen's presence chamber, to the great alarm of her ladies. Fearful that if the palace should be besieged, and the Queen's person seized, Mary was urged to flee. To her great credit, she did not, and counselled those around her to fall to prayer.

Such was her faith that, having brought her to queenship, God would not abandon her in the face of her present danger.

And how else, except by the workings of the Almighty, could the next turn of events be explained? In the streets of London, a strange thing was happening. Wyatt's men, who had followed him through the mire of the winter weather, were deserting him, and melting away in the darkness. He was alone. There was no convergence of his fellow conspirators, and he knew that the enterprise was ended. In the blackness of despair, he remembered, when he was a youth, the fate of those who were called "Pilgrims" in that great northern rising in the time of the Queen's father, and shuddered as he was led away into captivity.

Easter - The Tower

On the river at Whitehall, it was noted by a few bystanders that a barge pulled away from the palace, and was rowed quickly into midstream. In it, under armed guard, it was possible to see the slight figure of a young woman. It was Palm Sunday, the eighteenth day of March, the brightness of the spring morning hesitant, and inclined to rain. Then, as is so often in early spring, a few fitful rays of sunlight broke through a passing cloud. They touched the head of the prisoner in the barge, and kindled a fiery glint in the brightness of her hair.

"'Tis the Lady Elizabeth," one murmured to his companion. They watched the barge as it sped on, until it was only a speck in the distance.

"She goes to the Tower, I'll warrant" the other replied. He lowered his voice, for none knew who listened.

"God help her in that place," he said.

The cloud that moments before had parted before the shafts of sunlight, now lowered dark and threatening, and soon blocked out the feeble shine. Then drops of heavy rain began to fall. As if of one mind, both men glanced upriver at the fast disappearing craft, before seeking shelter, and each breathed a silent, heartfelt "Amen."

The oarsmen dipped in unison into the grey water of the river. In the barge, the Lady Elizabeth sat in silence between her guards, and had it not been for the rhythmic sound of the oars as they broke the water, she could have believed that the thudding of her heart must have been audible to her captors.

She breathed deeply to steady her jangled nerves, and sought to quell the rising wave of terror that threatened to overpower her. She was accused of complicity in the plot for which now poor Tom Wyatt was like to lose his head. At his trial, Tom had spoken up roundly for her, and though his prosecutors tried to trap him into incriminating her, they failed to move him. Nevertheless, their suspicion of her, and that of her sister, Queen Mary, was such that she was summoned from Ashridge, and despite her plea of sickness, by which ploy she was able to delay her arrival in London, she was charged with involvement in the plot.

It was an ominous sign that the Queen steadfastly ignored the repeated pleas of her sister and subject to be granted an audience, and only yesterday, when the two lords arrived at her lodging in Whitehall to escort her to the Tower, she had been reduced to begging them to be allowed to write to the Queen before she left. With great reluctance, they agreed, and Elizabeth drew upon all her powers of eloquence to move the Queen to allow her to plead her case before her in person.

"For, I have heard of many," she wrote, "cast away for want of coming to their prince." As an afterthought, she added post-scriptum "I crave but one word of answer."

Then she scored the remainder of the parchment heavily to its base with great lines of ink, mindful of the possibility of any additions that might be forged in her name. In the time it took her to compose the letter to her satisfaction, the tide on the river turned, much to the annoyance of her would-be escorts. Now they must wait until the following day for its turning again to convey their prisoner to the Tower.

All through the evening hours, and the beginning of the Sabbath morning, the Lady Elizabeth waited, hoping for the Queen's summons to her presence. It never came, and now, as the square outline of the Tower came into view, she contemplated two possibilities. Either her letter to her sister had been intercepted and never delivered, or worse, that it had, and Mary's heart had grown so cold against her that she stood already condemned.

With every stroke of the oars, the bulk of the Tower increased. A royal palace it might be, but it was a prison too, and to all who came this way, and there were many, her own mother included, it was a place of dread. Inside its stout walls, death might well be the only means of exit. They were there, and now between the two lords who escorted her, she too must enter. Armed men lined her path, and at a distance she glimpsed the scaffold upon which her cousin, little Jane

Grey, the unwilling nine-day Queen, had lost her head only the month before. Why had it not been taken down since then? Did it await another victim? Raindrops began to fall so heavily that Elizabeth was forced to quicken her pace and seek the shelter of the place where she least wished to be.

***

Three weeks and three days passed, and it was April. Tom Wyatt stood on the scaffold, and breathed in the sweet air of the English spring. He did not fear death. In his soldiering days he had seen the many, and often terrible ways of it often. His own, so near now would be quick and clean, providing, of course, that the headsman knew his trade. He regretted, however, that he would not live to see England governed in peace, a prosperous land, not riven by religious dispute, as he feared it would be so when the Spaniard came to share the English throne.

He looked back at the Tower. Somewhere enclosed within those walls, lay the Lady Elizabeth, so English, and with a natural rapport with the common people, the hope, surely, of better things to come. Never, throughout his examination had he admitted that she had any knowledge of the plot for which he must now die, and he knew his interrogators still hoped that, even upon the scaffold, he would still implicate her. A small crowd was gathered to hear his last words. This was the last service he could do for her. He looked down at the upturned faces, and flung wide his arms as if he would embrace them.

The moment had come. He raised his voice, so that all might hear. It was steady and strong.

"Good people," he cried, "it is said that I should accuse my Lady Elizabeth's Grace. It is not so, good people. It is not so."

***

May, and the Lady Elizabeth walked abroad in the sunshine. How good it was to feel the earth beneath her feet again, English earth, even though that earth was within her prison. But now that spring was merging into summer, she was allowed the freedom to exercise in the fresh air.

Even so, she knew that she was watched. Still, despite the visits of the Council and the probings of Bishop Gardiner, who would dearly have loved to trap her into admitting she had foreknowledge of the Wyatt rebellion, nothing could be proved against her. Yes, much was suspected of her, and for that reason, though she was soon to be released from the Tower on the Queen's orders, she knew her freedom would be limited. The old palace of Woodstock would be her next lodging, under the watchful eye of Sir Henry Bedingfield.

In her father's day, King Henry had often been accommodated at Woodstock with his riding court. Whilst on his many progresses, he had found the hunting in that part of Oxfordshire much to his liking. But since his death, the building had been allowed to deteriorate, and it was certainly not to the Lady Elizabeth's liking. Though she was relieved to quit the Tower with her head still on her shoulders, from the moment she arrived at Woodstock and realised the restrictions Sir Henry was ordered to place upon her, her incessant complaints and contrariness drove her unfortunate gaoler to near distraction.

The Lady Elizabeth must have no communication with the outside world, and he must accompany her when she walked in the parkland. It was clear that the Queen did not trust her sister, and while she prepared for her marriage to Prince Philip, Elizabeth must endure the tedium of her containment as best she might.

Spring – Wetheral

It was as Margaret Aspedaile had anticipated. William Winter and Ellen Grinton were to be wed at the end of June, and they, the Aspedailes, were bidden to the wedding. Margaret perched on her swing beneath the old pear tree, and set herself in motion, to and fro, in the spring sunshine. Would the Bowerbank family from Lazonby be bid too, she wondered? She hoped with all her heart that it would be so. Of course, there would not be so many bid as there had been to her father and Janet's wedding, for her father was well-known and reverenced for many miles around, and the house then had been filled to bursting with well-wishers.

But William Winter too, since he and his mother had settled in Wetheral, had gained a name for his honesty and fair dealings, and he and the Lazonby saddler were well acquainted, so Margaret's hopes of meeting with John Bowerbank again ran high.

In late April, pedlar Jack came again. He did a roaring trade with the Aspedailes and the Winters, both in earnest preparation for the forthcoming celebrations.

"Jack is not so strong as he was, I think," observed Isobel to Janet, after the old pedlar and his train departed Carlisle-wards.

"He is getting old, now, I suppose," Janet said. "'Tis a hard life, tramping across the countryside in all weathers. Did you see he only has three ponies now?" Isobel nodded.

"John says he has sold one to the Bowerbanks in Lazonby. The saddler there is buying more ready tanned skins from the tannery in Penrith, rather than tan so much himself. He needs an extra horse so he and his brother can carry them back home. But I wonder if Jack is finding it hard now, and is trying to lighten his load."

Isobel nodded again, and then a look of concern passed over her face.

"But did you hear the news he told of the new law?" she asked Janet. In her agitation, she did not wait for Janet to reply, but rushed on.

"It will concern poor Sister Galfride. You remember? She was one of the nuns turned out of the House at Heremitithwaite with Dame Dinah, God rest her soul." Isobel hastily crossed herself, then hurried on.

"Well, Sister Galfride married a friar from Penrith, when the religious were allowed to wed."

"What news is this, Isobel? I have heard nothing" Janet said.
Isobel hurried on. "It seems that all those who were once in religion, and were allowed to marry in the young King's reign, must now part .

The new Queen will have it so."

"Oh, Isabel, you must have known the Sister well when you lived at the Nunnery", Janet exclaimed.

"I did", Isobel replied. "And Dame Dinah, God rest her, once told me that Galfride had found great contentment with her friar, more than she ever found in the life she lived as a nun."

Janet considered for a while, and then she said, "So the Queen will take away what little happiness those poor dispossessed ones have managed to find in their new lives. Yet she herself will be wed come summer to one of her Spanish kin, John tells me. He had it in Penrith but yesterday, and there are those who mislike the match, so 'tis said. How will it be for her, I wonder?"

The weeks sped by. It was a cold May, and despite the fact that it was springtime, the wind blew relentlessly across the fells, and from leaden skies rain and even hail lashed the countryside. Then, the days of June dawned in welcome contrast, soft and balmy and bright. Once again, the bridal feast was held in the Aspedaile house, it being more commodious than the old farmhouse where the Winters lived. Again, the house rang with the sounds of merrymaking, and many a good wish, and sometimes the occasional uncalled for advice was offered to the newly-wed pair.

"I never thought to be so happy", Ellen whispered to William when the din subsided. "Nor I," said William softly, one arm clasped around his new wife's waist.

His mother and Mistress Mary Bowerbank sat together, deep in amicable conversation.

"We are fortunate to have good sons, Mistress Winter", Mary ventured. "And I congratulate you on your new daughter-in-law. She is a good girl, and I have no doubt they are well-matched. You must be glad for them."

"Indeed, that I am," Isobel assured her. "Most truly, they deserve their happiness.'
The hint of a cloud crossed Mary's face.
"I think it will be a long time before my John is wed," she sighed. "If his father had lived, perhaps it would have been different. But John, he works each and every day. Aye, and often long into the nights to keep my Andrew's trade from failing. There's no time for courting for him, though I know the Lazonby maids wish it otherwise."

"Mother, what nonsense are you telling Mistress Winter? I heard what you were saying."
John Bowerbank, his eyes twinkling with amusement, was standing unnoticed behind his mother, and laughing at her discomfiture.

"'Tis true, John, 'tis true", she cried, and tried to hide her confusion at being thus overheard. "T'would content me to see you happily wed, too, like Mistress Winter's son."

At that moment, John noticed Mistress Margaret Aspedaile, jug in hand, replenishing the beakers of those guests, and there were many, who claimed that their throats were still parched. Laughingly, she poured out copious draughts of home- brewed ale. He watched, and though his own beaker was in no need of refilling, he stepped forward and held it out to her.

"We meet again, Mistress Margaret," he said to her, and gave a little bow. "I trust I see you well."
With hands that were not quite steady, she poured a little ale into his proffered beaker, then summoning every jot of composure of which she was capable, she looked up into his face, and smiled.

"Indeed you do, sir, and I thank you", she replied.

Her face was enchanting, alive with the vitality of youth. He was taken aback at her beauty, her face, her eyes. Her eyes, where had he seen that look before? Something stirred in his mind, a memory long forgotten, hidden deep for many a year. As many years, in fact, as this beautiful maid now had, seventeen, perhaps? It was at the time of the Pilgrimage. He was a lad again, and Ben was with him.

Their father had left them, with his mother and Dinah, at the Priory at Heremitithwaite, while he rode on to Wetheral to deliver a saddle for John Aspedaile's wife. The Prioress had sent them out to collect eggs, and a beautiful young Sister was with them. Her face, her eyes! He was looking at them again!

"Your pardon, Mistress. I did not mean to stare. But now that you are grown, you reminded me of someone I remember from many years ago. She was so like you are now."

Margaret felt her heart miss a beat, and her eyes searched his face. "Did you know her well?" she asked, and strove to conceal the anxiety she felt. Perhaps he had loved her once?

"No," he replied. "I only saw her one time, when I was just a young lad. But I remember that she was very beautiful."

Margaret flushed with pleasure, and relief flooded through her. He had not loved another then, as she had feared, and he had let it be known to her that he thought her beautiful.

"I trust we shall meet again, Mistress. Soon, I hope." He bowed again, and she must move on. There were more beakers waiting for her to fill.

His mother and Mistress Winter exchanged glances.

"Yes," Isobel read Mary's thoughts. "She is indeed as her mother was. So beautiful."

"I only saw the Sister once," Mary replied. "But you are right. Margaret has all her mother's beauty. She is a lovely maid."

***

Riding home to Lazonby in the sweetness of the June evening, John meditated deeply on the events of the day. John Aspedaile might call Margaret his daughter, but her mother? Time and again he linked the two faces in his mind. At last, he turned to Mary, riding pillion behind him.

"Mother," he asked, "You mind the time father left us at the Priory, that time the Pilgrims were about, and a young Sister took me and Ben to collect eggs - who was she?"

"Yes, my son, you have guessed aright, she was Margaret Aspedaile's mother, long dead, the poor wronged soul." Mary said no more, but as John quickened his horse's pace, fragments of speech, shocked and incomprehensible to him then, crystallised in his mind. "The nun's child!" He remembered the murmured words passed on by scandalized neighbours behind cupped hands before the mouth, as though it was a shameful thing to relate.

They had no significance for him then, and were soon forgotten. But out of the depths of childish memory, now they leapt up into his consciousness in a flash of illuminating clarity. The nun's child - Margaret Aspedaile - she was the daughter of that gentle young Sister who knew all the places where the convent's hens laid away.

And then, he remembered that a man had been watching her, a stranger who had come with the King's men. He remembered that he had hailed her, approached her, and that she was anxious and hurried away.

Mary kept glancing round. Since John had quickened his horse's pace, they had drawn ahead of Ben and Dinah following behind. Now the distance between them was lengthened, and the two were no longer to be seen. Why did she have this feeling of unease, she wondered? Ben and Dinah had always been close from the very day that Andrew brought Ben home to Lazonby, a fatherless, motherless waif. Now they were full grown, and had eyes for none but each other. Nor was her anxiety dispelled that night when sleep, coming at last, she could not remember hearing the sound of the returning horse, and she wished with all her heart that Andrew was still with her.

***

The sun was already low in the sky when Dinah and Ben bid the Winters farewell. John was already mounted and ready to go, though Ben noticed that his brother had lingered taking his leave of the Aspedailes. William Winter helped Dinah to mount up behind Ben, and they followed John and Mary out onto the road. It had been a perfect day, the sun warm and bright, and Dinah felt a pleasant weariness overcome her. It was at evening's gate, that time when day was changing into night. A cool breeze began to blow, and fanned her hot cheeks. She wound her arms around Ben's waist, and laid her head in happy contentment on his back.

They spoke not a word, but rode on, each lulled by the rhythm of their horse's motion, into a private, timeless world.

When ahead of them, John quickened his pace, they did not, and the distance between them widened. The sky lost its fiery aftermath of sunset, and as dusk began to fall, it became a soft, pearly grey, and never truly dark. A young moon began to glow, a bright sickle in the deepening sky. In places along the wayside, the first wild roses scrambled.

"Let me down, Ben. I must pick some," Dinah cried, pointing at the pale blooms gleaming in the moonlight. Ben reined in the horse, and she slid down from its back. He too dismounted, and the horse seized the opportunity to crop the lush new grass at the side of the track.

"Here, let me," he said. "They have sharp thorns." The briar stems resisted his attempts to break them, and their protective thorns bit into his fingers.

"Oh, they have scratched you. You are bleeding" Dinah cried, when he gave the roses into her hands.

"'Tis no matter", he laughed. But she gathered his hands into hers, and raised them to her lips.
Often, in their childhood play, they had kissed a hurt place better, and assured each other that the pain was gone, because of the kiss.
Now, to Ben the significance of Dinah's instinctive gesture gave rise to an overwhelming need, an ache, a hurt that a single kiss could not redress.

How long they lay in each other's arms on the bank where the wild roses grew, neither could tell, but when a heavy dew began to fall, and the moon above climbed high in the sky, they roused, and rode back the rest of the way to Lazonby.

"We are wed now, Dinah", Ben whispered in the quiet dark of the houseplace. "We must tell them in the morning, my love."

When the impact of their tidings broke upon the ears of Mary and John, it was met by a moment of startled silence, by incredulity on John's part, and the confirmation of Mary's long held suspicions.

"Wed! What mean ye?" John burst out. "Ye are brother and sister. It cannot be."

"Brother, I have always loved Dinah. As a sister, 'tis true, since the first day I saw her, and she gave me a piggin of milk to drink. But we are both grown now, and she is not my sister by blood."
"How can ye call me brother, and Dinah not thy sister?" John raged.

In all their days together, from the closeness of the bond forged in their childhood years to this present moment, never had Ben seen his brother's face so contorted with wrath.
Then, in those tender years, their occasional and inevitable squabbles were quickly mended, each bereft at the loss of the other's companionship. Now, their eyes met, John's hard, implacable, and in that instant Ben felt a profound sensation of loss, and perceived a rift that was widening into a chasm between himself and his brother.

"'Tis because our love is grown into that of a man for a woman, no longer like that of children. And last night, we became man and wife. Can ye not understand?"

Mary stepped forward and without a word encircled her daughter in her arms.

"Mother, 'tis so," Dinah affirmed, will ye give us your blessing?"

Before she could reply, John leapt forward and smashed his fist into Ben's face.

"'Tis against the laws of God and nature for a man to lie with his sister," he yelled. The force of the blow caught Ben off guard, and sent him sprawling onto the floor of the houseplace.

"Get up, get up, I say, and fight." John spat out the words between clenched teeth. Ben rose to his knees, still dazed from the blow.

"I will not fight thee, John, for thou'rt still my brother, and will always be," he said.

But John seized him, dragged him upright, and aimed for another blow.

"Stop." Mary forced herself between them. "John, there is truth in what he says. There is no blood tie between them, so why may they not wed?" she cried.

"Oh, yes, John," Dinah pleaded. "Surely it may be so. You know that I love you, my brother. But I could not live without Ben." Her blue eyes searched his face in anguish. She laid a hand on his arm. "Be reconciled with us, I beg of thee."

John glowered, then considered. At length he spoke, grudgingly, his voice rough with the anger that still simmered within him.

"And where do ye think to find a priest to wed you in these changing times", he asked. "Whether it be at the church door, as in the old time, or by the rite of the new faith that even now is like to be cast out now the new Queen reigns. I tell ye, the priests know not what to do, and I can see trouble ahead", he said darkly.

When the young King died, the fortunes, and more particularly, the tranquillity of mind of his beloved tutor, Sir John Cheke, spiralled ever lower. From that fateful summer of 1553, when he watched the suffering of his royal pupil as he waited for death, Sir John descended from his place of high honour and learning, to the ignominy of imprisonment as a traitor, to exile, recantation, shame and death.

When the Duke of Northumberland left London with his troops to meet and engage the Lady Mary's forces, it had fallen to Cheke, as secretary to the Council, to despatch letters in the Council's name, urging loyalty to the newly proclaimed Queen Jane. But so fast did events run that it seemed the ink had hardly dried upon the same letters, but the Duke had surrendered, a triumphant Mary proclaimed Queen, and the Council turned about and made their abject submission to her.

Cheke, with his zeal for the reformed faith, and mindful of the diligence with which his dying pupil and King had striven to secure the continuance of the same, could not, in conscience conform.

Thus, with Queen Mary's accession, he found himself committed to the Tower, soon to be joined there, in September, by Archbishop Cranmer.

In the mellow sunshine one autumn day, they had met and talked briefly under the watchful eyes of their gaolers, as they were permitted to exercise within the Tower precincts.

"Right sorry I am to see you in this place, Sir John," the Archbishop said. "The Queen has no love for either of us, I fear."

"And certainly no love for our reformed faith," Cheke replied. "'Tis anathema to her."

"She will cast away all that King Edward achieved in his godly reign, and give England back to the rule of Rome" Cranmer pronounced heavily. They walked awhile in troubled silence, heartsore at the loss of the boy King they both held so dear.

"She blames us both, Sir John, for what she considers our ill-teaching of him in religion. If it were not for the urging of some of the Council, she would not have let him be buried according to the Protestant rite. But I thank God that she allowed me to do that last service for him" Cranmer said.

They walked together, each deep in thought, until the time allocated for their brief freedom was over.

Then they were escorted back, each to his gloomy cell. Winter came, its dank chill to be endured in the short days and the long, cold nights. It penetrated a prisoner's very bones, and denied him that small measure of forgetfulness he might have found in sleep.

With the coming of the next year, so too came Jane Grey and Tom Wyatt to the Tower, both to die. The Lady Elizabeth came too, one wet March morning, but she would live.

Then, the doors of their Tower cells were opened for both Cranmer and Cheke. The Queen's marriage plans were uppermost in her mind, so Cranmer was sent to Oxford, to be contained there under house arrest until such time as she should decide his fate.

Cheke sued for the Queen's pardon for his offence of supporting the Lady Jane's claim to the throne.

He was granted licence to travel abroad for a limited time, and so he joined that growing diaspora of those committed to the new faith who sought the safety of those places on the continent where they might practice their religion without hindrance. Sir John wandered in Europe, meeting again those voluntary exiles for conscience's sake, with whom he had been well acquainted in happier days. It cheered his heart to see again Sir Thomas Wroth, one of the chief Gentlemen of King Edward's Privy Chamber, whose sad privilege it had been to watch at the King's bedside in his last hours.

The Duchess of Suffolk too had fled her native country, so wedded was she to the reformed religion. Sir John remembered vividly the young and beautiful heir of Lord Willoughby, married at fourteen to the aging Charles Brandon. Always close to royalty, the young Duchess's mother had been Maria de Salinas, one of the high-born Spanish ladies accompanying Katherine of Aragon to England to be her Lady in waiting, and her friend until death. Katherine, Willoughby's daughter likewise was appointed Lady in waiting to Queen Katherine Parr, and it was at that time, in 1544 that Cheke was called from his life of study at Cambridge, to tutor the seven year old Prince Edward.

On occasion, he would see the new Queen and her ladies at Court, where, at that time, they were careful to present a semblance of religious orthodoxy, though in private, their leanings were suspected to be far more radical. Katherine, the young Duchess, dared to be more openly critical of the Catholic bishops, and mischievously named her pet spaniel "Gardiner."
The little pup gambolled and frolicked, until with mock severity, and to the barely suppressed hilarity of the Queen's ladies, the Duchess imperiously ordered him to heel. Cheke smiled, as he waited one July day in 1554 for the Duchess to receive him.

A host of memories flitted through his mind of that time when he was newly come to Court, fresh from his academic life at Cambridge, to instruct the fine mind of the young Prince. Those brief years of Kate Parr's queenship, her love of learning, which was shared by her ladies and her step-children, seemed to him now as an oasis of tranquillity, a precious place where quiet study and the sheer love of learning created an alternative world, unassailable by the ever present intrigues of Court life.

The Duchess came now to greet him, a handsome, mature woman, vivacious still, despite the losses of the past decade of her life.

"Ah, Sir John, I rejoice to see you come safely to these parts. England is no place now for those of our persuasion," she greeted him.

"Indeed, 'tis so, madam. I fear there are many who will pay a heavy price for it ere long," he replied.

"Tell me, Sir John," the Duchess was eager to know, "what news of Archbishop Cranmer? How does he?"

"We were together, Madam, in the Tower," Cheke explained. "You know that Cranmer stood for the Lady Jane, as I did. Though he did so with a heavy heart, I fear, for it was his opinion that the Lady Mary was Edward's rightful successor, under King Henry's will.

At first, he would not sign the young King's device that the crown should pass to the Lady Jane, and thus ensure the continuance of the reformed faith. But Edward pleaded with him, begged of him that he would not stand against him, and such was the Archbishop's love for his dying godson, that he was persuaded to sign the device."

The Duchess nodded. Cheke did not need to tell her this, she was well informed.

"Where is the Archbishop now, Sir John?" she persisted.
"After his secular trial, and found guilty, of course, he was removed from the Tower to Oxford, there to join Latimer and Ridley to await the Queen's pleasure" he told her. Both were silent for a while, then Cheke continued heavily.
"But I fear she wants him tried for heresy too, she hates him so. And the heresy laws; I fear they will be revived before long. What then?" he asked, with a sigh.

The Duchess did not answer, she turned her lively gaze upon Cheke, and asked. "And you, Sir John? what will you do now?"

"I hope to travel to Italy, Madam. To Padua, in fact, to read Greek there," he replied.
"They will be fortunate, Sir, to benefit from your great skill in that tongue. I am sure of that," the Duchess smiled.

They talked with ease, with that spontaneity that is so evident in the conversation of like-minded souls. They fell to reminiscing of the happy days of the young King's schooling, and of the close friendships formed when his lessons were shared with young Henry and Charles Brandon, the Duchess's sons, both now dead of the dreaded sweat.

"I doubt your boys would tell you, madam, that once I had to reprimand them for scribbling on the King's schoolwork," he said, for he was quick to see that a shadow clouded her face. The Duchess laughed softly, and brushed away a tear that rose to her eye, and Cheke was glad that humour had leavened the dense mass of grief she carried for her lost sons.

"And what of the future, Sir John?" she asked wistfully. "Will we ever be able to return home again?"

"I do not know, my lady," Cheke replied heavily. "The Queen will marry Prince Philip; he is even now embarked from Spain, and England will be given back to the Roman faith. If the heresy laws are revived, I fear there will be persecution in our land. There was silence between them, fraught with despondency.

"I cannot deny my belief in our reformed religion," the Duchess said at last.
"Nor I, my Lady," echoed Cheke.

"But, maybe there could be a way for it to live again in England," she ventured. Cheke met the bright gaze of the Katherine Willoughby he remembered. Her face was alive with intelligence, and now with hope, the flickering spark of which grew in intensity as her words tumbled forth.

"How so, Lady," Cheke enquired, though he knew she would speak of that which he himself contemplated, and there were many too, who dared not voice their hopes, but cherished and savoured them, as children might anticipate the fulfilling of a daydream.

"The Queen is old for childbearing", the Duchess's voice rushed on. "If there is no issue from this marriage, no Catholic heir... What then?" She hesitated, then spoke the words that implied treason.

"If the Queen should die? She has been sickly for many years. Would the English accept Philip, a foreigner, as their King?" She gave Cheke no time to answer, but leaned towards him, her eyes alive with hope. "Surely they would prefer the Lady Elizabeth to succeed, a wholly English princess?"

"Madam, I am thankful that you are not in England now," Cheke smiled at her animated face. "If your words should ever come to the sharp ears of Bishop Gardiner..." Cheke began.

"Oh, Gardiner, Gardiner", the Duchess broke in. "Who is safe, since the Queen let him out of the Tower?"

"Be careful, Madam. I doubt it will be safe in England for such as we, for many a year."

There was a scratching sound behind the partly open door, and through it waddled a small, fat spaniel, its greying muzzle betraying its advancing years. It came and sat quietly at its mistress's feet, and looked up at her with adoring eyes.

"Oh, Gardiner, Gardiner," the Duchess cried, and gathered the old dog up onto her lap. "If only your namesake were as gentle as you!"

The day lengthened, and Cheke made to take his leave.

Each was reluctant to part, and lingered as they bade farewell.

"God have you in his keeping, Lady. May we meet again in better times."

"God keep you too, Sir John", she replied. They would not meet again.

Summer

Southampton Winchester & London

Now the Spaniard came. The great armada of ships escorting Prince Philip that left the sunny port of Corunna on the thirteenth of July, a week later was seen entering Southampton water. Their sails hung heavy, rain soaked, and some of the bright pennants flying from the masts dangled ragged and torn, evidence of the severe storm that had lashed the fleet in the Bay of Biscay. Below decks, the high-born Spanish ladies on board lay prostrate in the aftermath of seasickness. The voyage had been a nightmare, the vessels pitching and rolling crazily in heaving seas. All in the Prince's entourage had suffered, nor had the Prince himself been spared. Now, entering in calmer waters, the great galleons sailed slowly along the length of the Solent, emerging from the sea-mist that shrouded the water on that dank summer's day.

Then the Espiritu Santu dropped her anchor. Philip and his nobles stood upon the deck of the great flagship and awaited the barge that would row them ashore.

All around them was grey, the water, the sky, the misted coastline. All merged into one dispiriting, cheerless whole.
"Is this what the English call summer?" some of the nobles grumbled. There was no sun, and whatever the season might be called, it was

cold and damp, the leaden skies ever threatening rain.

If, in that moment, when the barge drew alongside, Prince Philip yearned for the sunlit warmth of his homeland, for his mistress Dona Isabel and their two young sons in Valladolid, who could not but feel some sympathy for his unenviable situation? He was here in this dreary land to marry a woman he doubted he could love. She was eleven years his senior, and an aging virgin. To serve Spain and the Holy Roman Empire, it would be his duty, though not his pleasure, to get her with child, and that as speedily as possible, the Queen being well past her youth, and said to be of somewhat delicate health.

They were rowed ashore, and Philip looked back once at the Espiritu Santu, at the Imperial arms of the Empire over which his father ruled, emblazoned upon its mainsail. He needed no other reminder of his duty. It was to his father, the Emperor, the Holy Catholic Church, and if need be, the Inquisition, by which means this heretic land would surely be returned to the embrace of Rome. His own desires must be denied. Then, they were ashore, and the Prince turned and smiled courteously at the English lords escorting him, and was conducted to the lodgings made ready for him in Southampton.

For three days it rained almost incessantly. Not the fine, warm summer showers that refreshed parched earth, but cold, persistent rain that pelted down in torrents. They must, nevertheless, set out for Winchester, where the Queen already awaited her bridegroom.

When they arrived, chilled to the bone, their rich finery drenched and bedraggled, they were met at the Cathedral by Bishop Gardiner, who would perform the marriage ceremony. Philip and his party then gave thanks for their safe arrival in what his disgruntled nobles, to a man, regarded as a benighted, mannerless land.

Briefly, Philip met his bride. She was old, he perceived, with some degree of pity, for he realised the stresses and illnesses of her early life had taken toll of whatever beauty she might have had in youth, and gallantly, he hid his despair. But Mary, who had never known the thing called love, began to feel a late stirring of the heart. Thoughts of love, so long denied, need now no longer be suppressed, and the floodgates of emotion opened, as in a torrent of long pent-up waters.

"I will love him perfectly," she vowed.

The rain continued to fall. It was the twenty-fifth day of July, the day of the marriage of Mary Tudor, Queen of England, and Philip, Prince of Spain and newly created King of Naples by his father, the Emperor Charles. Disappointing as the weather might be, inside the Cathedral all was brilliance and light. The candlelight shone upon the rich hangings of cloth of gold, and struck shafts of colour from the jewel-encrusted clothing of the sumptuously dressed Spanish nobles awaiting the procession of the Queen. When she entered the Cathedral, escorted by her Council and English nobles, and attended by a great number of richly dressed ladies, the sword of state was carried before her by the northern lord, the Earl of Derby.

The ring that was placed upon her finger was an unadorned plain band of gold, for "so maidens were married in old time" she said.

In the Bishop's palace, they feasted and danced. When night began to fall, Gardiner blessed the marriage bed, and at last, the King and Queen were alone.

From his earliest years Philip was aware that, as Prince of Spain, he must before all things serve his father, his country and his faith. In whatever degree of importance these three obligations might be considered to be placed, as a child it seemed to him that each converged with the other, and to serve one, served all. Then, as he grew to manhood, he perceived that service to the Faith, the one true Faith, superseded all other considerations.

So, with the death of the young schismatic King of England, the son of that deviant rogue Henry the Eighth, who had defied the Pope and broken with Rome, his daughter Mary, that most staunchly Catholic of princesses, was come to the throne. Philip knew the workings of his father's mind. Surely, the Emperor would say, "Here is an opportunity devised in Heaven." Three interlocking purposes might be achieved by the joining in marriage of the still unwed Queen of England, and himself, the widower Prince of Spain. It would follow that England would be returned to the true Faith, and God willing, would continue so by the birth of a Catholic heir.

Not least in the Emperor's eyes, there would be the advantage of a foothold too in England, from where, because of that country's proximity to the continent, a vigilant eye could conveniently be kept on matters there. War with France, Spain's old enemy, was an ever present danger, and the Lutheran princes of Germany posed another threat to the Holy Roman Empire. Philip was the key to the neat solution to all these problems, and surely, his father reasoned, his son must see that Heaven was showing the way.

In his private thoughts, Philip could not help likening himself to the sacrificial Isaac of scripture. Unlike the Biblical Isaac however, he doubted that his own sacrifice would be rendered unnecessary by heavenly intervention. He married the Queen. He bedded her. He charmed her with his solicitude, and forced himself to hide the natural reticence he could not avoid feeling - that of a young man shackled to a woman eleven years his senior, and aged even beyond those years by grief and sickness. He pitied her, but he could not love her.

For Mary, the remaining months of that miraculous year were the happiest she had ever known. Whereas only four summers ago, she had feared for her life, and contemplated fleeing England, now she was brought to queenship as its rightful heir. After those long years of degradation and humiliation that she had endured, at last God had answered her unceasing prayers, and turned His face towards her. Now, she had a husband of her own choosing, and if the God of the many miracles He had wrought in her favour chose, she had faith that her union with Philip would be blessed with a Catholic heir. Now, she dreamed the dreams it had been impossible even to contemplate so short a time ago.

August
Kenninghall, Norfolk

In Norfolk, at Kenninghall, in the house restored to him by his Queen, Thomas Howard, third Duke of Norfolk lay dying. The old veteran of so many campaigns, so many in his long life that he had lost count of their number, knew that this last battle was one he could not win. Death did not come to him swiftly, as it might have done so many times in conflict, or by the axe, so close had its presence come then. No, death gave warning of its approach to his aged body, as his accustomed vigour declined. But those seven years of custody within the Tower had surely left their mark upon him.

Before claiming his victim, death gave the Duke time to reflect on the long years of life so few of his contemporaries attained. Since Queen Mary released him from his imprisonment in the Tower, he was restored to the high offices of state to which, as senior peer of England, he had long been accustomed. To him fell the duty in the very month of his liberation of presiding over the trial of the Duke of Northumberland, and soon after, of witnessing his execution.

Then, with pride, he rode before the Queen at her coronation, bearing the sword of state. Pride, Howard pride, was restored for all to see that day.

Then came the winter, and though his eighty-first year was upon him, he rode out again in battle, this time to quell those Kentish rebels marching upon London in protest against the Queen's marriage to the Prince of Spain. The weather was atrocious, and his men deserted, forcing him to retreat. It distressed him to think of it, that his last campaign should end so, in ignominy.

When springtime came, he was changed, and so began the inexorable decline to the inevitable. Still death tarried, content to wait, certain of ultimate victory. In the progressive weakness of his final days, whether sleeping or waking, or lingering between the two states, which is indistinguishable from either, he was young Thomas again, a stripling of twelve years growth. That same year, his father and grandfather rode out to join King Richard in battle against Henry Tudor at that fateful field of Bosworth. There, in the terrible slaughter that ensued, his grandfather was slain, and his father nearly so. But he survived his wounds, only to be committed to the Tower, and stripped of his titles and possessions. There he languished for upwards of four years, until the Tudor heart softened.

Sometimes, Anne drifted in and out of his dreams - Anne Plantagenet, a King's daughter, and a Queen's sister, the wife of his early years. Then another Anne danced by, dark-eyed and haughty, her laughter shrill and fearful. Katherine too came and joined her, their dresses whirling as they danced, their jewels flashing as they moved in graceful motion to the measure of haunting music.

Then came the time for no more dancing. Katherine, the reckless jade, she was indefensible. She asked for what she got. But Anne? Even in sleep the Duke sighed deeply. Was she truly as guilty as King Henry would have her be? And he, her own uncle, with his own lips, had passed sentence of execution upon her.

And once, whether wakeful or sleeping, he could not tell, nor whether it was by day or by night, he saw an ill-conditioned rabble pass before him - poor caitiffs he had called them then, those wretched rebels sentenced by him to hang at Carlisle, even though he doubted the guilt of some of them. Those others too, hanged in their villages, their bodies left to rot, they too disturbed his rest.

Then, he was at York, where Robert Aske stood before him; not dangling in chains from the walls of the keep from which he had ordered him to be cast, but whole and militant, with his throng of Pilgrims at his back.

"You tricked us with your fair words. You promised us the King's pardon", they cried, and pointing to the banner of the Five Wounds of Christ that Aske displayed, they called out, "We fought for the Faith, and Holy Church." The Duke struggled to answer them, restless and tossing in the great bed.

"I served my King", he shouted to them. But to the watchers at his bedside, no sound was heard.

***

After the days of drenching rain that coincided with the Spaniards' arrival in England, there was some respite in the weather as autumn drew on. But no two days could be relied upon to be alike. The climate in this unwelcoming land was fickle and capricious. One day might be bright, the breezes gentle and mild, the next, a cold storm wind might rage, and icy hailstones rain down to briefly whiten the ground. The Spaniards longed for the days of certain sun and warmth that blessed their native land. What might winter be like, they wondered, if this had been what was called summer, and they yearned to go home.

But while Philip stayed, so must they. As the weeks passed, heavy mists rolled in along the river, and droplets of moisture clung to their clothing when they ventured out. October gales lashed the branches of trees, and ripped off their yellowing leaves. The Spaniards clasped their cloaks tightly around themselves, and with bent heads, they walked against the wind. They did not see at sunset the glory of the late autumn skies, the heavens suffused with that shade of blue that is not entirely blue, nor green that is neither green, but is the colour of a thrush's egg. Ripples of primrose merged with wisps of violet and the flush of pink, the whole being illuminated by the gentle gilding of a declining sun.

Nor did they care to be about after nightfall. A gentleman might be set upon in the dark streets and robbed, and though he might cry out for help, the passers-by might have all been deaf, for no Englishman would come to his aid.

Even the ragamuffins that lived on the streets and slept in whatever shelter they might find in the stinking alleys that meandered like rabbit warrens throughout the city, even they aped their elders, and shouted insults as the Spaniards passed by.

It was fortunate that the proud grandees whose hot blood would never have brooked such insolence in their native land, understood little of the meaning of their raucous language, or hands would have flown swiftly to the hilts of their daggers. But there was no mistaking the nature of their crude jibes, so they seethed with suppressed rage, and strove to bear these insults for the sake of their prince.

One and all, their admiration for Philip grew, as the weeks of their stay lengthened into months. There were times when they barely recognised the demeanour of the prince they knew. It seemed to them that he put aside his natural disposition of unsmiling solemnity, and like a snake that casts its skin, he emerged, bluff and hearty, and amenable to the rough customs of his hosts. He even drank and expressed his liking for their foul-tasting ale, he who appreciated the fine wines of their native land.

And his wife, the Queen, that thin, aged virgin who was totally devoid of any feature to charm a man? What was she, stripped of her jewels and rich clothing? By her own admission, she was unknowing in the ways of love, and for the Empire and the Faith, this was the woman that Philip had espoused, and must get with child. It would be hard to find any Spaniard who was envious of his lot.

In the dank days of November, when the raw chill of winter began to bite, there came news of the imminent arrival of Cardinal Reginald Pole from the continent. For twenty years Pole had lived in exile from his native England, but now he came as the Pope's representative to bring the Holy Father's message of absolution to England. Once, as the studious son of the Lady Margaret Pole, Countess of Salisbury, his education had been funded by the Queen's father, both at the Charterhouse and in Italy. Then, King Henry's rage over the Pope's refusal to grant him a divorce, and his outrage at Reginald's less than complimentary pamphlets published from the safe distance of Rome, ensured the downfall of the Pole family.

Even Lady Margaret, his own daughter's lady governess and friend, was imprisoned and later butchered by an inept headsman. Now Reginald Pole was returning in power to his native land, and with the Pope's authority, the stain of schism would soon be purged from England, and the land restored to its ancient Faith.

When the last day of November came, Mary and her husband knelt before the Cardinal. Humbly, she offered the submission of England to the obedience of Holy Church, and asked that her country be received back into the one true Faith. With the pronouncement of the

Pope's absolution, her joy was beyond measure. Her fervent prayers were answered, long years of schism ended, and she was rid of her unwanted title of Head of the Church. Now England was again a Catholic country.

There was another reason, too, for her joy. She carried within herself, she believed, the fulfilment of her hopes of an heir. Was it any wonder that the words of the Magnificat sang in her brain, and there was about her a glow not seen before? After the long years in which she had endured sorrow, degradation, turmoil and danger, now in the few short months of her marriage, the face of God was truly turned towards her. In the Almighty's good time, He had given her the crown, a husband, the return of England to Catholicism and now, while there was still time, the hope of a child. Only one thing more could make her heart rejoice even beyond this present peak of exultation. It would be in the spring of the next year when, God willing, she would hold her son, a healthy prince, in her arms.

Autumn - Lazonby

The Plague

Old Jack the pedlar came early that autumn.

"'Tis my last visit," he told them, when he stopped at the Lazonby tannery. "Old bones," he laughed, "and too many drenchings over these bleak fells."

"So what will you do now, Jack," Mary asked him. "Where will you live?"

"Ah, that is what I want to tell ye," Jack replied. "I never wed, ye know. Neither chick nor child I have. But I have a nephew, my sister's lad - a good lad he is, too. so I am giving him my stock and train. That will be my rent, and I shall live with them in Carlisle."

He loosed his packs for them to make their choice of his wares. Strangely for Jack, he was unusually silent. He spread his wares upon the ground, then his eyes wandered over the expanse of countryside he knew so well.

"I shall miss the life sorely, I think, when the days are sweet, and the birds sing..." The old voice faltered, and John could see the look of regret on the wrinkled face. Like tanned leather it is, he thought, weathered over the years by the wind and the sun.

"We shall miss thee, Jack," he said with feeling, for he had known the old pedlar for as long as he could remember. When they were children, he and Ben had listened impatiently for the sound of the bell on Jack's leading horse, and rushed out to greet him. As if Jack read his thoughts, he asked, "Where is thy brother Ben?"

"In Penrith," John answered shortly. "Gone to buy more ready tanned skins. We're not tanning so much ourselves now. It takes too long now that we're making more saddles and horse gear."

Jack gave him a sharp look. "Have a care, John. Dids't not know the plague has broken out in Penrith? I came away when I knew. 'Tis not wise to go there." He was ready to go, his panniers packed and hoisted back over his pack horse train, and was leading the bell horse out on to the track.

"Oh, I am forgetting," he called. "I have not told the news." He halted the train, then turned to tell them, "The Queen is wed this summer to the prince from Spain. 'Tis said there are many who mislike the match. They fear she will bring back the old religion, and forbid the new."

"God keep thee, Jack. Farewell, old friend," John shouted after him, as he turned and waved, and above the clatter of his horses' hooves, he could hear that now Jack was whistling the merry notes of a jaunty tune.

***

It was a strange thing, the good folk of Lazonby thought, that after his accustomed stop at the Skin House, Jack the pedlar was seen riding astride his bell horse, the rest of his train clattering after him, through the main street of the village. He did not stop, as they expected, but waved aside the women gathering to inspect his wares. He was shouting loudly, and the one word that he yelled was sufficient to strike terror into all those who heard it. Plague!

The Lazonby tannery was located some distance from the main part of the village, on account of the noxious smells that were generated from the processes of that trade, and according to the saddler there, Jack had seemed well enough then. But something happened in that short distance between the Skin House and the village that alerted him to the knowledge that the pestilence was upon him, so swiftly did it strike.

It was many days before they found him. He had pulled his train off the trackway, and laid down on the fellside. From the evening of the first day when he knew he was a victim of the dreaded plague, to the night of the following day, his strength waned rapidly. He had not yet reached Wetheral. He might have reached it had he carried on, but in his more lucid moments, he resolved to shun all contact with human kind. Always, folk had greeted him gladly in the many years he had served their needs.

Now, he would not be the carrier of death to them. His ponies stayed close, cropping the tufted grass. In the moments when his mind cleared, he noticed that they were still laden, and with the last of his strength, he staggered first to his bell horse and set him free of the train.

Then, likewise he loosed the rest. The panniers containing his goods he was barely able to remove from their backs. He panted with exhaustion, but at last it was done, and his train was free to roam the fellside in search of food. Then, he lay down on the springy turf, as it had been needful for him to do many a night on his travels, when he found himself far from habitation and shelter.

Did he feel despair, or anger at being cheated of his well deserved rest after a lifetime of wandering, of time to spend with kith and kin? Maybe such thoughts flitted briefly through his disordered mind. But at the last, the plague bestowed one small mercy upon its victim - a state of indifference to both life and death, and the acceptance of the inevitable.

His ponies wandered near and far on the fell, as countless of their wild ancestors had done for generations past. But the old bell horse remained close by. He nuzzled into Jack's pockets in the hope of finding an apple there, and eventually it was the tinkling of his bell that guided those who discovered Jack's body to the place where he lay.

They buried him quickly, deep in the earth that had served him often as a bed, and sent word to Carlisle.

***

The villagers of Wetheral had cause to be thankful that by Jack's selfless act of charity, their community was spared the dreaded contagion, and none more so than the Aspedailes. At the beginning of September, Janet Aspedaile found herself to be with child. It was an unexpected joy, tempered by the knowledge that she was no longer young for childbearing. Nigh on twenty years had passed since the birth of the babe she had lost in that dreadful time after the Pilgrims' rout, and she would have starved in that bitter winter had it not been for the Aspedailes. John was exultant at the prospect of fatherhood, a condition so long denied him, and his hopes for a healthy child were ever in his mind. When he learned of the old pedlar's death, and the infection that he carried, his heart quailed at the realisation of how close the same danger had come to Janet and her precious babe, and to Margaret too, for they would have rushed out to meet Jack at the sound of his bell.

In Penrith, trading was restricted as the plague spread. All necessary business was conducted with the utmost speed, and none lingered in the town longer than he must. It was not until Ben arrived at the tannery there, which because of the unavoidable stink the processes of tanning created, was situated on the edge of town, that he became aware of the reason for the emptiness of the streets that were usually crowded on a market day. There was always some fever or other breaking out there in the heat of summer, and folk were accustomed to it. And as like as not they recovered.

But plague was different. It killed, and swiftly too, so he heeded the tanner's advice when he had purchased the skins he needed, and made haste to leave Penrith. It irked him though, that he had not sought out the ring that Dinah would be expecting upon his return.

When news of the pedlar's death came from Wetheral, and that he had carried the plague with him from Penrith, there was understandable alarm in Lazonby. Folk kept to the comparative safety of their own dwellings, reluctant to travel if it could be avoided.

"Jack seemed well enough when he stopped here," John said.
"That is the way of it", Ben rejoined. "They told in Penrith that a man might be hale and hearty before noon, yet stricken before nightfall, so quick is the pestilence to strike."

In the days that followed, they watched each other covertly, fearful lest the dreaded signs should appear. Ben feared greatly for Dinah, knowing she never missed an opportunity to buy from the pedlar. Night after night his eyes swept over her face, searching it intently, until she asked, "Ben, why do you stare at me so? Your looks are so fierce."

It was true. His eyes darted wildly, and before long, he began to rave. All through the night Dinah tended him, though he tried to push her away. Mary bathed his face to cool it, and as the night hours wore on, John struggled to restrain the flailing arms.

"Get away from me, all of you. Dinah, go. Get away," he would cry in moments when his wandering mind returned briefly to lucidity. On the third day, he quietened. His strength ebbed away, and in his weakened state, he lay passive, no longer able to resist what inevitably must be, nor seemingly to care that it must be so.

When death came, they knew there must be no delay. With all haste, they wrapped his body in a coverlet, then John lifted his brother up in his arms, and carried him out onto the fellside.

Word travelled fast to shun the Skin House where the saddler's young brother was stricken. Days later, the saddler himself was seen carrying a burden far out onto the fell, and digging a grave there.

No-one came to the Skin House for trade, and certainly not to visit a neighbour in distress. All such considerations were obliterated by the primal need for self-preservation. So, in their isolation there, each endured their own particular sorrow. At first, the sharpness of grief was blunted by shock, then when its analgesic effect was gone, came all the rawness of pure pain.

John worked alone, in unaccustomed silence. Work he had to do in plenty, and now only himself to do it. In the houseplace, Mary and Dinah worked and wept together. Mary was fearful for her daughter's wits, as Dinah alternated between uncontrollable fits of weeping and long periods of trance like lethargy. Still, there was work to do, whatever the pain.

All the while she watched with dread for any signs of the sickness in her son and daughter, but as day followed upon each day, there were none. Nor was there infection in the village, for which they knew they had old Jack to thank for his final service to them. By degrees, life returned to normality, and the saddler's services were in demand again.

***

That year, the rain beat down in torrents, and roads and trackways were churned into tracts of liquid mud. The Eden swelled and ran high and fast, and its grassy water meadows became submerged beneath an ever widening overspill of the river. In the early days of October, however, there was a respite in the downpour. The sun began to shine, feebly at first, in a dun coloured sky, then it gathered strength, and its fitful rays illuminated the sodden landscape with pale flashes of reflected light. On such a morning Dinah woke early, though her mother was already astir. The smell of the bacon Mary was frying at the fireside pervaded the house, and Dinah retched violently.

It had been so for several mornings now; the smell of frying bacon had become sickening to her. She wiped away the spittle from her mouth, and dressed slowly.

John was already fed and away to his workshop by the time she joined her mother in the houseplace. Mary brought two plates of bacon from the fireside where they had been keeping warm, and set them down upon the board.

"I do not think I can eat, mother," Dinah said, and pushed her plate away. "You must start to eat again, Dinah", Mary urged. "Little enough has passed your lips since......" She stopped abruptly, not wishing to say the words that by their utterance must only wound her daughter further.

"You are so thin now, child, just take a little for now," she coaxed. "Here, with some bread." Dinah took the collop wrapped in a piece of bread her mother held out to her. She bit into it, and began to heave. Then she rose hastily, and rushed to the door and spat. When she returned to the houseplace, Mary cast a searching look over her daughter. Yes, she was certainly thin, her gown hung about her shoulders so.

And yet, she looked again, alerted by something she had not noticed before. Could it be that there were signs of a pronounced thickening below Dinah's waist?

The hint of a rounding of her belly; that was certainly not caused by any surfeit of food. In that stark moment of realisation, Mary asked herself how could she not have seen what was now apparent? The absence of Dinah's courses she had attributed to the shock of Ben's death, to grief and her half-starved condition. It was well-known that such things could interrupt the natural sequence and regularity of a woman's times. But now, oh, how could she have been so blind?

"Dinah, are you with child," she asked gently, and drew Dinah into her arms.
"Mother, I believe it is so," came the whispered reply, and together they clung to each other for mutual comfort. Mary fussed, and made sure Dinah had the lightest jobs to do. No lugging of heavy buckets for the benefit of the pigs, yet all day, Dinah was conscious of a dull ache in her back, and as night closed in, she felt a recurring stab of pain in her belly.

She slept only fitfully, in snatches between the discomfort, and when she woke near morning, she was aware of a creeping flood of warmth beneath her. She reached down, and felt a slippery wetness between her thighs. It spread downwards, it reached her knees, and when she withdrew her hand, it was smeared with clots of blood. When Mary pulled back the bed coverings, amidst the mess of blood soaked bedding, she discovered a tiny, barely formed body. Though human, it reminded her of a newly hatched, unfeathered bird.

Much later that day, when the light was beginning to fade, John took up a spade again, and carried a bundle of no weight at all up onto the fellside. He made his way to a place where the sod was still newly dug, and opened up the soft earth beneath. He knelt, and with tender hands, he laid the tiny bundle where below he judged the position of his brother's heart to be.

Then he filled in the small space it had only been necessary to make to bury the tiny body the bundle contained, and carefully replaced the sod upon it. He continued to kneel, for how long he could not tell, but the moon was rising and the first stars glinting in the darkened sky when he rose to his feet. Tears such as he had not shed since childhood were coursing down his cheeks.

Tears of contrition, of bitter regret that in his heart he had held a grudge against his brother, and that the grudge was unresolved.
Time passed before he picked up his spade again and turned to go. In the darkness, it was no longer possible to see where the sod had been disturbed, only a slight rise in the level of the ground indicated the place. It was here, on this fellside in childhood that he had roamed happily with his new brother, showing him where to search for plovers' eggs, and carrying them home so proudly in their shirts.

He lifted the spade over his shoulder. "Forgive me Ben, forgive me, brother," his heart cried out, and then he walked slowly away. The moon now was hidden behind a cloud, and all was enveloped in a grey gloom.

Her body healed itself. It was nature's way. To appease her mother, Dinah responded to Mary's urgings that she eat to renew her strength. Her bodily health was indeed restored, but something was gone, some essential spark, a light put out....John took her by the hand one day, and held it in his own. "I'll take thee onto the fell, sister, to show thee the place" he offered. Dinah's eyes were bright with unshed tears, so blue they seemed to John to be the hue of the wild speedwells after rain.

"Not yet, brother, not yet," she faltered. "But in the springtime, when there are primroses. And in the summer, too. I'll go when the wild roses are in bloom. Oh, yes, the wild roses! I'll take wild roses to that place."

The days were shortening, signalling the dying of the year, but when there were days of pale sunshine, hesitant though the beams might be, Dinah took to wandering through the village, and folk cast curious glances as she walked silently by. The plague apart, and the death of Ben, it was rumoured that there had been something amiss between the brothers at the Skin House before Ben died, the nature of which was not known, but was the cause of much speculation.

Eden was running high and turbulent. It was swollen by weeks of rain, and it carried before it the limbs of trees wrenched off in the accompanying gales. In places on the river where their passage was obstructed, they formed great rafts of tangled branches, until a surge in the river's flow swept them onwards in a heaving mass that gathered to itself whatever debris it encountered in its transit.

Dinah lingered on the bridge that joined Lazonby to its neighbour, Kirkoswald. It was late in the day, and in a mackerel sky ripples of silvery blue dappled its wide expanse. Below her, the river was a rolling highway, widened beyond its normal bounds, so that the bridge was becoming isolated in the ever increasing flood. Dinah saw nothing of this, not the rising mass of water behind her, nor the ever widening sheet of water covering the opposite bank that cut off her means of escape.

On the Lazonby side of the bridge, two men rounding up their cattle from the flooded water meadow, saw her predicament. They were signalling wildly to her, urging her towards them. But a grey mist had clouded Dinah's mind again, blotting out reality, and she saw nothing of her danger. To the men on the bank, so high had the level of the water risen, and so fast, that she appeared to walk upon it.

Suddenly, a coldness gripped Dinah's ankles, and looking down she could see that the level of the river and that of the bridge upon which she stood had become one. In that moment, sanity returned and cleared the mist that fogged her mind. Leaden as it had been in these last terrible weeks, now it became as quicksilver. The men on the bank were calling to her. One carried a staff. He was wading out to reach her through the river's overflow, probing before him with his staff, testing for a sudden drop that would mark the edge of the river bank. Dinah recognised him as her means of rescue, and with the cold flood tugging at her feet, she sped through the water to the bridge's end. There, she was trapped by the ever widening encroachment of the flood. Dinah could hear his words above the sound of the rushing water. He raised his staff and held it out towards her.

'Take hold", he cried. "Hold fast, and I'll pull thee over to the bank."

Upriver, rainfall on the high fells gushed down and augmented the several streams racing to join the already swollen waters of Eden. The river scoured its banks, gathering fallen timber like flotsam into a fast-moving dam that carried all before it. The mass bore down upon the bridge, shattering its ancient oak timbers. They parted, and the torrent struck. It lifted Dinah high in the water, and carried her for a long moment, as if she travelled on a broad highway. There was no fear, no pain, for now reality had flown again, and she was running fast, the wind at her back, across the broad water meadows, as she and Ben had done in childhood. Where the light gleamed brightest, the shining figure of a young man hastened to meet her. Ben! smiling, healed of all hurt, whole again.

He opened his arms towards her, and borne upon the torrent, she raced to join him. Then the wave broke, but before the swirling depths sucked her down, Ben's arms closed fast around her, safe and strong. He was swinging her high, as he had done at their love's beginning, and together they entered that other Eden of perpetual bliss.

Late Autumn, early Winter – Wetheral

There were times, especially in the first years when Isobel and her young son first came to live in Wetheral that she would wake in the night screaming with fright. It was a recurring night terror that woke her, her heart pounding with fear. In that dreadful dream, Robert Winter was back. His face leered with malevolence as he threatened to wrest her from the new found peace and security she and William had found at Wetheral. Over the years, her fears had diminished. Robert had never returned to disrupt the settled tenor of her life, William was now a grown man, and more than a match for his father should he ever come back.

Nearby was John Aspedaile, by whose charity she and young William had found a refuge after Dame Dinah had pleaded for them to accompany her to Wetheral when her House at Heremitithwaite closed. And it was due to John Aspedaile's kindliness too, that William prospered. Truly, John in his wise guidance of her son had been more of a father to William than his own had ever been. Now too, there was William's wife, Ellen.

She also had known only repression, and there was a bond between the two women, each knowing, in her own time, how the human spirit flourished when liberated from the tyranny of abuse. Yes, Isobel considered, how good it was to have achieved the respect of friends and neighbours, to be Mistress Winter, the proud mother of an honest and trustworthy son. No longer did she feel herself to be the misused wife of a vicious scoundrel.

Yet one night, the dream returned, so vivid in its clarity that she woke in terror, bathed in the sweat of fear. The scream that forced itself from her throat only partially wakened her. But Ellen, conditioned by a lifetime of the necessity for alertness, and therefore a light sleeper, was instantly awake.

"William, wake up," she cried. "I heard your mother scream. Something is amiss."

"Ah," William roused sufficiently to mutter, "'tis but a dream she has. 'Tis no matter. It has happened before."

But Ellen pushed back the bedcovers and slid out of bed. "Nevertheless, I will go to her and see. It was a fearful scream."

Outside the window, the night sky was black. She waited only for her eyes to become accustomed to the dark, then she groped her way down the short passage and opened the door of Isobel's chamber.

"Mother, what ails you" Ellen asked. There was a whimper from the bed. The sound was muffled by the pillow on which Isobel's head lay. She was obviously not fully awake, and in a state of paralysing fear.

Vaguely, in the gloom, Ellen could see Isobel's body drawn up into the foetal position, her knees almost beneath her chin. Her head lay face downwards, burrowing into her pillow as if she expected a blow, and her arms were uplifted in protection against it.

"Mother, wake up. There is naught to fear." Ellen laid a hand on Isobel's shoulder, and felt her night-rail drenched with sweat. Then, as she wakened, Isobel's whole body relaxed with relief. She turned over in the bed, and grasped Ellen's hand.

"Oh, I thought it was him! I thought Robert was come back," she whispered. "I saw his face so clearly in that awful dream. So close he came. I could swear he was here."

"There is no-one here, Mother. Only the three of us. Never fear." Ellen's voice was reassuring, but Isobel pleaded "Do not leave me, Ellen. Pray stay with me till daylight comes." She threw back the bedcovers, and Ellen clambered up into the bed, and took the older woman in her arms.

"There now, Mother, rest yourself. 'Twas but a bad dream." She spoke soothingly, as if to calm a frightened child, and pacified now, Isobel slipped into sleep, When William rose at daybreak and quietly lifted the latch of his mother's chamber door, he saw that his wife still cradled Isobel in her arms, and that both women were sleeping peacefully.

They were not to know that in those hours of darkness, the surge that carried away the bridge at Lazonby also bore with it what might at first have appeared to be the body of a newly drowned man. But within the tattered clothing only a skeleton remained, proof that the river had held its victim in her embrace for many a year. A leather shoe still encased the bones of one of the feet. The other shoe was missing, so too were the bones of he who once wore it. The river played with him, loosed him to float upon its surface, then swept him between the outcrops of rock, trapped him for a. while, then sucked him out again, to carry him ever onwards, until at last, what remained of the man who once was, reached Wetheral.

There, in the night hours, his rag- wrapped bones snagged on the submerged remains of the fish- traps constructed there by the long departed monks. In the darkness, while the water swirled past him, he was held for hours in that same place where, years before, another dead man was trapped, a knife lodged fast in his back. Then, as dawn began to break, the river released him. It carried him towards the coast, upon ever broadening waters, until the ebb and flow of the tidal waters cast him onto the sandy flats governed by the waters of the Solway.

There, at each ebb tide, the waders and flocks of screaming sea-birds probed the exposed sands for the food they knew would lie beneath. Some pecked fruitlessly at the disintegrating rags that now only partially concealed what had once been a man, then on discovering no nutriment there, they resumed their more productive quest in the shining sands.

Far away upriver, in the place where Eden had at last let go of the body of Robert Winter, a leather shoe was still held fast in the narrow crevice between the great boulders that lay on the river bed. When the force of the surging water tugged relentlessly at the fragile bones still trapped within the shoe, eventually they had parted. Not far away lay a heavy bundle, unmoved by the power of the river's flow. It had lain there for almost twenty years, and its contents would not deteriorate. It might lie there for centuries to come. It was the silver treasure of the Priory of Heremitithwaite.

***

It was some days later that a man whose errand caused him to ride to Wetheral hailed John Aspedaile as he too was about to ride into the village. The man drew rein and waited till John was mounted, then rode alongside him.

"The bridge is gone at Lazonby," he said. "Dids't thou know it?"

"Nay, indeed I did not," John answered. "Tell me, is it completely gone?"

"It is," the man replied. "I saw it go with my own eyes." He turned in the saddle, and looked directly at John Aspedaile. "There was a young woman on it, but she took no heed of her danger till it was too late. The surge that smashed the bridge carried her with it. She could not have lived, I fear."

"And is it known who the young woman was," John asked.

"Aye," the man said heavily. "It was the tanner's sister, Mistress Dinah Bowerbank. And only lately, they lost their brother to the plague. In the village, they say that Mistress Dinah lost her wits at the grief of it."

"There is no doubt of this?" John queried.
"None", his companion answered. "I was with the man who tried to save her. He held out his staff towards her across the water, and bade her grasp it. But it was too late. The torrent struck, and the bridge was swept away. She with it."

They had reached the village, and there they parted. John hastily conducted his business, and rode speedily home. As he dismounted and led his horse to the stable, he could see Margaret in the barnyard.

"Father, we did not expect thee back so soon," she exclaimed. She searched her father's grim face, and asked, "Is all well, father?"
"Come inside, child, and leave your work. I have sad news to tell."

When John related his tale, Margaret gave a gasp of horror, and hid her face in her hands. "John, oh, John," she whispered.

Janet, always practical, spoke first.

"We should go at once to Lazonby", she declared. Mistress Bowerbank is in great need of comfort now. John, too." She glanced at Margaret, then significantly at her husband.

"I would go myself", she declared, "but for the sake of our babe, I dare not ride."

Margaret leapt up from her seat, and confronted her father.
"Oh, father, take me with you," she pleaded. John's eyes met his wife's, and Janet nodded. So Janet had been right, he thought, when she guessed the reason for the change in their daughter - those days when she sang blithe as a songbird in springtime as she went about her work, eyes aglow with a radiance that lit up her whole being.
Then, for no apparent reason, it seemed the light dimmed, and a sad silence replaced her joyful singing. So, it was the young saddler then that his daughter's fancy had fallen upon.

"You are right, Janet", he agreed. "You must not ride at this time." He looked into Margaret's face. There was an intensity in those eyes that could not deny the strength of her feelings.

"I shall be glad of your company, daughter", he said. "Mistress Bowerbank will have need of another woman, now. You ride side saddle, yes? Then we will take two horses, and go tomorrow, if the weather be fair." As an afterthought, he added

"Perhaps I will ask the saddler to make thee a new saddle. The one his father once made for Sarah is quite worn now."

***

It was a good day for riding, dry and still, and with only a hint of the oncoming winter in the air. Margaret's spirits alternated between sadness at the reason for the journey, and apprehension at what she might find at the Skin House. Also, she could not repress a feeling of elation at the prospect of meeting again with the saddler there. Then she felt shame that her heart lifted so, when his must be heavy with sorrow at the loss of his sister and brother. They rode through the village, and at the Skin House, her father lifted her down from the saddle, and greeted Mistress Bowerbank with grave courtesy.

"Oh, 'tis so good to see thee, John. And Margaret, too," she exclaimed. "Pray come to the fireside and warm thyselves. John is in the village. He will not be long."

"Mistress, we heard but yesterday of the happenings here, and we grieve for your loss." How empty his words sounded, he thought, and he wished that Janet was here. He saw a tear roll down Mary's cheek, and Margaret rose from her stool and took Mistress Bowerbank's hand in her own. He cleared his throat, and continued. "Janet would have come with me, but because of the babe she carries, she dare not ride. So I have brought Margaret with me," he finished lamely.

A tremulous smile touched Mary's lips. "Ah, Margaret," she said wistfully. "So dark! As dark as my Dinah was fair." She caressed Margaret's hand, loath to let it go.

"I always feared I would lose my Dinah," she said, in a voice that began to shake. "Ever since the day when I took her into the village when she was able to walk, and old Mother Benson looked at her and said, 'That child is too beautiful to live. The angels will take her.' Ever since, I have dreaded something would happen to her, and now it has." The shaking voice broke, and a great sob escaped as she hid her face in her hands.

"Oh, what a cruel thing to say," Margaret exclaimed. "Do not distress yourself so, Mistress Bowerbank, I beg of you."

When the saddler returned, he found his mother and the Aspedailes seated in amicable companionship at the fireside. John Aspedaile he greeted warmly, grateful for the promptness of his visit. His eyes slid round to where Margaret sat, his mother's hand in hers.

"Mistress Margaret, I thank thee for coming," he said. Margaret felt a flush spreading over her cheeks as she recognised the pain and longing his look betrayed, and in confusion, she stooped to fondle the sleeping kittens that huddled together in the warmth of the hearthstone.

Immediately, the mother cat flew at her hand, hissing with rage, and John darted forward to chase her away.

"Oh, no. Do not send her out," Margaret cried. "It was my fault to touch them. She was only protecting her kittens."

A memory stirred. I have heard this before, he thought, Margaret's face looked up at him, and he saw in it that of the beautiful young Sister at Heremitithwaite Priory, begging his brother Ben not to be angry at the little hen that pecked his hand when he tried to take her eggs.

"I trust she has not drawn blood, Mistress", he said, and lingered holding her hand as he examined it for scratches. The cat resumed her defensive position near her sleeping progeny, and Mary shook her head in disapproval.

"Winter kitlings again," she said. "They'll be wanting to lie at the fireside the winter through."

By the time the Aspedaile's must depart and were mounted again, a bond had been strengthened, one of sympathy, of kindliness, and where the young ones were concerned, one of deepening, but yet undeclared love.

"So you will make a new saddle for Margaret, then, John?" John Aspedaile asked as he turned his horse's head towards the road that would take Margaret and himself back to Wetheral.

"It will be my pleasure, sir," the saddler replied.
"Then we shall meet again soon," John promised. "Come, Margaret, we need to be home before nightfall."

Margaret looked down as John Bowerbank took hold of her horse's bridle and led it out to join her father on the road. He turned to face her, and their eyes met.

"God keep you, Mistress Margaret," he said, "I shall count the days till we meet again."

"And so will I," Margaret replied. "Truly, John, I will."

***

Preparations for the keeping of Christmas began early in December in the Aspedaile household. Janet's condition was now evident in the thickening of her body, and her altered stance and gait. Her health was excellent. Only rarely did she retch upon rising in the early weeks of her pregnancy, and there was a bloom about her that testified to her joy at this late promise of motherhood. But now was the time when, despite that joy, she must remember that freezing winter of seventeen years ago.
There was no fire then to warm her starving body in that bitter winter, no food but what a kindly neighbour could ill spare herself; her new-

born babe too weak to live, and Luke, her young husband lost in the bloody rout of the Pilgrims at Carlisle.

In the darkening days of December, the horror of those days now crowded her mind, and would do so for as long as she lived. Nor would she ever forget that it was to the Aspedailes that her own survival was due, and that in her arms a motherless babe depended upon her for its own survival. Her thoughts ran on as she worked the up and down churn until the butter began to come. Margaret pushed open the door, and set down the baskets of eggs she had collected from the outhouses in the barnyard. Her face was ruddy from the nip of frost.

"Mother, let me finish the churning," she said. "Rest your arms, do," and she set to working the churn with a will, until she judged the butter to be ready. Janet was glad of the welcome respite. Her arms did indeed ache, and the exertion of swinging the churn was making her breathless. She watched Margaret thoughtfully. Rising seventeen now! How comely she was! "I was married to Luke when I was her age," she reflected. Last night, when she lay in the snug warmth of the feather bed and listened to the low soughing of the wind in the trees, John tossed restlessly at her side. She reached out towards him, and laid a hand upon his arm.

"What ails thee, John," she asked. "'Tis past midnight, and not a wink have you slept."

He heaved himself over onto his side, the better to talk to her, and she, though unable to distinguish his face in the darkness of the curtained bed, turned her face towards him on the pillow.

"What think ye, Janet, if we should ask Mistress Bowerbank and her son to keep Christmas with us? There will be no cheer for them there in Lazonby. Not this sorrowful year." Janet smiled in the darkness, and replied, "I know that it would content Margaret greatly. And yes, company will help to lift a little of their grief. And the Winters, let us ask them too.

Isobel and Mistress Bowerbank find each other good company. And William knows John Bowerbank well."

"Aye, that young man I want to know better. We both know 'tis to him that Margaret's heart is turning." In the darkness, Janet heard his intake of breath, and the sigh that followed. "She is so dear to me, Janet," he said, "And it saddens me to lose her. But the time is coming that she should be wed, and I must be certain 'tis only to a good man that I give her."

"Good like you, John," Janet said softly. "That is what I wish for our daughter, too. A man as good as thee," she murmured into her pillow. "Now ease your mind, John, and rest," she said.

***

Dinah Bowerbank's body was never found. Whether the river held her always in its close embrace, or swept her far away, none ever knew. Little remained of the ruined bridge at Lazonby, and on their way to Penrith market one day, John Aspedaile and William Winter reined in their horses there and surveyed the destruction in silence.

"I mind the time," John said at length, "my father telling me, that in his father's time the bridges were kept in good repair by the monies raised by the granting of indulgences. By the old Church, I mean."

"Aye, so my mother told me," William replied. "But what was the way of it?" he asked. "What must be done then, for folk to obtain these indulgences?"

"Well, John reflected, "before the great changes came about in religion, if a man had the means, he might pay a sum of money to the Church to buy an indulgence to lessen the time his soul would spend in the torments of purgatory when he died. Forty days, I recall, was the time his pains there were lessened. And the money he paid would be put to the cost of maintaining the bridges in good repair. The roads, too."

"So," William said slowly, "that was of great benefit to a man rich enough to pay for such an indulgence. But what of those too poor to pay?"

"Ah," John smiled ruefully, "I fear it was their lot to endure the pains of purgatory for the full allotted time."

William was silent, his eyes fixed upon the fast flowing water that tugged at the scant remains of the old bridge.
"Then when the old order of religion changed," he said thoughtfully, "and such things ceased to be, then I suppose bridges such as this one lacked proper care."

"We cannot tell, William, whether that was the reason why this bridge was not strong enough to withstand that great surge, and the weight of the timber it carried with it. But, come, we must not dally here, we have yet to call at the tannery on our way back from Penrith."

They rode on swiftly, and when they were done in Penrith, they covered the few miles to Lazonby without delay. There was a sharpening wind that bit their faces, and promised a keen night frost. The Skin House stood only a short distance back from the road. The saddler heard the sound of their horses' hooves, and emerged from his workplace to greet them as they dismounted. He led them into the houseplace, where his mother brought small ale, and thrust the poker into the fiery embers on the hearth.

"Come and warm thyselves," Mary bade them, and when the poker glowed red hot, she thrust it into the ale and poured the heated contents into beakers. The three men warmed their shins in the welcome heat of the fire, while time and again Mary heated the poker and plunged it with a great hissing and spluttering into the ale. Their talk was desultory, for a while. John Aspedaile found it difficult to broach the matter upon which his visit depended, and wished, as he had upon his last visit to the Skin House, that Janet was with him.

He shrank from causing Mistress Bowerbank pain, for surely, he reflected as he supped the hot ale she poured, how sorely must she feel the loss of her children at Christmastide.

"I have taken on a lad from the village to help now that my brother is gone," John Bowerbank was saying to William. "I have plans to build up the saddlery trade. 'Tis not worth doing my own tanning now, when I can buy good skins from the new tannery in Penrith." He paused and drank deeply of the hot ale his mother poured into his beaker. "I like the lad well", he was saying, "born after his father was hanged at Carlisle for joining the Pilgrims. He looks well to his widowed mother, too."

"That he does", Mary agreed. "He takes on whatever work he can get, so that she does not want. And he sees to the pigs and fowl for me, too, now that..." Her voice trailed off, and she turned aside to hide the raw grief that contorted her face. John Aspedaile waited until she had control of herself again.

"Yes," she said at length, "'tis a blessing to have a good son. That I know well. And I pray that you, John, might know it too, in time to come.

How does Janet? Well, I trust," she asked.

This was the opportunity that John Aspedaile was seeking.

"I thank thee, Mistress," he said. "Yes, she does indeed do well, she has two willing helpers in Margaret and Ellen. Ever watchful they both are; they care for her well. And Mistress," he continued, "I have a favour to ask of thee.

And John, too. Janet bids me to ask wil't come and keep Christmas with us? It would please her and Margaret so. And William and Ellen, and Mistress Winter will be with us, as well."

"Aye Mistress," William urged. "Your company would content my mother greatly. Ellen too, for I know she still grieves for the loss of her brothers, though they often treated her amiss."

Mary hesitated. She looked at her son's face, and saw that it was alight with hope, with eagerness, and with longing. There was an intensity in his eyes, a wordless pleading, that willed her to accept. Ah, yes, plainly it was young Margaret Aspedaile he yearned for. The eyes of the three men at her fireside gazed intently at her.

She dismissed her own instinctive reluctance to stir from home, from the familiar surroundings where her inevitable sadness might be borne unobserved. Then, she turned to John Aspedaile, and forced herself to smile her thanks.

"Pray give Janet our thanks for her kindness. We shall be glad to come. Is it not so, John," she demanded.

"Mother, it is," John Bowerbank replied, and rising from the stool upon which he sat, he addressed John Aspedaile earnestly, and said, "Sir, I thank thee."

***

It was Christmas Eve, and at Wetheral, days of hard frost encrusted the branches of the trees that surrounded the old farmstead with a crystalline whiteness. It glinted, jewel-like, in the moonlight, and an owl, perched in the mighty oak that had seen the passage of centuries, fluffed his feathers against the cold. They hid the formidable claws that clutched the icy branch upon which he waited, motionless but watchful, as he listened for any stir of rodent life below.

In the soft greyness of dusk, he had roused himself, his great eyes peering out of the hole in the oak tree where he slept the hours of daylight away. In its close confines, he had stretched one leg, and then the other, before emerging to look out onto the greying world. He observed a man riding towards the larger house close by, with a woman seated pillion behind him.

With mild interest, he watched these two creatures of a genus of which he was aware, but which was of little significance to him. Two others of their kind came out from the big house to greet them. One, the man, strode quickly forward to assist the mounted pair, closely followed by the other human, an excited girl. In the bitter days before Christmas Eve, she had feared for a change in the weather, and that a heavy fall of snow might render the road between Wetheral and

Lazonby impassable.

This very morning, her father had smiled at her barely concealed agitation, and assured her, "'Tis too cold yet to snow. Never fear, Margaret, the ground is hard, and good for riding." She had blushed, knowing that her father was well aware of the reason for her anxiety.

"Come inside, Mistress," John Aspedaile was saying, as he lifted the woman down from the pillion. "You must be perished from your ride." Though she and her son had ridden at a fair pace, they were somewhat cumbered by leading a second horse upon which was laden the things they thought would be needed for their overnight stay at Wetheral. Mary's limbs were stiff, numbed by the intense cold, and had not John Aspedaile still been supporting her as he set her down, she feared they might have buckled beneath her. But her son was already dismounted and at her side, one strong arm around his mother's waist. The other he held out to John Aspedaile.

"I give thee the season's greetings, Sir," he said, and grasped the hand John Aspedaile offered in return. In the fading light, he could see Margaret's face. It was alight with joy, and was it....love? Yet she held back, overcome by sudden shyness. That look, had only he seen it? His pulses raced. He strode forward and grasped her hand. "Greetings, Margaret," he said. His voice was thick, and sounded strange to him, as though it was not his own.

"I wish thee joy of the season", that same voice said.

"'Tis joy indeed, now you are come, John." Her voice was low, intense as his own had been. He did not release her hand, and in the gathering dusk, she leaned against him. He smelled of new leather, and mingling with it, she caught the faint, but characteristic perfume of lavender, the dried flowers of which his mother had laid between the folds of his best, but seldom worn shirt when last she laid it away in her linen chest. For a fraction of time, in the welcome dark, he held her close, and cupped her head in his hand. When they drew apart, he to follow her father to stable the horses, and she to lead his mother into the warmth of the house, to each, those brief seconds were a foretaste of what a bliss as yet unknown to them might be. Each was changed, elevated in a vibrant awareness of a newness of life.

At length, the door of the big house closed, and only the glow of soft light that streamed from the windows broke the night's darkness, though the owl's acute hearing could detect the faint murmur of voices within. He could not know that many seasons of owl-life ago, one of his own kind had listened in puzzlement in this same tree, to the sounds that precede the opening of the gateway to human life.

Suddenly, his great eyes widened. Something stirred on the ground below. Without a sound, he glided aloft, quartering the ground where the barnyard and the stables stood.

A young rat, disturbed by the presence of the two strange horses in the stable where he sheltered from the cold, was eagerly devouring the few scattered grains of corn the fowl had neglected to find at feeding time.

He never heard the noiseless approach of the owl as he swooped. Only the slight movement of the air created by his silent wings alerted the rat to his peril.

Then, powerful talons gripped his body, and he felt himself swept upwards and carried high into the branches of the oak tree. He struggled, of course, and emitted frantic screams of terror, until the owl's powerful beak crushed the bones of his skull with ease. The owl dined well that night, after which he sat replete upon his favourite branch. Then, snow began to fall, covering the frost-laden branches of surrounding trees and settling upon the hardened ground. He shook the flakes from his white feathers, and sought the shelter of his hole in the oak tree. There would be no more hunting that night.

***

The company gathered in the big house dined well, too, unaware as they ate at the laden board of the whitening world outside the snug confines of the houseplace. Mary's cold body was warmed, and in the congenial spirit of good fellowship, the ice that encased her heart began to melt. John Aspedaile sat at the head of the board, well contented with the scene before him. His wife, with her unborn child faced him, her hands resting upon her high belly. Janet surveyed the remnants of the feast she and Margaret, and Ellen too, had laboured long to prepare.

The two fat geese, lately carved by John, were now reduced to skeletal proportions, and the great ham was pared down to the bone. Likewise, the custards, the sweet pies and pasties baked from the orchard's fruits were now being eaten with relish. She caught John's eyes upon her, and they assured her of his tacit appreciation of their efforts. From time to time, the eyes of John Bowerbank and Margaret sought each other across the board, holding for a while, and conveying messages they could not yet speak.

A great log that had dried out in the stable since the March gales felled it, rested upon the hearthstone. William and John Bowerbank took hold of each end and lifted it together, then set it in the glowing embers of the turf fire.

Soon it was ablaze, and all the company gathered their seats before it, the dense wood burning slowly and long. The young folk chattered eagerly together, glad of this rare chance of conviviality. Mistress Winter and Mistress Bowerbank sat close, deep in amicable converse, each finding a mutual comfort in each other's company. Each too recalled times spent at Heremitithwaite priory, and spoke with loving reverence of Dame Dinah.

Time and again, they heated the poker to fiery redness, and thrust it spluttering into the ale, and talked, as folk do at Christmastide, of times past and hopes for future days. All was warmth, kindliness and amity. When midnight approached, the great log was almost burnt through, its glowing heart sheathed in a powdering of white ash. Mistress Bowerbank began to nod.

Soon too did Mistress Winter. It was time for the company to seek their beds. The Winters bid their goodnights, and John Aspedaile flung wide the door, so that they might make their way back to the old farmstead. Outside, the snow had ceased to fall, and it was as bright as day. The moon stood high in the sky, and countless stars twinkled in its cold light. The world was white, pristine and pure under its coverlet of virgin snow. Before daylight dawned, and man sullied that purity, the only marks upon its surface would be those of wandering trails of tiny feet, where hungry birds foraged to find food.

"There has been a fall of snow," John Aspedaile called. "It will not be so cold, now." Margaret rushed to the door to see. "Oh, it is so beautiful" she cried in delight. "Look, John, just see the branches of the trees. I love to see them so." She turned to John, her face alight with happiness. "This is the best Christmas of my life," she murmured, so that only he could hear. He looked down at her glowing face, and gently caressed her cheek with the palm of his hand. "Of mine, too, my dear, dear Margaret. Might I call you so?" he asked.

"With all my heart. Oh, yes, with all my heart," was her impassioned reply. Janet appeared, candle in hand. "John, your mother is abed now," she said. "And Margaret, 'tis time that you were, too. 'Tis Christmas Day, now." She was tired herself, and longed to lie down.

John Aspedaile took the candle from her hand. "Come, John," he said. "I'll light thee to thy chamber. Janet, go to bed thyself," he urged, when he came down the stair again. "Go and rest. I will not be long."

When all were gone to their beds, and he was alone, he opened the door again, and stood looking at the white world beyond. His eyes travelled to where the old pear tree stood, clothed like the others in a gown of purest white. Marguerite!

Always he must remember her, as now, in the beauty of newly fallen show, unsullied by the world upon which it lay. One day, he must tell Margaret of that terrible morning, when he had lifted her mother's frozen body out of the drifted snow there. But not yet, for he shrank from burdening her with that sadness. He would wait, he decided, until she should be wed, and there was another she would love, in another, different way that she loved himself. That one would then share her sorrow, and lighten it with his love. He closed the door, and returned to the warmth of the houseplace.

The great log still glowed red through its white powdering of ash, and he sat in the darkened room and watched until its bright heart burnt out. On the morrow, he determined to speak to the young saddler, and discover where his intentions lay.

***

John Bowerbank lay deep in the warmth of the feather bed. He woke early, as dawn was breaking. Christmas Day! Somewhere near, under this same roof, lay Margaret, his dear love. Of that he was sure, though until now he had never fully realised, she was what he had unconsciously been seeking all of his life. And that she should feel love for him, it seemed a miracle. He was wide awake now. All was still, and he watched the light beyond his chamber window grow brighter. Today, he resolved to speak to her father, and ask his leave to court her.

No doubt John Aspedaile would wish to know -no, he would demand to know of him, in what condition he proposed to maintain his daughter. And rightly so, John mused, for no-one could fail to realise the depth of John Aspedaile's love for her.

There was not a sound in the house, so he continued to lie snug in the hollow his body made in the warmth of the well stuffed feather mattress. Only his nose, of necessity, emerged above the heavy bedcovers, and he felt the sharp nip of the night's frost. Then, when he heard the sound of footsteps descending the stair, he rose and dressed himself quickly. He found John Aspedaile dragging his boots on, Christmas Day or no, there were beasts to tend and feed. William Winter was already abroad, at the milking, so they made their way to the stables.

The snow that had fallen the night before was light enough, and there was no drifting. Where they trod, their footprints compressed its unmarked surface to icy greyness in their wake.

Inside the relative warmth of the stable, when the cleaning out was done and the horses fed , there would be no better opportunity than this, John Bowerbank judged, to approach Margaret's father for his consent to pay his addresses to his daughter.

"Sir, I have brought with me the new saddle you bade me make for Margaret. 'Tis here", he said, and he retrieved the saddle from the corner of the stable where his own two horses stood. "And by your leave, Sir, I would give it as my Christmas gift to her."

John Aspedaile viewed the saddle, marking the quality of the leather, and the fine stitching upon it. Without a doubt, he perceived that this young man was a master of his trade.

"'Tis a fine saddle, John," he said at length. "I admire thy workmanship; I do believe 'tis even better than the one thy father once made for Sarah. A deal of years back, that was."

"I remember, Sir. At the time of the Pilgrims, it was. My father took my mother and us children with him as far as Heremitithwaite, and left us with the nuns there for safety, before he rode on to deliver that saddle to you. We stayed overnight at the Priory, and when he returned and took us home, we found that the Pilgrims had made off with our pigs and fowl while we were away."

"Ah, I did not know that," John Aspedaile said thoughtfully. So, the lad was at the Nunnery, then. Perhaps he saw Marguerite there - but he would not speak of that now. It was of Margaret they must talk. He rubbed his chin, and considered what he should say. It was not in his nature to dissemble, so he asked directly, "Tell me, John, how does thy business, now that thy brother is gone? Does it prosper?"

"Indeed it does, Sir" John Bowerbank replied eagerly. This was the opening he hoped would lead on to what he desired to ask of John Aspedaile.

"I have work a-plenty. Not only saddle making, though that demands the greatest skill, but also bridles and horse collars, and the long reins that are needed for snigging in the woodlands, and all manner of repairs needed for leatherwork. In fact, I have so much work, I have taken on a lad from the village. He is quick to learn, and I have a mind to apprentice him, so that he can begin to learn the lesser skills of the trade. That would give me more time to attend to those things that only a competent saddler can do."
He paused for breath, and John Aspedaile smiled. How the lad ran on in his enthusiasm. Aye, Andrew had taught his son well, he thought.

"William tells me thy mother has a care for this young lad," he intervened. "That is so," John replied. "He sees to the pigs and fowl for us. Before we came, she gave him leave to take her all the eggs he collected while we are away." He grinned with amusement. "And" he said, "she cut some thick slices from one of our hams, so that they should not want at Christmas. Long widowed, his mother is, and sickly, too."

"Her charity does her credit", John Aspedaile agreed, He looked quizzically at the young man before him. Neither he nor himself had so far broached the matter each had determined to raise the night before, and it was getting cold in the stable. The horses shifted and stamped their feet in the newly laid bracken, whilst their breath billowed in clouds of grey-white vapour on the frosty air. He determined to bring the matter to a head. He rested his hand upon the new saddle, and looked directly at John.

"I can see that this has taken thee a deal of thy time to make, and I would gladly pay thee for thy work.." He stemmed the protest he could see the young man about to make. "Nay, hear what I have to say, and take care how you answer. I must ask, how stands it between thyself and my daughter, for 'tis plain thou'rt drawn to her, and she to thee?"

"Sir, 'tis true", John answered. "What I feel for Margaret, I have never felt before, for I have had neither the time, nor indeed the inclination to dally. Sir, in all truth, I believe that I love her." He drew himself up to his full height, and looked John Aspedaile directly in the eye. "And Sir," he spoke ardently, "I came to thy house this Christmastide to ask permission to court her in all honour. As to the saddle, 'tis a gift of love that I would offer her, with thy consent, that is."

"Well answered" John Aspedaile said. "Then thou hast it. Give her the saddle, John. She will like it well. But take heed. Meddle not with my daughter's affections unless thy desires and intentions be true, for I will not see her wed into heartbreak. Remember, John, for 'tis upon this condition that I give my consent, for she is very dear to me. We will speak of this again, but come now, my belly tells me 'tis time to break our fast." He clapped John heartily on the back, and opened the door of the stable.

"Sir, I thank thee. I shall abide by that condition, and pray I shall never be the cause of hurt to Margaret," John answered earnestly, and held out his hand to John Aspedaile.

"Then come, let us go in and give Margaret her new saddle." John Aspedaile took the proffered hand in his own firm grasp, and there was mutual respect between them.

The day passed in feasting, good humour and contentment, and between the lovers, joy abounded.

It was a hard winter. Snow began to fall the night after the Bowerbanks rode home to Lazonby, and continued, relentlessly, drifting in white waves across the fells cutting off access between villages and towns, for days and even weeks. Life was hard, both for man and beast. It was a time to be endured until the coming of spring. Even then, the high places retained the ragged remnants of snow on their tops, and lingered there tenaciously after the lower tracks and roads were clear again.

1555
Spring – Wetheral

At the beginning of April, John Aspedaile rode again to Penrith market. It was a cold, blustery day, the feeble sunshine uncertain, and more than once he was caught on the open road in a drenching shower. But his business in Penrith was urgent, and once there, he lost no time in seeing about it, then hastening on to Lazonby to see how the Bowerbanks did. He dismounted quickly, and found John in his workshop.

"'Tis not fit yet for Margaret to ride." he said. There was a look of disappointment on the young saddler's face, when he saw that he rode alone. "The roads are full of mire, and besides, Janet is near her time. But Margaret would be glad to see thee, John, I know it, if there is time for thee to spare to visit."

"Is all well with Janet?" Mary asked, as she poured him hot ale in the houseplace.

"It is," he replied, "I thank thee. And so I pray it may be, for 'tis not long before the birth." He was anxious to be on the road again, and so soon they parted.

"Come soon," he urged John as he mounted up again, "for I know Margaret longs to see thee."

It was springtime, and in the small hours before daybreak, Janet Aspedaile woke. There was a faint stirring in her belly. It was not a pain, not yet, though her instinct warned her it preceded the pains of labour soon to come. There was a dull ache in the lower region of her back, and she grasped the edge of the bed and heaved her swollen body over in an effort to ease herself. John still slept at her side, undisturbed by her movements, his breathing rhythmic and deep. She lay still, waiting for the stirring to consolidate into the pangs that would indicate the certain onset of childbirth. But it would not be yet. Not for many hours might it be before, God willing, she held John's precious child in her arms, safely brought to birth.

Her thoughts slipped back to that other time, when it had been winter, and bitter cold. She was famished. There was hardly a crust left to eat, and Luke gone. If it had not been for the kindly old crone who knew of her plight, and came to help birth her child, Janet was sure she would have died that night, nor would she have cared. The puny babe that slipped from her body into an unwelcoming world, barely uttered a weak cry of protest. Neither did it cry lustily for nourishment, as robust babes do.

It lingered, cold, pale and silent, until one night it slipped imperceptively from sleep to death. In the darkness, Janet wiped away a tear. Ah, but she was a different woman now. She was strong and well-nourished herself, and that terrible time was many years ago. The thought reassured her; but then, with the passing of those years, had she not become old for childbearing? Conflicting thoughts battled in her mind, tempered by that persistent edge of fear.

She turned again, slowly, in the bed. The Queen, her time was come, too, it was said. How did she, Janet wondered? She too was past her youth. John slept on, undisturbed by her movements, and some time before dawn, she drowsed into half sleep. When she woke, the sun was up, and John was gone. Beyond the chamber window, the May morning shone. The sky was a cloudless blue, and somewhere, in its never ending vastness, a skylark sang. Oh, that was indeed a pain! Yes, her labour had begun.

The door latch lifted, and Margaret entered quietly. "Mother, you are awake now", she said. "I will fetch you a posset of new milk, with the best ale." She cast an anxious look at Janet, and asked, "Is it well with you? Father said you must be left to sleep."

Janet smiled, lest her own anxiety show. "It is, Margaret," she replied. "I would be glad of the posset. Something woke me in the night, and now I am sure we shall have our babe, ere long."

Margaret ran to the bed, and flung her arms around Janet. "Oh, mother, I will pray for you," she murmured. They clung together wordlessly, their love for each other not needing words, too deep for utterance. At length, Janet raised Margaret's head from where it rested on her shoulder. "I know that you will, my dear, dear daughter." She kissed Margaret tenderly upon her forehead.

"Now," she said, "go and find John and tell him. And Isobel, too. I shall have need of her."

The day wore on. Pains came and went, then came again and grew in their intensity. Isobel sat by the bedside, and wiped away the sweat from Janet's face.

Her labour was hard and protracted. The shadows of evening deepened, then merged into the star-lit night. The moon rose, then rode high in the sky, then dipped and paled as another dawn began to break. In the great bed, between her recurring pains, Janet fell for a while into an exhausted sleep.

"How much longer can this go on?" John asked wearily. There was fear in its voice, though he strove to hide it, lest he add to Margaret's obvious concern.

"Have patience, John", Isobel spoke reassuringly. "This little sleep will give her strength, and the babe, too. When she wakes, I think it will not be long, now." It was so, when the sunlight broke through the morning mists, Ellen came with new milk, and Janet woke, refreshed.

"I have such a thirst", she gasped, and drank deeply from the beaker that Margaret held to her lips. Then the pains came sharp and fast, and with each pain, she mustered the strength she did not know she had. Guttural sounds forced their way from deep within her throat as she strained with all her might to bring her son to birth.

He yelled lustily, as Isobel quickly wiped away the streaks of natal blood from his sturdy body, and laid him in the receiving cloth held out in Margaret's arms.

There was joy, and laughter, the laughter of relief. For all, their exhaustion was dispelled in the wonder of the eternal miracle of new birth. Hours later, John Aspedaile sat in the quiet chamber, and listened to the sound of birdsong on the evening air. His eyes travelled alternately between the sleeping form of his wife and the old wooden cradle close by , where his new son too was sleeping.

When Janet woke, he took her hand, and raised it to his lips.

"Sweetheart," he said "I have been thinking. Would it please thee to name our son Luke?"

Janet's eyes filled tears, but these were tears of joy, of heart-wringing emotion. This, she knew, was a good man's supreme offering of love.

"Oh, indeed John, it would, if it would content thee, too," and she raised his hand that cradled hers to her lips.

Spring - Hampton Court

A miserable winter had been passed by those at Woodstock. The Lady Elizabeth objected volubly to her lodgings there. It was cold, despite efforts to heat the place. It was damp, because the rain seeped in where the palace had been left in disrepair for years. Icy draughts penetrated through ill- fitting doors and casements. But most of all, it was the monotony of each dreary day in her isolation there that drove the royal prisoner almost to distraction. So too, Sir Henry Bedingfield. His task of keeping his fractious charge contained was no sinecure.

She fussed, she complained, sulked and continually demanded an audience with the Queen, and when such requests were ignored, the conscientious Sir Henry bore the brunt of his irate prisoner's displeasure. But with the coming of spring, release came for both. The Lady Elizabeth was ordered to Court for the Queen's expected lying-in, there to await the delivery of the prince who would supplant her in the line of succession to the throne. April came, and went, so did May, and still there was no child.

"A miscalculation", the doctors attending the Queen assured her. "Your time has not yet come." But the unease they felt was growing. In June, the Queen received a woman who demanded to see her on account, she said, of the Queen's condition.

"Your majesty", she mumbled, her speech impaired by the loss of most of her teeth, "the doctors' reckoning is not always right. My son was nigh three months overdue his expected birth time, and there were those who mocked me, and said I was not with child. Madam, I was over forty years old at that time, and now my son is a grown man, with children of his own."

Mary's generosity, even before she became Queen, was well known. The bearer of even the simplest of gifts when she lived a rejected princess, never went away unrewarded. A dish of apples, a basket of new-laid eggs offered in sympathy, always elicited its own reward. How much more so this woman's words cheered her. To Mary, they were a gift of great price, and the woman was rewarded accordingly. It was not long before grandmothers were flocking to Court with their own daughters' babes, and claiming them to be their own.

When another month passed, and there was still no sign that the birth was imminent, it seemed that only the Queen herself believed that she carried a child. All things were possible to Almighty God she wholeheartedly believed. Had not this been proved in the last two years of her life? Her faith was steadfast that He would not deceive her now. July! She must be told, though all shrank from the task. The child existed only in the fixation of the Queen's mind.

***

Philip stared at the despatches newly arrived from Brussels. His father needed him there, and urgently. It was the Emperor Charles's intention to abdicate and return to Spain, there to spend the rest of his life in contemplation in a monastery at Juste. Perhaps, Philip mused, the fact that mad Queen Juana, his grandmother had died in March, had hastened this decision for a peaceful retirement from the worldly cares of governing the vast Hapsburg Empire. The greater part of his father's life had been spent travelling between his far-flung territories. With weariness and declining health, now he wished to relinquish his vassal states to the care of his son.

Philip's immediate thought was "I can leave England now with justification. I have done all that I can here." True, he had been chiefly instrumental in facilitating Cardinal Pole's return to England, and with the Pope's absolution, now the country was returned to Holy Church. For the sake of the Church, his father and his country, Philip had borne with all the fortitude he could muster his marriage to Mary Tudor. For the sake of the expected child, the child that never was, he had remained at her side. It was never intended that he should remain indefinitely in England, it was only until an heir should be born. But now it was evident that Mary was ailing, and was unlikely ever to bear a child. Poor Mary! She was distraught, and he pitied her. But how he longed to get away, and he must hide that longing from her.

The Queen's distress, when finally she was forced to accept the bitter truth that her distended body contained no child, was terrible in its intensity.

Of her ladies, only those two favoured persons, Susan Clarencius and Jane Dormer, were witnesses to the depth of Mary's grief. They bathed her face, swollen from weeping, and brought soothing draughts to calm her. Her doctors prepared potions, which she was persuaded to swallow, and by and by, the swelling in her belly was reduced. Those of her gowns that had been let out to accommodate her increasing girth, were skilfully taken in again by the seamstress hastily employed for that purpose.

As ever, in the many periods of anguish she had endured in her life, and there were many, prayer was her refuge. God had brought her to queenship, and those duties that state entailed, she would not shirk. All the paraphernalia of her expected lying-in must be dismantled at Hampton Court. The palace badly needed cleaning, and the Court returned to London. Susan Clarencius found her one day carefully folding away the christening robe Katherine of Aragon had brought with her from Spain so long ago.

"Ah Susan," the Queen said sadly, "my mother grieved for the loss of her real babes. I grieve for the loss of the one that never was." A tear rolled down her cheek, then fell upon the exquisite whiteness of the little gown.

July - London, Smithfield

In the corner of one of the crowded London gaols a man condemned to die as a heretic bent low over the prostrate form of his son. The lad, a youth of some seventeen years, and also condemned to die the same appalling death, was already burning up, but more mercifully, by a fever. It was July, and both father and son had been confined in the fetid air of the prison since their trial in January, under the revived heresy laws. All over London, the prisons seethed with overcrowding, and fever was rife.

Through his cracked lips, the lad murmured "Water, water", so his father rose and made his way to where a leather pail was chained to the wall, and a ladle, similarly chained. The man looked around, hoping to find something in which to carry the water, but there was nothing. So he tore off a piece of cloth from his ragged shirt, dipped the ladle into the pail, and teemed the water over the rag to soak it. He hurried back to where his son was lying, and dripped the water thus collected between the lad's dry lips. But now it was not possible for him to swallow. Then, the father laid the wet cloth tenderly upon his son's burning brow.

The lad had always been slow witted. He was not an imbecile, he did not rave, but perhaps simple would best describe his condition of mind. He certainly was not capable of understanding the import of his examiners' questions at his trial.

What could he make of that most vital question - "Do you believe in the corporeal presence of Christ in the sacrament?" He did not understand, and he did what he often did to hide his confusion - he laughed. Repeatedly, he was asked the same question, until his examiners lost patience with him and asked, "Is your answer 'yea' or 'nay'?" Confronted. with an easy choice, he answered "Nay," and thus condemned himself.

Execution was to be carried out the following day. So great now was the need to empty the crowded gaols that this was to be a mass burning. If his son was still alive by the morning, he would be carried to the fire. The lad was quieter now, his breathing so shallow it was barely perceptible. His father knelt down at his son's side, and clasped his hands together in prayer. He needed no priest to intercede for him. In the young King's reign, he had learned to speak directly to his Maker and had found the comparative simplicity of the reformed religion to his liking. Now he would continue steadfastly in that faith to his life's end.

"Almighty God," he prayed, "Father of all men, look mercifully upon my beloved son, and take him into Thy loving care before men harm him in Thy Name."

The lad seemed to be sleeping peacefully now. His father took hold of one limp hand. It felt cooler to his touch. He held it within his own, and listened to the noise of the unseasonable rain that poured down in torrents outside the gaol. An hour passed, maybe two, he could not tell. The hand that he held had grown colder. The noise of the rain ceased, and he heard another sound. It was the gentle rush of his son's last breath as it left his young body.

***

Five were to burn at Smithfield that day. A crowd waited in the square where the bundles of faggots were stacked. When the pitiful procession arrived, each man was chained to a stake, and the faggots stacked in a circle around him. A makeshift pulpit was made ready, and a priest began to speak. Queen Mary was insistent on the value of good preaching at these events. The attitude of the crowd was mixed. Had not the punishment for heresy always been burning? Might not a foretaste of the eternal flames of Hell persuade a burning man to recant, and thus avoid his soul's damnation? Such was the mind of the conservative Catholics gathered to watch. But there were others too, those who were convinced of the truth of the new faith, who gathered close to give their support and encouragement to their brethren facing martyrdom.

At the front of the pyre stood the man whose son, by his timely death was spared the flames. In the crowd, he noticed a man, unknown to him by name, but recognised as one who worshipped as he himself had done in the time of young King Edward. The man smiled at him, and moved forward to be near him.

"Heart up, neighbour," he called. "The fire is but the gateway to Paradise." The priest's exhortation was ended. There was a brief silence. If a recantation was expected, there was none. "Fiat justitia," the cry rang out.

The attendants approached with their blazing torches, and held them at the base of the faggots. The fire was slow to start, the wood damp from the previous day's rain.

Smoke, acrid and choking, billowed up into the faces of the five chained there. More wood was brought, and stacked at their feet, and this, being drier, began to kindle. A slow flame rose up, and licked at the feet of each victim.

"Courage, friend," the man in the crowd called, and drew closer. "Beyond the pain is salvation." He spoke directly to his neighbour, willing him to summon all his strength for the ordeal. The flames were climbing higher now. A spark flew up, and ignited first his beard, and then his hair. In seconds, it burst into a fiery halo encircling his head. There was a gasp from the watching crowd, and to some, those old enough to recall such things, it brought to mind the images of those sainted beings once painted on the walls of their churches.

But the countenance of the burning man bore no resemblance to the calm demeanour of those painted, holy ones. His face was hideously contorted as the fire bit into his scalp, and his mouth opened wide to emit his agonised screams.

The stench of roasting flesh hung upon the air. Time froze. None who watched could rightly tell how long the tortured body endured before there came the merciful oblivion of death. But at last, there was silence, broken only by the roar of the flames leaping high now, and feeding on the fat that oozed from the blackening bodies.

The agonised writhing was ended, the bright halo faded, the hair upon which it fed burnt out. The scorched head slumped forward to meet the engulfing flames and the ghastly spectacle was over.

***

It was August when they finally removed from Hampton Court and came to Greenwich. There, Mary must school herself for the formal leave taking of Philip and the chosen party who would accompany him to Brussels, where his father, the Emperor waited to invest him with the sovereignty of the Netherlands. A barge waited on the river to carry him downstream to Gravesend, and embarkation at Dover. He was anxious to be away, to be free of the wife he could not love. She, wretched at his imminent departure, and not knowing when or if he would return, stifled her inner misery, and watched from a window until the barge carrying the Spaniards vanished from sight. Then, she wept in as much privacy as the royal state afforded, with only her ladies to witness the desolation of her wretchedness.

In Brussels, the Emperor Charles made ready for his departure to Spain, having laid the burden of the government of the Netherlands on Philip's shoulders. He longed for the peace of the monastery of Juste, and to be done with travelling and warfare.

Despite her sadness, Mary must nevertheless attend to all matters of state and religion that, in her unique position as a reigning queen, devolved upon her. The autumn days faded, and winter approached. There had been rain and floods, and much loss of harvests. So great was the flooding that the Thames broke its banks, and the little wherries that plied their trade upon the river were able to sail into the streets of London.

The Lady Elizabeth, called to attend her sister in the months prior to the expected birth of the royal heir, now obtained the Queen's permission to return to Hatfield, where before long she was again suspected of plotting, and vehemently declaring that she had no wish to marry Duke Emmanuel Philibert of Savoy, the husband her brother-in-law Philip had proposed for her. Mary, with some justification, suspected that her wily sister had her sights set upon her own eventual succession to the throne.

***

After his parting with the Duchess, Sir John Cheke travelled into Italy. He was made welcome at the University of Padua, which benefitted from his deep knowledge and pronunciation of the Greek tongue. Upon his return, he settled at Strasburg in company with a great number of his compatriots exiled there, where they were free to practice their reformed faith. The news that filtered through from England was dire. The heresy laws had come into force on the twentieth of January 1555, and two weeks later, the first of many fires that would be lit at Smithfield consumed its first victim.

A man newly come to join the exiles that year witnessed the burning of Bishop John Hooper at Gloucester.

"Market day it was," he told them. "There was a great crowd gathered; I saw it with my own eyes. There was a wind that day. The wood was wet, slow to light. Yet when the flames took hold, the wind blew them away and he died slowly, like meat roasted upon the spit."

"For God's love", he pleaded, again and again, "let me have more fire."

Cheke's licence to travel expired, and when he failed to return to England, the remainder of his lands and estates that had been granted to him in King Edward's reign, were confiscated to the Queen's use. What monies he had taken abroad to sustain himself had now been spent, and he must find a means to earn his bread. Then he fell sick, but when he recovered, he made shift to read a Greek lecture at Strasburg, preferring to live in exile in his reduced circumstances, rather than return to England and renounce his principles.

In that dreadful year, fires burned, not only in London, but at sites over the south of England, as the persecution of those stalwarts for the reformed faith who would not recant gained pace. News came of the burning of Bishops Hugh Latimer and Nicholas Ridley at Oxford in October. They were bound together at each side of the same stake. Latimer died quickly, but for Ridley, it was not so. Some of the faggots were green, and would not take hold. Then, the slow flames that began to lick at the soles of his feet were carried away by fitful gusts of wind.

They veered towards the timber stacked around the side of the stake where Latimer stood. Suddenly, some of the drier wood ignited, and a sheet of flames leapt up! Through the crackling of the now fiercely burning timber that engulfed Latimer's body, he could hear the older man's voice calling to him.

"Be of good cheer, Master Ridley. We shall this day light such a candle, by God's grace, in England as I trust shall never be put out."

The flames roared, and mounted higher. He could smell the stench of burning flesh. Latimer's voice was silent now. He could not burn, and in the extremity of his pain, he begged for the fire to come to him. To Cheke's distress, he learned that his friend Cranmer had been taken to the top of the gatehouse of Oxford's town gaol, and made to watch the horrific progress of the bishops' agonising deaths.

Autumn - York, Lazonby & Wetheral

The pedlar was late that autumn. In York, he fretted for two whole weeks as he waited for the commodities he needed to arrive there. It was October before he left the city, and he should have been across the high fells and on his way home to Carlisle by that time. He was mindful of the dire warnings his uncle had given him, to avoid crossing that wild territory when the weather was likely to worsen, though at any season it might change without warning.

"Take heed of the helm, lad," the old man had warned him often, "for when the cap sits atop Crossfell, 'tis bad for man and beast alike, any's the time I've been caught in that icy wind that blows then, strong enough to blow thee over the edge, it is."

Nevertheless, though he chafed to be away from York, he made good use of his enforced stay, for there was much news to be had, and he must commit it to memory so that he could recount it wherever he went. And what news it was! Fearful news; York was agog with it. The burnings had begun. At Smithfield, in London, the first of many fires were lit at the beginning of that year of 1555. Then, further afield they blazed, in Gloucester, Rochester, Dartford and Coventry. England was Catholic once more, and the dreaded heresy laws were in force again, and heresy to the Queen was the greatest sin. She would stamp it out, if not by good preaching and persuasion, as she hoped, then by fire.

As the pedlar made his train ready to depart from York, came the news of two bishops who died chained together at one stake, staunch in the reformed faith of the Queen's young brother's reign. Hugh Latimer died quickly, but the other, Nicholas Ridley, not so. To him, the fire came slowly, so that he suffered a protracted death, begging for more fire to end his agony. And the folk of York remembered that he was a northern man, born, some said at Newcastle, and it angered them that one of their own should die so. Neither did they forget the barbarous execution of their own Robin Aske.

He bade farewell to an old pedlar who, like himself, had dossed down in the outhouse where their horses were stabled.

"'Tis a lonely life, this, lad, ever travelling the roads," the old man reflected one night as they ate together. "But I reckon 'tis better than being mewed up in alleys like this one." His cheery face clouded over as he went on. "I had it from a pedlar once, one whose route crossed mine. He was used to travel to London town once a year, perhaps, though a long, weary way it was, and he would take his dog with him for company. He did not know it, but the plague had broken out there, and he saw blue crosses being painted on the doors of the dwellings where it raged. Folk thought that the infection was carried by dogs, so the authorities employed dog-catchers to round up and kill any they found roaming the streets." The old man heaved a sigh, then continued. "He saw them catch and kill his own dog, too. He quit London, then, and never went back again."

The day was bright as the loaded train clattered through the narrow streets of York. The pedlar was glad to head out into the surrounding countryside, the morning air sharp and clean. He needed to breathe its freshness again. The fetid stinks in the crowded alley where he had been forced to lodge repelled him. But just as much did he feel his gorge rise at the repeated tales of horror that flew from mouth to mouth, as news from the south travelled up-country. That news he was now the bearer of, and in every hamlet and village where he stopped to sell his wares, folk clamoured to hear it. The telling of it delayed him, but the weather held, and at last he was over the high fells safely, and dropping down into the green Eden Valley.

"Make sure ye stop at the saddler's place in Lazonby," his uncle had reminded him before his death. "He will doubtless be in need of more strong needles for stitching his leather. He lives at the Skin House, a way out of the main part of the village." He found the saddler awaiting him at the roadside, the sound of his horse's bell giving notice of his approach.
"I feared some harm had come to thee, lad," John Bowerbank greeted him. "Thou'rt overly late for the time of year."
"Aye," the pedlar explained, "I was some time delayed in York. A bad time I had of it there." He shook his head sadly, and as he had done wherever he stopped, he recounted the sorry tales he had learned there.

Mary came out of the houseplace to make her purchases, and listened as his news unfolded.

"How cruel men are to their own kind," she exclaimed. The bell horse nuzzled her hand, and took the crust she held out to him. "Even a beast does not kill for malice," she said, and stroked his soft nose. It was old Jack's bell horse, his companion of many years, a bond broken only by Jack's death on the lonely fell.

Winter – Greenwich

No sleep would come for the Queen. She tossed and turned restlessly in the great bed. A fire warmed her chamber, and the hangings that enclosed the bed kept out the rawness of the wintry air. Already, preparations for the celebration of the Twelve Days of Christmas were well in hand, though Mary had little appetite for such jollity. This year of 1555 had begun with such joy, Philip at her side, England returned to Rome, and the promise of the longed-for child within her. It had all begun so well. And now? Well, there were fewer heretics in the land! The heresy laws had been revived, and the burnings had begun at the start of the year. Bishops Hooper, Latimer and Ridley had already died the death prescribed for heretics. And Cranmer?

"He shall not escape." she cried out with such force that Susan Clarencius appeared beside the bed.

"Majesty! Is it well with you?" she enquired. "I heard your cries. Did you dream?"
"Nay, Susan, I cannot sleep," Mary replied. "I think of the wickedness of unrepentant heretics. And now Gardiner is dead."

It was so. News came in mid-November that that most diligent seeker-out of heretics had died, to stand his own examination, the reformers hoped, before a much higher authority.

"Dear Majesty, do not let such concerns rob you of your rest," Clarencius answered gently. "I will bring you a soothing drink to help you sleep."

The soporific effect of the spice-infused posset began to lull the Queen into that state that is not yet sleep, nor yet is wakefulness. Tormenting images from the past revolved in the turmoil of her mind. Cranmer! How she hated him. How could she rest while he lived? He who had pronounced the divorce of her beloved mother from the King, her father; to this man was attributable all the pain and misery of her early life. He had led her father into schism, and her brother into heresy.

She continued to move restlessly beneath the heavy bedcovers until, near dawn she drifted into a world of inestimable bliss. She held a babe in her arms, and Philip was with her. The transport of joy into which the dreaming Queen's spirit wandered, burst the bounds of sleep, and she woke again to reality. There was no babe. It had never existed, and Philip was gone. Between them stretched the cold sea, and for Mary, the bitter realisation that despite the outpouring of her love for him, he had never loved her. She moaned, and drew the coverlet close about her. The fire had died down, and the winter cold penetrated the chamber. Morning was near, and soon it would be time to rise for Mass.

1556

Spring, Wetheral

When the pedlar came again, it was in the following springtime. Again, he brought doleful news.

"I tell thee", he confided to John Aspedaile as he loosed his packs, "I would not live in London town for any money. All manner of folk are being burned there now; not only the great men of the Church. They were the first though to taste the fire." He spread out his wares, and looked enquiringly at John. "Now the common folk are suffering, too, those that stand fast in the reformed faith. One was a woman born and bred hereabouts, in Greystoke 'tis said. Isobel Foster her name. Wed to a cutler from Fleet Street in the city. Haply she was known to thee?"

"Nay, I cannot recall her name," John answered thoughtfully. "When did she die then?" he asked.

"In the winter-time, in January, so I heard. There was another younger woman with her, five men, too. None would turn from the reformed faith, so they bound them to stakes and stood them in tar barrels, and set them alight. 'Tis said a great crowd came to watch."
John Aspedaile was silent. He felt sickened at the pedlar's tale. He went about selecting his purchases, and the pedlar continued to tell his news.

"Archbishop Cranmer is burnt, too. They say the Queen hated him. Determined she was he should not live. Aye, the fires are burning for high and low alike. And I tell thee," he said, "there was a strange happening in the sky at that time."

"How so?" John asked.

"I tell thee how I heard it," the pedlar replied. "The same month they burned the Archbishop, March it was, a great blazing star appeared in the sky. It continued to burn for several nights, shooting out fire, and flickering like a torch being waved in the wind. Folk marvelled at the sight, and many feared it. Fire upon earth, and fire in the sky, like the flames of a great burning in the heavens, too."

"Does it still burn?" John Aspedaile asked.

"Nay. It continued several nights, they say. Then it grew fainter, and now 'tis died away", the pedlar said.

John paid for his purchases, and the pedlar began packing up his train. "I heard it whispered" he said, as he turned the bell horse ready to lead the rest out onto the road, "that the great star that blazed across the sky signifies the reformed faith that shone brightly in King Edward's days. Now, like the star, 'tis fading, and likely to be put out."

He laid his hand on the bell horse's bridle, and walked beside it towards the road that would take him into Wetheral, and thence to Carlisle.

"I shall be glad to get home", he spoke heavily. "Everywhere go, I see fear in folk's eyes."

Summer – Wetheral

Young Luke Aspedaile sat bawling in the dirt of the barnyard. It was a fine June day, and his first birthday was now past. His fat young legs were still unreliable, and in his quest to see why the cockerel was pecking determinedly at the hardened earth, they buckled beneath him. It was at that moment that the cockerel pulled out a worm from the ground and it dangled invitingly from his beak. It fascinated Luke. He made a grab for it, and unsurprisingly, the cockerel retaliated. He flew at the child, his hackles up.

He pecked at him furiously, and in the process dropped the squirming worm from his beak. More scared than hurt, Luke roared in alarm, the sound of which brought his mother and sister running from the henhouse to investigate the cause of the uproar. The enraged cockerel wisely departed at speed, without the worm, which Luke immediately stuffed into his own mouth, and swallowed with obvious satisfaction.

"Oh, what will he do next?" cried Janet, in mock despair. She gathered her now smiling son into her arms, and gently thrust her finger between his gums to dislodge what remained of the worm. Margaret produced a cloth from her pocket in an endeavour to clean up the mess from the child's mouth. Evidently, his mother's finger was just as good a substitute for the worm, and he chewed upon it contentedly instead.

Margaret retrieved the baskets of eggs they had left behind in the henhouse at the sound of the commotion, and Janet swung her son up onto her hip and carried him back to the houseplace, where young Luke's antics were recounted with pride to Isobel and Ellen.

At the end of the day, when their work was done, they sat with Isobel and Ellen in the still of the evening. It was their pleasure to sit together for company, though they were never idle. Always there were rents to be mended in the men's working clothes, and their coarse stockings checked for wear. Young Luke's smallclothes too, needed to be folded and laid into piles. Then, when all their necessary tasks were done, Margaret would unfold a length of linen cloth lately purchased from the pedlar. This she marked into sections, and drew designs upon it, maybe a bird or a butterfly, a flower or a leaf.

"'Tis for a bedcover", she announced, "for when I am wed," and a flush of shyness crept across her face. "Will it not look well," she asked, "when I have sewn it with these coloured threads? I got them from the pedlar when he last came."

"Indeed, it will look well." they assured her, and watched as her nimble fingers guided her needle through the coarse fabric.
Isobel Winter watched her closely. Margaret worked quickly, she had a natural ability with the needle. No-one had taught her. No-one had the skill, nor the time to do so. But the Lady, Isobel reflected, had she lived, she would surely have passed on the skill of the nuns to her beloved Marguerite's child.

The nun's child, ah, yes, the nun's child. Isobel began to nod. The pendulum of time began to swing backwards. Why did the swift hands of the little nun work with such a coarse fabric and thread? And why did she seem so afraid? Isobel slipped further into sleep. Ah, that was how it should be! A great cope of lustrous velvet lay spread upon the young Sister's lap. Her needle was threaded with bright thread that gleamed golden under the rush-light where she sat. Under those flying hands, the rich velvet was becoming encrusted with intricate designs of shining gold and silver flowers and entwining leaves, of flying birds and holy symbols.

There was the clatter of horses' hooves, and men's voices shouting. The cope was gone! Outside it was raining, the ground churned up by the passage of a cart that carried away what little wealth the poor House was deemed to possess. One of the King's men turned the great key in the door and walked towards his horse that stood tethered nearby. Over its back, he slung the shining cope, then he mounted and began to ride away at speed.

John Aspedaile and William strode into the houseplace, their ringing laughter filling the room.
"Hush, pray do not wake Luke," Janet whispered. "And see, Isobel is sleeping."

"Ah, my mother does a lot of that, now," William said. "A little sleep refreshes her, though sometimes I fear she dreams of things long past that disturb her."

Isobel whimpered in her sleep. Men were laughing.

"'Tis a fine horsecloth he has found," one jested. But over the horse's hind quarters, the stiff cope was sliding away. It dangled until the flying hooves entangled it and trampled it into the muddied ground. There was a whinny of alarm, then the frightened beast reared, and threw its rider into the mire. He cursed roundly, and kicked the ruined cope from beneath his mount's lunging feet.

Margaret began to fold her work away. At evening's gate, the light was fading, and soon it would not be possible to see clearly enough to sew, and she would not risk a misplaced stitch. The men finished the ale Janet poured for them, and William gently roused his mother from her sleep.

"Come, mother, 'tis time we were abed." He spoke softly, and took hold of Isobel's hand. He felt her fingers tighten upon his own, and she woke with a start. William caught a look of stark fear in her eyes until she comprehended that the man towering over her was her son.

"I did not mean to startle thee, mother," he reassured her. "Come, there is naught to fear. Was it a dream again that frightened thee?"

"I thank God that it was," Isobel's voice trembled ."But it was so real."

Ellen gathered up the mending they had brought with them to work upon as they sat. She too knew the terrors of those dreams that were rooted in past memory, such a small thing was needful to bring them bursting in all their terror upon a sleeper's mind. She entwined her free arm around Isobel's waist, and felt a tremor shake the aging frame.

"Come, mother, I will bring thee some warm milk to drink in bed. It will help thee to sleep well," she soothed.

Autumn – Lazonby

There was free stone to be had on Lazonby Fell for any willing to hack out the warm hued sandstone for his building needs. For months, John Bowerbank laboured thus. It was slow, back-breaking work, and only when he had liberty from his saddlery work could he spare the time to take his horse and cart up onto the fell and bring back whatever stone he could prise free. Once he had it back at the Skin House, he dressed it into blocks in whatever moments of leisure he might have.

To this end, he laboured early and late, so long as there was light to see, and slowly the walls of the new addition to his workshop took shape. As the height of the walls increased, he was grateful for those times when John Aspedaile and William Winter came to help him to lift the heavy blocks upwards, for then he needed help.

Summer was gone, and in the shortening days of Autumn, the new building was ready for roofing. John harnessed up one of his horses between the shafts of his cart, and the second horse followed behind. A day's snigging in Baronwood was before him, and he set off at daybreak, with bacon and bread, and a good quantity of ale. Thirsty work it would be, dragging the long timbers out of the clearing where the felled oaks lay.

It was nearing sunrise as he drove through the village, and from several chimneys thin curls at smoke were ascending skywards, a sure sign that folk were up and about.

He was reminded of the many times he had made this same journey with his father and Ben to gain the oak bark each springtime for their tanning needs.

Ben! He stifled a surge of pain that welled up inside him. Would that sensation of inconsolable regret never leave him, he wondered?

Margaret, he would think of her, and of their hopes for the future. Indeed, she was never far from his mind. He drove on, past the few mean dwellings that clustered on each side of the road.

Dogs barked at the sound of his cart's rumbling wheels, and one, more ferocious than the rest, ran snapping determinedly at his leading horse's legs. John leaned down, and took aim at it with his whip. It retreated out of his range, and stood snarling, fangs bared, until he had passed. At the Church, he turned and drove on until he came to the place in Baronwood where the felled oaks lay. He loosed the second horse and drew out the long reins attached to its collar.

These he made fast around each log he selected to use to carry the roof timbers of his new workshop, and by the time John Aspedaile and William Winter joined him, he already had a fair number ready for loading.

They had brought another cart with them, and the three men raised the heavy timbers onto the tail of each cart.

It took all their strength to lift them, but by dint of pushing and shoving, panting and sweating, by the time the sun stood overhead, the carts were loaded with the timbers John Bowerbank had dragged from the woodland, ready to drive back to the Skin House.

"By all the saints, I swear 'tis a young man's game", John Aspedaile gasped. He wiped the sweat from his face, and flung himself down to rest against the wheel of his cart. William laughed.

"Rest thyself, John," he said.. "Here, take a sup of this, and let us eat." He handed a leather bottle of home brewed ale to John, and lost no time in attacking the rest of the supplies their womenfolk had packed for them. Likewise, John Bowerbank sank his teeth into the hunk of cold bacon he found in his own hamper. The day was warm, and the bread was becoming dry, but no matter, it took the edge off his hunger, and the great gulps of ale he swallowed slaked his parched throat.

John Aspedaile began to nod, and the regular rise and fall of his chest, accompanied by the odd snort, signified that the noonday heat and the morning's labour had overcome him. William caught John Bowerbank's eye, and winked.

"It was so with my father," John smiled, "when we came for the barking. Many a trick I played on him while he slept. "With my brother, I mean... His voice trailed off. The memory hurt. "It was a good time," he recalled wistfully.

"I can call to mind no such times," William said bitterly, "The less I saw of my father, the better it was for me. My mother too. We were but a burden to him, and he took his ill will out on both of us. 'Tis no wonder my mother still has bad dreams."

He searched at the bottom of the hamper, and withdrew a couple of ripe pears. "Here, catch." He tossed one to John.
"Margaret told me to be sure to give thee these. From her favourite tree, she said." He dug his teeth into the ripe flesh, and with the back of his hand wiped away the sweet juice that trickled down his chin.

"So, when wilt thou be wed," he asked, and cast an enquiring glance at John, as he flung the pear's core away.

John bit into his own pear, savouring it's refreshing juices, before answering. He looked at the still sleeping form of John Aspedaile, and said thoughtfully, "When her father says we might." He jumped to his feet, and aimed a friendly kick at William's recumbent rear.

"Get thee up, William," he ordered. "The sooner the building is finished, the sooner that might be."

***

It was in the springtime that Sir John Cheke had occasion to journey to Brussels, and it was on his return, somewhere between Brussels and Antwerp, that he was waylaid upon the road and dragged from his horse. His captors threw him into a waiting cart, and bound him to it by means of a halter. They blindfolded him, and carried him to the coast where he was put on board a ship bound for England. There, once more, the Tower awaited him, and the mighty battle for mind and soul began. At first, his courage was high. He knew that the Queen held himself and Cranmer blameworthy for their part in the guiding of the young King's mind in matters of religion. Cranmer, he knew, she had already sent to the flames, and he, Cheke, was determined to be resolute in the new faith, even if it should be in the face of death.

Perhaps he did not realise that he was of more value to the returned regime of Catholic orthodoxy as a living convert, than as a dead martyr of the reformed faith. To persuade him to return to the one true Church was paramount, and hour after hour he listened and disputed with two of the Queen's chaplains sent to bring him to compliance. When they were unable to turn him, then came John Feckenham, the Dean of St Paul's, the Queen's own confessor. He and Cheke were well acquainted.
Ironically, in the previous reign, it had been Cheke's endeavour to reduce Feckenham, likewise imprisoned in the Tower, to comply with the then established new religion, and in this he had failed. Two men, similarly pitched, learned and possessed of fine minds, were each

resolute in upholding those tenets of faith in which they were diametrically opposed. But Feckenham had the advantage. If persuasion by disputation should fail, Feckenham was empowered to demand a choice. It was one never made of him by Cheke - if not compliance, then death.

Night after night, Cheke tossed sleepless upon his pallet, his mind churning, unable to find respite, until dawn lightened the sky beyond the bars of his cell. Then his brain would conjure up those morning dreams, so vivid that he would wake with a start, his body bathed in sweat. Once he dreamed of Cranmer standing in the fire, his right hand extended to the flames. That hand, the old man declared, must burn first; it was the hand that had signed his recantation. In that tortured dream, Cheke's body writhed as if it too could feel the flames.

He felt them licking at his feet, and a scream of terror forced its way from his throat. Waking or sleeping, he was beset by anxiety. Nothing in his previous life had prepared him for this. Born to a peaceful life of study in Cambridge, he had progressed from grammar school to university, from his position as King's scholar to King's Greek professor, then he was called to Court to tutor the young Prince. His life spent as an academic had sealed him away from the harsh realities of the outside world.

The days of June came and went, and Cheke realised that at some time in those uncounted days, his forty-second birthday had passed unnoticed. What did isolation do to a man, he wondered? His courage and resolution began to waver, and because he longed for freedom, and to ascertain by what means this might be achieved, he sought an audience with Cardinal Pole, the new Archbishop of Canterbury. The price was a high one. He would not burn, but he must submit himself wholly to the doctrine and authority of the Roman Church.

The carnal presence, the very true real presence of Christ in the most blessed Sacrament - 'this is my body, my blood', that tenet the reformed faith rejected, he must accept. There was a desperation about him now, after hard questioning by the Cardinal, and twice in one day, he conferred with Feckenham. By mid-July he dared hold out no longer, and with a heavy heart, he penned two letters which he gave to Feckenham to deliver.

In the one to Pole, he signified, most necessarily, his acceptance of the carnal presence, and begged the Cardinal to have so much compassion on his frailty as to spare him from making a public recantation.

In the other, to the Queen, he declared his willingness to obey her laws and orders in religion, and humbly beseeched her to favour his suit for liberty.

Next, he was required to declare his repentance for the sin of his rejection of the Pope as Head of the Church. He knelt before the Cardinal to make his solemn submission, whereupon he was absolved and received back into the Roman Catholic faith. The compassion he had begged of the Cardinal did not materialise. For a further two months, until the beginning of October, Sir John was left to languish in the gloom of his Tower cell, awaiting the shame of his very public recantation.

At last, he came before the Queen, and bowed low. By his side stood John Feckenham, his accredited converter. Feckenham began to speak. He was a skilful and eloquent orator, and Cheke remembered well his fearless delivery in the previous reign, which had resulted in his own sojourn in the Tower. Feckenham's voice seemed to come from far away, though he stood so close. Cheke's eyes were downcast, he felt giddy, his head was swimming. He did not meet the Queen's gaze, but stared fixedly at the richness of her black gown, at the chain of bright jewels that hung upon it from her waist. In her eyes, had he met them, he would have seen the lingering accusation that said, "You harboured my brother in his heresy. It was your mis- teaching of him that endangered his soul."

Feckenham was saying, "I put myself in place for him...I
open my mouth for him."

His words pierced Cheke's consciousness. "Most dangerous error and wicked heresy - he is a very sorrowful and penitent man...he doth submit himself to recant the same...most humbly beseeching your Highness to take him to your great mercy."

The Queen's look was cold. Upon his knees, he read the words of the recantation prepared for him by the Cardinal. "Now I believe firmly in the real presence of Christ's very body and blood in the sacrament....I do most humbly give thanks unto the ministers of mercy in Christ's

Church, whereof I do acknowledge the Pope's Holiness to be the Head."

Nor was this enough. To satisfy the Cardinal and the Queen, yet another, a third recantation he must make, this time before the assembled Court. Had he not, in the two previous reigns, lived long at Court, and with his pestilent opinions, infected the young minds of the youthful nobility there? This was his sin. Upon his knees, he must acknowledge it. Again, the faith he held dear he must deny. It was the price he must pay for his life. He read the long recantation prepared for him. The words with which he must besmirch himself bit into his soul. "Amen," he said at its end.

"Betrayal, betrayal....." the word hammered repeatedly into his brain. Such must have been the agony of the Apostle Peter consequent upon his thrice denial of Christ.

1557

Spring - Greenwich Palace

War reared its ugly head again in Europe, and his father gone, Philip must deal with it. Again, there was enmity between Spain and France, and would not Englishmen, he reasoned, relish the opportunity to fight with him, their nominal King, against England's ancient foe? King though he might be, empowered he was not. His was, to his intense chagrin, but the crown matrimonial. Therefore, he must return to England and sue for the agreement both of his wife and her Council, before an English force could be committed to fight the French.

Husband and wife had been parted for nineteen months. For him, it was release from an onerous marriage, for her, unutterable sadness.

It was mid-March when he returned, and as he rode from Gravesend to Greenwich he could not but be aware of the fresh beauty of the breaking of the English spring. At Greenwich, Mary awaited his arrival with joy that was tinged with trepidation. Her health was much improved, and now she hoped most fervently that the intervening months had not accentuated her increasing age. For days past, she had incessantly demanded of her ladies their opinion as to what she should wear to greet Philip. They laid out her gowns for her to inspect, the black, the purple, the violet and the white, the velvets and the satins, all richly embroidered in gold or silver thread.

"Jane," the Queen demanded of Jane Dormer, "fetch me my jewels." Then the ladies spent hours conferring as to the suitability of each glowing set of gems in Mary's personal collection. At length, after much argument, the choice was made, and with a note of wistfulness in her voice, Mary said, "I will wear the gold cross my mother brought with her from Spain."

Then, he was there, smiling and greeting her with all the deference due to her rank, and she, almost forgetting her rank, embracing him with the exquisite joy born of long months of privation. Susan Clarencius watched anxiously, and prayed that the rumours of Philip's running wild in the streets of Brussels at night, and his illicit amours, had never reached the ears of her beloved mistress.

The Queen's happiness was complete. Her husband was returned. For love of her? That was a question that at the beginning of their reunion, she chose not to ask herself. Then, as her euphoria lessened, she must address the question she had pushed to the back of her mind. Of course, he had come back to persuade the Council to take arms against the French. No, her happiness was not entirely complete. He would not stay; that she had always known. It was so with princes. So it had been with the Emperor, his father, always journeying far from home. So too it had been with her own father. He also, on occasion, had felt it necessary to accompany his troops in battle. But how it would content her if, before they must part again, she could conceive, and in the fullness of time bring forth the longed-for Catholic heir. Was there not still time? Surely, if God willed it, even now it could be so.

Philip got what he wanted, in spite of the Council's reluctance to commit to the inevitable expense of raising and maintaining an army, and by early summer, several thousand English soldiers were gathered, ready to embark for France. He himself was more than ready to be free of the matrimonial bonds he had found it necessary to endure in order to obtain his wife's consent to the English contribution to Spain's European quarrels, and on the third of July, he took his leave of the Queen.

This time, she was resigned to their parting. His duties lay on the continent, and she was fully aware that the burden laid upon him by his father was a heavy one. The loneliness of separation she must bear now was the price royalty must pay for the high position into which God had seen fit to place them, and Mary's unshakable faith in the Almighty did not question this. Besides, a faint hope flickered within her, daily growing stronger. It was the glorious hope that she was with child.

In the weeks that followed, as with the wife of any soldier on active service, it was the Queen's lot to know, in some degree, the anxiety of awaiting news as to the outcome of battle. She knew that in France, the town of St. Quentin was under siege, and Philip was commanding a combined force of the newly arrived English army and his own Spanish troops based in the Netherlands. The French desperately tried to relieve the town, but they were beaten back.

Still, St. Quentin held out for a further two weeks, until after a ferocious attack by Philip's men, it fell on the twenty-seventh of August.

Now was the time to march on unimpeded and take Paris; it was a heaven-sent opportunity the Emperor would have recognised. But militarily, Philip was not the man his father was. He was sickened by the terrible slaughter that followed as his troops sacked the fallen town. Besides, both men and money were in short supply, and with the decline of the year, and the approach of winter, always a dead time for soldiering, the opportunity of inflicting a devastating blow upon the French was lost.

In England, the victory of St. Quentin was celebrated with enthusiasm, and in due course, the English troops were disbanded. Philips finances, stretched as they were to pay even his own soldiers, did not permit of his maintaining the English in idleness over the winter months, and those who had not left their carcasses to rot in foreign fields, returned home.

Autumn – London

In the house of Mr. Peter Osborn in Wood Street, London, a man lay dying. There was nothing remarkable about that. Many a man in London would die that September day. But this was a most singular man who, in his forty- three years of life, had risen to the highest honour, and descended to the deepest shame. Soon, the life he had bought at the terrible price of betrayal of his faith would be over, and he would be glad, for that life had proved most bitter to him, and worthless.

The three recantations of his faith had scourged his soul. Not for John Cheke, like Cranmer on the way to his burning, had been that valiant reaffirmation of the faith he too had denied. In the black depression of his own soul's night the Archbishop had recanted that faith even six times. Then, on the twenty-first of March the previous year, to the fury of those onlookers who expected him to make a public admission of his heresy, he revoked his recantation, and was dragged to the terrible death he too had dreaded. Next day, while the ashes of that fire yet retained a little warmth, a new Archbishop of Canterbury was consecrated. It was Cardinal Reginald Pole.

Sir John Cheke's lot was to live, and become a tool for the turning of those brought for examination before the heresy courts. What a prize he was, to be exhibited in persuading those accused to return to the unity of the Church. Their eyes! What did Cheke see there? Incredulity, anger, accusation?

"Here is a man," those looks said plainly, "so zealous for the new faith in fair weather, yet unable to stand for it now, for craven fear of the fire." And he accepted their scorn. What he could not bear to see was pity for himself in the eyes of those condemned. What he had become was odious to him, and burdened with shame, and regret, he wasted away .Then, no longer of use to his Catholic task-masters, he languished in the care of a man he could call his one true friend, one who neither questioned nor condemned.

"Peter", he called from the bed where he lay, drifting in and out of sleep, "Peter, when I am dead, bury me in the Church of St. Albans, here in London."

Peter Osborn came to sit close by the bed, and asked gently, "Would it not be your wish to lie in your native soil of Cambridge, John?"

"Aye, it would," Cheke answered sadly. A tear glistened on his sunken cheek, and rolled down upon his pillow.

"But I have had a dream, so real it was." He paused to gather his strength, then continued. "I was a boy again. So hot was the day. I walked along the banks of the Cam till I came to a spot where the willows drooped over the water, and I swam in the cool river.

Then, all was turmoil. The river seemed to boil, and the surge of the water forced me back to land. I clawed at the bank, but I could get no purchase. Peter, it seemed that both water and land rejected me.

"It was but a dream," Osborn spoke soothingly. "Surely 'tis of no account." He took hold of his friend's thin hand, and sought to pacify his agitation.

"Yet I would lie here, Peter, in London, where the passers-by will soon forget me. Not in my beloved Cambridge, where they will rightly say, 'He was once our honoured son, but his own frailty brought him to shame.'

"Then it shall be as you wish, John. Now lie easy," Osborn comforted him, for he could see that his friend's strength was all but gone. The September sunlight flooded into the room. A clock ticked on a table nearby, and reminded the now calm man of happier days. It was the little French clock King Edward had given him, the one that had told the many hours of their studies together.

"Ah," he breathed, "lessons are over now. Listen to them! Those Brandon boys are at their tomfoolery again." A smile lit up the sharp features of his wasted face. "My little King! How he dotes on Henry Sidney, and that wild Irish lad from Upper Ossory. See, they are shooting at the butts. But, ah they are going now." For an hour, he slumbered peacefully, then he woke and fixed his friend with a loving smile.

"Peter," he said, and his voice was low, "I am lying in a boat, and it is carrying me downstream on the waters of the Cam. I am drifting towards a great light and there is a peace there such as I have never known." The tired voice sank to a whisper, but Osborn was able to catch the last confident words. "I know now that God's mercy is for such as me."

The little boat sailed on, and to the one who lay within, over the water came the faint, sweet sound of bells. The clock on the table continued to tell the hours, but by then, the sorrows of John Cheke were over.

Autumn - Whitehall & Hampton Court

It was not the sweating sickness, nor was it the plague. Both these well-known diseases carried off their victims with great rapidity. This new sickness did not strike and kill, often within hours. No, it toyed with its prey, like a cat with a mouse. Death was slow in coming, but almost certainly inevitable. It began in the summer, in town and country alike. Rich and poor, high and low, irrespective of degree, were afflicted. They complained of strange fevers, "the burning ague" they called it. It was a malady that sucked out their strength, until over time their weakened condition collapsed, and could resist no more.

In the palace of Whitehall, Queen Mary held a jewel in her hand. It was from the will of the Lady Anne of Cleves, briefly her father's despised fourth wife, one time queen consort, and eventually, when the King knew and liked her better, the newly-styled "King's sister." She had raised no objection to the divorce that set him free to marry the nubile Katherine Howard, upon whom Henry's fancy had lighted.

Rather than return to her native Germany as damaged goods, she had been content to live in England, and seemingly happily, for the rest of her days. Now she had died, and had been interred with due honour in Westminster Abbey in early August.

To her step-daughters, Mary and Elizabeth, she had bequeathed each a jewel from her small personal collection, as a token of her esteem for them.

As she cupped the jewel in her hand, Mary remembered with affection the Lady of Cleves, a friendless stranger at her father's Court, unable to understand, or to express herself in the language of the country where she had come to be queen. Nevertheless she had tried to be kind to herself when she was but the unhappy Lady Mary, the King's daughter. Mary Tudor was not a woman to forget a kindness.

The autumn days passed, and soon the sharpness of early winter frosts rimed the hedgerows and grasses overnight. Ships began to bring back the residue of fighting men sent earlier in the year to join with Philip's forces on the continent. Philip was loath to keep them over winter, when in that dead time of year hostilities were not expected to occur. But the French, humiliated by their defeat at St. Quentin, roused themselves to devise a plan that would heap as much mortifcation as possible on the English.

To capture Calais, that last foothold the English possessed in France, how sweet that revenge would be! Warfare in winter was rare indeed.

But the French marched upon Calais in early January, and took it by surprise. The loss of Calais had its desired effect upon English prestige. It was a severe blow to national pride, and as the cunning French had anticipated, it caused resentment between Spain and her English allies, the latter having been reluctant to participate In Spain's quarrels in the first place.

1558

Spring – London

With the loss of Calais, the new year of 1558 started ill, and would continue so. Mary had made her will in late March, thinking herself to be with child, and conscious of the great perils women faced in childbirth. But who else thought so? Clarencius and Dormer might soothe the Queen with soft words, but Mary was conscious of the querulous looks that passed between those of her household and members of her Council. Was this pregnancy any more real, those questioning glances implied, than the last non-event? Still, the Queen maintained her belief in the true state of her condition. It was nine months since Philip's departure, and though there was some swelling of her body, was it not, most thought, more likely to be a recurrence of her previous ailment?

April came, and still no child was born. By May even Mary must acknowledge that her hopes of motherhood must be abandoned. By day, she carried out her sovereign duties with the innate dignity bred in her. But when night came, she gave herself up to her own private Gethsemane, and in the depths of her misery, she cried out that agonised question - "Why hast Thou forsaken me?" Then, when the morning came, like the good daughter of the Church she undoubtedly was, she disciplined herself to accept the will of God.

What was the Almighty's will then? All had seemed so clear five years ago, when against all the odds, her path to the throne had miraculously been swept clear for her. A bridegroom, too, from her mother's kin, and he the most Catholic of princes. Moreover, to their joy, England was returned to the one true Faith. Why now, despite all her fervent prayers, did God withhold that ultimate blessing of a Catholic heir to succeed her?

The succession! The thought tormented her. Elizabeth! Her father's daughter, yes, and by his will next in the line of succession if there should be no lawful issue from her own body. But, the daughter also of that woman whose name was anathema to her, whose name she could not bear to say. So clever was this red-haired sister of hers, yet so crafty, so able in her manipulation of the truth that her mind remained an enigma. She was no true Catholic, of that, Mary felt sure, no matter that she paid lip-service to the Mass.

Should she succeed, she would pull down all that she, Mary, had restored from the devastation wrought in the last two reigns. Why, oh why, Mary agonised, did it seem that God's face was now turned from her? What was she to do? She could find no answer, and as she had done all her life, she turned to prayer for divine guidance.

In June, Count Feria came from the Netherlands, Philip's special envoy, and he carried dispatches for the Queen from her husband. Mary stifled the pain she felt. Of course, Philip's affairs in the Netherlands, and on the continent, prevented his presence in person.

But Jane Dormer! Her whole being glowed with the radiance of true love. And Feria, that high-ranking, handsome Spanish noble? Who could doubt that his betrothed, so long admired at her own Court, had indeed captured his heart? The lovers were reunited, joyously, though briefly. Feria's efforts on Philip's behalf, to levy more troops after the debacle of Calais, came to nothing. Despite the Queen's efforts as a dutiful wife to comply with her husband's requests, the Council remained obdurate, and would make no decision. Feria's patience was mightily strained; he found he could do nothing to persuade a stubborn people to do something they were determined not to do.

***

With the onset of summer, that strange new beast that had appeared in the land the previous year, now rose in strength and stalked its prey without mercy. Those stricken did not die swiftly as those did when smitten with the plague or the sweat. They lingered, their strength sapped, sucked remorselessly out of them, until the last sparks of life flickered out. In the countryside, it was reported that much corn lay in the fields unharvested for lack of workmen to cut it. The townsfolk suffered equally; no-one was immune, as death cut its remorseless swathe across the kingdom.

At Hampton Court, Jane Dormer sat with the Queen and her ladies. It was hot, but a cool breeze blew in from the river, and it was a relief to them. The embroideries upon which they worked were destined to adorn a church in dire need of refurbishment. Its former elaborate pieces were destroyed in the former reign.

Each lady kept a cloth nearby, in order to wipe away any moisture from her hands, so that the fair material upon which she worked should not be marked. The Queen rested her eyes. Her eyesight was not good, and the fine stitching she did was a trial to her. She noticed that Jane Dormer's attention seemed not to be focused upon her own work. With the back of her needle, she was pulling out the costly thread from the stitches she had done in error. Then, in frustration, she reached for her cloth and dabbed away a tear that threatened to roll down her cheek. Since Count Feria's departure, the Queen noticed that a light seemed to have been extinguished in the girl, and though she was never neglectful of her duties, her thoughts were obviously far away.

"Jane." The Queen's hand lay lightly upon the girl's shoulders. Her eyes, when she raised them to the Queen's face, were bright with unshed tears.

"Majesty," she murmured, and a tremulous smile hovered upon her lips. No wonder Feria loves her, Mary thought. She is so beautiful, so easy to love, not like me, and she fought down a pang of jealousy. It was an unworthy thought, and she felt shamed by it.

Yet, how could she not compare the ardour of the dark eyed young Spaniard for Jane, to the cold restraint of her own husband's pretended love for herself?

"Put down your work for a while, Jane. Tell me, how go your plans for your marriage?" she asked.

At this, the ears of the other ladies pricked up acutely. Marriages and births, and intrigue of course, these were their unfailing interests.

"We hope to wed at the year's end", Majesty, so long as our duties to yourself and the King permit," Dormer replied.

"I shall miss you, Jane", the Queen spoke with a hint of sadness in her voice. She smiled at the young woman she remembered as a six-year old child, one of those young ones chosen to study and play with her young brother Edward. How fond of her he had been then! "My Jane," he had called her.

"I shall miss you, Jane," she said, again. "But it is a fine match for you. You will travel across the seas, and see, as I have never done, the land my mother left when she was even younger than you."

There was a wistfulness in the Queen's voice. It betrayed a yearning for her Spanish heritage, known only to her by description, and in her own imaginings.

"Ah, you will know the warmth of the Spanish sun, and the scent of the orange groves. You will see the antics of the mischievous monkeys - my mother had one once, I remember. She was fond of it. But that woman could not abide it." She did not say the woman's name, but all knew to whom the Queen alluded.

"Jane, you will be a great lady in Spain, and one day, God willing, a duchess. I shall pray for God's blessing on your marriage, and for your happiness.'
"I thank you, Majesty", Dormer replied. "And I will write and tell your Majesty of all that I see in the land I hope soon to make my own."
"How eagerly I shall await your letters, Jane." The Queen smiled, and cast an amused glance at her elder lady.

"Now, Susan, I trust you are not thinking of leaving me, too?" she asked in jest to lighten the sadness of the parting to come. But Clarencius did not join in the laughter of the other ladies.

"No, dear Majesty", she answered solemnly. "I shall never leave you. Only death can part me from you."

Autumn – London

Jane Dormer sickened in the sultry heat of the summer. But she was fortunate; her constitution was strong, youth was on her side, and eventually, she recovered. Then, when autumn came, the Queen was plagued by intermittent bouts of fever, from which she too would recover, temporarily, only to succumb again, until her progressive weakness made it clear to those who tended her, that her life was ebbing away. Often Mary lay delirious; as the fever ravaged her body and clouded her mind. Clarencius and Dormer scarcely left her side, and it was then that they became privy to the thoughts that tortured the Queen's mind. When the fever raged, it loosened her tongue, and unwittingly she betrayed the jealousy and doubt she harboured in her secret mind.

"Philip, Philip." She would cry, as they tried to cool down her heated body. "You will marry Elizabeth when I die. She is young, and you admire her, I know," She moaned, then they heard the whispered words, "You will soon forget me."

"Hush, dearest Majesty," Clarencius begged. "Do not distress yourself. It is not so." Though in her heart, she doubted the truth of her own words.

When the fever abated and her mind cleared, the Queen recognised the time was come when she must name her successor. There was no help for it - Elizabeth it must be.

Outside her chamber of sickness, the late October winds ripped off what remained of the year's dying leaves from the branches of trees. A message was despatched with all haste to the Netherlands to inform Philip that his wife was not likely to survive her present illness. Perhaps he doubted the urgency of the summons. Mary had been ill before, many times. But the husband she had vowed to love perfectly did not come to give her what she most desired - the comfort of his presence one last time. Instead, he sent Feria with his greetings, and his excuses that with the deaths of both his father and his aunt in Spain, his immediate duties in arranging their funeral rites prevented his coming.

With resignation, Mary added a codicil to her will, "Thinking myself to be with child," at the end of March, she had made provision for the expected lawful issue of her body. Now, all hope of that cherished dream was abandoned, and in sorrowful acknowledgment that "for as much as God has hitherto sent me no fruit nor heir of my body," she charged her successor to honour the provisions of her will, in which the payment of her debts, charitable bequests and provisions for those who had served her in life, were set forth.

So too, parted so wretchedly in life, it was Mary's wish that Queen Katherine's body, interred at Peterborough, be brought and laid beside her in death. And to Philip, she wrote in her own hand, "I do humbly beseech my said most dear lord and husband to accept... and to keep for a memory of me, one jewel, being a table diamond."

It was the one his father, the Emperor Charles had sent to her upon their betrothal.

Mary slept, and though weak, she woke refreshed. Clarencius managed to get her to swallow a little nourishing broth, then, in full possession of her mind, she lay back upon the pillows and ordered "Jane, bring me my jewels. I have an errand for you."

Jane brought the coffer containing the Queen's jewels, and laid it down beside her, and at length Mary spoke.

"Jane, I want you to go to Hatfield, and take these jewels to my sister Elizabeth. She will be Queen of England soon, when am gone. Tell her that I ask her to honour my will."

With the arrival of Count Feria, Jane Dormer was transformed by an inner radiance. Mary could see the new sparkle in the girl's eyes, and the fresh pink flush that tinged her cheeks. The sheer joy of life pulsated within her, strong and eager in the confidence that she was loved.

"God grant that it may be always so for her", she prayed.

In the days that followed, the fever returned. In Mary's wandering mind memories came and went, some bitter, some sweet.

Once, conscious that Clarencius and Dormer were close by her bed, she asked, "Mind you the time we walked abroad, to take our baskets of food to the poor?"

"We do, Majesty", they replied. "And none could tell us one from the other, so hooded and cloaked we were. Just, 'From the Lady Mary's Grace' we said, and they blessed you."

The grey November days slid by, and daily the Queen's body sank closer to death. She drifted in and out of consciousness, murmuring that she saw little children, like angels, singing before her. Then, those watching at her bedside became aware that a deep peace enveloped the Queen. The cares of state, and those of her own unhappy life melted away.

Outside, on the river, a grey mist gathered and merged with the grey ribbon of its waters. Whilst the Queen slept, Jane Dormer stood and looked out at the gathering dusk. She felt a touch upon her arm. She turned, and saw that Susan Clarencius stood beside her. Susan's face was haggard with weariness, and her eyes reddened by weeping and lack of sleep. For days, and nights too, she had remained at Mary's bedside, refusing to leave the Queen she had served for so many years.

"Her sleep is deep, now, Jane," she said. "The doctors say it cannot be long…" Her voice trailed off, her meaning plain.

Together, they stood watching the dying light.

More candles were brought in, and the doctors conferred solemnly together. A priest was praying.

"Susan," Jane turned to face the older woman. "Will you come with me to Spain?" she asked. "Count Feria assures me you will be most welcome there, and I shall be glad of your company when I leave England behind."

Clarencius wiped away a tear. She did not answer immediately. Jane took her by the hand, and looked earnestly into her face.

"Susan," she urged. "I beg of you to consider. There will be nothing left for those of our faith when Elizabeth reigns. I do not believe that she will do as she has promised. Come to Spain with me. My grandmother is most desirous that you join us when we leave."

Clarencius looked towards the bed where Mary lay, her sleep undisturbed and tranquil now.

"I will think on it, Jane, when we have done what we must, here, and that, I know, must be soon. And I thank Lady Dormer for her consideration," she said.

The doctors withdrew, and the two women resumed their watch at the Queen's bedside throughout the night hours. As dawn approached, Mary woke. She heard the Mass that was so dear to her, then she lapsed into sleep again. When morning came, the troubled life of Mary Tudor was over.

Hatfield Palace

Those who rose early to go about their daily tasks soon after dawn on the morning of the seventeenth day of November in the year 1558, heard a lone horseman galloping at a speed that was less than safe through the heavy mists that lay over the streets of London. He was riding north, out of the city, and when he reached the open countryside, he raced on at a breakneck pace.

The morning was still, only an occasional ruffle of wind stirred the grey vapour that clung low over the sodden fields. Where the mist parted, horse and rider emerged briefly as pale spectral wraiths, then quickly were swallowed up again in the swirling mist.

On the rider sped, through scattered hamlets, where the mean dwellings of the country folk were clustered. There, the lanes narrowed, and often he raised his hand to brush away a film of wetness from his face. He did not see the delicate tracery of the spiders' webs that festooned the leafless bushes along his way, but as the morning light strengthened, he saw that their gossamer threads were hung with droplets of shining moisture. Soon, shafts of weak sunlight began to disperse the mist. He urged his pale steed on, ever faster, until at last Hatfield was near.

As usual, William Cecil had risen early. Already, he was at his desk at the palace, as he had been for several weeks. There was much to do, the business of government to be put in place for the new reign, and he had the trust of Elizabeth.

Neither could know that that trust, though often marred by the Queen's petulance, would endure for some forty years. He heard the sound of a horse approaching, and soon its rider stood before him. He brought the prior information he had been awaiting. Queen Mary was dead. His informants in the capital served him well. Now he must prepare the new Queen Elizabeth, to receive those members of the Council who doubtless, even now were riding to Hatfield bearing the news of her accession.

Elizabeth too had risen early, to walk abroad in the parkland, deep in contemplation. She too, like Cecil, had her informants, who reported that her sister was close to death. But those perilous years through which she had lived, and survived, had bred in her very psyche extreme caution. Mary had been sick before, many times, and had recovered. Proof - she must have proof!

The sound of horses at full gallop could be heard, even before she saw them speeding towards her through the mist. As they drew close, she could see that they were flecked with foam. Their riders flung themselves from their saddles, and knelt before her. "Majesty!" they said, and kissed her hand. "Proof. Have a care," that inner voice insisted. She waited, in silence, and looked down at their bowed heads. But they held out a ring towards her. It was the proof she needed. Only in death would that ring have been taken from Mary's hand.

She slid to her knees on the damp ground. "This is the Lord's doing," she quoted from the hundred and eighteenth psalm, "and it is marvellous in our eyes."

November – Penrith

The pedlar's route in the late autumn of 1558 took him by way of Penrith. He was over the high fells at the end of October, and because the old pedlar who served some of the villages that lay on Penrith's eastern outskirts was lying fever racked in York where the plague raged again, he had agreed to travel that way, so as to serve their needs. Their needs, before Christmas, and to carry them through until spring, were prodigious, and though he carried extra goods in anticipation of their wants. So it was with some relief that he made ready one morning at the end of November to quit Penrith, and begin his journey home.

He paid his dues for the stabling of his train, and for his own uncomfortable accommodation there on a flea-ridden heap of straw. He was not known to the keeper of an ill-conditioned hostelry, where he at last found lodging in that busy town, and was therefore considered by him to be fair game for fleecing.

"'Tis daylight robbery to charge so for a night's lodging", he complained volubly the following morning. "Not a wink of sleep could I get for the biting of thy fleas....." ."Fleas!" the innkeeper yelled. "If there were fleas, then thou must have brought them with thee", he retorted. A small crowd of onlookers gathered to listen in obvious enjoyment as the volume of choice insults escalated. The entertainment was only cut short by a deafening peal of bells. They were ringing wildly to attract the townsfolk's attention. The crowd lost interest in the altercation at the stable yard; the innkeeper would win the argument - he always did!

It was useless arguing with the innkeeper, he was giving no quarter.

A man wearing a handsome coat and a superior pair of breeches was standing with a scroll in his hands and about to make an announcement of obvious importance. It was news, and news was meat and drink to a pedlar. He could only hear snatches of what was being said, as the man's words were lost to some degree by the shuffling and murmuring of the gathering crowd. But those close enough to hear clearly what was being said quickly passed on the stupendous news.

The Queen, Queen Mary was dead. The new Queen, her young sister Elizabeth, now reigned in her place. The pedlar could not leave yet. Such news it was! He listened, garnering the reactions of those willing to speculate upon it, and there were many that day who did. Tongues were being loosened by the copious draughts of ale in which the new Queen was toasted - tongues whose owners, in their more sober and careful moments, would have remained still.

"Another woman on the throne" snorted a red-faced farmer. "I tell thee, 'tis no good."

"No good," echoed his companion, and lurched upon unsteady legs to a nearby wall for support. The farmer followed, beaker in hand. He drained its contents, then belched loudly and spat derisively upon the cobbles.

1559

January - The Tower of London

In her bedchamber in the royal apartments, within the Tower of London, the new Queen sat and gazed at her reflection in the mirror. It was Saturday, the fourteenth day of January, in the new year of 1559. Tomorrow, the crown of England would be placed upon her head. Kat Ashley was brushing her loosened red gold hair with long, sweeping strokes. They were alone together at last, all the other Queen's ladies dismissed, for it was with Kat that she could speak with the freedom of long association. Their eyes met in the mirror.

"Well, Kat, we are better served today than when we were here last, prisoners in this place. Is it not so?" Her eyes searched Kat's face with an intensity that recalled the memory of that time, when neither could be sure of keeping their heads upon their shoulders. Kat laid aside the brush, and bent to kiss the top of the Queen's head.

"'Indeed, 'tis so, little Majesty", she murmured softly. "And tomorrow, the crown that is rightfully yours will be placed upon this little head. There is none that can deny your right to it. You are safe at last, my sweeting." Kat brushed away a teardrop that fell on Elizabeth's bright hair.

"At last, at last", she breathed." There were so many times I feared that day would never come."

"But it has come, Kat, and I thank God for it." Elizabeth turned in her chair, and rested her head against Kat's outstretched arms.

"Tell me, Kat," she asked, "what do the people say about me? The common people, I mean."

Kat smiled. "They say 'Our Queen is all English. She has no foreign blood. She is like us, merely English.' That is what they say."

"Ah, merely English!" Elizabeth sat upright in the chair, and met Kat's eyes again in the mirror. "And that is how I would keep it, Kat. No foreign husband to meddle in English affairs. I am minded there shall be one mistress here, and no master."

"But, dear Majesty, the succession?" Mistress Ashley spoke softly, and resumed brushing the Queen's long hair. "If you do not care to take a foreign prince to husband, then what think you to an English lord?" There was a long moment of silence, and in the mirror, Kat saw the quick flash of Tudor anger in her young mistress's eyes. The slender white hands, of which Elizabeth was so inordinately proud, tightened upon the arms of her chair, and she gave a harsh laugh.
"This is Nan Bullen's daughter, too," thought Kat. "So she would laugh, not in mirth, but in anxiety."

"So which of my noble lords would you have me bed with, Kat? For the sake of the succession?" she added tartly. Kat recognised the note of irony in the Queen's voice, and wisely forbore to name the one young lord she knew found favour in her eyes. Lord Robert Dudley, she had known him since childhood, and as a prisoner like herself in the Tower. The bond was deep and unforgettable, forged in fear of the axe, neither knowing what the future held, or if indeed there was a future to be contemplated.

What did each hope for then, Kat wondered, apart from life itself? Freedom, doubtless, but what would they do with such freedom, should it ever come? Neither could be free of circumstance, she of her royal blood, and he the son of Northumberland, the attainted, executed traitor. What dreams did they dream, what impossible hopes sprang from those visions of freedom in this fearful place? Here, in the Tower, fear distorted judgement.

Kat sighed. "Sweet Robin", the Lady Elizabeth called him then. On the leads, or the green sward of the Tower they met and walked together for a brief time, breathing the fresh air that blew from the river, watched but not overheard. What secret hopes did they harbour then, when hope was a tenuous thread, slender, gossamer thin, that might be broken with no warning. Even then, in the close companionship that grew between them, they must have known that should freedom come, they must follow different paths.

For Robin already had a wife, young Amy Robsart, wed to him at the peak of his father Northumberland's power.

Kat forgot protocol, she leaned forward and gathered the haughty figure of King Henry's younger daughter in her arms. How many times, she wondered, since she had come as nurse and governess to this motherless child, had she comforted her thus?

"Nay, nay, dear Majesty", she soothed. "Do not take on so. There is time enough to consider such matters. Come to your bed now and sleep. Tomorrow is your coronation day."

Kat drew the coverlets close around the Queen, and closed the heavy bed curtains against the winter cold, for despite the fire burning in the chamber, the Tower was still a cold, cheerless place, no matter what the season.

"God keep you, little Majesty," she said, and withdrew. In the great bed, Elizabeth lay wakeful, despite the hot posset laced with wine and aromatic spices that Kat had insisted she drink. She could hear Kat moving softly close by, fussing no doubt over the robes and all the paraphernalia needful for the morrow. Dear Kat, so loyal. And there was another upon whose loyalty her instinct told her she could depend. He, she knew she would always trust to guide her. She had appointed Sir William Cecil to the all-important post as Secretary and member of the Privy Council in November. So great was her trust in him, she had given him this charge. "This judgement I have of you, that you will not be corrupted with any manner of gift, and that you will be favourable to the state, and that WITHOUT RESPECT OF MY PRIVATE WILL, YOU WILL GIVE ME THAT COUNSEL THAT YOU THINK BEST."

England, her England now, riven for years by the conflicting teachings held oh, so sincerely, first by her brother and then equally sincerely, by her sister. Could there not be a middle way, she thought, where men might differ in the opinions they held dearly, yet live together peaceably and unafraid? Eventually, whatever Kat had put in the posset began to take effect. Despite the chill of the January night, a pleasant warmth suffused the Queen's body, and in her mind a resolution formed. No more would the innermost thoughts of law-abiding Englishmen be wrenched from their very souls, with threats and dire consequences.

"I do not wish to make windows into men's souls," was her last waking thought. Then, sleep enveloped her.

Spring -Lazonby & Wetheral

The winter was past, and the new addition to the Skin House was roofed and watertight. A fair building it was, the saddler thought, and he was well pleased with it. All his tools were laid out, ready to hand, his pricking irons for accurately marking off the distance between holes prior to stitching the leather, his needles and threads, and his mallet and stuffing stick for ramming straw into horse collars. But pride of place went to his new saddle tree. It was made of beechwood, and he displayed it in a prominent position, so that it could be seen in the light of the new, wide window by any who passed by. And many did, out of curiosity at this seeming upturn in the young saddler's fortunes.
"He is marrying into money," the envious ones said.
"He deserves his good fortune," was the fair-minded judgement of those who had witnessed his labours in the years since Andrew, the tanner's death.

John laid aside the piece of leather he had selected to form the upper part of a new saddle he was intending to make. The light was beginning to fade to the pearly glow of evening. Dusk would gather quickly, and he would not risk his reputation for fine workmanship by marking the costly leather in error.

Tomorrow, he would begin the process of building up the saddle on his new tree, and he resolved to start at daybreak when the morning light would be good. Outside, somewhere in the branches of the ash trees that stood on a slight knoll behind the place where his father's old tanpits lay, a bird was still singing.

He listened; it was the joyous, full-throated notes of a throstle that carried on the still, evening air.

Mary appeared at the door of the new workshop. "Son, will thou not come for a bite to eat?" she asked.

"Mother, I will, I thank thee," John said. He could tell that she craved his company, and he felt a stab of guilt, because of late, there was a change in their relationship, though each loved the other dearly. Soon, and it was inevitable that it should be so when he took a wife, he would look to the future, and she, increasingly, would dwell upon the past.

"I will not be long, mother," he said gently. "Go inside, for 'tis growing cold." She nodded, and turned to go, then asked, "What hast thou done with thy father's old beam, son? 'Tis old, I know, for it served his own father, too."

"Never fear, mother, 'tis still here, in his old workplace. I would not be rid of it, for it may well still be needed, if times should change. And my young apprentice can learn its use, like once I did. And Ben, too," he added, and felt that familiar ache that accompanied any reminder of his brother's death.

"Ah," Mary smiled in the darkness, "how your clothes did stink from the rotting flesh and the hair you both scraped from the skins Andrew brought home from Penrith, and soaked them in the tanpits. I cannot think how many hides have been scraped across that beam."

John laughed, and laid an arm around Mary's shoulders. He noticed that they felt thinner now, and realised with a shock that she was growing older.

"Go inside now, mother. I will just make sure the fowl are all inside, lest Tod is about," he urged.

It was silent now, the birdsong done. Outside the henhouse, he could hear the sound of agitated squawks from within. He made the door secure, and stood against it, and waited. It was not long before a fox emerged from the shadows, and slunk purposely towards the door. It was a thin, scrawny thing, its brush nigh as wide as its emaciated body, a female with hungry young to feed. She began to circle the henhouse, seeking a means of entrance, and a cacophony of alarm rose from within. John stepped forward, flinging wide his arms, and letting out a menacing yell. The vixen was swiftly away, swallowed up by the deepening dusk. Man was no friend to her kind, but she was famished, and she had young cubs to feed. So of necessity she was driven to seek elsewhere for supper.

***

In the early May morning, Mistress Bowerbank was mounted up behind her son. Today they would ride to Wetheral, and on the morrow, he and Margaret Aspedaile would be wed there. Afterwards, she herself would stay at Wetheral for several days, and lodge with the Winters, whilst the newly-wed pair returned alone to the Skin House.

Then, John Aspedaile would ride her home, and there would be a new young mistress there. Try as she might, Mary could not dispel a certain heaviness of heart.

"Are ye ready, mother?" John asked. He turned in the saddle, and sensed her thoughts.

"Never fear, mother", he said. "All will be well, I know it."

He rode out, and turned his horse's head in the direction that would take them through Lazonby village. Mary looked back. Years ago, so many now, it was she who had come to the Skin House as Andrew's bride, and somewhat in awe of his formidable mother.

In time, the two women came to respect each other's differing abilities, but it was only when the old dame was old, and prostrated with sickness, that Mary knew herself to be truly mistress there.

She determined that it would not be so with her son's wife. They were passing the place where the old bridge had once been, and Mary turned her head so that she would not see the place where Dinah was swept away. She wound her arms around John's waist, and leaned forward in the saddle to speak earnestly into his ear.

"Your wife shall be to me as my own daughter", she said. "Like Ben became my dear son."
With his free hand, John lifted one of her hands to his lips, and without a word, he kissed it. The morning sun touched the moving waters of Eden, and a freshening breeze whipped up dancing lights on its surface, and mother and son rode on in the harmony of their deep understanding of each other.

***

He saw her sitting on her swing beneath the branches of the old pear tree. It was in full bloom, again, and laden with white blossom. At the sound of horse's hooves. Margaret turned and ran to meet him, her arms outstretched.

"I have been waiting for thee," she cried. The breeze ruffled the pear blossom, out now for more than a sennight, and a shower of white petals drifted downwards, so that it seemed she ran through flakes of falling snow. John leapt from the saddle and threw the reins to William Winter, who strode to meet him.

"Come Mistress," William said to Mary. "I will take thee to my mother. She longs to see thee again."

John caught Margaret up in his arms as she reached him. He brushed away the pear blossom that rested on her dark hair, and kissed her tenderly.

"And I have been waiting all my life for thee," he whispered against her ear. Their arms entwined, and for a few precious moments, he drew her into the shadow of the pear tree's broad trunk.

"Come, I must pay my respects to thy father," he said at length, as he released her. "And tomorrow, we shall be wed."

***

The old priest met them at the church door. He could scarcely remember how many years had passed since he had come, as a young man, to serve the spiritual needs of the folk of Wetheral. This he had done through the vicissitudes of three reigns. Like a reed, he had learned to bend with whichever wind of religion was blowing in those tumultuous years. He had seen the going of the monks at the nearby Abbey, and the coming of the ill-fated Pilgrims, and all had ended in sorrow.

But he was no firebrand for faith, no martyr for conviction. Instead, by conforming with the dictates of whichever faith prevailed, his priestly tenure at Wetheral remained uninterrupted.

He had outlived most of his contemporaries, and consigned their mortal remains to the earth. He had baptised and married their children, their children's children too, and buried those not destined to live out their mortal span. But always, throughout his many years, he had given solace and kindly succour to the seemingly endless number of his needy flock, and they loved him for it. And they did not care if, on this marriage day, the old priest's mind slipped back and forth, so that none could tell for sure by which rite the pair were wed.

Now, with a new young Queen upon the throne, all was changing again.

Under a cloudless blue sky, it was a merry throng that made its way back the short distance from Wetheral church to the Aspedaile homestead. There, with appetites whetted by the still sharp air of spring, the guests bidden to the wedding fell with unrestrained enthusiasm upon the victuals the womenfolk had risen early to set out upon trestle tables in the houseplace.

The ale flowed, and many a toast was made, often to the discomfiture of the newly wedded pair. At length, as the day wore on, the guest's bellies filled, and the remains of the feast cleared from the tables, Ellen beckoned to Margaret.

"Come into the dairy with me," she whispered. "There is something I would tell thee," she said. Her face glowed with happiness. "Margaret, I can scarce believe it," she breathed. "I am with child. The babe will be born before the year's end." Margaret threw her arms around Ellen. "I am so glad," she cried. "Tell me, does Isobel know?"

"Yes, we have told her, and William will tell John and Janet after all the guests are gone," Ellen smiled. "His mother is so joyful, and I suspect she has already told Mistress Bowerbank. Like cats that have been at the cream they both are."

"Ah, dear Isobel," Margaret said. "'Twas she who brought me to birth. Oh, Ellen, this is such glad news. I thank thee for telling me before we leave for Lazonby."

"I could not let thee go without telling, for I can scarce keep it to myself. But William said that this is your day, yours and John's, so he will not say until all the guests are gone. And you must go soon too, if you are to reach Lazonby before nightfall."

Amidst tears that were both of joy and sadness, Margaret said her farewells. With an ache in his heart, John Aspedaile laid his hand upon the bridle of the saddler's mount, and led the newlywed pair towards the road that would take them to Lazonby.

He was glad that Margaret could not see his face, riding pillion behind her new husband, lest the pain that he felt at losing her should show, and thus cause her sadness. Then, he forced himself to turn and look up into her face, and smile. How could she guess what it cost him to let her go, and yet give no sign of the acuteness of the pain he felt at this impending loss?

On, past Sarah's potherbs, and a faint waft of their perfume was released where his boots brushed past them.

On they went, towards the ancient pear tree. There was a sudden rush of wind. It came as though from nowhere, in the stillness of the day. It rippled through the white blossom, full out now and ready to fall from its laden branches. To the watchers still waving their farewells at the farmstead door, it seemed that the whirling drift of petals enveloped Margaret in an unseasonal fall of snow.

Isobel Winter clutched Janet's arm. "See, 'tis her mother's blessing upon her," she breathed in wonder.

The moment was come. John Aspedaile stepped forward as they reached the road. He laid his hand upon the saddler's arm.

"Remember thy promise," he said.

John Bowerbank held his gaze steadily, and replied, "Thou hast my word, Sir. I will keep it."

Turning to Margaret, her father felt the words of farewell constrict his throat.

"My daughter," he choked. She leaned down from the saddle, and rested both her hands in his. "My father, my dear father...." Margaret's voice too, was shaking. "I thank thee for all thy care of me."

"My blessing upon thee, my child," John said. "Now go, and God go with thee."

He watched them go until they were out of sight, then with a heart fit to burst, he returned the way he had come.

***

Their way descended by a path that led to the river. It wandered by way of wooded tracts, where new green fern fronds rose upwards towards the light, and late primroses still clustered on banks along the river path. Beneath the hooves of their mount, the lush wild garlic released its pungent odour. John felt Margaret's arms around him, holding him closely as the path dipped and rose, then dipped again. They cleared the wood. Once they gained the lower levels, it was safe to ride at a faster pace. He closed one hand over Margaret's that were clasped tightly around his waist.

"Is it well with thee, my love?" he asked.

"It is very well," she replied softly, and leaning forward, she rested her head upon his shoulder

They rode on in silence, in the contentment that has no need of words. The fiery afterglow of sunset began to fade, and when the last coloured vestiges of its departure left the sky, the soft pearly light of the long spring evening never darkened into deep nightfall. The miles lengthened behind them, their rhythmic rise and fall in the saddle governed by the smart pace at which John urged on his mount. The sound of its hooves became mesmerising, and the riders spoke little to each other.

With every turn of the river's route, their path deviated also. Sometimes they lost sight of it, then the bright flash of Eden's waters reappeared. The river was never far away. The sky deepened to a vibrant blue. The moon they had seen rising as a ghostly presence in the sky at Wetheral, to Margaret's mind the colour of milk skimmed of its cream in the dairy, now rode as a bright sickle overhead.

Then, a dark smudge of trees indicated that Baronwood was near, and beyond it lay Lazonby. John turned his horse away from the river. Not a soul was about as he rode through the village. All, that is, except an ardent young swain returning late from an assignation with his sweetheart. He turned again, where the road led out of the village and up towards the fell. Then, the long, low outline of the Skin House emerged beyond the little knot of trees that stood close by his father's old tanpits.

In the last miles, he had felt Margaret's arms begin to slacken about him. He guessed that sleep had begun to claim her, and he tightened his grip upon her hands. He drew rein, and the absence of the horse's familiar motion roused her. John turned his head towards her.

"We are home, my love," he whispered. Quickly, he dismounted, and lifted her bodily from the saddle. The night was cold now, and her limbs stiffened from the long ride. She stumbled, and had he not been still holding her, she might well have fallen.

"Come, I will carry thee," he said. He lifted her high in his arms, and strode towards the door.

***

Margaret laid a caressing hand on his face, so close to her own. She spoke to him earnestly, then reached up in his arms and kissed him long and lovingly upon his lips.

He laughed then, a triumphant laugh of sheer joy. Swiftly, with one hand, he searched for the great key he carried in the pouch at his side. Then he turned the key in the lock of the stout door, and Margaret still in his arms, disappeared from sight.

The river, though no longer visible, was always close. Silently, under the spring night, Eden's waters flowed onwards, as they had for uncounted centuries, and as they would for uncountable time to come.